D0411295

Leste Jann Cla

SHATTERED ICON

Also by Bill Napier

Nemesis
Revelation
The Lure

SHATTERED ICON

Bill Napier

headline

First published in 2003
by HEADLINE BOOK PUBLISHING

Cataloguing in Publication Data is available from the British Library

ISBN 0 7472 6925 4 (hardback)
ISBN 0 7472 6926 2 (trade paperback)

Typeset in Sabon by Avon DataSet Ltd,
Bidford-on-Avon, Warwickshire

Printed and bound in Great Britain by
Mackays of Chatham plc, Chatham, Kent

HEADLINE BOOK PUBLISHING
A division of Hodder Headline
338 Euston Road
London NW1 3BH

www.headline.co.uk
www.hodderheadline.com

To Calum

Things called Stars appeared, which robbed men of their souls and left them unreasoning brutes, so that they destroyed the civilization they themselves had built up.

Nightfall, Isaac Asimov

Part One

God's Longitude

1

The bird circles gracefully, high in the mountain thermal, a slow, lazy motion. Delicate fine-tunings of its wings, the product of ancient evolutionary forces, keep its head perfectly level in the updraft and its black eyes steadily fixed on a spot five hundred feet below. These eyes are focused on a large, motionless animal. Ancient instincts tell the bird that this big animal is in trouble.

A shadow flits briefly over the man. Something big, but he can't think what. He forces his eyes open but at first sees only the harsh sun. Then a high, black shape: a bird, a beautiful thing, soaring in the mountain air.

And another. And another.

Need to drink. Tongue a lead weight. Face hot, beaded with sweat.

Lots of them now.

They're circling around me. Getting lower.

A buzzard lands, about twenty yards away. Not graceful at all: powerful tearing beak, bald head, long scraggy neck, big talons. And those black shiny eyes.

Strong flapping behind me, from big wings, and a scuffling noise, like two birds squabbling. And then a quiet rustling sound, very close. Almost at my neck.

I can't move!

Several pairs of eyes now. No pity in them, no way to plead or reason, no way for our minds to connect. Closing in, in cautious little hops. Indians round a wagon circle.

They'll go for the softest parts of me first, the eyes. Then maybe

3

my ears and nose. Then they'll start on my neck and cheeks, tearing at the flesh.

Don't die, not like this. Not eaten alive by vultures.

'It's not like forensic entomology, for example.'

The Professor – at least that's what he appears to be – is a small, weedy, wrinkled man with a sweaty, pinched face and a turned-down mouth with thin, mean lips. He is wearing a cheap grey nylon suit, an absurdity in the Jamaican climate: it is stained with sweat from his armpits. A gaudy tie is pulled wide at the neck. His eyes are small and black. He is leaning over a small wooden artefact on the table in front of him. It is in three panels, hinged together so that the two side panels can fold on top of the central one. This central part contains a little rectangle of gnarled wood. The other two panels are painted, a mother and child on the left panel, Christ crucified on the other against a black and stormy sky. He is scanning this strange object with a large magnifying glass.

'Entomology?' A second man scratches his head.

The Professor smiles primly. 'Insects. If this was an insect we would have a large DNA database. But as you see, this is a piece of wood, not an insect, and wood, after all, is dead. There are some special tests we can apply to test for particular types – staining, shining ultraviolet light on them and so on. But these are only useful for identifying unusual families of trees, usually obscure species from South America. The Vochysiaceae family, for example, accumulates aluminium from the soil, and its wood turns blue if we apply a special reagent.'

As execution chambers go, this one is comfortable, even luxurious. The room is large. One wall consists of nothing but French windows. Beyond it there is a broad balcony, and beyond that the black expanse of the midnight Caribbean. Expensive air conditioners whisper, barely audible, from the corners. The floor is laid with imported Italian marble, in big multicoloured squares. The furniture is heavy, dark brown and ornately carved in the Mexican style. Exotic lampstands and vases are scattered around, and Jamaican artwork in bright primary colours decorates the walls.

Three people are seated on a deep, low, white leather sofa. In the middle is a bearded man, tall and well-built, in his early thirties. He is sitting upright, tense and watchful, calculating the odds. A teenage girl to his left, casually dressed in jeans and white sweater, is breathing in big gulps, hyperventilating. She has a bruised cheek. Her eyes are wide with fear and she is trying hard to keep herself under control. On the man's right is a woman also in her early thirties. She too is casually dressed and calculating the odds, coming up with the same hopeless answer. They know that, so long as the Professor keeps talking, they stay alive. Their problems begin when he shuts up.

Two men are standing across from them at a table. One of them is the Professor; the other is of Mediterranean extraction, probably Greek. He is short and stocky, with a deep-wrinkled, angular face. He is wearing black trousers and an open-necked shirt with a silver cross – or swastika – hanging around his neck on a chain.

A heavy black revolver lies on the polished table in front of the Greek, within his arm's length. His companion is talking.

Apart from the Greek, six others in the room are armed with guns, five men and a woman. The woman is leaning back, relaxed, in an armchair in one corner. She too has Mediterranean features; she is wearing a long, slim, pink evening dress and a lot of gold. She has a revolver resting on her lap. The five men are sitting around on casual chairs, with the exception of a young, black Jamaican with dreadlocks. He is sitting cross-legged on a bean cushion and is rolling a large joint, his gun on the floor. He seems to be more interested in his joint than in the prisoners. The woman, however, is watching them carefully, a cat eyeing up a mouse, a distant half-smile on her lips. From time to time she rotates the barrel of her gun, a chamber at a time, as if checking that it is loaded.

'A scanning electron microscope is a lot of work, and to tell you the truth, my most useful tool is this magnifying glass. For example,' the Professor says, peering closely at the wood, 'there are about eighteen thousand species of tree worldwide, but I can already, after a few seconds with my lens, narrow this wood down to a few hundred possibilities.'

He drones on. His small black eyes are shining enthusiastically and his lips are puckered primly. 'Tree trunks are really marvels of plumbing. There are chains of large cells which carry water from the roots to the leaves, and more chains which carry the sugary liquid made by the leaves back down through the tree trunk. Different species have different patterns of plumbing, you know. Ah, now this is interesting. Here we have big structures mixed in with the smaller, finer cells. That means I can eliminate a whole swathe of trees, in particular the softwoods. I believe we are down to ash, hickory or oak.'

The young Jamaican says: 'Ya.' He has finished rolling the joint. He pulls out a thin blue lighter, flicks it and puffs. Whorls of ganja smoke begin to drift upwards. He watches them rise towards the ceiling, a look of contentment settling on his face.

The Professor looks up from his magnifying glass. 'Jesus Christ was most probably crucified on a cross made from a white oak, a common tree in the Middle East then and now. Something like a boat was discovered some decades ago on Mount Ararat in Turkey. It turned out to be made from white oak, and enthusiasts have seen it as evidence that the boat was Noah's Ark.' Again that prim, superior smile. 'There are several types of oak, quercus robur, quercus rubra . . .'

'Doctor . . .'

But the Professor seems insensitive to the volcano of impatience building up inside his companion. '. . . and I can tell you that this particular wood is white oak.'

The Greek says, 'What are you telling us, Doctor? That the wood is from the Middle East?'

'Unfortunately white oak is also found in North America. It was often used for shipbuilding two hundred years ago. However, in my opinion this wood is much more than two centuries old. And there are subtle differences between North American and Middle Eastern white oak. It is my opinion that this is not North American white oak. Yes, it comes from the Middle East. And yes, it is very, very old.'

The Greek's temper has reached its limits. He asks: 'Is it the icon or not? Yes or no?'

The Professor smiles triumphantly. 'Of course proper verification would require carbon-14 dating. But I can safely rule out some sort of elaborate modern forgery.'

For the captives, the remark is a death sentence.

'Thank you, Doctor.' The Greek exhales air as if a pressure valve has been opened. 'I think you can leave us now. Cassandra, would you see to the Doctor's fee?'

The Professor gives a slight bow of his head. 'I would like to be well clear of this island before' – he glances briefly at the captives – 'before there is any unpleasantness.'

The Greek exposes his teeth. 'You will be long gone before anything happens here.' The woman in pink uncrosses her legs, stands up and walks towards the prisoners. Her high heels click-click sharply on the stone floor.

The Professor gives a last glance at the prisoners, this one slightly anxious. 'They have seen my face, you know.'

'Doctor, you have absolutely no worries in that direction.'

She raises her gun.

2

It was more or less closing time. Janice had left with her usual cheery 'Byee!' and I was about to set the alarm when a maroon Rolls-Royce drew to a halt on the double yellow lines outside the door. It was pouring with rain and the man was wet in the interval between leaving the Roller and scurrying into the shop.

I'd seen him around the streets of Lincoln from time to time. He was small, rotund, white-haired, with a tiny, prim mouth, piggy eyes and a complexion which told of a lifetime's devotion to port. The voice was middle-aged, English public school, with the faint air of disdainful superiority which affronted my proletarian roots. 'Mister Blake? Harry Blake?'

'The same.'

'My name is Tebbit. Toby Tebbit.'

The Tebbits. Our local gentry, tucked away behind a thousand or so acres of woodland, back of Lincoln, surrounded by a high wall. 'Sir Toby?'

'The same.' He brushed a few drops of rain from his camel-hair coat. 'Mister Blake, if I can get to the point. I'm looking for some help. I've had a parcel delivered from Jamaica. It's a heap of paper, basically. Very old, so far as I can see.'

'How did you come to——?'

'In due course.' Spoken in the slightly irritated tone of a man who is not used to being questioned. 'I'd be grateful if you could evaluate the papers for me.'

'That'll be fine. Do you have them here?'

'I felt it better to have you come and see them.'

'No problem. My assistant will keep shop. I'll call for them at ten o'clock tomorrow, then.'

Tebbit nodded curtly, turned his collar up and left to brave the rain between shop entrance and Roller again. He hadn't bothered to tell me where he lived.

The next morning was blue sky, but dark clouds were on the horizon. I took my elderly Toyota out of Lincoln and along a country lane. After a few miles I turned into a single-track road guarded by a lodge house. A notice on a stone gatepost displayed the words: PICARDY HOUSE. A sign on the other gatepost said: PRIVATE. NO UNAUTHORISED ENTRY.

The road was tarmacked and lined by low metal fencing, and it meandered through fields scattered with oak trees and sheep. About a mile along there was denser woodland. I drove past a small lake on the left; a rowing boat was tied up at a short pier. Then I curved in towards a large gravelled courtyard with fountains, manicured bushes and statues in the Italian style fashionable amongst people who had gardeners on their staff a century or two ago. Ten generations of family wealth looked coldly down on me as I climbed moss-green steps and tapped a heavy brass knocker. The door opened almost immediately.

She was about nineteen, with dark eyes and black hair swept back in a pony tail, and she was wearing a black sweater and jeans. She gave me an appraising look. 'Daddy will be along.' I followed her down a broad corridor and into what I took to be the study. It was about thirty feet by twenty, and wall-to-wall Axminster. One wall was taken up by a bookcase: old books, expensively bound, neatly laid out and, I suspected, never read. She motioned me to an armchair, eased a Persian cat on to her lap and sat facing me. The room was chilly.

Again that appraising stare. 'So you're Harry Blake.'

I said, 'Yes.'

'I'm Debbie. What do you do?'

'I'm an antiquarian bookseller. I specialise in old maps and manuscripts, mostly.'

'That sounds boring.'

'Not if you have an imagination. What about you?' I asked. 'Any interests?'

'Clubbing and horses, mostly.' She smiled wickedly. 'And fit guys.'

Daddy came in, dressed in an old sweater and baggy trousers. 'This is private business, Deb. Shut the door on your way out.'

Debbie dropped the cat and flounced out, glowing with teenage angst.

Sir Toby waved me towards a desk next to a big bay window. Beyond it was a lawn and then trees. In the shadows of the wood I could just make out a thin man with wellingtons, a black labrador and a rifle.

'Didn't even know I had a relative in Jamaica,' Sir Toby complained.

He paused, as if waiting for some comment; I gave him a nod. He sniffed and continued, 'A man called Winston Sinclair. I'm his next of kin apparently. The man died without property.' Spoken in a slightly ashamed tone.

'You want me to take a look at the material?'

'You do deal in antique documents, do you not?'

Under the bay window was a wooden box about the size of a biscuit tin. Sir Toby heaved it on to the desk. Stencilled lettering on its side spelled out *Silver Hills Coffee. 20 kg*. He rummaged through wrapping and handed me a wodge of quarto-sized papers about three inches thick. 'Can't make sense of it. What about you? It is a manuscript of some sort, is it not?'

The condition of the pages was good, although the ink was browned with age and the page corners were lightly foxed, as we say in the antiquarian book trade. The first page was taken up with a title written in a sprawling, slightly immature hand: *MY TRAVELS TO AMERICA AND THE ARCHIPELAGO OF MEXICO, WHERE THE ISLANDS OF CUBA AND JAMAICA ARE TO BE FOUND*. Below the title was the author's name: *JAMES OGILVIE*. I'd never heard of him. A faded watermark ran through all the pages. I held the top page up to the window. I could just make out a crown surrounded by concentric ovals. Between the ovals were the words: HER MAJESTY'S STATE PAPER OFFICE. At a guess I put the manuscript at four hundred years old. But the words were incomprehensible;

they seemed to be written in a sort of shorthand.

'More like a journal,' I said. 'It could take some time to transcribe it.'

'How long?'

'Days, probably.'

'I'm driving down to London this evening and won't be back until Sunday.'

'No problem. We'll leave it until you return.'

Sir Toby hesitated. 'Actually I'm anxious to be shot of it. Why don't you take it away? Give me a valuation when I get back.'

'I'm not sure I want the responsibility. What if I had a fire or a burglary?'

Another hesitation while Sir Toby weighed the odds. Then he said, 'I'll run that risk. But there is one thing.' He lowered his voice in the empty study. 'Confidentiality. For reasons which need not concern you, I don't want to be connected with this journal.'

'I'll put it in my flat. I live alone. Nobody will know about it but myself.' I tried to take the baronet by surprise: 'Sir Toby, is there something about this document you're not telling me?'

'Of course not, what an absurd idea.' He managed a sardonic laugh.

'Who was the Jamaican lawyer?' I asked.

The lips pursed disapprovingly. 'What on earth does that have to do with you?'

'If there's something of historical interest in here, I might want to chase up the source.'

Sir Toby froze. 'You will do no such thing. Confine yourself to transcribing the document. Just give me your translation, your valuation and your invoice.'

I lifted the parcel. 'I'll get back to you after the weekend.' Sir Toby nodded curtly. He turned to the bookcase; as I left the study he was pretending to read a book.

Outside, Debbie was being a femme fatale, lounging on the bonnet of the car like a model in a car show. 'People find Daddy a bit abrupt sometimes,' she said.

'Not me,' I lied. 'I'll probably be back next week.'

11

She rolled off the bonnet and leaned into the car window. 'Do you ride?' she asked, her eyes wide with enquiry. I gave her a sideways look and roared off. There was a spattering of gunfire in the woods to my left.

3

The shop was quiet and I gave Janice the afternoon off and closed early.

In my flat, I took the manuscript from its box and put it in the safe in my bedroom. The safe was an elderly Guardsman with twelve-digit combination, a separate key and fire-resistant lining, and it had a wooden surround which made it look like a bedside cabinet. Normally it held nothing more valuable than my passport, a few near-the-limit credit cards and a thin pile of banknotes.

The Crown and Martyr was crowded, as usual on a Wednesday night, but I found myself a corner. Barney and I went through our ritual: he asked me what I wanted, I said the chicken curry and a pint of bitter, and he went off to collect it. The pub was ablaze with light and chatter, good after the grey silence of the Tebbit mausoleum. There was a birthday party at the next table and half a dozen office girls were letting their hair down. Somebody was leaning forward and speaking *sotto voce*. I caught snatches: '. . . honeymoon . . . rubber gloves . . . I'm told you have to *touch* the beastly thing . . .', followed by shrieks of female laughter. I settled down to my pint, vaguely disturbed by the events of the day and unable to make sense of them.

I'd finished my meal and my second pint when I spotted Barney waving a telephone receiver at me from the far end of the bar. I pushed my way towards it, surprised that anyone would know to contact me here.

'Mr Blake?' Her English was good, although the consonants were a bit harsh. The accent was Mediterranean or Turkish, and I put her age as about my own, thirtyish.

'You have something in your possession, given to you by Toby Tebbit?'

How the hell did she know that? Cautiously: 'Perhaps.'

'And Tebbit has told you nothing about the contents?'

'Who am I speaking to, please?' I asked.

'You may call me Cassandra. I have information about the item which I'd like to share with you.'

There was another outburst of female laughter in the pub. I put my hand over an ear. 'I'm listening.'

'We should meet, but we can't be seen speaking together, Mr Blake. Do you know the prayer room in the cathedral?'

'You mean the Langland Chantry?'

The line went dead.

The night air was cold after the warmth of the pub. I trudged up Steep Hill, my mind buzzing with possibilities, none of them sensible. The cathedral was still open. I nodded to the lady at the collection box. There were a few late evening tourists, sparsely scattered around the huge, mind-emptying interior. I made my way towards the far end, past the big transept, before turning right into a small stone room with a heavy door and bars on its window. A notice said: HERE IS A PLACE TO BE QUIET WITH GOD. Another said: SILENCE PLEASE.

The centre of the room was taken up with a small table on which candles were burning. A wall was taken up with a plain wooden cross, another with tall, narrow stained-glass windows. There were hard wooden chairs against the walls, and there was a gargoyle, mother with child, with squat faces like Easter Island statues. The room was empty.

I waited. After about ten minutes the room began to feel vaguely oppressive; maybe it was the silence, maybe it was the overbearing presence of the iconry. I turned to leave and was startled to see a woman standing silently at the door, watching me.

She had short black hair and a hooked nose and dark eyes, and she may have been Greek, Italian, or even Turkish. She was dressed in a business suit, and she wasn't a local. Her dark eyes looked directly into mine. 'Mr Blake?'

'Yes. And you are?'

'I'll come to the point, Mr Blake. I'd like to buy it.'

I shook my head, mystified and uneasy. 'You'll have to discuss that with Sir Toby. By the way,' – I lowered my voice in the empty cathedral – 'how do you know he had the journal? That information is confidential.'

She waved a hand dismissively. 'Unfortunately Tebbit is in London and I need to acquire the document quickly.'

I asked her, 'It's cold here. Can we talk about this someplace warm? Over a glass of wine, maybe?'

She shook her head impatiently.

I shrugged. 'I'm sorry, I can't help you.'

'I'm authorised to offer you twenty thousand pounds for it.'

In Sir Toby's study I'd mentally bracketed the journal somewhere between one and three thousand dollars. For a moment I wondered if the woman was some sort of lunatic. There was something not right about her; whether it was her body language, or the direct way she had approached me, or the slight air of fanaticism which she seemed to exude, I couldn't say. 'I'd like to help, but it's not mine to sell.'

Again that impatient shake of the head. 'I have no time for horse-trading. We need the journal immediately. Let me go to my limit, which is fifty thousand pounds. You can have that by tomorrow morning, in cash if you like.'

Fifty thousand! I began to feel a sense of unreality, as if I was watching a scene in a movie. The woman was peering at me, trying to read my mind. 'I'm sorry, but if it's not mine to sell, how can I sell it?'

'That is a conundrum.' She nodded thoughtfully, running a finger absentmindedly up and down her neck. Then, 'Is a hundred thousand pounds the answer?'

I think I must have gone pale. Certainly I felt my mouth going dry. The woman was deadly serious; I could see it in the tense downturn of her wide mouth and her steady, disconcerting stare. If twenty thousand was silly money, a hundred thousand was scary. It would also clear my overdraft, car loan and credit cards, and make a big dent in the mortgage on the flat. I actually hesitated for a moment. But then I was saying, 'I'm sorry, but there's no further point in this conversation. Why don't you just find out where Tebbit is and ask him to phone through his authorisation to sell?'

'The fact is, the journal is not Tebbit's to sell. It belongs to the people I represent.' She paused. 'And you have no right to be holding it.'

The tone of menace came with a touch so light that I wondered if I had imagined it. I asked, 'The people you represent?'

Curtly: 'Don't concern yourself with that.'

'I don't understand. If the journal is yours, why are you trying to buy it? Why not just prove ownership? Go through the courts if you have to.'

She shook her head. 'It would create . . .' – she struggled for the right word – 'complications.'

'As would my selling it to you without Sir Toby's permission. Look, he'll be back on Sunday. Why don't you speak to him then?'

'You must not return this article to Tebbit. But I see we will have to find other ways to persuade you.' She gave me a smile of undiluted malice, and said, 'We'll meet again, Mr Blake.'

'I look forward to it.'

The smile intensified, and then her high heels were clattering along the stone slabs of the nave.

I gave myself five minutes, feeling a bit shaky. There was a light drizzle outside, and a little cluster of merry revellers around a hot dog stall: I recognised the office party from the Crown and Martyr. I took the road round the side of the cathedral and turned off towards my flat, at the end of a cul-de-sac shared by half a dozen upmarket houses. The lane was deserted.

Feeling exposed in the street lights, I turned into the gravelled courtyard, fumbling for my keys and expecting heavies to jump out of the bushes. Cursing my overactive imagination, I inserted the Chubb key and turned it. Then the Yale, the wrong one, of course. Trying again, with an unsteady hand; finally I got it right and the door opened.

I groped in the dark for the light switch. The hallway was empty; through to the living room: empty. Of course. I padded through to the bedroom, resisting the ridiculous temptation to look under my bed. Then I went round the flat checking doors and windows. Back in the hallway I hung up my jacket and kicked off my shoes, grinning and sighing with relief and mentally calling myself an idiot.

I was in the kitchen, rustling up a tomato sandwich and still grinning at my own silliness, when I spotted the rainwater on the windowsill. Just a few drops.

This time, when I went through the flat again, breadknife in hand, I opened wardrobes and looked under the bed. Finally I opened the safe, a feeling of dread washing over me. But the Model G400 Guardsman with key, keypad and fire-resistant lining was undisturbed, and I went weak with relief.

I threw my clothes off and ate the sandwich in bed, flicking through the journal pages but unable to make any sense of it. Finally I put it back in the safe and switched the light off. Things were swirling round in my head but I could make no sense of them either. I listened for sounds, but heard only the steady patter of rain on the roofs of cars and an occasional shudder from the refrigerator. From time to time I peered into dark corners of my room.

As I dozed off I thought that, if it hadn't been for the rainwater on the kitchen windowsill, I'd never have known someone had been through the flat.

In the event I didn't sleep much. Partly it was the foetal comfort of lying in bed and listening to rain battering off the window pane. Partly it was the mystery of the journal; a journal which Sir Toby had known nothing about from a relative he didn't know he had, but which was sending him into a state of mild paranoia. Mainly, though, it was the dark shadows in my room, and a vague foreboding of trouble to come.

4

Round about eight in the morning I rustled up scrambled eggs, and while I watched low, black clouds sweeping in over the fields behind the flat, I made a telephone call.

'Sir Toby?'

'Yes?'

'Harry Blake here.'

A hesitation, then, 'Blake. How the hell did you find me?'

'Your daughter tells me you usually stay at the Cavendish. There's a problem. Someone's trying to get hold of the manuscript.'

'What?' Surprise and consternation came down the line.

'I was offered a lot of money for it, in fact a ridiculous sum. I referred them to you but they thought you wouldn't be interested. The woman concerned also claimed rightful ownership.'

A slight hesitation. Then, 'That's nonsense.'

'And something else. My flat was broken into. That can't be a coincidence.'

'You mean you were burgled? What about the manuscript?' There was alarm in his voice.

'They didn't get to it. Sir Toby, I think I'm entitled to know what I'm getting into here.'

'Getting into? I don't know what you mean.' The man was lying. I knew it, and he knew that I knew it, and he didn't give a damn.

His arrogance was getting to me. I said, 'I guess I'll go to the police.'

Tebbit's response was gratifying. 'No. On no account.'

'Oh, but I will, Sir Toby. Unless you tell me what's going on here.'

This time the silence was longer. Finally he said, 'I would

like you to trust me on this. I really cannot tell you what this is about.'

'When I put this phone down, Sir Toby, I'm going to pick it up again, report a burglary and mention your journal.'

'I'm not used to begging, Mr Blake.'

'Talk, Sir Toby. Either to me or to the police.'

'Whatever fee you had in mind, I'll double it.'

'That would make things damned expensive for you. We're dealing with some sort of Elizabethan shorthand. It'll take me days to transcribe it into modern English, even if I can track down the shorthand system, and that may no longer exist. There was a lot of secret writing in those days.'

'Look, just do it, will you? Triple your blasted fee. And for Christ's sake keep the manuscript secure and your mouth shut.' The line went dead.

I gave it a minute of serious thought while the black cloud approached. Then I lifted the phone again and dialled another number.

Janice was used to my sudden absences and could be trusted to look after the shop for a few days. All right she didn't need the money, but she was long overdue for a salary increase and I kept waiting for that elusive rarity, a map or a document that would fetch half a million at Christie's. I filled a holdall, tossed it in the boot and took the M1 past Nottingham. Mozart took me on a long, slow crawl around Birmingham and on to the M40, and some mid-Atlantic DJ with ten times my income drivelled me towards Oxford. The road was congested and I kept clearing greasy spray from the windscreen. I also kept having fantasy thoughts about being followed, but there was no sign of anything odd in my rear mirror. But then, I wondered, would there be?

In Oxford I trickled along Woodstock Road, parked in St Edwards School and made my way diagonally across the quad in the rain, past the school church. The man waiting for me at the entrance to the common room was about fifty, with a haphazard mop of white hair which offset the formality of his suit. He grinned at me over the top of his half-moon spectacles. 'Harry, good to see you again. Well, what have you got? Let's be at it.'

We sat on soft armchairs in the upstairs gallery, next to the bar. It was just after two o'clock and the common room was deserted. I sat down and took the journal from my briefcase. He turned over the pages, his eyes scanning them carefully.

'Fascinating. You're right, Harry, it's Elizabethan, no question, and written in an early system of secret writing.'

'Can you identify the system?' I was speaking to one of the world's authorities on Elizabethan secret writing.

Fred Sweet grunted. 'It looks like a very early one. Very like that of Timothy Bright himself, which would put the manuscript at 1588 or later. Except that there are minor differences. He might have been using an earlier version of Bright's system.'

'But look at the watermark, Fred. It's Spanish Netherlands. What's an Elizabethan journal doing written on Spanish Netherlands paper?'

He held a sheet up to the window and peered at it through narrowed eyes. 'You're right. The paper comes from the Spanish Netherlands.'

'That's weird. Like seeing a 1940 British government memo written on Nazi notepaper.'

He shrugged. 'Maybe, maybe not. The Dutch had more or less loosened their Spanish chains by the late 1500s. And the Netherlands was crawling with agents of the English. But I agree, it's odd.' He looked at me curiously. 'Where on earth did you get this?'

'Sorry, Fred, but my client wants to stay anonymous.' It came out sounding excessively conspiratorial. 'But I do need to crack that code.'

'Try Bright's *An Arte of Shorte, Swifte and Secrete Writing by Character*. The Bod's bound to have it.'

I thanked Fred, left the car in the school car park and took a crowded bus into the centre of Oxford. Normally my reader's card took me into the Map Room in the New Bodleian, but Timothy Bright would come into the Rare Books category and hence the Old Bod, across Broad Street. I passed through the first security point and climbed the spiralling wooden stairs into the Arts End, a hundred feet of light, airy Gothic fantasy. Through a second security barrier, whose guard was struggling with the *Daily Mirror* crossword, and I was into the inner sanctum, forever beyond the Great Unwashed: Duke Humphrey's Library, almost as old as the book I was seeking.

I ordered Bright in the Graduate Study and waited for an hour at the reserve counter, soaking up the grotesques, the coats of arms in the ceiling, the light smell of ancient books. It was dark by the time the woman arrived with a small, leather-bound book and a smile. I found an empty chair in one of the narrow alcoves and sat down between an elderly scholar with a nervous tic and a miniskirted girl with a pink laptop computer. I laid out the book on the long, narrow shelf. I carefully turned its pages. And I recognised words. My old friend Fred had been right: Bright's system was the secret key to Ogilvie's journal.

Strict rules are enforced within this *sanctum sanctorum*. Conversation is strongly discouraged. A manuscript older than 1901 may not be photocopied. Hand-held photocopiers are strictly forbidden. Photography likewise, even of the library interior itself. Pens may not be used. This means that if something is to be copied, you are down to a laptop computer or a pencil. I decided on a pencil and settled down to a long slog. The professor disappeared about six in the evening, and the girl shortly thereafter. I was alone in the alcove.

Just after nine o'clock, with my bladder beginning to complain and my fingers aching, I became vaguely aware that someone was standing next to me. I paid no attention until he cleared his throat apologetically. 'Mr Blake?'

A young man, with short, neat black hair and a brass earring. Smartly dressed in a three-piece suit and green tie. A stranger addressing me by name. Again. My stomach flipped. 'Yes?'

'You have some papers that don't belong to you. I want you to hand them over.'

I tried to suppress the sudden rush of alarm. 'Forget it, chum.'

'I don't think you grasp the situation. I'm instructed to retrieve it by whatever means.'

21

'And I suppose you have a shoulder holster with a Beretta automatic pistol?'

'No, just a pen with a poisoned tip.' His expression didn't change. 'We're serious people, Mr Blake. We're not even asking you to do anything wrong. Just stand up and walk away, leaving the manuscript where it is. Go back to your flat in Lincoln, and there you will find an envelope whose contents will give you a great deal of satisfaction. It's in your own interests to do this, believe me.'

'If you're a *bona fide* scholar, I'm a monkey's uncle. How the hell did you get in here?' I was drawing bravado from the security of the library.

'Ssh!' A white-haired old woman was glaring at us from the alcove across the passage. We were breaking the rule of silence and her face was lined with indignation.

The young man stared at me with ice-brittle eyes, then left as silently as he had come. He was gone by the time the shaking started.

I gave it five minutes and returned Bright to the reserve counter. A quick check with the guard confirmed that he had never set eyes on the gentleman before, but we get so many foreigners these days sir and he did have a reader's card. I quickly retrieved my bag from security and mingled with the students on the wet, shiny pavements of Broad Street. I crossed and recrossed roads, doubled back, dived in and out of narrow lanes and the side entrances of pubs and generally behaved like an idiot before making my way to Gloucester Green bus station. It was standing room only on the bus but it quietened after a few stops and I took the opportunity to look at the assorted passengers, every one a heavy from a gangster movie. In dribs and drabs the heavies got off at various stops. At St Edwards School I reached my car safely, gratefully sank into the seat and took off smartly, heading away from Oxford. I found a hotel near Bicester, some miles out of town. I grabbed a beefburger and ate it in my room with a chair jammed up against the door. The food lay like a heavy lump in my stomach the whole night.

The next day I left my car and took a bus into Oxford. There was no sign of the polite thug from the previous evening. It would have been easy to dismiss him as a fantasy. At lunchtime I sat with my back to the wall in the Kings Arms. By the end of the evening I was through copying Bright and my hand ached from writing. I repeated my backtracking routine and shared the Thames Transit bus with a handful of tired travellers.

Bicester was almost deserted apart from a few harmless drunks. I turned left off Sheep Street onto a quiet lane. A young couple about twenty yards ahead of me suddenly seized each other and began to waltz. I thought this was strange until the edge of a hand hammered painfully into my kidney and a heavy fist smacked into my eye a second later. I collapsed in agony just as my briefcase was snatched from my hand. As I lay groaning on the pavement I thought it had been a fine piece of distraction.

I heaved myself up, using the wall of a house for support. I thought I'd better get to my hotel quickly, before they discovered that the briefcase was empty. I returned the receptionist's welcome with grunts, covering my bruised eye with my hand. Hopefully she thought I was drunk.

In my room I went through the routine of jamming a chair up against the door handle. My mouth was dry and I was shaking, but mainly there was an intense pain in my kidney. I eased Ogilvie's manuscript from inside my shirt and tossed it onto the bed. *Something.* Somewhere in its pages was *something.* The cold water stung my eye and there was more pain as I patted it dry. I phoned down. Sandwiches were off but the bar had crisps and soft drinks. After they had arrived I threw off my clothes.

Now at last I had everything I needed for the long, slow business of turning Ogilvie's shorthand into English. I fired up my laptop. I saw no point in writing Elizabethan English and put the words into modern form for Sir Toby's benefit, even changing phrases where things would have sounded too archaic.

It was a diary, or at least a journal. The writer was a boy, James Ogilvie. Here and there he had written poems, verses and Latin script in longhand, and I copied them down just as they were, Shakespearean spelling and all. I ignored the shaking, I ignored the pain. And as I rattled away at the keyboard, hovering somewhere between determination and anger, a few packets of crisps and cans of Seven-Up dwindling at my side, the 21st century began to dissolve and a time machine gradually transported me four hundred years into the past, into the strange and dangerous world of the young James Ogilvie.

5

Do not think that I am the ignorant son of some poor shepherd, driven by starvation to seek my living in distant realms. My father was a shepherd, yes. But he was also a farmer who owned much of the valley of Tweedsmuir. When he died, my mother married in indecent haste to a man who was dour, unpleasant and low of stature, in mind and body. He came from a Drumelzier family, some leagues to the north, who were reputed to cut the throats of passing travellers for their purses. He was barbarous and foul-smelling, like many of my countrymen. But my mother was a shallow creature, vain and easily led by his flattering words. And so it happened that this unworthy man, by a low form of cunning, became heir to the land which should have been my brother's and mine.

No, I am not an illiterate herder of sheep. In fact I had, through industry and with immeasurable help from the Dominie of our church, gained the ability to read and write. Dominie Dinwoodie was a strange man. He was not of these parts. Some rumoured that he had been a pirate, others that he was a refugee from the English Queen, having failed in a plot against her. Others again saw in his long, sad face some tragedy in his past. His sermons were full of gloom, but then, I believe, so were those of all men of God in those days. But he was also a learned man who, for whatever reason, seemed to draw comfort from the solitude of our valley.

It was through the Dominie that I became familiar with Euclid's *Elements Geometrical*, and with the writings of the Greek and Roman scholars. My father's will had put money aside for an education, and so, with my brother Angus, and with the smiddy's four daughters, we learned to read, write and count. Often I would stay on after the lessons, and the Dominie and I would talk of many things. He had travelled, that was sure, but he never revealed why or in what capacity. He was fond of the bottle and sometimes, in evenings when his tongue was loose and the peat threw a red glow around his room, he talked of matters which, I suspect, could have had him hanged for heresy. All of this I absorbed like a parched plant absorbs water. I confess that, in my enthusiasm – even desperation – for learning, I many a time took one of the Dominie's books into the hills when I should have been looking after the sheep.

It was a strange irony (a word often used by the Dominie: it comes from the Greek *eironeia* and means the unexpected opposite; Socrates made use of irony in his speeches) that the Dominie, a man of great learning, chose to hide himself away in the valley, while this same learning gave rise, in my soul, to a growing sense of dissatisfaction. I began to feel that the hills were prison walls, closing me off from a great world outside. In truth, I began to think that to spend my life tending sheep was to do little with it.

My increasingly unsettled state was not helped by my stepfather. He turned out to be as ignorant a man as any you could ever meet. Not only that, but he was also one of the most violent, especially after whisky. He would often beat me for little reason or none, although never when my brother was nearby; Angus, stronger and bigger than me, he left alone.

After a few months of my mother's marriage, and after a particularly vicious kicking, I laid about my stepfather with a shovel in a great rage. He retired whimpering and bruised to the Crook Inn and I saw no more of him that night. The next day I told my mother that I was going south to England, perhaps even to London, to make my own way in the world. There were tears and protestations, but I sensed that in her heart she was happy to be rid of her youngest and most troublesome son, who after all was of little use on the land and whose head was full of strange ideas and nonsenses (and indeed, if she only knew it, heresies).

On the evening before my departure from the valley, I walked the half-league to the Dominie. The moon was full, and it seemed that its light came down through a tunnel made of high swirling clouds. The hills glowed with an unearthly light and it was easy to see warlocks in the dark shadows. The Dominie – I only ever knew him by that title – had been busy with the bottle and did not hear me enter. The room was warm and red from the glowing peat and he was sprawled on a chair, gazing into the fire, a Bible and a near-empty bottle on the floor next to him. He spoke without looking up.

'Is that you off, then? To the English Queen's city, the great dunghill?'

'In the morning.'

He turned to me. His cheeks and eyes were red, whether with whisky or the fire I could not be sure. 'You know nothing of life outside Tweedsmuir, James.'

'How can that be? Look what you have taught me.'

He shook his head. 'Education is a fine shield and a deadly weapon, but it will take you only so far. You lack experience, and you are going alone into a city with more sins than Nineveh.'

'I've been to Lanark.'

He laughed briefly. 'Lanark is not Nineveh.' He paused, and then asked, almost as if he was speaking his thoughts aloud, 'Will we ever see you again?'

'Sir, who but God can say?'

'Who, indeed. Aye well, you have learning far beyond ABC, and the sharpest wits I've seen in any lad of your age. But you'll need more than that.' He stood up unsteadily and crossed to a small black chest in the corner of the room. I had wondered many a time what was in the chest, but had never dared to ask. But now he was turning a key in a padlock and pulling up the lid. 'This will supplement your wits.' To my amazement he produced a black leather sheath and from it pulled out a long, thin, two-edged dagger. He handed it to me, almost reverently. 'Mariners call it a ballockknife. It has been places and done things you don't want to know about. Roll up your sleeve,' he said. I did so. He buckled the sheath on to the back of my forearm. 'You will not see many handles like that. It is called ivory and is carved from the tusk of an elephant.'

But the edges of the blade were of more interest to me. I touched

them and gasped with the unexpected pain. They were sharper
than those of any knife I had come across.

'Put it back in its sheath. Then pull it out quickly, and try not to
slice your skin as you do.'

I did so. There was a ridge inside the leather sheath which held
the dagger in place but was easily overcome simply by tugging at
the ivory handle.

'Do it again.'

I did so several times. I found I could pull the knife out in an
instant.

'Now roll your sleeve down and repeat the process.'

I did so.

The Dominie nodded. 'Again, faster.'

I did so, until I felt confident that I could snatch the knife out
from under the sleeve of my tunic in an instant.

The Dominie nodded in satisfaction. 'That is your friend,' he
said. 'Put your trust in no other. Use him only when you must. But
when you must use him, do so suddenly, and with great rage and
boldness.'

I began to thank him, but he silenced me with an impatient
gesture. 'Another good friend. He has served me well but I no
longer have need of him.' And from under the bed he produced a
pole, about shoulder high, with a sharp metal spike on its end. 'He
is happier in the open air than hidden under a bed. The mariners
call it a boarding pike. It needs little skill but is very effective. There
is no defence against this—' and he suddenly swept the pike from
knee height upwards towards my stomach, stopping its point an
inch from me. He laughed at my sudden fear. In the red light of the
peat, his eyes watery and gleaming, he looked satanic. 'And if you
thrust your opponent here' – he moved the point down to just
above my groin – 'he will take hours, maybe days, to die in agony.'

'I would not wish that on any man, even if he was not a
Christian.'

The Dominie looked as if he had something to say on the matter,
but then changed his mind. Instead he pulled aside a curtain.
'Perhaps one last friend.' Over his unmade bed was a single shelf of
books. He pulled one out and thrust it into my hands, almost with

embarrassment. Again I started to speak, but he shook his head and turned my shoulders towards the door. As I left he said, 'I can give you no better advice than this, James. Hold onto your weapons, keep your own counsel, never get too close to any man. Now go, and God be with you, if there is a God.'

I left, my head swirling like the clouds above me. Surely the world beyond the valley was not as dangerous a place as my drunken teacher implied? The Dominie was a man of God. But of what God, in truth I was beginning to wonder.

The following morning, I crawled over my sleeping brother and stepped quietly down the ladder. Heavy snoring came from behind the curtain screening the hole in the wall where my parents slept. One of the pigs stirred. My satchel was prepared. As I lifted it I heard my name whispered: 'James!' Angus looked down at me, his face pale and strained. There was nothing I could say to him. I waved silently, my heart filled with sadness. Outside, the air was chill and damp. I took the drover's road running alongside the chattering Tweed and, with the mist coming down from the dark hills, turned south, away from the cottage where I had spent my life.

After half a league the road took me past the smiddy, its windows shuttered. Fiona's home; Fiona of the long black hair and the cheerful smile; Fiona who, had I stayed in that valley, might some day have become my wife. She was fifteen years, my age. My will almost failed me at that point, knowing that if I walked past I might never see her again. But walk past I did, although with trembling knees and pain in my heart.

Presently the mist began to lift, and the road skirted the broad marshland which was the source of the Tweed, and then wound along the rim of the Devil's Beef Tub. I took this dangerous road, treading carefully. The great cauldron below was filled with mist, as if water was bubbling within it. Then the road descended steeply towards Moffat, where plumes of smoke were drifting up from a dozen chimneys. By noon I was walking through the village, having met not a soul on the way.

I had now reached the boundary of my world. Beyond Moffat, the landscape was unfamiliar. I began to feel a sense of adventure, mixed with apprehension. I carried on south and by the evening the drover's road merged with a broader track heading towards Carlisle and beyond.

My mother had given me enough silver coins to purchase food for some weeks. The Dominie's pike was in my hands and his ballocknife was hidden in my sleeve, its sheath strapped to my wrist. I was to wonder many times, in my long journey, what lay in this strange man's past and what tales the dagger could tell. Be that as it may, pike and knife gave me a sense of security; the robber who attempted to waylay me would be risking a cut throat.

My satchel held not only a purse of coins, but also a small Bible and – God bless the Dominie – Thomas North's translation of Plutarchs's *Lives*. Useless baggage? My mother would have said so. But in the days to come the wisdom of these men of liberty – Solon, Publicola, Philopoemen, Titus Quinctius Flamininus and Caius Marius – was to shine through the mists of time, lighting my way through terrifying darkness, and I was the stronger for their companionship. I truly believe that I would not have survived to this day without them.

You may think that a country boy going alone into unknown territory would be prey to the wiles of clever tricksters, who would present themselves as affable companions but whose true purpose would be to lighten me of my coins. And indeed some tried, even at the end of my first day when, with darkness falling, I stopped at a hot and cheerful hostelry. But I will not trouble you with the adventures of my long journey south – I write this in circumstances where parchment must be used sparsely, and indeed in circumstances where I must write quickly, for my survival is far from certain. Suffice to say that I found myself equal to all that I encountered, and that when I entered London three weeks later, with my last coin gone and the soles of my shoes wearing thin, I had been measured and not found wanting in the world of men.

I saw the haze of that great city a full half day before I saw the city itself.

6

As I approached the city I began to pass houses the likes of which I had never before seen. They were like palaces, almost as grand as the castles I had glimpsed in the distance on my way south. Some were reached through long, broad paths and were surrounded by trees and shrubs cut in patterns which were clearly the work of man. The road broadened and from time to time horsemen would pass, sometimes singly, sometimes in twos or threes, dressed in fine clothes and with long, thin swords in scabbards. Then the houses became smaller and more clustered, with little space that I could see for gardens.

Individuals began to pass me, paying me little attention. In my long walk from Scotland I had preferred to travel alone – keeping my own counsel, as the Dominie would have said. Unwelcome companions had been met with dourness and taciturnity and had soon found excuses to part company with me. Here I had no such problem. There was not even a nod of greeting.

Within an hour of reaching the border of the city I was walking past rows of houses stuck together, and people in their hundreds walking on roads covered with filth. The air stank worse than our byre. I had to step around dung and garbage many times. I wondered how people could be content to live in this way. I began to notice that I was receiving curious stares, and I surmised that my tunic, my breeches, my cap and my pike were the objects of this attention. Indeed, two young women ran past me giggling, covering their mouths with their hands. I noticed that their faces seemed to be covered with some white powder, which I found very strange.

All the time, as I approached the centre of this great town, the bustle and noise increased. There were men pulling carts full of vegetables, shops displaying fly-covered meat, women carrying bags of bread and flour, and more horsemen, wearing stockings like my mother, and tunics with frills of white cloth around their necks. These men too had swords, and usually carried themselves with a certain swagger, the horses seeming as grand and arrogant as their owners. And there were others in flea-infested rags, sitting on the street with hands cupped, looking for coins. One or two played on mandolins like those of the Lanark beggars.

Soon I found myself walking along narrow streets, full of inns and bustling with merchants and carts carrying barrels, timber, bales of wool and many other products. I passed a great tower on a hill, square in construction and with flags flying from each of its four turrets. But it was not the tower which caught my eye: it was a scaffold next to it, from which the bodies of three men were hanging. Further along I saw a great archway and close to it four high poles with what looked like turnips stuck on top. As I approached, I saw to my horror that these were human heads, drained, discoloured, the jaws hanging open and flies buzzing in their ears, eyes and mouths. Dark stains had trickled down the poles from the heads. I could not believe such barbarity. Whatever they had done, were they not Christians, and so entitled to Christian burial? Trying not to retch I passed under the arch. None of the crowd milling around me seemed even to notice the ghastly sight.

In the late afternoon, with the sky growing dark and thundery, I walked alongside the broad river which I knew to be the Thames. Small ships, many of them loaded with cargo, were sailing up and down this stretch of water. I had seen pictures of ships but this was my first sight of real ones. I was enchanted by them and almost forgot the gruesome heads which I had earlier passed under. I walked along the embankment, past a timber crane which was being used to unload casks of what I believed to be French wine, until I came to a bridge, and joined the throng which was crossing it. By now it was almost dark, I still had no money and no place to sleep, and I was filled with great weariness, having walked four leagues that day.

South of the river, London was clearly an area of great poverty, but there was also much merriment, or so it seemed. The streets were crowded with drunkards. A woman of great age, perhaps forty, with bright red lips and face powdered white, gave me a strange, unpleasant smile. I ignored her and passed. She smelled of flowers and sweat. I had hardly gone fifty paces when my path was blocked by four youths, some years older than me. They wore flat caps with feathers and had long, thin swords dangling from their belts. I did not like their demeanour.

The oldest, a flat-faced individual with a dull red tunic and thin breeches, stopped me with a raised hand. 'So where have you crawled from, country boy? Scotland?' There was an outburst of coarse laughter from his friends, who were spreading themselves around me. 'And where did you steal these clothes? From the back of a sheep?' More laughter. I tried to push on past but the man shoved at my chest and said, 'I'm not finished with you, boy.' His face was a foot from mine and his breath was disgusting, with a strong smell of port.

'And I don't like the look of you,' I replied.

He looked at me with angry amazement and then slapped my face. The blow was hard and unexpected and I staggered, almost knocked to the ground and dropping my pike, which he stood on. I recovered my balance and suddenly, with rage and boldness, pulled my dagger from its sheath and lunged at his throat. He froze, wide-eyed in terror. I pricked the skin of his neck, drawing blood, and said loudly, making sure anger was in my voice, 'I am indeed from the land of the Scots, sir. Do you have anything to say about that?'

White-faced, he shook his head and backed off, but from the corner of my eye I saw one of his companions reach for his sword. I judged the weapon to be about an arm's length, but my pike was longer, about two arms' length.

There is no defence against a pike thrust upwards from knee level towards the stomach. I dropped my dagger, snatched up my pike and put my weight behind it, since I perceived myself to be in mortal danger and was in any case by now very angry. The metal tip of the pike sank into the man's belly to about a finger's depth. He collapsed like a dead weight and rolled on the ground, screaming in pain and holding himself, while blood spurted between his hands. His companions ran off shouting – brave fellows they! – leaving him howling on the ground. I noticed that the woman who had smiled at me a moment earlier had disappeared. I picked up my dagger and went on my way, hardening my heart against the man's cries of pain.

No more than a hundred paces had passed when I was stopped yet again, this time by someone of my age, dressed in little more than rags. 'I saw that,' he said in an accent which I could scarce understand. The word 'saw' came out as 'zorr'.

He added, 'You are a stranger in these parts?'

'I am, and what of it?' My voice came out harsh and trembling with the excitement of the last moments.

'This is Southwark, a dangerous place to be after dark. There are many thieves and cutpurses here.'

'Aye, and you are perhaps one of them.' My ballocknife was inside my sleeve again but could be at his throat in a flash.

He laughed. 'My name is Michael,' he said. 'As you are a stranger in these parts, I swear to God you are at risk.'

'You have just seen me dealing with Master Risk.'

'Have I not!' Behind me, the man was still threshing around and howling. Others were stepping around him, paying him little attention. I believe there was admiration in Michael's voice, though why I do not know. 'Where are you staying?' he asked.

I hesitated before confiding in this complete stranger, but judged that he presented little immediate danger. 'I have no place to stay, and in case you think to lighten me of my purse through some trick, save your effort. I have no money.'

'And what about food?'

'I ate yesterday.'

'Come with me.'

I decided that the risk of being on my own in this hostile area was greater than that of following this boy of my own age. With every sense alert, I followed him along the streets. There was a whiff of human excrement in the air, mixed with wonderful smells of food coming from taverns which we passed. Presently he turned into a noisy, well-lit tavern. Over the entrance was a sign on which was painted a galleon like those I had seen in the Dominie's books. Inside, the noise was greater than any I had ever heard, even in the hostelries where I had stayed on the way down. It was hot, from the crush of bodies and a roaring fire near the entrance.

'Find a space,' he said, and disappeared towards a far corner of the room. As it happened, three men, all drunk, were standing up and about to leave a table. I pushed my way through the crowd, attracting no small attention, I suppose because of my pike – although I had wiped the blood from its tip – and sat down. My companion soon appeared with two large jugs of beer. 'Put that down you,' he said. 'Food will be along shortly.'

'Why are you doing this?' I asked. 'I am a stranger to you. And I judge that charity is not in your heart.'

My companion grinned, raised his jug. 'I have my reasons,' he said.

'To do with those roughs?'

'To do with the way you dealt with them.'

I sipped at the beer. It was strong. It was clear that if I finished the jug I would be as drunk as many of those in the tavern. I decided that out of courtesy I would sip at it but take no more than a mouthful in total.

'A Scotchman, then?'

'Aye.'

'Come to look for employment in the big city.'

'That is true.'

'With no money and no place to sleep?'

'You have me in summary. But not all of me. I am also alert, angry and armed.'

The boy smiled again. 'And rightly so in these parts. But you need have no fear of me.'

'I have none, I assure you.' A woman about the age of my mother, with the upper part of her chest shamelessly exposed, approached with two plates of stew, bread and cutlery. I hardly knew where to look for embarrassment. She looked at my pike with some alarm but said nothing. I began to eat hungrily. I noticed that my companion, while eating, glanced at me surreptitiously from time to time. The leather holster of the dagger was comforting against my forearm.

'Armed, you say.' He nodded at my boarding pike. 'That is of little use at very close quarters.'

I wondered if he had seen my work with the dagger in the near-dark. 'For close quarters I have other devices.'

He grinned again; a happy one this, I thought. 'I do not doubt it. Are all Scotch such warriors?'

My companion waved and shouted to a man in the far corner of the room. The man was completely bald and had dark skin, the likes of which I had only seen in Dominie Dinwoodie's illustrations of the travels of Sir John Mandeville. He was wearing a green blouse, of a sort which I had only ever seen on women at the markets in Lanark and Biggar. His arms were muscular and painted. His face was dominated by a large nose and he had a row of decaying yellow teeth. He sat down at our table, putting his jug of beer on the table.

'This is the Turk.'

I returned the man's nod warily.

Michael leaned forward, although his voice would scarcely carry above the din. 'This is a Scotchman. He killed a man not ten minutes ago. I saw it with my own eyes.'

The Turk's eyes widened.

'He may not be dead. And I was defending myself.'

The Turk looked at my pike. 'What fool thinks he can walk into a crowded tavern with that and attract no notice? Why are you not fleeing? Do the Scots kill with such impudence? And do you not see curious eyes on you from every corner?'

'In truth, sir, I have seen so much that is strange in this town that I am paying them little heed.'

'Did others see this killing?' The Turk was still wide-eyed.

'The man had three companions, who fled for their lives.'

'I am not surprised.' The Turk drank from his jug. 'Describe them.'

'They wore fine tunics with white frills around their necks, flat feathered caps, they carried swords and were little older than me.'

'Not cutpurses,' the Turk said. 'The sons of gentlemen.' He made a hissing noise through a gap between his teeth and then shook his head. 'You have put your head in a noose, my little Scotch. Even now you are surely being hunted. And before the night is out, perhaps even within the hour, you will be found and imprisoned in Newgate. And then, unless you are rich . . .' He made a throat-cutting gesture and grinned.

'But I did nothing wrong,' I said in dismay. My thoughts went to the heads I had seen aloft on poles.

The Turk continued to grin. 'You understand nothing. They may have wealthy fathers. The magistrate will know where his duty lies, and if not, a pouch of gold will remind him.'

Fear and despair began to seep into my bones. I pushed my bowl away. 'Then I must get away from here,' I said, glancing fearfully at the door which, as it happened, opened that second. I snatched at my pike in fright, but only two women of middle age came in, their faces thick with powder and paint, and their dresses gaudy and stained, the hems lined with the filth of the street.

'Aye,' said the Turk, imitating my accent crudely, 'but where to?'

'Back to Scotland. From what I have seen of this dunghill, I wish I had never left.'

'But can you outrun horsemen? You are, forgive me, what is the word? Visible. Yes, visible.' The man looked up and down at my clothes and grinned unpleasantly.

'I have a better idea,' said Michael.

I sensed a trap, but did not know what to do.

'The Scotch man here is looking for a place to stay, and for employment.'

'Employment?' The Turk's voice was strong, even harsh, but there was something else in it. Already alert, I was on the verge of leaving their company on the instant. 'I can offer him that.'

'What is the nature of this employment?' I asked.

The Turk was still grinning. 'It is of a nature which will let you escape the hangman. That should be enough.'

A girl approached. She bore some resemblance to Fiona, but she was a little older, or at least seemed so. Again there was the strange white powder on her face, which I began to think was some London fashion, and her lips were painted bright red. Like the tavern servant, much of her upper chest was exposed. She affected a smile. 'Business, gentlemen?'

My companion dismissed her with a wave, as if he was getting rid of a fly. To me his attitude was insulting but the woman seemed to take no offence and walked over to the next table.

'What business?' I asked.

The men looked at me with astonishment, then at each other, and then burst out laughing. The Turk said, 'You mean you do not know?'

Michael leaned forward. 'The women here sell their bodies in exchange for money. Many gentlemen cross the bridge in the evening for amusement. There are several such even here.'

It took me some seconds to understand, and when I did, I could not believe such depravity was possible. I thought of Fiona, of similar age and appearance, but shy and kind and cheerful, and could not understand how women could be so different. 'Has she no concern for her soul?' I asked, shocked and intrigued all at once.

The Turk laughed as if I had made some jest of great wit. 'In this place, Scotch, our souls are damned.' At that moment I wondered if I should have stayed in the valley, or if I should even now take my chance with the constables and walk the fifty leagues back home. But the Turk interrupted my thoughts.

'We stay in the basement of a house not far from here. The rent is cheap but you can be our guest for tonight. Tomorrow we will talk of the work.' He slapped a flea on his muscular arm.

'I had thought to work in a shop, or perhaps use my ability to write.' I asked again, 'What is the nature of this work?'

The Turk gave me a sly grin and tapped the side of his big nose. This annoyed me and I said, 'Tell me now or I will thank you for the meal and be on my way.'

'You barely have time to finish your beer,' Michael said. 'Your gentlemen will have crossed the bridge and may at this moment be recrossing it with friends in tow. Make your decision, Scotch. The Turk or the hangman? Which is it to be?'

7

I did not trust my new companions and was determined not to sleep. I lay on damp straw with my satchel under me and my arm wrapped around my pike. It was not long before my whole body seemed to be crawling with fleas. In the dark I listened to the sounds of snoring from a dozen or more bodies in the cramped room, and a mysterious rustling in a corner. There was a smell of sweat and damp and bad wine, and presently urine. It was disgusting in my nostrils.

I must have fallen asleep nevertheless. For when next I opened my eyes a bleak grey light was shining through a small window high in one of the walls.

I sat up. My limbs were itching and covered with little red bite marks. I looked around and longed for the warm companionship of my brother rather than the vile strangers sprawled around me.

Michael was asleep in a corner, mouth agape, in his ragged clothes, but the Turk was gone. With satchel and pike I stepped over sleeping, wretched bodies. Then, in a narrow passageway outside, I gulped in what passed for fresh air. There were privies round the back, shared, it seemed, by hundreds of tenants to judge by the windows which overlooked me on every side. A dog was urinating at a single water pump.

I stepped back to the passageway, my mind made up to find my way out of this wretched city, but the Turk was already standing in the street. He gave me a wide, yellow-stained grin. 'Scotch! We must get you away from here as quickly as possible.'

Michael appeared, rubbing his eyes.

'Get rid o' that,' said the Turk, nodding at my pike.

'Never. It saved my life last night.'

'And it will hang you this morning.'

I shook my head.

'Stubborn fool,' said the Turk. He turned and led the way smartly north, towards the bridge I had crossed the previous night. We passed a dark stain, larger than a man, where I had split my attacker's stomach. I wondered if he had survived the night, whether he might now be dying in agony somewhere. Michael muttered something to the Turk, pointing at it.

The Turk said, 'Scotch, if the constables approach, or a gang of young gentlemen, cut and run. You will have to save yourself if you can.'

In the dawn light, without the noise, bustle and drunkenness, this was a dreary place indeed. Filth and stench were everywhere. Here and there a woman staggered along, or sat slouched in an alleyway.

Once over the bridge we turned right. Here there was activity, even at this early hour of the morning. Several gentlemen approached on horseback. The Turk's eyes widened with fear. 'Your pike, you Scotch fool!' he hissed. 'Get rid of it!'

I shook my head, although my legs were trembling. The gentlemen passed.

Further along the embankment we began to encounter merchants pulling carts loaded with bottles and sacks. The Turk was walking ahead eagerly, almost running, as if approaching sanctuary. His anxiety was infectious and I too began to walk quickly, although I feared the attention our haste might draw. My companions did not choose to reveal the nature of the employment they were leading me to, and I saw no purpose in asking.

I had seen a picture of one in one of the Dominie's books, but the reality made me open my mouth. The Turk saw my amazement and, in spite of his evident tension, laughed.

The ship had three tall masts, sails furled. Joining mast and deck was a mass of rigging which reminded me of a spider's web. There were square holes along its sides. Men were toiling up and down a gangplank with barrels, sacks and chests. A group of men, dressed in satin finery of muted greens, yellows and reds, and wearing swords, were talking together on the dock.

40

I began to see the nature of the employment which the Turk was offering me.

At this point, I believe I could have turned and run. Instead I asked, 'Where is she bound?'

'Nobody knows. Do you come willingly?'

I had my dagger as well as my pike, and knew I could outrun this heavy man. But run to where? Back to a stinking basement in Southwark? Into a noose? I did not doubt that the Turk would cry 'Murderer!' to collect whatever reward might be going. My imagination saw my head perched on a pole, flies buzzing in every orifice. In any case, I had come to find my way in the world, not become a fugitive or a beggar. And there was a strange allure about this magnificent ship, the sharp commands of the officers reaching us from the deck, the smells and the bustle, and the mystery of the lands that it might visit and which I would never otherwise see outside of Dominie Dinwoodie's pictures. And I thought that, whatever happened, I would have something to eat, and a better place to sleep than a flea-infested basement or a condemned cell in Newgate. 'How long will the voyage last?'

The Turk shrugged. 'I do not know.'

My companions waited. I looked at them, and then again at the ship, and then continued towards it. Michael and the Turk joined me on either side, grinning from ear to ear. I suspected that they might share some small reward for enticing me on board.

'Let them know that I boarded of my own free will as a freeman and was not pressed.'

The Turk nodded happily. Whether he did would depend, I suspected, on the size of his reward.

We joined a short queue of men. A red-faced man was sitting at a barrel on which paper, pen and ink were laid out. Recognition passed between him and the Turk. 'Joining us again, Ferhat?'

'Aye, Mister Twiss.'

'Not even the tavern scum are volunteering. Your experience will be useful. And perhaps we will have better hunting this time.' Mr Twiss looked at me. 'And what minnow is this you have brought along, Ferhat? Your name, boy?'

'James Ogilvie, sir.'

41

'And what is that?' He eyed my pike curiously.

'I use it for catching fish, sir.'

I could sense the Turk catching his breath.

'This lad's impertinence will see him well flogged before the journey is over,' Mr Twiss said, half-jokingly.

'This is the ship's quartermaster, Scotch. You cannot speak to him that way.'

'He'll learn soon enough,' said Mr Twiss. 'I dare say you are in trouble of some sort.'

I stayed silent, although my heart began to thump in my chest.

'Serious trouble, perhaps?'

Not knowing what to say, I still said nothing. He was looking closely at me.

Then he shrugged. 'No matter here. Do you have sailing experience?'

'No sir.'

'Can you do anything?'

'I can read and write.'

'I meant anything useful.' I believe he was using irony in the Socratic style. 'What is your employment?'

'My father was a farmer.'

'Aha! Why did you not say so? We will have livestock on board presently. You can look after it.'

He wrote my name on a sheet of paper. 'You are now on the Queen's list for the duration of the voyage. The penalty for desertion is death. Find a berth and then help with the loading. Do not idle. We have a morning tide to catch.'

I felt a tremendous surge of excitement and relief.

On deck, a chain of men was coming in and out of an open hatch. I followed the Turk, clambering awkwardly down steep wooden steps. Then there were more steps and a long, gloomy corridor.

'The ship will become crowded,' the Turk predicted. 'Let the others sleep between the cannon, as cannon there will surely be.' The corridor opened into a large, low room. I had to duck my head to avoid hitting it on the beams. Long, narrow nets were strung between these beams. 'Choose a hammock and put your things on it.' I dropped satchel, pike and jacket on one of the nets and rejoined the circulating procession of men on the deck.

I spent the morning with the other mariners, rough-looking men, all of them, rolling huge barrels of water and beer into a net suspended from a wooden crane. A team of men heaved this great weight into the air and swung it round so that the heavy barrels could be lowered down through a hatch into the dark depths of the ship. I helped with the storage of these great barrels in the gloom of the hold.

By mid-day my muscles were aching and my back was sore. Presently, smoke began to drift up from the depths of the ship, mingling with the smells of tar and sweat which were everywhere, and at the instructions of Mr Twiss we stopped and climbed down broad ladders to a large room with benches and tables. Here the smell of wood-smoke was strong, and came from an adjoining open kitchen. We queued and I was given biscuits and a huge jug of beer. The biscuits turned out to be as hard as rocks. The air was filled with bangs as they were tapped against corners and edges of benches.

'Hunger!' cried the Turk, next to me, waving at a sailor. A small, muscular man, carrying a bowlful of biscuits, grinned and sat down opposite us. 'Still avoiding the pox, then? And keen for more punishment, it seems?'

'Aye,' said the man called Hunger. 'Where do you think we are bound? I surely don't know.' He leaned forward. 'But this is a very small crew for such a large ship.'

The Turk nodded. 'I thought so too. And supplies are meagre. They say Sir Walter Raleigh lies behind this expedition.'

'Tavern rumour,' replied Hunger contemptuously.

'Will you not venture a guess?' The Turk, amazingly, broke a biscuit with his teeth and began to crunch noisily. I drank my beer greedily: the work had been hard and my throat was dry.

Hunger said, 'We'll be in search of Caribbean gold. You'll have seen the gunports – ten of them, enough to put the fear of God into any Spanish captain.'

'Aye, empty gunports. Where are the cannon to fill them? And the gunners to work them? We have scarce enough men on board to unfurl the sails.'

'Which we shall do shortly, I'll wager.' This from another man who had joined us. The smoke was beginning to sting my eyes but nobody seemed to be paying any attention to it. I coughed and drank more beer. I was not used to it and it was beginning to have an effect on me, not an unpleasant one.

'Caribbean gold. I do not doubt it, Mr Chandler,' the Turk agreed. I began to wonder if everyone knew everyone else on this voyage.

'And the *auto-da-fe*, unless the ship is better manned than this.'

'*Auto-da-fe*?' I asked.

The man looked at me in surprise. 'You do not know of the *auto-da-fe*?'

I shook my head, bewildered.

The man threw back his head and laughed. 'And the Turk, no doubt, enticed you on board?'

'I had my reasons for wishing to join the ship and had no need of the Turk to persuade me.'

'Be careful not to offend young Scotch,' the Turk said in a half-joking voice.

Michael joined in with enthusiasm. 'He has a short temper and is capable of extreme violence. I have seen him, with my own eyes, leave three men howling on the ground, trying to push their bowels back in place.'

I chose not to dispute these assertions, thinking that such a reputation might afford some protection amongst my new companions in the days ahead.

'The light loading is a ruse, I'll wager,' said the man called Hunger. 'Intended to confuse Mendoza's spies. I believe we will sail round Portsmouth and take on more men and supplies. Then we'll see.'

Full of curiosity, I asked, 'Mendoza?'

The man called Chandler looked at me. 'What backward people the Scots are. Do you know anything?'

'I know how to cut a throat,' I said.

Chandler looked at me through narrowed eyes. No doubt he was trying to assess how much of my speech was bravado and how much was meant. But he had no time to say more. A squat, burly man was walking amongst the sailors, a short cudgel in his hand.

He held it strangely and it was a second before I noticed that he had two fingers missing. His face was so covered with black beard and whiskers that he looked like a furry animal. Now he was standing at our bench. Small, pig-like eyes, hard as rocks, stared at me. 'Finish up and get on with the loading.'

'Aye, Mr Salter.' The tone of humility in the Turk's voice surprised me greatly. Somehow I did not think that my reputation as a fifteen-year-old cutthroat would make much impression on this man.

I cannot describe the magic of the next few days. In response to the harsh commands of Mr Salter, we climbed the rigging and unfurled the sails. From the high masts I could see much of London and even the countryside beyond. Then, as the wind caught the sails, we began to slip along the Thames. The Turk pointed out Greenwich and the Isle of Dogs as we passed, and the river slowly broadened until, by the end of the first day, we seemed to be a mile from the nearest shore. Then a great lantern was lit at the rear of the ship and we sailed on through the dark. It was not long before a sense of nausea overcame me, and to the laughter of the others I had to hurry along a corridor, climb stairs in the dark and find my way to the edge of the ship, where I emptied my stomach into the sea.

On the third day, following shouted instructions from Mr Salter, the ship began to turn towards a large town with an enormous harbour. Rows of pretty white houses and shops stretched away on all sides, and its streets were bustling with people. It happened I was furling a sail, whose name was mysterious to me but which was high enough for the act to cause me some fear, with Hunger and the Turk. 'What town is this?'

'Plymouth, Scotch!'

We were slipping alongside a long quay, heaped with sacks, barrels and other supplies. A few children waved. We drifted past a sailing ship not much smaller than our own. 'The Lyon,' said Hunger in a tone of admiration.

'And the Roebuck,' said the Turk. 'But what ships are these?'

The Turk, I believe, could not read. Hunger said, 'The Dorothy and the Elizabeth.'

But there was little time to admire the sight. Having docked, there was loading to be done. There were scores of soldiers. I was surprised to see that many of them carried pikes like my own. And there was such a supply of provisions as I had never seen: chests, casks, crates, sacks, hogsheads and creels full of dried fish and prunes. And enough barrels of cider, wine and beer to keep the whole assembly drunk for months.

There was a harsh shout on the dockside: 'Make way!' A large group of men in naval uniform, carrying short cudgels, were bundling several dozen men of all ages, haggard and grey-faced, between them. Several of these men seemed drunk.

'Who are they?' I asked the Turk. We were rolling barrels on to a net for the crane men to lift.

'Prisoners, by the looks of them,' said the Turk. 'And tavern scum.' He seemed to have forgotten that he was in a tavern when I first saw him.

'Press-ganged,' Hunger informed me. 'Men are afraid to serve. And little wonder, after Sir Humphrey's expedition.'

Another sailor, whose name I later learned was the Hog, stopped to stretch and wipe his brow. He said, 'They say that, before the disaster, there was strange voices heard at the helm of the ship and strange sea-creatures were caught with their harpoon. And before the storm which sank them, Mr Cox saw white cliffs which vanished as they approached.'

'Nonsense,' Mr Chandler told me. 'That was twenty years ago. It's the astrologers who keep men from this voyage. The planetary conjunctions are not good. Jupiter and Saturn came together in eighty-three, starting the age of the Fiery Trigon. We are entering a period of great catastrophe. Thomas Porter predicts much violence against travellers, and Euan Lloyd tells us there will be tempests, fogs, mists, storms and shipwrecks.'

'Tales fit only for women,' Hunger informed me. 'It is true that many sailors are prone to such nonsense. But no, Scotch, what is truly keeping men from this voyage is something of this world, not the spirit one or the celestial one. It is the fear of *auto-da-fe*.'

That phrase again, always spoken with fear: *auto-da-fe*. Not even the lure of Caribbean gold, it seemed, was able to overcome that fear.

It took three days of backbreaking work to stuff the hold of the Tiger. Ten massive cannon were dragged on board in pieces and assembled. I had the impression that these great guns were reassuring to the Turk and his friends. After that, the mariners and soldiers climbed aboard, and the ship suddenly became cramped, with hardly space to move. And then, at last, there came the gentlemen. It was late afternoon when the Turk beckoned me urgently towards the side of the ship. We leaned over the rail and looked down on a small group of men. 'That is Walter Raleigh,' he said with something like awe. 'He is the Queen's favourite, newly knighted. And the man next to him is Thomas Harriot.'

'Christ! Philip Amadas,' said Hunger, dismay in his voice as a tiny man emerged from a carriage.

'And who are these?' I asked. For two men of very strange appearance had emerged from a second carriage, accompanied by more gentlemen.

'All London knows of them,' said the Turk. 'These are Manteo and Wanchese. Savages from America.'

'And now it's clear enough,' said Hunger. 'We are heading for America.'

'By way of the West Indies, I do not doubt,' said the Turk. 'And a little plunder.'

'Thank Christ for the gunners,' said Hunger.

I was kept busy for the rest of the day: chickens, pigs and goats had come aboard. There was little room for them in the narrow square of deck assigned to me by Mr Salter, but I believe that I organised it well, and I felt some pride that I had found a place, however modest, in this great enterprise. At last, the gentlemen came aboard, most of them joining the Tiger. Raleigh remained on the dock, then left in a carriage. When, at dawn the next morning, on the ninth of April 1585, the ships slipped quietly out of Plymouth harbour, I felt a strange mixture of excitement and apprehension.

But it was a full thirteen days before I summoned up the courage to ask the Turk about the *auto-da-fe*.

8

It was not long before I had my first encounter with Mr Salter. I am grateful for the beating he gave me. Not because it filled me with hatred for my assailant, which it did, but because it filled me with determination to leave the ranks of the tavern scum at any price and attach myself to those of the gentlemen.

Following instructions, and imitating the Turk closely, I had climbed riggings, crawled along masts, hauled on ropes until my hands were raw, scrubbed the deck and done all the things that the deckmaster Mr Salter had demanded of us.

A strange sensation which had slowly been growing in my head somehow connected with my stomach. A feeling of unease, hard to describe, increased slowly as the day progressed until it filled my whole being with wretchedness. It was not long before I was wishing that I was dead.

The incident which precipitated my beating happened at the very highest point of the ship, on the main topgallant sail. The Turk was sitting astride the yard while I, in a state of terror, hauled at a rope following his instructions. From here I could see the other five ships of the expedition spread around us on the sparkling sea. They were rolling from side to side, and up and down, and corkscrewing, as the wind blew them through the waves. At this height the roll of the ship was greatly exaggerated. I seemed to remember a principle about leverage enunciated by Aristotle, but was too miserable and frightened to think it through. As the mast swayed from side to side the dreadful feeling intensified. 'Turk,' I said. 'I'm going to be sick.'

'It's the rolling of the ship, Scotch.' He seemed unaffected by it. 'Now catch this and heave. Harder, are you a girl?'

'How do I stop the ship rolling?'

'You cannot, foolish boy. But you will grow accustomed to it.'

I doubted it: far below me, several experienced mariners were hanging grey-faced over the rails. One of them began to vomit into the sea. It was too much for me. 'I must go down now.'

'You cannot, Scotch.' The Turk glared at me. 'Not until we have unfurled the sail.'

But I had to. At any cost I had to reach the side of the ship and empty the contents of my stomach as quickly as I could. Carefully, I sidled along the yard and picked my way past the Turk. To pass him I had to lean outwards, gripping him by his shoulders while feeling my way along the rope with my feet. A foot slipped, and for some seconds of horror I teetered between life and death on the swaying ship, while the Turk's nails dug deeply into my forearm. But I passed him, reached the mainmast thankfully, and began to clamber quickly down the ratline, the wind fluttering my shirt.

Mr Salter was looking up at me, his eyes a mixture of hostility and mystification. He opened his mouth to shout at me. Unfortunately, at that very moment, bile rose within my mouth and I retched out the contents of my stomach: a white frothy stream poured out, containing within it half-digested lumps of biscuits, dried fish and peas. Mr Salter tried to leap aside, but because of the rolling of the deck his jump was clumsy and my vomit went cleanly onto his head and down his jacket. There were gasps from around the rigging. Someone muttered, 'God, lad, he will kill you.'

I started to climb back up the rigging, wishing it extended to the clouds above, but Mr Salter's roar of command brought me down. He was using a handkerchief to wipe the vomit from his head and neck while I stood before him, trembling. Then he took off his jerkin and placed it on the deck, and slowly picked up the cudgel which he had dropped as he jumped. It was short, polished, narrow at its handle and broad at its base. He tapped it a few times in the palm of his three-fingered hand. He said nothing, but his brittle blue eyes were filled with fury.

The first blow was to my stomach. It was a hard, upward thrust with the cudgel, which he held with both hands. The blow doubled me up and put me to the deck, unable to breathe. Salter then hauled me up by the hair and began striking me on shins, arms, legs, ribs

– anywhere he could reach. When at last he let go of my hair and I fell to the deck, the blows continued on my back and buttocks. I began to wonder if his fury would last all day and if I would be alive at the end of it. Then at last, while I lay prostrate and moaning, I heard a distant voice say: 'Now clean the deck, you Scotch bastard!'

That night, lying in my hammock, unable to find any sleeping position which did not cause agonising pain to one bruise or another, Mr Bowler, a Cornishman who had sailed with Frobisher in eighty-four, told me: 'He doesn't like you, Scotch.'

'Why not?' I could hardly speak. 'It was an accident.'

'You can read. You make him feel ignorant.'

'Aye,' came a voice out of the darkness. 'But at least it will keep Salter off *our* backs.'

'Keep up the reading, Scotch boy.' The sound of men laughing rumbled around the berth. At that moment I hated them all with a great and passionate intensity. And as I lay stiff and throbbing from a beating far worse than any my stepfather had ever given me, and thought, if only I had never left home!, I decided that somehow I would have to find a position below decks, away from Mr Salter and his needle eyes and his truncheon. For if I did not, the day would surely come when I would thrust my ballockknife into his stomach again and again and again, and that would be the end of me.

For several hours I turned every way I could, drifting in and out of nightmares, listening to the creaking of the ship and the snoring of the men around me, and smelling the stench of sweat and tar. Sometime after midnight I heard the rhythmic tap-tap of footsteps on the deck above. Someone was pacing to and fro, to and fro. The nightwatch, I supposed.

Once, in the early hours, the sound of low, muttering voices came down through the hatch. Then, strangely, there was a muffled thump followed by silence. This was followed some moments later by a scraping sound, which I did not understand. It was consistent with something being dragged along the deck. And then there was silence again, apart from the thousand night noises of the ship. In other circumstances my curiosity would have been roused to the point where I would have gone up to investigate. But my exhaustion was too great and my bruises too painful for me to care.

By the next morning I was so stiff that I was unable to leave my hammock. My arms were swollen and every breath brought pain to my ribs. The Turk brought me water but I had no strength for the biscuit which he offered me, even after he'd broken it into pieces with his yellow teeth. Two mariners played a game of backgammon awhile, rattling their counters on the big table. But after that, the berth-hold was empty for much of the day and I lay alone, slipping in and out of half-sleep.

In the afternoon, the sound of feet coming down the hatch ladder wakened me from a bad dream. As my eyes focused I saw that Mr Harriot was examining me closely. He said, 'You cannot help me.'

'Sir?' My voice was a whisper.

'You have not been above deck these past few hours, am I right?'

'That is so, sir.'

'Aye. We have lost a Mr Holby. He was last seen at dinner yesterday.'

Mr Holby. One of the gentlemen. A faint recollection came back to me. Was it a dream? No, it was real. 'Sir, I heard a strange disturbance in the early hours of this morning. It may have no connection with Mr Holby.'

Mr Harriot said nothing, but his eyes encouraged me to continue.

'Two people were talking on the deck above. Then there was a faint thump, and then the sound of something being dragged. After that, silence.'

The man's expression did not change. Then: 'I hope you are not saying that Mr Holby was knocked down and dragged overboard?'

Uncertain what I was getting myself into, I said in some alarm, 'No, sir. I only report what I heard.'

'Did you hear a splash?'

'No, sir.' I struggled to a sitting position. My throat was parched. The wind was fresher and the sway of the ship was steepening. Through the hatch I saw dark, fast-moving clouds.

'What is your name, boy?'

'James Ogilvie, sir.'

'And what happened to you?'

'I vomited over Mr Salter, sir.'

For a startled moment I thought I detected a glint of humour in the man's eyes. I thought, I will never have another opportunity like this again. Boldness and desperation made me add, 'And I can read and write. And I have read the *Lives of Plutarch* and I know the propositions of Euclid.'

The man peered at me in astonishment, as if a cabbage had spoken to him. 'Indeed? What, then, is the theorem of Pythagoras?'

'That the square on the hypotenuse of a right-angled triangle equals the sum of the squares on the other two sides.'

His astonishment increased, and I could not help but add: 'And I have found a way to prove it other than by using shears and rotations of triangles in the manner of Euclid. I can prove his theorem by dissection. I take the large square on the hypotenuse and divide it into pieces which I can rearrange to fit exactly into the two smaller ones.' I remembered this well. I had played the game with sticks in our barn one afternoon while, I fear, our cow had gone unmilked.

He stood silently, his mind grappling with the notion of a speaking cabbage. Then: 'God's wonders will never cease. We will speak further of Pythagoras, Mr Ogilvie. But for now, you will tell nobody what you heard on deck last night. Keep your mouth firmly shut.'

'I will, sir. I will.'

On the stairs, Mr Harriot paused briefly and looked back at me, puzzled. As his footsteps receded, I almost forgot my bruises. I am not ashamed to say that I wept with happiness. I had told a gentleman that I was not tavern spawn, to be worked to death on the riggings. I would tell him of my new proof of the theorem of Pythagoras. Who could say, perhaps Euclid had been my salvation? Within the hour, stiff and light-headed, I was on deck again, breathing the spray-filled air and thrilled to be a part of this voyage.

But I did not have time to reflect on my good fortune, if such it would turn out to be. Mr Holby was still missing and a search of the ship was underway. The Turk spotted me and I joined him and Michael in the bowels of the ship. We carried burning tar-covered ropes for light. I was still unfamiliar with the ship and soon became lost as I followed the Turk down ladders and along dark corridors. The smell of wood-smoke was strong as we passed the galley. In the very depths of the ship, when it seemed the next stage down must be the sea, the smell was truly vile.

'Seawater in the bilge,' Michael explained to me.

'What is the bilge?' I asked.

Michael laughed. 'Scotch, it is the space between the hold and the keel. The seawater leaks into it and creates the foul stench. Is your ignorance so great that you will ask me what is the keel?'

I ignored him and followed the retreating Turk, whose flickering shadow reminded me of some genie. In the black hold we clambered around the barrels and sacks, while chattering and scurrying surrounded us and red eyes in dark corners reflected the light from our ropes. Once I accidentally trapped one of these large and dangerous creatures. It reared up on its hind legs and glared at me furiously. I stared uncertainly. Suddenly something hissed by me. There was a thump and a cry of delight from behind as the Turk's knife thudded into the body of the big rat. It lay quivering, impaled on a sack of grain. As I leaned over it I saw dozens of fleas spreading away from its body. Had I tried such a trick with my ballockknife I would have hit the rat with the hilt, or more likely have missed it altogether. The Turk didn't need to say anything; he saw the wonder in my eyes. His yellow teeth were exposed in a knowing, triumphant grin. A valuable lesson. My conceit after having defeated the four men in Southwark had led me to fancy myself as something of a fighter. But against such a one as the Turk, I was no warrior at all!

Now the effects of the beating were stiffening my muscles. Every time I moved I was in pain. 'You carry on,' I said. 'I will search for Mr Holby on my own.'

We split up. I had little doubt that Mr Holby had gone overboard the previous night, and that there was a murderer in our midst. But following Mr Harriot's instructions, I could say nothing about this.

It soon became clear that a man could stow away in the ship with ease. There must have been a hundred quiet corners where a body could have been concealed. I grew more and more confused in direction as I stumbled through storerooms and along dark passages, up and down ladders, sometimes coming across sacks of food, sometimes piles of wood, huge jars of olive oil, meat pickled in salt water, heaps of rope, bales of sailcloth, barrels of water and beer, racks of cannonballs. Rats were everywhere, in their hundreds or thousands. And when I thought I had explored every inch of the ship, I would find another room with another cargo. My tarred rope had all but burned out, and I was seeking a ladder to take me up to the fresh air, when there came a cry from the forward part of the ship.

There was already a crowd of sailors clustered around the barrels when I reached the unfortunate Mr Holby. At least I assumed it was Mr Holby. All we could actually see was a pair of bare, blotchy feet protruding from under a stack of beer barrels twice the height of a man. The dark liquid oozing out from around his feet was not, I believe, beer. It was blood from his crushed body.

9

I had been spared the task of extricating Mr Holby's squashed body from under the barrels. A bell had summoned everyone on deck. Mr Salter was standing as we emerged from the hatch. There was more work to be done on the sails, and he bawled instructions at us. I did not think that the man knew how to speak in a normal voice. The wind was stronger but I no longer felt the *mal de mer*, as the French call it, of the day before, and wondered whether the beating had removed it from my body.

I could scarcely walk, let alone set about climbing. Mr Salter, seeing my predicament, approached me. 'Do you need help up the ratline, Ogilvie?'

I knew what the help would be. 'No, sir,' I said in a humble tone which by no means came naturally to me. I forced my limbs to haul my body up the ropes. At least I would be out of range of the cudgel.

I had not been aloft ten minutes when Mr Salter called me down, iron in his voice. I thought of his cudgel hammering at my already painfully bruised ribs and limbs, and was gripped with such fear that I thought to jump off the foremast to my death rather than face another beating. But when I stood before him, close to fainting, he said simply, 'The captain wishes to see you this moment.'

I cannot describe the emotions which flowed through me as I stood at the desk of Sir Richard Grenville in his great cabin. The man had a face of granite. Mr Harriot stood next to me. I told my story exactly as I had given it earlier, of my beating by Mr Salter, my sleeplessness because of the pain, and my hearing a strange noise, like something heavy being dragged on the deck overhead. And when I had finished, he stared at me coldly and then both men spoke of me as if I was elsewhere. 'What do we know of this boy?'

'You see as much as I do, Richard. There is one thing. He seems to have acquired learning in patches, his mind is lively and he has a mathematical ability, perhaps considerable, which I have yet to test to its limit.'

'Another damned sorcerer in the making, by the sound of it,' growled Sir Richard. 'But what we need to know is, can we rely on his testimony? Is he reliable?'

'Damn me, Richard, Holby has vanished. If he is not onboard ship then he is at the bottom of the ocean. He didn't jump. He was not pushed or he would have cried out. Ogilvie's story is consistent with the only reasonable possibility. Holby was stabbed or knocked out and thrown overboard.'

'First Holby and then the carpenter.'

The carpenter! So the man under the barrels was not Holby after all, but a second victim.

'It seems we have a murderer in our midst, Richard.'

'Aye. For what motive, Harriot?' The two men were looking grimly at each other. At that moment I sensed – no, I knew – that this voyage had some secret purpose. And whatever that secret purpose might be, someone onboard was trying to frustrate it.

Sir Richard suddenly became aware of my presence again. 'Leave us,' he ordered brusquely.

I had reached the door when Mr Harriot said, 'Ogilvie. I need an assistant. I think you would be more usefully employed in my service than on the masts. Are you agreeable, Richard?'

Sir Richard waved his hand casually in agreement. I wondered if St Peter, waving his hand to direct an undeserving soul towards heaven, could have induced greater happiness.

'Do you recognise the pole star?'

'I do, sir. The Bears guide us to it. There they are, at the end of the Little Bear. And we have the pointers of the Great Bear. The Bears circle the sky but never dip below the horizon. All the other stars in the sky seem to rotate about the pole star, but this is an illusion. It is really the earth which rotates. The stars are fixed in the sky, embedded in a crystal sphere.'

'And if you were standing at the North Pole, where would Polaris be?'

'Directly overhead. All the stars move in horizontal circles about it.'

We were mid-ship, far enough away from the great lantern on the afterdeck for our night eyes to be unaffected by it. Mr Harriot had a strange bowl, made of clay and filled with some burning herb. He was sucking the smoke along a hollow tube and into his mouth. 'Now put on magic boots. Take giant strides over the surface of the earth towards the equator. What do you see in the sky as you move south?'

I took a moment, unsure what answer Mr Harriot expected of me. 'Sir, the pole star would no longer be overhead. As I strode to the equator in my magic boots, the pole star would sink lower and lower in the sky.'

'And at the equator?'

'The pole star would then be lying on the horizon. All the stars would move in big vertical circles around the axle joining north and south. And if I moved south of the equator, Polaris would disappear from sight. Except that I would then see the other pole star, the one at the South Pole.'

'Except that there is no such star. The Italian traders and missionaries, travelling by overland or on coastal routes around the tip of Africa, have described the southern skies. Marco Polo travelled even further south than the missionaries. He saw many wonders in the southern sky. He saw a star as big as a sack, and four bright stars in the form of a cross. He even saw the south pole of the sky a spear's length above the horizon. But he described no southern pole star. Even so, we in the North have an infallible way to find our latitude on the surface of the earth.'

He paused. I said, 'Find the altitude of the pole star above the horizon. If it is overhead, you must be at the North Pole. If it lies on the horizon, your ship must lie on the equator. And if it is sixty degrees from the zenith, we are sixty degrees from the north pole of the earth and so thirty degrees from the equator. That is, our latitude is thirty degrees.'

'And I have an instrument for the very purpose of measuring altitude. It is called a cross staff, and I will train you in its use shortly. So, Ogilvie, you see how to determine how far north or south we are. But now the question arises, what about east or west? Here we are, sailing on an empty ocean. There is nothing around you but waves and sea monsters. Are we a hundred leagues from England? A thousand? How close are we to the Caribbean or the Americas?'

I felt that I was being tested. As anxious to please as a puppy with a new master, I searched my brains desperately for an answer. It was with extreme reluctance that I had to say, 'I do not know, sir.'

Mr Harriot laughed, while clenching the tube between his teeth. 'Neither does anyone else, young Ogilvie, do not be so downcast. Consider a line drawn from the North Pole of the earth, through London, to the South Pole. This is a line of longitude. If the sun is at its highest point along that line, then at that same moment the sun is also at its lowest point along the opposite line of longitude, one hundred and eighty degrees away.'

A light dawned, vaguely. 'But if we know the moment of noon in England, and if noon on our ship comes six hours later, then we must be a quarter of the way round the globe, since the sun takes twenty-four hours to travel around the earth. Therefore our longitude is ninety degrees away from that of England.' I could hardly contain my pride in providing the answer.

Mr Harriot smiled. 'But how can you tell when it is noon in England?'

'Set a clock to noon when you leave England! Whenever it reads noon on the clock, whatever the time of day or night on the ship—'

'What clock? A sand glass? An Egyptian water clock? A pendulum clock? These barely keep time on stationary ground. On a heaving ship they are useless.'

'Then I am baffled, Mr Harriot.' I could see that I was failing, not only as a warrior, or even as a mariner, but also as a scholar. The dreadful thought came to me that perhaps my level in life was that of a shepherd after all.

Harriot laughed again. 'Don't look so dismayed! The problem has defeated the best minds in England and elsewhere. But with half the globe still to be discovered, and trade routes to be found joining us to Cathay, and vast treasures being brought from the Americas, the man who solves the problem of accurate navigation will become rich beyond measure.'

10

A secret purpose!

Somewhere around three in the morning my eyes refused to stay open a minute longer. I staggered to bed and slipped under cool sheets. I sank into dreamland with a jumble of sailing ships, ballockknives, heads on poles and a hardwood truncheon rising and falling, rising and falling, thumping again and again into the body of a fifteen-year old boy; and Salter, vomit trickling down his head, his face contorted in anger, shouting, 'Secret purpose, secret purpose, what is the secret purpose?'

In the grey light of the morning I skipped breakfast, paid the little Italian landlady, threw my holdall with the manuscript into the back of the Toyota and took off, following the signs to The North. Once on the motorway I pushed ninety, keeping in the fast lane most of the way. I was feeling angry.

Partially it was professional pique. Tebbit got up my nose. I didn't like being treated like one of the servants, excluded by a snap of the fingers from what might just turn out to be a superb piece of historical research. Certainly not by some minor gentry who seemed to think he was master of the universe. The Roanoke expedition was the first attempt to colonise North America; Tebbit had been handed a journal with something to say about that, and I wanted to know what it was. In any case, I doubted if he had the proprietorial right to deny me my slice of history.

And I felt entitled for another reason: my kidney was still aching. All the way up the motorway, the words *secret purpose* kept going through my head.

I'm damned if I'm going to let this slip through my hands; just translate and walk away.

I was in my flat by noon. I kept ringing the Tebbit number, but it was permanently engaged, and I finally drove out to Picardy House. I was met by an impressive array of Bentleys and Jaguars, and thought for a moment I'd stumbled on a party until my eye caught the uniformed policeman and the people in white overalls fussing around the back of a police van.

A policeman with a yellow traffic jacket circled his finger at me and I wound my window down. 'What's your business here?' He was trying for an authoritative tone, but he didn't have the Salter touch.

'I want to speak to Sir Toby.'

'You're not a relative, then?'

'No, I hardly know the man.'

'He's been dead for two days, sir. Don't you read the papers?'

It took some seconds for the news to sink in. Apart from his florid cheeks, Tebbit had seemed healthy enough three days ago. I wondered if he'd had a heart attack. 'Maybe I should clear off.'

At that moment Debbie appeared at the front door, speaking to someone who looked like a lawyer. She was dressed in a dark grey cardigan with a long black skirt. She seemed matter-of-fact, cool even. She spotted me and waved. I waved back.

The policeman leaned forwards, spoke in a confidential tone. 'You've met the daughter? A real goer if you ask me. The mother died years back and she's the only sprog. Imagine inheriting this lot at her age.'

'If this is the funeral . . .'

'No, sir, he's on ice in town. This is just grieving friends and family. You might say Sir Toby was well-heeled.' The policeman leaned even closer; his breath was garlicky. 'And this lot look as if they own half of Lincolnshire.'

The lawyer was heading for his top-of-the-range BMW, and Debbie came smartly down the steps towards me. 'Mr Blake? Harry?'

I didn't know quite what to say. 'Debbie, I was sorry to hear about—'

'Of course, you've been away. Daddy was killed, you know.'

'What?'

61

'By burglars.' Spoken conversationally. 'Do come in.'

I picked up the manuscript, feeling a bit dazed, and followed her into the house. The study door had blue and white tape across it, with the words POLICE LINE DO NOT CROSS. 'The forensic people say they're nearly finished. They had the whole house until this morning.'

She led me into a long, dull room whose centre was taken up with a massive table surrounded by about twenty chairs. There were drinks and canapés on the table and a couple of dozen people standing around. Subdued conversation filled the air and there were curious glances in my direction.

'I feel I'm intruding,' I began.

'No you're not. Did you finish the translation?' she asked, nodding at the manuscript in my hand. She was unconsciously chewing a lip. Her eyes were a bit glazed and I thought she was probably doped with sedative.

I had no chance to reply. A small, stocky man, a white-haired forty, detached himself from a group and sidled up. There was a startling resemblance to the late Sir Toby; the same small, bullet-like eyes and turned-down mouth. He looked at Debbie and then at me. And like Sir Toby, he made no attempt to be friendly. 'What's your business here?'

'My name is Blake. I'm an antiquarian bookseller. Sir Toby asked me to translate and value a manuscript. I was sorry to hear—'

'Never mind that. Just leave it there.' He nodded at the table.

'The translation isn't finished. I wanted to discuss the manuscript with Sir Toby.'

'Well, that will no longer be possible. Just leave the manuscript on the table.'

'Forgive me, but I don't know who I'm talking to.'

'I'm his brother.' Spoken an octave higher, to show his irritation at the impertinence. 'If you're worried about your fee, send it to me at this address.'

'That'll be fine.' *And next time I'll use the tradesman's entrance, you repulsive toad.*

'What did you find, Harry?' Debbie's voice was quiet and

solicitous, and I wondered how such a nice kid could have come from this arrogant family.

I opened my mouth but the Tebbit brother got in first. 'I'm sure it doesn't matter now, Debbie. And I expect Mr Blake has other things to do.'

'Uncle Robert, that journal belonged to Daddy and he wanted to know what was in it.'

'Maybe I should just go, Debbie,' I suggested.

'I think you should,' Uncle Robert agreed curtly.

I told Debbie, 'It's a journal kept by a cabin boy who sailed on an Elizabethan voyage. He used some sort of secret writing, which I've managed to decipher. You should know, Debbie, that I was offered quite a large sum of money for it, in fact silly money, far beyond its market value. I don't know why.'

Debbie's eyes widened. 'Wow! That sounds cool! I know that Daddy was very excited when the journal turned up. He thinks it might have something in it about our family. What do you think could be in it?'

Uncle Robert said, 'Goodbye, Mr Blake.'

Debbie said, 'I'd like you to dig deeper, Harry. Why should people offer a lot of money for this journal? There must be something interesting in it. Maybe even something valuable?'

'As I said, Mr Blake. Goodbye.' The man's face was getting florid.

Debbie was adopting an imperious tone, which was impressive coming from a teenager. 'Harry, I'd like you to take this further. Find out what's in this journal that made Daddy so excited and made people offer silly money for it.'

Uncle Robert's face was lined with anger. 'Debbie, you're handing a blank cheque to a complete stranger. Don't you see he'll rip you off? I'm not going to stand by and watch that happen. Now' – pointing angrily at me – 'get out.' A circle of silence was beginning to spread around us, as people picked up vibrations.

Debbie's face was flushed. 'Uncle Robert, you have nothing to do with this. Unless Daddy's will says otherwise, that journal belongs to me. And you don't pay the fees, I do. Harry, will you take it on?'

'I'll do whatever's necessary to protect you from—'

I interrupted the flow. 'Delighted to do so, Debbie. I'll keep you informed.'

The inspector was polite.

She sat, long-faced and attentive, while I told my tale. Next to her, her sergeant took notes. He reminded me of Chief Sitting Bull: squat, white-haired, wrinkled and impassive.

'So, the value of this manuscript?'

'It would be of great interest to historians of the period.'

She nodded patiently; I'd missed the point. 'I was thinking of the commercial value. I mean, sixteenth century is old, isn't it?'

'Yes, but it's not as if it's a first edition by Buenting or Theodore de Bry, or even something by Walter Raleigh. Who ever heard of James Ogilvie? You could maybe sell it to a gallery in New Bond Street or East Fifty-fourth for fifteen hundred dollars. A private collector might pay more.'

'Ah.' There was a world of deflation in the way she said it. 'What did you say its date was?'

'1585. Three years before the Spanish Armada.'

'And it describes an expedition to North America?'

'Exactly.'

'Was there anything in the manuscript which might be of commercial interest? Maybe something that could lead to buried treasure?' She gave a polite smile to soften the insult embedded in her question: she was humouring a lunatic.

'Nothing like that, nothing I could see. It was a straightforward cabin boy's account of an early Walter Raleigh expedition.'

'No reason to commit murder for it then?' Another polite smile.

'Absolutely none that I can see. All I can say is that some very funny people were anxious to get their hands on it.'

She nodded. 'The journal came from Jamaica, you said?'

'Yes. Sir Toby had a relative he didn't know about, a man called Winston Sinclair. This man died and his lawyer sent on the journal.'

'Well, thank you for that, Mr Blake. It's always helpful to get a rounded picture.' The inspector stood up and extended her hand, and Chief Sitting Bull snapped his notebook shut with a sigh.

I turned at the door. 'How did Sir Toby come to be killed?'

'Haven't you been told? It looks as if he disturbed some people in his study. They tied him to a chair, gagged him and caused him a great deal of pain. I can't tell you too much about that except to say there was a lot of blood. He actually died of a heart attack. His daughter was at a night-club while all this was going on. Very upsetting thing for her to come home to.'

'Surely an ordinary burglar would just have knocked him on the head? Isn't this consistent with people looking for something?'

The standard reply: 'We can't rule anything out at the moment. What time did you meet this woman in the cathedral?'

'Around ten in the evening.'

'That was on Wednesday?'

'Yes.'

'And when did you phone Sir Toby?'

'Seven o'clock the next morning. Thursday. When was Sir Toby killed?'

'Between ten o'clock and midnight that evening. He took the train back to Lincoln just after you called him. Where were you at that time on Thursday?'

'Tucked up in bed in a Bicester hotel. On my own.' I gave her the address. 'A woman tries to get hold of the journal and twenty-four hours later Sir Toby is tortured and killed. And you say there's no connection.'

The inspector managed a smile. 'It's what *you* say, Mr Blake. There's nothing of interest in the journal. That is right, isn't it? Nothing to kill for?'

'Dr Khan?'

'Zola Khan speaking.'

'My name is Blake, Harry Blake. You don't know me, I'm a dealer in antique maps.'

There was a pause, and then, I thought, a touch of coolness in her voice. 'From Lincoln?'

That surprised me. 'Yes, that's right.'

'We did meet briefly, Mr Blake, at the Ross-on-Wye bookfest a couple of years ago. The Terra Nueva.'

Damn. I remembered the woman now. I just hadn't connected Zola Khan the marine historian with the creature I'd encountered at the bookfest.

'I remember,' I said. 'The 1548 Gastaldi, which you misidentified as a Girolamo Ruscelli.'

Frost came down the line. 'The misidentification was entirely yours, I assure you.'

We'd had different opinions on the authorship of the Terra Nueva, a 16th-century map. The issue at stake wasn't the six hundred dollars valuation, of course; it was professional pride. It had been one of those jolly, bibulous events. Things had got heated and she had ended up calling me an ignoramus in front of goggle-eyed colleagues. I'd called her a poisonous witch.

I cleared my throat, beginning to wonder if this call was a good idea. 'Dr Khan, I've come across a journal written by someone on board Raleigh's 1585 expedition.'

'What? The Roanoke expedition?'

'Yes. The first one.'

'And you found a journal kept by someone on board?'

'Yes, a cabin boy by the name of James Ogilvie.'

'But that's fantastic! Where on earth did you find it?'

'It's fantastic all right, but it's more than that. Frankly, I need your help. I think there's more to the journal than meets the eye, and the question of ownership is, shall I say, clouded. Can we meet?'

'Yes, of course. And, naturally, bring the journal. Where are you?'

'Lincoln. But I can come down right away. The sooner the better.'

'I don't suppose you could make it to the National Maritime Museum by this evening?'

She sounded as anxious as me. 'Sure. Probably by five o'clock.'

'I make a damn good paella.'

So long as you don't add poison, I thought.

She said, 'And I promise not to poison it.'

'Pull its head off. No, pull harder, that's the idea. Now cut the tentacles just above the eyes.'

'What do I do with this?' I asked, picking up a glistening body.

'There's a bin under the sink.'

'I'm not very good at this,' I said, struggling with bits of cephalopod.

'The problem is, Mr Blake—'

'Harry, please' – I dropped the slithery body, retrieved it, then carried it to the bin, trying to overcome a slight feeling of revulsion.

'The problem is the Tebbit murder. You can't seriously connect that with the manuscript?'

I took a second to glance surreptitiously in her direction. She was much as I remembered her, late thirties, black hair reaching to her shoulders, long dangling earrings, a smooth complexion and an accent which told of some years spent in the States. I had picked her up at the National Maritime Museum and driven the short distance to her flat. It had turned out to be three flights up, spacious and modern, with a fine view of Greenwich Park. Traffic noise was effectively muted by the heavy double glazing. The walls were dotted with obscure paintings, but no family photographs. As far as I could see she lived alone.

'They could have been trying to persuade him to make me hand over the journal. But his heart gave out.'

She gave me an are-you-serious look. 'That's embarrassing. It's just a fantasy thing.'

'What do you know about my fantasies?' I said it jokingly.

'What do you know about mine?' She was slicing through a monkfish with a long, thin knife which seemed to me to be razor-sharp. 'You need to get rid of the cartilage,' she said. 'Not with the knife. Squeeze it, like so.' A round bit of cartilage like an eyeball popped out of the end of the tentacle. 'Good. Now get rid of that membrane – the brown stuff.'

I clawed around, up to my elbows in fishy slime.

She said, cutting briskly, 'And you're satisfied with its authenticity? Look how you screwed up on the Ruscelli.'

'You mean the Gastaldi. The Spanish Netherlands watermark would be hard to fake. And I showed the manuscript briefly to Fred Sweet at Oxford. He didn't raise any question about authenticity. This is vile.'

'I'll say it again, Harry. Your notion that something in the journal was motivation enough to have Sir Toby murdered is just plain fantasy.'

'To me it's a serious proposition.'

'Which the police don't buy.'

'They think I'm deluded, like I have the male menopause or something.'

Zola managed an eloquent silence. Then: 'Okay, run cold water through the tube, and when you've done that, start cutting the tails into thin rings.'

'I guess I'm a bit squeamish,' I said, struggling with the slippery tentacles.

'What could possibly be in a four-hundred-year-old manuscript to justify murder?'

'Exactly my question.'

She sizzled stock and rice into a big two-handled pan on a heavy gas cooker.

'The answer is: nothing.'

'Don't forget I was attacked. They snatched my briefcase. I'd anticipated that possibility and was carrying the manuscript under my shirt.'

'People get their bags snatched all the time. Okay, that's fine.' She gave me a sweet smile and said, 'Now you can start pulling the heads off the prawns.'

'What do you say? Maybe you think I forged it?' I said it to provoke.

Zola rubbed her eyes. It was two o'clock in the morning. We had left the dining-room table in a clutter and were on a white furry rug in front of a gas fire, papers sprawled around us.

'You don't mind if I change into something more comfortable?' she asked.

'Of course not,' I said, wondering what was coming.

She disappeared into her room, and returned a few minutes later wearing white silk pyjamas covered with moons, stars and teddy bears. 'Wild Nights' was written across the pyjamas in small yellow letters. Her dressing gown was ankle length, red, silky, and had a Chinese dragon on its back. She was still wearing her long, pendulum-like earrings. I poured the last of the wine – our second bottle – a Chablis I'd picked up from Sainsbury's.

She said, 'There are things which don't fit.'

'Such as?'

'Thomas Harriot was the navigator. In those days the navigator was called a pilot, and it's on record that the pilot was Fernandez. There are lots of little things like that. And one big thing. Harriot is smoking a pipe. Every schoolboy knows that Walter Raleigh brought tobacco back to England, but Harriot must have got it from the earlier Amadas and Barlowe expedition.'

I put my hand to my head. 'But I can't make sense of that. Look at the spiderweb cracks. This is a standard iron gall ink, working on the paper for centuries. If it doesn't get phytate treatment in the next ten years the manuscript will be gone. It can't possibly be a forgery.'

'You don't get it, Harry, but that's okay, I've known since Ross-on-Wye that you're not very bright.' She giggled. 'My point is that anyone who went to the immense trouble of forging the journal would also take the trouble to get the details right. My guess is that the historians have been getting things wrong. The inconsistencies are a strength, not a weakness.'

I stretched my legs. 'These attempts to get hold of the manuscript. Could they have something to do with the secret purpose of the expedition?'

'The secret purpose. Yes, that really has me going.' Zola picked up the pages and started to flick through them. 'Let's keep reading. Unless you're ready for bed.' She looked at me speculatively.

I thought about that. 'Let's keep reading.'

11

At first I believed that only the captain, Mr Harriot and myself knew of the murders. I glowed with pride in being part of this small inner circle of knowledge. But I knew little about the way in which whispers travelled through the confined space of a ship.

And indeed, with the death of the carpenter and the mysterious vanishing of Mr Holby, rumours began to sweep through the Tiger like a plague. You saw how carefully the stowers spread the weight of the stores, Hunger explained to me. We were in a quiet corner of the anchor room playing a complicated game which he called chess. Otherwise, if they shifted during a storm or even a heavy swell, they could upset the balance of the ship and cause it to overturn. Could you have raised the water barrels, slid the carpenter underneath them, and let them subside again, crushing his body? he asked. Of course not. No man could have. Some diabolical force must have been summoned up. I did not think much of this explanation, but could come up with none better, and in any case my mind was soon distracted by my pleasure in forcing Mr Hunger to what he called 'checkmate'.

As the days passed and routine began to impose itself on the life of the ship, the mysterious deaths became something remote. Death, I soon discovered, was part of the ship's life. Some of the more experienced men took to jumping from one ratline to another, to save themselves descending from one mast and then climbing another. But the procedure was not without hazard, as I heard one day – there was a thump on the deck behind me, and I turned to see a mariner plainly dead, with his neck broken and his companions looking down at him, horrified. That same afternoon the man was wrapped in sailcloth weighted with stones and thrown overboard with only a cursory ceremony. It was as if he had never existed.

Towards noon each day – or the time I estimated to be noon – I would make my way to the afterdeck. Noon being when the sun reached its highest point in the sky, Mr Harriot, by measuring its altitude, was able to calculate the latitude of the Tiger and its fleet. But as we passed the islands known as the Canaries, the sky darkened and there was no Mr Harriot and no sun, only low, fast-moving black clouds, a heavily rolling ship and fearful mutterings from the pressed deckhands. Even some older men, like Mr Bowler, had acquired a grimness of expression which added to my sense of unease.

In the afternoon the Hog told me that I had been summoned by Mr Harriot. I was required to serve the gentlemen with aqua vitae and biscuits. For days the talk had been of nothing but the murders, but as I entered, one of the gentlemen, a pale, curly-haired young man called Marmaduke StClair was telling some long tale which ended in an outburst of laughter. Mr Harriot was seated in a corner, reading. His short pipe, ending in a bowl, again projected from his mouth. The burning herb in the bowl, I was to learn, had been brought to England from the reconnaissance voyage of Amadas and Barlowe only the previous year. Its smoke had an acrid but not unpleasant smell.

This new air of nonchalance amongst the gentlemen restored my confidence. Between men of superior breeding and education, and the illiterate spawn of taverns and prisons, I knew where to place my trust, and I left their common room with a light step. And in the gloom of the berth-hold, while the rogues and ruffians exchanged complaints and fears as they played with dice and picture cards, I read the life of Philopoemen, the slayer of the tyrant Machanidas in 208 BC, and felt inspired. If only my life could be lived like those of the great lawmakers, soldiers and philosophers of the past!

But all that afternoon the roll of the ship slowly increased, and the wail of the wind in the rigging grew louder, and the mutterings of the crew grew more alarming.

As Mr Harriot's assistant and steward, I waited at the table of the gentlemen and officers, moving swiftly between galley and the great cabin in which their meals were served. It was a duty which I carried out with the greatest pleasure. I would stand quietly in the background. They soon forgot my presence, except when aqua vitae was to be served or plates were to be removed. Sir Richard had brought musicians on the voyage, but I must confess that the screeching of their instruments at the dinner table gave me little love for music. But when the musicians had gone and the aqua vitae flowed, the conversations of the gentlemen began to flow also. I listened with great eagerness, and each evening I was able to learn as much as Dominie Dinwoodie had taught me in all my years as his pupil. And at night, lying in my hammock, I heard a different set of tales. It was as if there were two worlds occupying the same globe, neither of which intersected.

I soon learned that Mr Harriot was regarded with suspicion by some of the gentlemen. His passion was mathematics. But, I was surprised to learn from him, this was seen as one of the black arts, to do with conjuring or magic, even though geometry, arithmetic and astronomy were being taught in the new universities. He talked of the Pythagorean's claim that the ratios of the integers were connected to musical harmonics, and also to the motions of the planets – this latter no more than a rumour emerging from Europe.

But when the talk turned to the Copernican heresy, which placed the sun and not the earth at the centre of the universe, I sensed that it was becoming dangerous. Faces became serious; men began to hunch forwards, listening earnestly. And after too much aqua vitae, Mr Harriot discoursed boldly on the strange beliefs of the Italian monk, Giordano Bruno. 'He was in Oxford four years ago. He believes that the stars are globes like the sun scattered through infinite space, with worlds around these stars and creatures living on these worlds.'

'And what do you believe, Thomas?' Sir Richard's tone was dangerous, but my master seemed not to notice – or chose not to notice.

'That on this matter at least he is correct.'

'In the minds of the simple, such ideas are dangerous,' Anthony Rowse complained.

'The man is a Neapolitan heretic!' cried Marmaduke. 'He was

expelled from the Dominican order. Some day the fool will burn at the stake.'

'I too heard him at Balliol,' said Rowse. 'He spoke well of the heresy of Copernicus, that the earth spins and the stars stand still. In truth it was his own head which turned round, and his brains which did not stand still.'

All this was too much for Sir Richard, who, furious at such extravagant heresy and equally drunk, roared like a bull and fired a pistol in the air. The ball bounced off a beam, sending a splinter flying, and struck the hand of one of the musicians, who fled howling from the room, blood spurting, while the captain's roaring transformed itself into raucous laughter.

'But it is mathematics which allows you to traverse the globe, Sir Richard.' This bravely from a young man, Abraham Kendall, who was fresh from Oxford University. 'Where would you be without the navigational skills of John Dee and Thomas Harriot?'

Anthony Rowse, the parliamentarian, had a face purple with drink. He waved a scornful arm in the air. 'To hell with the School of the Night and your occult heresies and your hellish triangles. Give me a bear pit and a brothel any day.'

'Much good would those do you out here, Anthony.' Harriot was now refilling his smoking-bowl.

'There is too much fancy in your reasoning, Thomas,' Rowse persisted. 'Planets orbiting the sun! Men on other worlds! You cannot believe these things.' He took a big gulp of aqua vitae, his eyes bulging.

'But Anthony, I do.'

Rowse sneered derisively. 'You will tell us next that one day men will fly like birds across the oceans.' He flapped his arms like the wings of a bird.

'Or fly to the moon!' Sir Richard roared, his face also turning purple in the process. I thought he would slide off his chair. He bit his wine glass, crunched the glass and spat out the shards, glaring angrily at Mr Harriot. He wiped a trickle of blood from his chin, and at that moment I believed I was in the company of lunatics. The musicians had not yet recommenced their screeching; the three still in the cabin were cowering in a corner.

And yet, in the midst of this bedlam, I was becoming aware that the roll of the ship was steepening, and that the sound of the wind in the sails and ropes was becoming angry. I drew comfort from the fact that none of the gentlemen seemed to notice or care.

The night brought gloom and squalls, and the Tiger wallowed up and down in waves as tall as itself, rolling from side to side like a pendulum, in a manner to make me want to vomit once again. As usual I followed Mr Harriot on to the deck, carrying cross staff and lantern. I had to clutch at rigging more than once to save myself from a fall, and once I stumbled and almost dropped the cross staff, with what outcome for myself I did not dare to think.

We planted our feet on the afterdeck, the lantern swinging and our bodies swaying to counter the movement of the ship. Whenever we broached the crests of the waves I could see little pinpricks of light all around, from the other ships of the fleet, but then we would plunge down and there was nothing but black water and a blacker sky. We stood on deck for a good half-hour, the rain penetrating our garments and soaking us to the skin, without sighting a single star. Finally Mr Harriot, his long black garment clinging to his sodden legs, said, 'Very well,' and we gave up.

I climbed into my hammock in my sodden clothes and lay shivering while sleep tried to overcome me. The Tiger creaked and grumbled from all directions, all but drowning out the snores and dream-mutterings of the men. Listening in the dark, as the waves crashed against the hull, and the wind howling *Whee!* in the riggings, my mind tried to grasp the reality that we were in some vast, swirling ocean which could swallow us up like a morsel. And as I slipped into that strange other-world between wakefulness and sleep, I wondered what God's purpose had been in creating so vast a kingdom of salt water, and how far down it went, and what creatures might lurk in its greatest depths. It was easy to feel fear.

I was awakened by the sound of a crash. Disoriented, in the near-dark, I did not recognise my surroundings, and it was a moment before my eyes penetrated the gloom and I saw that the berth was on its side, the deck timbers having turned to form a near-vertical wall while my hammock stayed horizontal. I thought

that the ship was about to founder, and turned in terror, anticipating that a great wall of water would pour through the gratings
and into the ship. None came, but the Tiger was groaning loudly, as
if she was in pain. The long table, chairs and two chests were
heaped up against the hull. As my eyes adapted I could make out
that a chest had burst open and its contents – clothes, mainly –
were sloshing in water. Almost immediately they began to slide in
the opposite direction. To my dismay I was alone in the berth-deck.

I rolled out of my hammock and was instantly half-thrown, half-
rolled along the wet deck timbers towards the side of the hold,
where my ribs struck the corner of the long table and I cried out in
agony. There was a *Bang!* and I swear that the hull flexed inwards,
as if struck by a great hammer. I rolled aside as the ship began to
level and the table threatened to right itself on me. I stood up, my
side aflame with pain, gripped the table for balance and half-ran,
half-stumbled to the ladder and scrabbled up. Halfway up I had to
hang on or I would have fallen back.

I thought it was still a pitch black night before I saw that the
hatch was battened down. The door was tightly shut and refused to
move. I had to force it against a powerful wind. After the dark of
the lower deck the grey light made me screw up my eyes. Driving
spray stung my face like sharp glass. I found myself looking straight
down into black foaming water and had to grip the handle for my
life while my legs dangled over the sea. Then the ship rolled over to
port and the door slammed shut and I wrapped my arms around a
hand rail.

Low, black clouds were rushing past, barely higher than the
waves, which were now like small mountains, taller by far than the
Tiger.

Seamen were aloft from jib to spanker, while Mr Salter, gripping
rigging on the deckhead, bawled obscenities and orders which I did
not understand nor, I am sure, did they hear above the cacophony.
His eyes were black with fatigue.

A wave tall as the hill behind our Tweedsmuir farm rose up. I
looked up at it stupidly, convinced it was going to break over us,
smash us to pieces. But the Tiger rode it like a bobbing seagull,
rising up its steep side.

From the top of the monster wave I glimpsed a sea of yet more white-capped monster waves, stretching to the horizon and overlain by horizontally driven spray and rain. There was a solitary mast in the distance. But then the Tiger was sliding down into a black trough and tilting steeply as it did.

Four men on the bowsprit, gripping it with hands and legs, were pulling at lashings. As the Tiger gained speed the mast went under water, and when it next surfaced only three men were gripping it. It was some seconds before a head bobbed up, and an arm waved frantically, but then the ship was rising again on the next wave and the man was drifting sternwards. I recognised Mr Treanor, the Irishman. He passed yards from me, shouting, gulping water, eyes full of terror, but his words were lost in the storm. There was nothing to be done and the crest of the next wave took him from my sight.

A sudden gust of wind tore at the ship and she veered to port, tilting almost on her side. 'Get aloft, d'ye hear me?' Salter was roaring at me, pointing up at men clinging desperately to the foremast yardarm. 'Get up there, ye Scotch bastard! Release the foreshroud!' His voice was high and close to hysterical. I had no idea what the deck master meant but he was approaching me, bent double against the wind, with an axe in his hand, and the expression on his face told me it would be better to jump into the sea than disobey. He thrust the axe into my hand and I timed the sway of the deck to run towards the main mast, clutching it with arms and legs when it leaned over open water and the sea rose to within inches of me. Another brief run, slithering on the deck, racing a wave to a ratline, and then I was scrambling up the flapping rope ladder with the master's obscenities barely heard above the wailing *EEEEE!* of the wind from all around.

Aloft, the Turk, his bald head glistening and veins throbbing in his neck, snatched the axe from my hand and began to chop at a line which was snarling the corner of the sail. It took all my strength to grip the wet spar with both arms, and it was a miracle that the Turk, gripping with one hand while the other wielded the axe, was not thrown clear of the ship by the violent sway of the mast. The wind was stronger here and the water hitting my face like little stones was salt even at this height, and so was spray as much as rain. I could now see several masts scattered around a massive white sea.

Mr Salter was yelling something. The ship plunged until, even on the foremast yardarm, I found myself looking up at a huge wave. It broke over the deck, catching Salter at waist height and snatching him from the line he was gripping. He was swept across the deck and banged his head against the port side. He lay dazed, and seemed unable to stand up. But now there was another wave. The deck of the Tiger tilted towards it. Mr Salter was trying desperately to get to his feet, but the big wave would be on him in seconds. I clambered down at speed, racing the approaching monstrous wall. The wave reached him first, and for a moment he vanished in the swirling water. Then, as it receded, he was gripping the deck rail, his body dangling out over the ocean. There was a large purple swelling on his forehead. I tried to heave him on board but with his sodden clothes he must have been twice my own weight. How he held on I do not know. But then Manteo, the savage, appeared and was heaving at the man's dead weight, and we dragged him onto the deck. By now water was pouring out of his mouth and his eyes were rolling. By the grace of God and brute force we reached the hatch, pulled it open and managed to ease his now unconscious form down the ladder and into the berth-deck, where we heaved him into my hammock.

I stumbled back towards the gentlemen's quarters, stepping over some grey-faced soldiers, in search of the physician, Mr Oxendale. I found him, snoring, tied in his bunk bed by wrappings of sheet, his head banging off the bulkhead as the ship swayed. Two empty flagons of wine rolled back and forth across the cabin floor. His cabin companion, Anthony Rowse, was standing silently, gripping an overhead beam. He watched me without a word said; he had the eyes of a hunted animal. I could not help a feeling of contempt. I left him.

I do not know how long we stayed in that dark and swaying place, holding on to the timbers. At times Mr Salter seemed not to be breathing and I wondered if he was dead. The savage, from time to time, would put his finger under the mariner's nose and give a reassuring grunt. Presently I began to feel nauseous and my teeth began to chatter. At first I thought it was the motion of the ship, but my symptoms became worse and I began to feel hot and cold in turn.

It was, I think, an hour before light and spray flooded in from above, during which a dull ache in my belly slowly grew into a sharp pain. I thought at first that the door had blown open, but then the captain was coming down, gripping the ladder. Water was pouring off his clothes. He staggered hand over hand towards us, gripping timbers and overhead beams, and looked at Mr Salter silently. I wondered whether I should dare to speak, but then said, 'He is alive, sir.'

Sir Richard, both hands gripping the side of the hammock, stared at me with his intense blue eyes. 'You are coming down with some fever, laddie. Since you have seen fit to put Mr Salter in your hammock, find his bunk and tie yourself into it.' He turned and clambered back up the ladder on all fours.

The savage seemed to understand. He nodded and waved me away. I clambered back towards the gentlemen's quarters, past the still-sleeping physician and the terrified Mr Rowse, towards the cabin which Mr Salter shared with Simon Fludd, the architect.

Simon Fludd was in his cabin. He was on the floor. His face was a deep purple and his tongue, sticking out of his open mouth, was almost black. His eyes were so wide they looked as if they would jump out of his head. They were black, and it was a moment before I saw that this was because the pupils were so distended that they almost filled the eyeballs. His arms and legs were stretched out like those of a child in a tantrum, and they were trembling violently. He was scarcely able to breathe, the sound coming from his mouth being that of a man who was choking.

I knew then that the murderer, or Satan, had not finished his business with us. And as the Tiger began to heel over, groaning and crashing, and Mr White wheezed and choked, and I shivered, and the sweat poured down my face and the bile rose in my mouth, I thought that I too had become his victim. And I thought that it no longer mattered: poisoner and victims, captain and gentlemen, soldiers and ship were about to sink under the waves, taking their secrets and their conspiracies down to depths beyond measure, obliterating all.

12

Later, they told me that I had been in a fever for three days. I have
vague memories of my mouth and gullet being on fire, and my face
and brow being mopped, and I remember opening my eyes to see
Manteo, the savage, raising a cup to my lips, and warm goat's milk
trickling down my throat.

On the morning of the fourth day I awoke in my hammock,
weak as a girl, but knowing that whatever had ailed me, whether
poison or fever, had passed from my system. Two sailors interrupted
their backgammon to help me out of my hammock and lead me to
the stairs, which I climbed slowly. On deck, the sails were billowing
in a fresh wind, and although there were still clouds, they were high
and light and the air was warm. The sea was calm. Mr Chandler,
the man from Devon, gave me a friendly wave,

'There have been hangings. Two of them. Aye, we have had a
busy time while you have been ill.'

'Hangings?'

'Two soldiers. They tried to start a mutiny, declaring that the
ship was cursed and nobody would reach the New World alive.
They at least will not.'

I went down to Mr Harriot's cabin. Fernandez and he were
looking at a chart.

'Are you ready to resume your duties, Ogilvie?'

'Yes, sir.'

'Good. We have need of you this afternoon.'

As the day progressed it became clear that some extraordinary
meeting was to take place. All the captains came on board the Tiger
by longboats. Their faces were agitated, stern, hard. The kitchen
had been warned, and the smell of roasting pig was drifting along

the galleys, up and down ladders, and through all the hatches and berth-holds of the ship.

Five captains. Sir Richard Grenville of the Tiger, of course. George Raymond, captain of the Lyon, had come aboard first. Then John Clarke of the high-sterned Roebuck, a square-rigged flyboat of Dutch design. It was almost as grand as the Tiger, but I had heard Master Fernandez tell the Turk that he would not wish to sail it in a storm. Mr Clarke was small and round and had a mean mouth which put me in mind of my stepfather.

But then I was summoned to the kitchen and missed the arrival of both Arthur Barlowe, from the little bark Dorothy, and the red-faced Thomas Cavendish, captain of the Elizabeth.

Another six gentlemen shared the table with the captains: John White the artist, a quiet man; next to him was Philip Amadas, whose sudden tempers rivalled those of Sir Richard and made him a man to avoid. On Sir Richard's left was Mr Ralph Lane, the commander of the soldiers and as hard a man as I ever saw outside Drumelzier. I could hear his two huge mastiffs under the table, gnawing and cracking bones. On Sir Richard's right was Simon Fernandez, the Portuguese sailor and a man of huge arrogance: out of his hearing, the mariners called him 'the swine'. And then there was the man who was becoming my guide and teacher, Thomas Harriot, and next to him Marmaduke StClair.

My role in the meeting was modest enough, to keep the officers and the gentlemen supplied with wine and aqua vitae. It still gave me a thrill to be part of this inner counsel, even as a humble servant.

As to the purpose of the meeting, this became clear with Sir Richard's first words, when all were seated in the great cabin: 'First Holby, then the carpenter. Once is misfortune – maybe Holby fell overboard drunk. Twice is suspicious, even though I cannot understand how the barrels came to be on top of the carpenter. But three times? Three mysterious deaths? Mr White's death by poisoning puts the matter beyond dispute. There is a murderer on board the Tiger. What do you say, Harriot? Is he a Jesuit or a witch?'

'Or both', Raymond suggested, pointing at his goblet. I moved forward in haste to fill it, and then went slowly around the table with a flagon of the red wine, trying to appear as a servant should, invisible, and yet lingering to hear every word.

'I smell a Jesuit behind this,' Ralph Lane declared, without allowing Mr Harriot time to answer.

Sir Richard growled from the depths of his chest; to me he sounded like a dog. 'And behind him, the hand of the Spanish throne. Am I truly forced to believe there is an assassin in our midst? Someone whose purpose is the failure of the expedition? Perhaps a man at this very table?' Sir Richard's icy blue eyes went around everyone, as if he was trying to peer into the soul of each man. There was a long, embarrassed silence. Marmaduke StClair's cheeks were flushing.

John White broke the silence. 'But the carpenter's body was squashed under the weight of the barrels. No Jesuit – or anyone else for that matter – could have raised such a weight and lowered it on to the man's body. It required a supernatural force. I say there is a witch at work. One with the ability to summon up diabolical powers.'

'But our goal was a closely guarded secret,' George Raymond said. 'How could it be discovered?'

Sir Richard stood up and stepped over to a cabinet. He produced a large brass key from within his tunic, took a flintlock pistol from a rack, along with a box, and sat back down with them, placing box and pistol next to his goblet. I felt a twinge of apprehension. 'Don't be a fool, Raymond. Mendoza's nest of spies—'

'But Richard, Her Majesty expelled Mendoza just before—'

'The viper is gone, yes. But will you tell me that amongst all the workers on Plymouth harbour, and the victuallers and vintners who came and went on the dock, there was not one agent of the King of Spain? And that they would not see the chests of dried beans, and the hessian bags of peas and other seeds for planting? What fool could fail to see that we intended to establish a colony for Elizabeth?'

I had already guessed as much from my wanderings through the great hold of the Tiger. But it was knowledge I should not possess. They had decided that I was of no significance or, more likely, had just forgotten my presence. I stood back, quiet as a mouse, still as a rabbit.

'A clever assassin would allow himself to be pressed on board,' said Mr White.

'Perhaps,' said Mr Harriot. 'But if this is an attempt to destroy us, it was planned months ago, by someone who knew of the expedition. That means someone close to the Queen.'

'Christ in heaven, Harriot, do you hear your own words? A traitor in court?' Amadas's cheeks were flushed, almost purple. He gulped more aqua vitae and snapped his fingers without looking at me. I hastened over to replenish the soothing liquid. There was a menacing growl from one of Lane's mastiffs as I passed.

I could sense that Mr Harriot was not at ease. I guessed that he was judging Sir Richard's temper. At the moment the captain seemed even enough, but the man was like Stromboli, a mountain of which the Dominie had told me. We all feared him for his unpredictable rages.

Harriot said, 'Not all Jesuits or Catholics are traitors, Richard. Simon here is of the Catholic faith.'

'He is Portuguese.' Spoken as one would say 'he is a servant' or even 'he is a thief'. Fernandez shrugged off Sir Richard's remark with a smile, but for the briefest of moments – and it may have been my imagination – I thought I glimpsed huge malice lying behind the mariner's dark eyes.

'I hope my loyalty is beyond doubt,' said Marmaduke StClair. 'And I am a Catholic.'

'Aye, damn your soul, but at least you are not a recusant.' Richard casually poured powder into the barrel of his pistol, tamping it down with a rod.

The soldier looked across at Harriot. 'Sorcery? Do you say such a thing is possible?'

Sir Richard grinned demonically. 'There are times when I suspect Thomas of sorcery.'

'I do not believe in the spirit world,' said Mr Harriot baldly.

Marmaduke StClair leaned forward earnestly. His face too was flushed and I am sure that the goblet of wine I had just poured him was his fourth. 'Have you not heard of the exorcisms which have taken place in Toulouse and Carcassone? Seen by thousands of witnesses? And the fact of exorcism can only mean there are spirits to be exorcised in the first place.'

Sir Richard scowled. 'Jesuit nonsense. Staged by priests to impress the Huguenots and trick them back into the false doctrines.'

'With great success, I hear,' Raymond said.

Marmaduke took a nervous sip at his wine. 'The reality of demonic possession is further proved by Marthe Brosier.'

'I have heard of her,' said Raymond in a sceptical tone.

'Speaking Latin and Greek, languages of which she had no prior knowledge. Discerning secrets to which she could have had no access. Becoming seized with convulsions when scripture was read or she was touched by holy water.'

'Did you leave your brain on Plymouth docks, Marmaduke? And do you expect me to swallow Continental Catholic lies along with my wine?' Sir Richard's hatred of Spain was as legendary as his temper; I began to pray inwardly that Marmaduke would have the sense not to mention the exorcisms of Cadiz and Madrid.

'And what of William Weston . . .'

'What of him? Another Jesuit and thus another liar.' Sir Richard's voice was raised somewhat; I began to fear another Stromboli. He was now tapping a ball into the pistol. But Marmaduke seemed insensitive to the atmosphere. He pounded on: 'Then there is John Darrell . . .'

'God damn you, the man is a Puritan!' Sir Richard banged his flintlock pistol on the table and I feared a discharge in my direction.

But Marmaduke StClair, it seemed, had more courage than sense. His face was growing ever more flushed. 'If there is no possession and no witchcraft, why should we believe in devils? And if there are no devils, why believe in angels? Think on it, sir! You are a sheet of parchment away from denying there is a God!'

In the silence that followed, even StClair saw that he had gone too far. He grew pale, while Sir Richard's complexion slowly turned a deep purple.

Thomas Harriot filled the intense silence. 'I know of herbs which, when inhaled as smoke, produce the illusion of flight or conversion of the body into that of a cat or dog. Yet an observer sees that no flight and no transanimation takes place.'

'The Devil's instrument,' Marmaduke suggested.

'I think not,' Harriot replied. 'Their use is sanctified by the Bible. Consider Psalm One hundred and four, verse fourteen in the vulgar: "He causes the grass to grow for the cattle, and the herb for the service of man." I believe that much of the belief in witchcraft comes from such illusions induced by herbs. Also, those who believe such things are mostly women, and we know them to be gullible creatures, prone to hysteria and illusion.'

'Aye. On that at least we can agree.' Harriot's words were calming the captain. 'You argue for a poisoner, Thomas, rather than a caster of spells or a summoner of demons?'

'In all cases of sorcery and witchcraft known to me, a natural explanation lay behind the apparent possession. In any case, how can there be a spirit world?' There was an outraged gasp from Marmaduke. 'Incorporeal bodies could exist only where matter does not. But Descartes has defined matter as that which has dimensions. It follows that a true void cannot exist because it can have no length, breadth or height. And without a void, there is no place for spirit bodies. Marmaduke's devils cannot exist. Amongst thinking men, there is no place for the supernatural.'

'There is a chain,' Marmaduke insisted. 'If we please ourselves whether to believe in witches, then we please ourselves about belief in devils or spirits, resurrection of the body, immortality of the soul, even belief in God. Break a link in that chain and we endanger the central tenets of faith.'

Little Philip Amadas finally spoke. I could scarcely understand his accent. 'Marmaduke's right. Only a fool denies the evidence of faith. You presume a thing is impossible, Thomas, because it cannot be proved. But thousands of persons have seen things done which go beyond nature. By denying sorcery you exalt your own opinion above the testimonies of men through the ages and you deny the possibility of an invisible world which lies beyond your senses. This is a mark, not of a rational man, but of one filled with conceit and self-importance.'

Mr Harriot's response was to throw back his head and roar with laughter.

I had never in my life heard Tweedsmuir men talk of more than the price of sheep. To question things which had never even been mentioned in my world, to explore them with their minds, and what minds! The spirit of Plutarch's *Lives* was alive, the philosophers who came before Christ were alive, here in the gentlemen's room. In my enthusiasm I blurted out, 'But did not Democritus say that the world is made of indivisible particles, forever jostling each other? Perhaps spirits could occupy the spaces between these atoms.'

A cabbage had spoken.

In the stunned silence which followed, the only sound came from the jaws of one of Ralph Lane's mastiffs, greedily crunching a bone under the table. Then Amadas, his face a picture of horrified disbelief, said, 'Hang him.'

Captain Clarke said, 'No. He is only a boy. Flog him until his spine is exposed.'

I did not understand. What had I done wrong? I froze with fear.

'Never.' Harriot spoke in a firm voice. 'The boy is from Scotland and knows nothing of rank or protocol. I have taken him under my wing, and I encourage him to think, a rare enough commodity these days.'

'Then encourage him also to keep his mouth shut, Thomas,' Sir Richard growled. 'He is here to serve aqua vitae, not to join in our deliberations.'

Mr Harriot said nothing, but he turned to me and put a finger to his lips. I needed no such instruction; from now on I would speak only when spoken to.

Raymond said, 'But the boy has a point. How could one man have lifted the barrels onto the body of another? It would take the strength of three men. It is clear evidence that someone on board has been assisted by a diabolical power.'

'Or else,' Mr Harriot suggested, 'there are three assassins.'

13

The meeting of the captains had reached no conclusions. As it happened, no further meetings between them were possible, for a second storm shortly afterwards separated the ships: the sea was empty as far as the horizon apart from one of the Tiger's pinnaces – the other had sunk. Mr Chandler told me, however, that without doubt Sir Richard had fixed a rendezvous somewhere in the New World.

Whether the hangings had put fear into the heart of the murderer I do not know, but the violent killings stopped. Gradually, as each day passed without an event, the atmosphere of fear began to subside and we began to look forward to our first sight of the Americas.

I had never known anything like the sticky heat of the Cancer tropic. My undergarments were wet with sweat. I washed them in seawater, dried them in the breeze and they were wet again within the hour. As noon approached, the sun rose high and the riggings threw short patterns of shadow on the deck, which moved like pendulums as the Tiger rode the swells. Modesty forbade me from appearing almost naked as some of the older mariners were prepared to do.

But the sails were full, and if Master Fernandez's chart was correct – and it would be a hanging offence to question it – we would be in sight of a land called Puerto Rico within days. A pestilence-ridden jungle, the mineral man Joachim had told me, under the control of the Spanish. But Sir Richard needed fresh fruit and water and cattle, and he was prepared to use his cannon to get them. The lookouts seemed more alert than usual, and other mariners were at the bow, little specks of spray cooling their tanned skins.

In the morning, having attended to the gentlemen, I had little to do but catch up with my journal. When the sand in the glass had less than an hour to go, I went searching for Master Fernandez. He was on the afterdeck, in serious conversation with Mr Harriot and Sir Richard. The captain's flintlock was tucked in his sword belt. I stood quietly, at a respectful distance, while the sun crept towards its highest point. If I interrupted I would be cudgelled for insolence. If I did not, and the sun passed the meridian, I would be cudgelled for not alerting the navigator. My position was not helped by the fact that the captain and Fernandez seemed to be at odds. Both were red-faced and talking in loud, angry voices, with Mr Harriot trying to calm them. I had no right to hear this. They were arguing about very little, as I recall.

I cleared my throat. As the moments ticked past I stepped closer. Still I was not seen. Finally I had a spasm of coughing. Fernandez turned and glared, suddenly directing his ill humour at me, but I had placed myself out of arm's length.

'Sir, the noon sighting.'

Harriot looked at me in surprise. 'Ah. Then fetch my cross staff, Scotch.'

I clambered down the ladder and along the gentlemen's short corridor. Mr Harriot's cabin was small and neat. The cross staff was in the navigation chest up against the wall opposite the door, directly under the reading desk. It was locked, and the key was in the left-hand desk drawer.

And to the right, underneath Mr Harriot's bunk, was his chest of cedar wood. It too had a large brass key, in the right-hand drawer.

I looked at it, burning with curiosity. I swear that it was a living thing, speaking to my inner mind. It was saying, 'Open me up, discover my secrets. None will ever know.'

I could retrieve the key from the right-hand drawer, pull the cedar chest out, open its lid, look quickly at its contents, close it, return the key and run upstairs with the cross staff from the navigation chest, all in the space of a minute.

Some lunatic impulse made me open the forbidden drawer. And there was the key, in amongst feathered pens, little bottles of black ink, chart dividers and parchment carrying some insignia which, in my excitement, I did not take the time to examine.

I quickly moved to the bunk and went on my knees, noting the exact position of the cedar chest before pulling it towards me. It was heavy and took much longer to pull clear of the bunk than I had expected. I almost gave up and pushed it back, but there was the lock and here was the key. I strained my ears but the only sounds reaching me were the hundred little creaks and groans of the Tiger as she clambered up and down the ocean waves. The key turned easily, although my hands were trembling. I opened the lid.

There was a black cloak, neatly folded. There were books, many of them. And oh, what books! With pleasure I saw Thomas North's translation of Plutarch's *Lives*, which had comforted me on the long journey from Tweedsmuir. But I had not even heard of the others. For some, the titles revealed their topics: *The Book of Falconrie* by Turbeville, *Theatrum Mundi* by J. Alday, *The Book of Martyrs* by John Foxe, and *A Treatise of the New India* by Richard Eden. Others seemed to be stories, like *Golden Epistles* by Guevara, translated by Sir Geoffrey Fenton. There was also, a hasty glance told me, poetry such as *Astrophil and Stella* by Sir Philip Sidney. I did not dare take the time to discern the nature of other works, such as *Canaans Calamitie* by Thomas Dekker. And there were books which, I suspected, dealt with forbidden matters: *Decem Rationes* by Edmond Campion, a man executed, I had heard, for treason, and *Secret Alchemy* by Humphrey Grindal. And I thrilled to see *De Umbris Idearum* by Giordano Bruno, the monk who was risking death by heresy. I flicked quickly through its dangerous pages: it was filled with Pythagoras and magic and occult writings.

I didn't dare to delay any longer. But when I began to push the chest back, I heard a strange rustling noise near the bottom of the box. Curious, I looked down the side and saw a small slit. I had my ballockknife. I pushed my knife into the slit and, to my utter astonishment, a drawer slid out. The chest had a false bottom!

And in this false bottom there was a chart. I thrilled at the sight of it. Its title was written in a corner: *Indiarum Occidentalium, Pascaert van Wesindien ende Caribise Eyelanden*. Underneath was written WGB in tiny letters. It was in brilliant colour. There were the islands of the West Indies, and lines marking the four voyages of Columbus, place names, coastlines, shoals, sea monsters and galleons. And most of all, lightly penned, was a single line of longitude running through the Americas, from a land called Virginia in the north to one called Guyana in the south. Marked on this line was a faint spot which, I believe, was the secret destination of which I had heard Sir Richard and Thomas Harriot speak. It was some miles inland from the shore.

And there was a manuscript, a simple bundle of parchment. This told another story. With a surge of horror I realised that by merely setting eyes on it I had become a spy. I knew now that if I were caught, if Mr Harriot were to enter his cabin at this instant, I would be dragged straight to the yardarm and hanged.

The title was written in a small, neat hand:

A playne Discourse and humble Advise for our Gratious Queen Elizabeth, her most Excellent Majestie to peruse and consider, as concerning the needful Reformation of the Vulgar Kalendar for the civile yeres and daies accompting, or verifyeng, according to the tyme trewly spent.

The author was John Dee. The English Queen's astronomer! Above the title someone had written: *The Secret Cycle of Doctor Dee, and the Secret Purpose of our Expedition.* And at the foot of this page there was a line of writing by a third hand. I could barely make out the Latin scrawl: *Quod defertur non aufertur. E.R.* This line had been scored out and the same hand had printed above it: IACTA EST ALIA.

Acutely aware that if I was caught I could not escape execution, I looked at the page below. Perhaps the extreme danger of my situation had sharpened my senses, but I recall the exact words.

> *ELIZABETH our Empress bright,*
> *Who in the yere of eighty three,*
> *Thus made the truth to come to light,*
> *And civile yere with heaven agree,*
> *But eighty foure, the Pattern is*
> *Of Christ's birth yere: and so for ay*

Eche Bissext shall fall little mys,
To shew the sun of Christ's birth day.
Three hundred yeres, shall not remove
The sun, one day, from this new match:
Nature, no more shall us reprove
Her golden tyme, so yll to watch.

Footsteps clattering down the ladder.

Mr Harriot's footsteps.

I was overwhelmed by a wave of terror. Now the footsteps were walking briskly along the short corridor. There was no time to lock the chest or return the key. Frantically, I heaved the chest back, thrust the key inside my tunic next to my purse and rose quickly, turning towards the navigation chest.

My back was to Mr Harriot as my hands reached the cross staff. I sensed his hesitation, felt his eyes taking in the cabin.

'What keeps you, boy?' His voice was sharp. I heard suspicion in every syllable.

'I had difficulty with the lock, sir. But I have it now.'

'Quickly, or we will lose the sighting.'

I picked up cross staff, easel and chalk, and followed Mr Harriot up the steps, weak at the knees and knowing that I would have to repeat the whole process, putting the maps and books back neatly, locking the chest and returning the key before he discovered it had gone.

I cannot describe the agonies of fear which consumed me the whole of that afternoon.

I was summoned to the kitchen and made busy with preparation of food for the evening. Moving between the gentlemen's room and the galley, I frequently passed Mr Harriot's cabin. After the noon sighting he, Sir Richard and Master Fernandez had all gone down to Sir Richard's cabin. Shortly afterwards, Thomas had left and gone straight to his own cabin, and there he stayed.

He could not fail to see that the chest had been moved. He could not fail to look for chart dividers in the desk drawer and see that the great brass key was missing. He could not then fail to find that the chest was unlocked and its contents disturbed. I carried my death warrant in my tunic, in the form of the key, and yet I dared not lose it as it had to be returned if I were to survive the day.

My imagination felt the rough hemp round my neck, the mariners pulling on the rope, the terrible constriction of my throat, my feet clearing the desk, my body swaying and a sea of faces seen through red as I danced . . .

The Turk was tapping my shoulder.

It must have been late afternoon. The table had been set and the musicians were grumbling up from the berth-hold.

'Mr Harriot requires you this instant.'

I knocked at the door and entered on his call. He was writing and had his back to me. The cross staff was on his desk. 'Ogilvie.'

'Sir?'

'You fail your master.'

'Sir?' I felt the noose tightening around my neck and thought I might faint.

He turned. 'Are you well, boy? You look pale.'

'I am well, sir. I just have a little sea sickness.'

'And I am neglected. Fetch me some wine.'

I took care not to show the surge of relief which went through my body. I fetched a flagon of red wine from the hold. He seemed not to notice my trembling legs and hands. I took care again this time not to spill the wine.

The evening brought a great oval of blood-red sun touching the horizon, and a sky of rapidly deepening blue, and the screeching of the musicians.

Hope, a desperate hope, began to seep into my bones. With Mr Harriot's feet safely under the dinner table, and with my fetching and carrying between great cabin and galley, I might be able to slip into his cabin and return everything to its former undisturbed state, replacing the key.

Dinner was dried beef, fresh bread, butter, honey, prunes and great quantities of ale and wine. The Turk and I were in constant movement. At the end of the first course we began to return the heavy gold plates to the galley. In the corridor I added my pile to the Turk's.

'What are you doing?' he asked in alarm.

The great cabin door was swinging to and fro with the ship. I raised a finger to my lips and opened the door to Mr Harriot's cabin.

The Turk was round-eyed and open-mouthed. 'You fool, Scotch!' he hissed. 'Are you so anxious to hang?'

I shook my head and closed the door quickly behind me. I crossed over to the chest and pulled it out. At first it was too dark to make out any detail, but light from the great cabin was shining under the door, and slowly – oh so slowly! – my eyes became used to the dark.

I pulled the cedar chest out, put the books neatly back as I had found them, turned the key in the lock, jumped over to the writing desk, put the key back in the drawer, ran towards the cabin door and stopped, frozen with horror.

Voices, on the other side of the door, Marmaduke's among them. I caught his words: 'Come and see for yourself,' and then the door handle was turning.

14

I was in terror of death. But what could I do?

I shrank behind the chest, using its bulk to shield me from the sight of the men. I counted four pairs of legs, one pair belonging to the savage, Manteo.

'Be quick, StClair.' The voice was low and urgent. It belonged to Kendall, the young mathematician. 'We are running a terrible risk.'

'It was you who asked to see the evidence.' Marmaduke StClair, but this was not the carefree Marmaduke I knew from the gentlemen's cabin, full of jokes and banter. This was another Marmaduke, a man with purpose in his voice.

'Stop bickering, you fools.' I was not sure of this voice. It was harsh and distorted by tension. It might have belonged to Rowse, the parliamentarian. 'Show us the map and the relic.'

To my horror, someone was bending down and pulling at the cedar chest. I shrank against the cabin wall. The chest was hauled to the middle of the floor. They only had to bend their heads to see me. But now the key was being taken from its drawer and I heard the distinctive click of the false bottom being opened.

The silence was so long that I thought I must have been seen. But then there was a rustling of paper and sounds which told me that the map was being spread out on Mr Harriot's table. Rowse was speaking. 'This is the line?'

'Yes. Seventy-seven west,' said Kendall.

'*Longitudinem Dei*,' StClair said.

'God's longitude indeed.' Rowse's tone was impatient, and his voice was edged with fear. 'But five leagues inland and the devil to reach, by the looks of it.'

'Richard is no fool. And he has Lane. He will succeed.' StClair too was catching the contagion of fear.

'And the relic?' It was Kendall; his voice was strained. Fear, certainly, but there was something else in his voice: avarice.

Footsteps towards Marmaduke's bunk. I could not understand what was happening. For all my terror, I could not resist poking my head out. To my astonishment, Marmaduke was sliding back a panel on the bulkhead above his berth. Then he was lifting something out very carefully. Whatever it was, it was flattish, wrapped in black cloth and clearly heavy. I shrank back under the bunk as they turned, and could not see what it was. There was a sound of cloth unwrapping. Then a gasp and someone – I think Kendall – praying quietly in Latin.

Rowse, his voice harsh, said, 'This is it?'

'This is it,' StClair was saying. 'And kissed by the Queen.'

There was another long silence.

'In God's name, gentlemen, we must succeed.'

'Aye, Kendall,' said Rowse. 'But it all ends here if Harriot walks in the door.'

'Then for God's sake let us get out of here quickly.' Kendall's voice was an agony of suspense.

There was the sound of the panel being slid back into place, and then things were being put back in the chest, the secret drawer was closed, and Manteo was down on his knees and pushing the chest back under the bunk. It came solidly up against me. He pushed harder, and then he was looking under the bed and staring straight at me. He showed no surprise, and his expression did not change at all. At that moment I believe I would have run from the ship and jumped in the ocean rather than face the fate which Grenville and the Devil would impose on me. But then the savage stood up, without a word, and the men left, leaving me trembling in the dark and trying not to weep.

Part Two

The Byzantine Cross

15

Zola jumped up and skipped out of the living room. I heard her footsteps pacing up and down excitedly in the corridor. She was shouting, 'Yes! Yes!'

'A conspiracy?' I called through.

'Yes, Harry. People trying to ruin an expedition whose purpose was supposed to be a secret.' She came back into the room, head bowed and fingers steepled.

I shook my head in bewilderment. 'It has to be connected with this longitude. What's special about seventy-seven degrees west? God's longitude?'

'It rings a bell.' She put her hands on the top of her head, closed her eyes and screwed up her face.

'How did they find longitude, anyway? They had no clocks on board.'

'I know. The Harrison clocks didn't come in until the 1730s. I guess they had to rely on eclipses happening at predicted times. Get the local time of the eclipse, compare it with the time it happened in London, and you've got a time marker. But it must have been a protracted business.'

'So what were these people up to? And what the hell was in the panel?' A grandfather clock in the hallway chimed three. Suddenly I just couldn't keep my eyes open any longer. 'Zola, about that spare room.'

'Of course, I'm forgetting. You've been chased by thugs and questioned for murder and beaten up. I expect you want some sleep.'

I followed her up some wooden stairs. Three doors led off from a small landing and she opened one of them. There was a neat, single attic bedroom. It had a faint smell of *pot-pourri*.

97

'This okay?'

'*Benissimo*.' I'd have said it, and meant it, if the bed had been a pile of flea-infested straw.

Dolls from fifty countries stood side-by-side on shelves lining the little room: Inuits with little spears; American Indian girls with hunting knives; Scots with kilts; Greek men with short skirts which would have had them arrested in Leicester Square; Indian boys with turbans, all looked silently down on me. Feeling a bit self-conscious I threw off my clothes and slipped between the sheets. I found myself lying on a horsehair mattress, almost unobtainable in the age of tractors, but unbeatable for comfort. Headache, bruises, thugs, huge bribes, obnoxious gentry, man-eating teenagers, Elizabethan voyages – all merged into a lurid pastiche as I drifted into oblivion.

I wake suddenly.

The dolls have come alive, are pattering around the house. Am I awake?

Sense a presence.

That has to be nonsense. I don't believe in telepathy. The dolls are getting to me: fifty pairs of eyes staring at me in the dark.

A sound, on the limit of hearing. I place it in Zola's bedroom. Maybe she's getting up to go to the bathroom. Then a moan, or maybe a whimper, so muffled that I'm not sure I hear it.

I lie still as a corpse, ears straining, heart thumping in my chest.

Crash! A scream so loud that it hurts my ears. I leap out of bed and dive for the door. It's flung open as I reach it and it slams against my nose. I feel warm blood and a lot of pain. A dark shape. It might be Zola except that it hits at me, a fist connecting with my shoulder. I kick in the dark at stomach level, make contact with something soft, hurt my toes. There is an *Oof!* and I kick again, now with the side of my foot. I wonder if Zola is dead.

Now the man is punching in the dark. The blows are ineffective and I charge at him, using my fourteen-stone body as a battering ram. He falls backwards through the door and I hear two distinct cracks as the back of his head makes contact first with the door frame and then with the floor of the hallway. I fall on top of him. He grabs my hair and I put my thumbs in his eyes and squeeze. He shakes his head violently from side to side, panicking, but I keep finding his eyeballs. Then he changes tack and a finger jabs repeatedly at my eyes. I have to let go and roll aside, and now my assailant is on me, punching and then digging his thumbs into my neck. I try to pull his hands off but his full weight is bearing down on my throat, I can't breathe, I'm beginning to panic. I grope for his eyes, I'm beginning to see flashing lights; still his nails are digging into my Adam's apple.

Then there is a metallic clang and the man yelps like an injured dog. He lets go, staggers to his feet. There is a brief scuffle and another clang and then he is crashing noisily down the stairs, and there are footsteps along the corridor below and the front door slams shut with a bang which shakes the flat.

The lights go on and Zola is standing triumphant and angry, flushed and gasping, all teddy bears and crescent moons. She is holding a frying pan with both hands. It's bright yellow, cast-iron, and looks as if it could smash a skull. 'That beat the shit out of him.'

Zola is in the shower, wisps of steam filtering under the bathroom door. The faint hum of London traffic penetrates the double glazing.

I feel nauseous and put my head in the kitchen sink, unsure whether I'm going to vomit. The feeling passes and I turn on a tap and run my head under the cold stream. I gently pat my head dry with a towel – rubbing is too painful. I pour some water into a kettle and watch the fierce blue flames under it. I don't have the nerve to check myself in a mirror. Not just yet. I am becoming aware of pain. It comes from all over, from my head, my throat, my midriff, my nose. Especially my nose. At least the bleeding has stopped.

The shower stops and in a moment Zola appears, with a yellow towel round her body and a pink one wrapped round her head. She has a bruise on her forehead. For the first time I realise I'm dressed in nothing more than boxer shorts.

'Let's call the police,' I suggest. The kettle is coming to the boil and I search around for instant coffee and cups. My stomach is still dodgy.

Her voice is tinged with anger. 'There's something in that manuscript, Harry.'

I ask, 'Do you want the good news or the bad news first?'

She waves her hand angrily.

'They didn't get the manuscript,' I tell her. I've brought it down from my bedroom. It's on the kitchen table and I give it a reassuring pat.

'And the bad news?'

'They got my laptop. It has Ogilvie's journal on file.'

'But they don't understand what's in the journal any more than we do,' she said.

'Wrong, Zola. They must know what they're looking for.'

'So let's beat them to it.' She is rubbing her hair, carefully avoiding the bruise on her forehead, and her voice is coming from somewhere underneath the pink towel.

'Are you serious? You still want to carry on with this?'

Zola pauses, peers out from under the towel, gives me a puzzled look. 'Nothing else crossed my mind.' She plugs in a hair dryer and starts to do mysterious things with tongs. 'Can we solve this one, Harry? If I take a couple of weeks' leave . . .'

'Let's do it.' I say it casually. 'God knows what we're getting into here but I have an obligation to a client, even a teenage maneater. Look, if we're in a race, we've competition.'

'Which means they could be back. There were two of them. One waiting downstairs.'

'The next time, maybe with guns,' I suggest. I'd done guns and had had enough of them. I'd done Northern Ireland, Kosovo and the Gulf before I'd left the army, opting for the quiet life. Much like the Dominie, I suppose.

'You're still going along with that fantasy thing? That Tebbit was murdered to get at the journal?'

'Admit it, Zola. I was right again.' I'm beginning to shake all over.

She switches off the hair dryer, sits down at the kitchen table, pours milk, picks up a mug of coffee with both hands, hitches the yellow towel up an inch, gives me a sultry look. 'You're a single man, right?'

'How did you know that?'

'Nobody could live with such smugness.' She takes a sip at the coffee and sighs.

'I don't see any sign of a partner here.'

'I was married to a lovely man. We met in Venice seven years ago. We're divorced.'

'I'm not surprised. Presumably he found you impossible to live with?'

'In a way. He couldn't keep up with my sexual demands.'

I splutter into my coffee. The action sends a shooting pain up my shoulder blade and Zola chuckles gleefully. Then her smile disappears and she says, 'With guns, you think?'

'Maybe. Which is one good reason for calling the police.'

'No, Harry. They'd just hold on to the journal for six months and I don't want to live like Salman Rushdie or a Mafia informer. Our best protection is to find whatever's in Ogilvie's journal before the creeps do. Beat them at their own game. What do you think?'

'Be sensible, woman.'

She says nothing.

'We don't know who they are or what we're up against.'

Still nothing, just a steady, disconcerting stare over her coffee cup.

I think, what the hell. 'We'd better clear off.'

The subdued hum of early morning motorway traffic came in through the double glazing. The mirror showed a face more comfortable than handsome, with an eye which, although still interesting, was well on the mend. I'd had maybe two hours' sleep, but so what? I was still alive. I made my way back from the public toilet.

The smell of frying bacon drifted over from the kitchen. Zola was at a window table, dressed in black sweater and jeans and wearing the gypsy earrings from the previous evening. The journal was in front of her on the table. A lorry driver at the next table was tucking into an all-English breakfast, and a young couple with two bleary-eyed children were across the passage. Otherwise the motorway stop was empty.

'This doesn't seem right in the cold light of the morning. Why should we be fugitives?'

'We're not. We're going undercover to beat the opposition.'

Zola's statement was arguable, but it was too early in the morning. I helped myself to toast. 'By the way, where are we going?'

'Devon. I have a hideaway, my parents' holiday cottage.' Zola leaned forwards, lowering her voice. 'And I know what Harriot and the rest were up to.'

16

'Okay, Harry, this is going to fry your brain. I doubt if you have the intellectual capacity for it.'

'Shoot.' I thought maybe the word 'shoot' wasn't the best, but it had come out.

'Go back to the bit about the secret cycle of Doctor Dee.'

I hadn't expected Zola to drive anything ordinary, and true enough we were in a thirty-year-old classic, a Reliant Scimitar with three litres of engine powering a light, silver fibreglass body, and a dashboard like the cockpit of an aeroplane. There were little hairline cracks on the massive bonnet but the black leather seats showed no sign of sag. Not that the latent power was doing us much good: we were crawling along at a few miles an hour on a roadwork-infested M25. The smell of perfume and leather were light in the air.

I flicked back the pages. 'Okay, there's the rhyme. Something about making the "*civile year with heaven agree*". And something else about "*Three hundred yeres, shall not remove The sun one day from this new match*" . . .'

'Exactly. First clue. It has something to do with calendars.'

'With you so far,' I said.

'But not for much longer. Now here's the second clue. What's the connection between Thomas Harriot and John Dee?'

'They both belonged to the School of the Night.'

We were approaching the end of the roadworks. I sensed Zola scanning the road ahead, judging accelerations, looking for gaps. She said, 'I'm impressed, Harry. I didn't expect a grubby shopkeeper to know something like that.'

I said, 'I know that some of the best minds of the day used to meet in Walter Raleigh's London pad, Durham House. People like

Francis Drake the explorer, Molyneux the globe maker, Christopher Marlowe the playwright, John Dee the Queen's astronomer, Thomas Harriot the mathematician, and a few others. I know that several of these people had a private ear to the Queen. I know they were accused of being a school of atheism and blasphemy, practising strange rites, but in fact they were discussing things like the truth of the Old Testament, the Copernican theory, the new mathematics and navigation. They were dipping their foot into modern science, carving a future for global exploration and turning England into a global power. Apart from that, no, I don't know much about the School of the Night.'

The road was opening out. Zola had spotted a gap, dropped a gear. I felt a hard push on my back, and with a roar we were accelerating clear of a herd of cars. She said, 'There's a magic triangle in there: Raleigh, Harriot, John Dee. Now let me give you clue number three. Look at what Queen Elizabeth scribbled on John Dee's report.'

I read it out: '*Quod defertur non aufertur*. Okay, she's telling Dee that what is deferred will not be abandoned. But it's been scored out and replaced by *Iacta est alia*: the die is cast.'

Zola was accelerating smoothly beyond a hundred miles an hour. 'What die, Harry?'

'Something to do with a secret cycle, and a calendar?'

'Good boy, you're coming along. Now let me tell you about John Dee's secret calendar. We have leap years because the year isn't exactly three hundred and sixty-five days long, right? There's about a quarter of a day left over at the end of each year. We count too fast.'

'So every fourth year we add an extra day to stop the drift. We have a leap year.'

'A device which goes back to Julius Caesar. Except that the drift isn't exactly a quarter of a day. The count still isn't quite right and the seasons still have a tiny drift in relation to the calendar. Not a lot, not enough to notice over a human lifetime, but over the thirteen centuries since the Church began to use this Roman calendar, the slippage had amounted to about ten days. Eventually we'd have Santa Claus appearing in the summer.'

'But the Gregorian calendar sorted this, a calendar we still use. I seem to remember it works by missing out some of the leap years.'

'All the century years are excluded unless their date's number can be divided by 400. The year 2000 was a leap year, but 1900 wasn't. The Gregorian calendar repeats on a four hundred year cycle. But there were problems with it, Harry. For a start it was Catholic. It was introduced in 1582 by Pope Gregory XIII, alias a drunken womaniser called Ugo Compagni. So the Protestant states had a choice: they could either stick with their calendar, which could only get slowly worse year by year, or they could grit their teeth and adopt the superior Catholic one. These things were life and death. The calendar dates gave your religious festivals, and the Catholic and Protestant ideologies were in a no-holds-barred war.'

'What are you saying? That John Dee had invented another calendar?'

Zola nodded. The needle of the old Smith speedometer had now steadied at a hundred and ten miles an hour. Signs for Southampton were zipping past. She said, 'It was a beauty. For a start, it performed better at achieving a major goal for the civil calendar, which Pope Gregory and Philip of Spain both aimed for. That was to keep the date, March 21st, the starting point for Easter calculations, as close as possible to the vernal equinox. Vernal being Spring, and equinox being equal duration of day and night.'

'Zola, I'll grant you I went to a comprehensive school, but I did know that. But so what? What's the significance?'

'What we're seeing is an underground war fought four centuries ago, and still simmering even now. A secret war. Even today we know almost nothing about it.'

'A war?'

'Between Christ and the Antichrist.'

I looked at her in surprise. She wasn't joking. 'You're serious, right?'

'Deadly so, Harry. It was a battle for the soul, and it involved the calendar. The modern calendar, the Gregorian, works on a four hundred year cycle, a sequence of ninety-seven leap years in four hundred. Boring numbers, meaningless to the toiling peasantry. But Dee had worked out a much better system of leap years, a system which paced the calendar dates smoothly with the seasons. Eight of them repeating in a thirty-three year cycle.'

'Thirty-three years?'

'The lifetime of Jesus. You're getting there, Harry. For the common man in the sixteenth century, a calendar which paced not just the seasons but also the life of Christ would have to be divinely inspired. It would capture his heart and his mind. Pope Gregory's four hundred year one would become mincemeat. If the Protestant nations had adopted the Dee calendar they'd have completely turned the tables on the Catholic Church.'

'And it's all done by leap years?'

'Good boy again. The first Dee cycle is AD 1 to 33. Its leap years are AD 4, 8, 12, 16, 20, 24, 28 and 32. The second cycle repeats the first, running from AD 34 to 66 and so on.'

'A four-year gap between leap years? Like the Gregorian system?'

Zola shook her head, put her foot down, accelerated past a convoy and said, 'Not quite. There's a five-year gap between the last leap year of one cycle and the first leap year of the next.'

'Isn't that complicated? How are these leap years worked out?'

'Piece of cake. Take 2004 AD. Split it into 20 and 04 and add to get 24. You can divide 24 by four which makes 2004 a leap year in Dee's system. Is your brain frying yet, Harry?'

'It's not even warm. Is this as fast as you go?'

'With timid passengers, yes. And it had another priceless feature.'

'Uhuh?'

'I said that Dee's calendar is better than the Pope's at matching the spring equinox to the same calendar date each year.'

'Brain's beginning to fry,' I confessed.

'I know, Harry, you're not very bright, but I'm sure we can find a use for you. In the Gregorian calendar there can be gaps of seven ordinary years sandwiched between leap years. During those years the spring equinox slips by almost forty-one hours. It's impossible to hold to a fixed date from one year to the next. But according to the Gospels, Jesus was resurrected on the first Sunday after the first full moon following the spring equinox. Result: because of this slippage, Easter doesn't always take place on the correct biblical Sunday, astronomically speaking. A bad business if you're a devout Christian.'

'And in Dee's secret calendar? The Jesus one?'

'In Dee's calendar there are never more than four ordinary years between leap years, so the equinox drifts by less than six hours for each of these years until the fifth year brings it back with a leap-day. It never drifts by more than twenty-four hours. Now suppose that every thirty-three years, at the beginning of the big five-year gap between leap days, you could get the spring equinox to happen very soon after midnight. In that case it would cycle within the same calendar date forever. Meaning that Easter would hold more closely to the biblical expectation. I'm losing you, right?'

I hated to admit it. 'Brain's sizzling. How can you arrange for the equinox to happen just after midnight on a particular year? Surely it happens when it happens?'

'But which midnight? Midnight in Honolulu or midnight in Greenwich? The Earth being round, Harry, midnight happens at different times at different places. You have the freedom to measure your universal time from a particular meridian on Earth, some prime meridian which defines zero degrees longitude.'

'Let me guess,' I said. 'You have to fix your prime meridian at seventy-seven degrees west.'

Zola was slipping through the gears, overtaking a lorry on the wrong side, moving swiftly up to a hundred and ten miles an hour again. She nodded. 'Measure longitude from Virginia instead of Greenwich, introduce Dee's secret cycle of leap years, and you've won the game.'

'But Philip of Spain's Catholic empire had a monopoly on God's longitude,' I said. 'The line runs through Cuba, Jamaica, Panama, Peru and so on.'

'You're nearly there, Harry.'

'Okay I get it. The English establish a colony on the seventy-seven degree meridian, operating in secret. Once they've established it, they announce the Dee calendar to the world. A calendar that paces the life of Jesus, that's more true to the Biblical Easter, that holds more closely to the seasons. Irresistible! England's influence with other Protestant nations is increased, and the Antichrist, in the form of the Pope, is stuck with flogging a second-rate ecclesiastical calendar which they'd only just introduced. Game, set and match to the Protestants. Quite a lad was our John Dee.'

'You don't know the half of it. He developed the concept of the British Empire, he was into navigation and mapmaking, he translated Euclid, he had the greatest library in England, he owned the Voynich manuscript – a cipher which hasn't been broken to this day, he founded the Rosicrucian Order as an antidote to the Jesuits, he advised Queen Elizabeth on matters celestial and he spied for her in Europe, using the codename 007.'

'Double-Oh-Seven? You're kidding!'

'I kid you not, Harry. He was the original James Bond.'

'Okay I'm persuaded. The School of the Night couldn't possibly have missed this. Anyway, how else can we explain Harriot's secret map? Or Ogilvie's instinct that the expedition had a secret purpose?'

Zola was scanning the road ahead, a General on manoeuvres. She moved down a gear. 'It also explains the murders onboard ship. Grenville talks about Mendoza's spies being everywhere. They must have penetrated the expedition. They were trying to destroy it from within.' Three litres of engine growled in complaint as she edged into the slow lane.

'Marmaduke StClair, Anthony Rowse, Abraham Kendall. Traitors and murderers.'

'Or patriots and freedom fighters. Depends where you're coming from.'

She was gurgling us on to a slip road, frowning. 'But it doesn't explain the desperation to get hold of the journal. It doesn't explain Toby Tebbit's murder. It doesn't explain last night. Hell, all this happened four centuries ago.' She shook her head in frustration. 'We still haven't got to the roots.'

I was flicking through the pages of the journal. 'Well. Well, well, well.'

Impatiently: 'Well what?'

I said, 'Nice try, Zola. But there's a lot more to this than calendars.'

'Harry!'

'This would fry your brain if you had one.'

'Talking about murder...'

'Just concentrate on the road, woman. I need to think about this.'

17

'Any further south and we'll need a boat,' said Zola. She was trickling her Scimitar round a small square towards a narrow, steeply descending lane. I got a glimpse of sea between the houses. Then we were clear of the little village and turning right up a stony track lined with a few whitewashed cottages. She stopped at the last one.

'The key,' she said, and I accompanied her back down the track to a cottage. A door opened and a spaniel came sniffing at my legs, and a middle-aged, dumpy woman said, 'Hello, Zola, how are you? Down for the weekend?'

'That's right, Mrs Murgatroyd. This is a colleague, Harry Blake.'

Mrs Murgatroyd gave me a lightning appraisal and a 'So you're just good friends?' look. 'Do you need eggs or milk?'

In her parents' cottage, Zola went through cupboards and then got busy at an Aga. I dumped Ogilvie's journal on a big farmhouse kitchen table and wandered. The cottage was large, comfortable and old. It looked out at a cultivated garden and a vineyard just beyond it, a bonus of global warming. A grandfather clock was ticking quietly in the hallway. It was just after 9 am and it felt like four o'clock in the morning. I turned back to the kitchen and hunted for instant coffee.

'So,' she said. We'd finished a breakfast of bacon, eggs and soft cornflakes and were on our third coffee of the morning.

'So. Ogilvie went back to Harriot's cabin. He wanted to find what was hidden in Marmaduke's secret panel.'

'What? Did the boy have a deathwish?'

'Do you want to know what he found, or would you prefer to resume your interrupted sleep?'

She yawned. 'Later. We're in a race, remember?'

18

I know that some day my curiosity will hang me. Even as I leave Mr Harriot's room with my heart pounding in my chest, I know that, at some stage of the voyage, I will have to find the secret lying behind the panel. The Devil is whispering in my ear: 'What is it? What is the sacred thing? Why is it so important?'

The next two days were spent in a routine of noon sightings and star measurements, serving the gentlemen at meals, washing their sheets and clothes and looking after the few hens and goats we had on board. It kept me busy day and night and protected me from the attentions of Mr Salter, whose dislike of me now showed itself by nothing more harmful than piercing stares. I wondered if I dared risk an insolent smile or even some remark, knowing that he could not easily touch me, but decided against it. Why torment an angry bear? Some day its cage door might be left open.

Every evening, of course, I shared the berth-hold with Manteo and a score of others, but we were never alone together. More than once I passed him in a corridor, or saw him in the galley. Once, leaning over the rails on deck, I had the strong sensation of being watched. I turned and there was Manteo, squatting cross-legged on the deck like an Indian Buddha, staring at me impassively. I knew that a word from him could hang me. And still, as my fright began to recede, my determination to invade the gentlemen's room increased. The urge to slide open the panel and discover the secret lying behind it became overwhelming. My curiosity was a disease, or a present from the Devil.

I committed this second crime of curiosity on the third day after I had almost been caught for the first one. Four sailors on the pinnace had now died of the plague and three replacements were being sent over from the Tiger. My young friend Michael from Southwark, Hunger, and a man I did not know were being transferred. Instead of rowing over in the longboat, the ship drew alongside, a rope was thrown across, and a harness attached to each man in turn. He then had to pull himself across the gap, hauling arm over arm on the supporting rope. The sea was calm but still the rope tautened and slackened, sometimes hurling a man in the air, sometimes plunging him in the water, to the delight of the watching sailors. The musicians played merry tunes while the transfer was in progress. On the afterdeck the gentlemen were watching the entertainment – the captain, Rowse, Harriot, StClair, Kendall and the others. The time would never be better.

Down ladders: nobody could hang me for that. Along the corridor abaft: still secure. There were no sounds over and above the hundred groanings of the Tiger. Everyone was on deck, watching the entertainment.

I knock, open the door, close it behind me. The panel pushes and slides easily. There are some jars, one with dried green insects – strange! – another with black curled leaves, others with white powders. But it is the black silk, wrapping something, which draws my attention. Its weight surprises me. I unwrap the layers of cloth – already I am shaking and my ears straining for human sounds – and this is what I find.

There are three wooden panels. The central one is about a foot high and nine inches wide. Two other panels are attached to it by wooden hinges so that they may either fold on top of the main panel or open out flat. The central panel contains, sunk into the wood, another piece of wood, a small gnarled rectangle. This central piece of wood is surrounded by a wide border of silver, and scattered through the silver like raisins in a pudding are diamonds, rubies, sapphires, emeralds and yellow stones whose name I do not know.

The left-hand panel, when opened, has a painting set into the wood. It shows a woman with large, cow-like eyes, an unbelievably long, thin nose, a tiny mouth and a pointed chin. Only her face is exposed: her head, hair, ears, neck and body are covered with a dark green shawl. Resting against her chest, and pressing his cheek against hers, is a baby wrapped in a long gown. It has long curly

112

hair and tiny hands and feet. The painting shows halos around the heads of mother and child, and there is writing of a kind which I have never seen before. All this against a blood red background.

On the right-hand panel there is a familiar enough picture: Jesus on the Cross, against a black sun in a stormy sky, women weeping at his feet and men averting their eyes, hands thrown up as if to defend themselves from the sight.

How long I gaze at this marvel I do not know. I wonder where it comes from, who made it, what it signifies. Somehow I feel the pattern, the symmetry, is designed to draw attention to the little rectangle of old wood in the very centre of this strange construction.

The sound of laughter and footsteps on a ladder bring me back to the present and remind me of the danger in which I have placed myself. Hastily, I fold the wood, wrap it in its cloth, put it back in its secret place and slide the panel closed. I am out of the door, along the corridor and up the stairs into the fresh air and the sunshine without, so far as I know, being seen.

19

Stay awake, I told myself. Stay awake. 'Let's apply some logic to this. What we have is some sort of relic, or secret object. It has to be what Tebbit's murderers are after. Not the gold, not the diamonds, just the wood at the centre of the thing. He's describing a triptych.'

Zola was stretched out on a couch, using a cushion as a pillow. I'd have had to be made of stone not to notice her figure. That trim stomach. Those breasts. 'What's a triptych?'

'The thing he's describing. It's an icon. A religious relic.'

'Okay, Harry, but so what? All you're giving me are words.'

'An icon being carried on a secret expedition by Catholic conspirators. There has to be a religious purpose to it.'

'With you so far, Harry. Would you like to go for a walk?'

'I'd much rather go to bed.'

'But we can go for a walk together.'

We both laughed.

I carried on. 'What religious purpose? They're trying to destroy the expedition, and if we believe your story about seventy-seven degrees west, they were trying to establish a Protestant colony and a new calendar. But look at the date – 1585. Look at the beautiful coincidence with the attempt to overthrow Queen Elizabeth in 1586, when the colonists were supposed to be setting up home.'

'You're talking about the Babington plot? The one where Mary Queen of Scots got her head chopped off?'

I sipped at my coffee; it was half-cold. 'I think there's a connection. There was a plot for a Spanish invasion of England once Elizabeth had been assassinated.'

'Keep the meter running, Harry. Tell me how that connects with the sacred relic.'

'I think it's a piece of wood from the Cross of Christ.'

Zola blinked nervously, sat up and gave me an intense stare.

Interesting eyes. Dark, intelligent. Eyes that look into your soul. 'What are you saying, Harry?'

'If a relic from Christ or the Virgin Mary was touched by a monarch it would authenticate that monarch's divine right to rule.'

Zola spoke carefully. 'So far so good. That's a matter of historical record.'

'Okay. Now, say that wood had been kissed by Mary Queen of Scots, and transported to seventy-seven west.'

Zola gave me a cautious nod.

I continued, 'Now say the Babington plot had worked. Say there was a punch-up between Mary Queen of Scots and Elizabeth, with Spanish troops invading England. Then Mary's right to North America would have been authenticated by the kissing of the Cross. It would have been a tremendous boost to the Catholic cause. And once Mary was safely on the throne, the Catholics would have had control of the magic longitude both north and south. Dee's calendar couldn't have been introduced by the Protestants. It even left Rome the option of introducing Dee's calendar and claiming the credit. Game, set and match to the true religion. The Protestant heresy would suffer a catastrophic blow, and might eventually collapse.'

'That's a nice theory, Harry. It's very neat, just like mine. But I have another one. I think maybe the knock on the head has done something to you. There's only one problem with it. To get your theory to work you need a piece of genuine wood from the Cross. Now how in hell's bells do you get hold of that?'

'The Crusaders had it, or believed they had. They called it the True Cross.'

'Harry, this is the twenty-first century. Stuff like that is just legend.'

'I know.'

Zola was looking straight at me. She stared at me for a moment, tilting her head to one side, and then spoke coolly. 'I respect you, Harry, I really do. The trouble is, you see yourself as some sort of superior creature, with idiots like me having to be coaxed up to your level of thinking. You're sitting there assuming I'm going to laugh you out of court.'

'You're right, Zola. I assume that an imaginative idea is beyond your grasp.'

'In fact, your theory explains a great deal. For example, it explains why people are prepared to commit murder to get hold of it. Think of the commercial value of a genuine piece of wood from the Cross. Think what a museum would pay for it. Think of the kudos of owning it.'

'Okay. But to test my theory, it looks as if we need to get hold of an expert on religious relics.'

Zola didn't blink. 'I know someone.'

'And if there's anything in my story there has to be some connection between Marmaduke StClair and the Tebbit family, a connection going back at least to the Crusades. All of a sudden we need to know the Tebbit family history.'

'Where do we get hold of that?'

'Debbie, of course. My teenage maneater.'

20

'Debbie?'

'Harry!' She sounded as if she had been crying. She also sounded pathetically pleased to hear from me.

'I know this is a bad time to call. Any time is a bad time to call right now.'

'Not at all.' She sounded genuine. I wondered if she was rattling around in the big mausoleum on her own, or whether it was still stuffed with grieving relatives, or whether Uncle Robert had decided to esconce himself there and take over her affairs.

'It's about the journal. I think we may be on to something.'

'On to something?'

'I'm not sure yet, but there's something in it needs chasing up. Look, Debbie, I would appreciate some help.'

I could practically feel her curiosity buzzing down the line. 'Of course. What can I do?'

I took a deep breath. 'I need to know something about your family history.'

'You mean, like what my grandfather did, stuff like that?'

'No, Debbie, I want to know about your family as far back as it goes. I mean, right back to the beginning.'

'Wow! We go back a very long way, Harry.' There was a hesitation, and then suddenly she adopted a cool, businesslike tone, as if she was speaking to the butcher: 'I'll ring you back—'

A male voice on the end of the line: 'Is that Blake?'

Uncle Robert. The tone had been harsh before, but this time it had an extra edge to it.

'Speaking,' I said, my stomach sinking.

'I will say this once again, Mr Blake. You are to have no further communication with my niece. If you do, you will hear from my lawyers. Have you understood that?'

Zola was standing at the end of the hall with coffee cup in hand and eyebrows raised. I jabbed a finger urgently towards the kitchen. It took her a second, but then she padded quickly through. I heard a faint click as she raised the kitchen receiver.

'Mr Tebbit, I'm a free citizen in a free country and I'll talk to anyone I damn well please.'

I guessed that Tebbit, like his brother, wasn't used to being contradicted. At any rate, he could hardly control the anger in his voice. 'You, sir, are working some sort of scam. Your sole interest in my niece is to extract as much money from her as you can. You are also in possession of a journal which belongs to our family. I want it delivered to me by registered post within twenty-four hours. If it is not, I will take action to have it returned and hold you responsible for the legal costs. Apart from the return of the journal, you are to have no further contact with this family.'

'Do you want some brandy in that?' Zola was nodding at my coffee cup. She had her feet up on the kitchen table and was teetering dangerously back, balancing a chair on two legs. I don't usually feel intimidated, but the unexpected confrontation had left me a little shaky. 'Are you going to do what he says? Stop any more contact with Debbie?'

'Are you serious?' I said. 'Stuff that.' Spoken with more bravado than I felt.

Zola frowned. 'Has it occurred to you that Uncle Robert seems remarkably keen to get his hands on Ogilvie's journal? And to keep you from looking into it?'

I sipped at the coffee. 'You bet it has. But what good would it do him? Would he recognise Elizabethan shorthand if it punched him on the nose?'

'Don't be stupid, Harry. He'd just hire his own expert. And he knows his own family history. If there's something in there, he could beat you to it.'

'Maybe depriving Debbie of something which is rightfully hers,' I speculated. 'By the way, where do your parents keep their brandy?'

* * *

I telephoned Janice later that afternoon and asked her nicely to look after the shop on her own for the next couple of weeks.

'There's a message,' she said, a little mischief in her voice. 'It came in a fax.' She read: ' *"You can't phone me at home with Uncle Robert prowling around. Where can I reach you? Debbie."* Who's Debbie?'

'We're just good friends,' I explained. I gave Janice Zola's number and told her to give it to Debbie in confidence next time she phoned. Now all I had to do was wait. The phone rang at 7 o'clock, just when I was thinking it was time I treated Zola to a dinner out. I gave her time to pick up the kitchen extension before I lifted it up.

'Harry?'

'Debbie, hi.'

'I'm in the study.' She was speaking quietly. 'I can't find my mobile phone. I'll bet Uncle Robert has taken it away. He's been hanging around all day. I feel like I'm the Prisoner of Zenda or something.'

'Can you be overheard, Debbie? Are there extension phones?'

'Yes, in one of the upstairs bedrooms. But Uncle Robert's playing snooker with one of his cronies.'

'You mean the house is empty?'

'No, Harry, he's in the snooker room. It's overhead.'

'It doesn't sound safe.' Unconsciously, I was beginning to whisper myself.

'Never mind that. Okay, here we go. I found this all written up in a book in Daddy's study, but I knew most of it already. I think there are lots of estate papers and family correspondence held in the University of Hull archives, though how they got there I have no idea. Are you ready?'

'Go.'

'Okay, we come from two large landed families, the Tebbits of Lincolnshire and the Maxwells of Scotland. We're really Tebbit-Maxwell but we dropped the double barrel in the 1920s, due to a great-great-grandpa wanting to be a socialist MP or something. There's also a small landed family, the Greenacres of Yorkshire.'

'So far so good,' I said encouragingly.

'I'll give you the Maxwell side first. I don't really think of myself as a Maxwell, maybe just because we dropped the name. It's really complicated, and mostly boring, with everyone marrying everyone else just to keep money in the family. The line nearly died out at the beginning of the last century, when there was only one daughter, Gwendoline. She had twenty thousand acres of land in East Riding and Lincolnshire and Dumfriesshire, with Caerlaverock Castle thrown in. But then she married the Fifteenth Duke of Norfolk in 1904, and that kept the line going and the money in the family.'

'Can you go farther back, Debbie?'

There was a rustling of paper. 'Well, the Maxwell side had problems about three hundred years ago when they backed the wrong team during the Jacobite rebellion. The Fourteenth Lord Maxwell escaped from prison dressed as a woman with clothes brought in by his wife. The poor things had to spend the rest of their lives exiled in Italy, along with Bonnie Prince Charlie. They lived in a big hill town called Frascati, just outside Rome.'

'It's a hard life,' I agreed. I wasn't making any connections.

'Still, the family's stuffed with barons and has estates all over Scotland.'

'Can you take them further back in time? Earlier than the Jacobites?'

'Sure. The Maxwells can trace themselves right back to Undwin and his son Maccus in the eleventh century. Maccus turned into Maccuswell who turned into de Maxwell of Caerlaverock castle, and so on.'

Still no connection, or none that I could see, with the Ogilvie journal. 'Okay, Debbie, what about the Tebbit side of the family? Are you sure it's still safe to talk?'

'What's Uncle Robert going to do?' She said it defiantly, but she was still whispering. 'The Tebbit connection with the Maxwells goes back to about 1600, when one of the Tebbits married Lady Joyce Maxwell. Let's see. Yes, here we are. Things were going wrong for them in the fifteenth century. There was a Sir Stephen Tebbit. He and two sons joined the Duke of Norfolk at Flodden in 1513 and they were all killed in battle. The youngest son inherited, but then he got his head chopped off for his part in the Lincolnshire uprisings. The estates and manors were forfeited, but Queen Elizabeth gave some of it back to the grandson. Hold on.'

The line went quiet for some moments. Then: 'It's all right, he's just gone to the loo. Right, there was another Stephen Tebbit who backed the wrong side during the English Civil War. Cromwell's parliament swiped their estates.'

'It seems to be a family custom, Debbie. Backing losers.'

'Thank you, Harry. So how come I'm living in Picardy House and you're in some hovel in Lincoln? The Tebbits only stayed afloat for the next hundred years through the generosity of the Greenacre branch. Then there was some smart intermarriage and the family fortunes grew again until we had five thousand acres in various counties, a couple of dozen palaces and an abbey. Not bad going for losers, I'd say.'

'Not bad going at all, Debbie. But can you take your family further back?'

'You mean really far back? Like to the dinosaurs? Let's see.'

More rustling paper. Then: 'Right. We can trace the Tebbit side as far as Baron Philip, son of Carr. He'd been given half of Cheshire by William the Conqueror. One of Philip's descendants married into a French family, StClair from Picardy, originally de Clari. That lot made a fortune out of the Crusades, and the family fortunes thereafter extended to Lincolnshire and York. They had sixty manors in total. I don't know what the heating bill must have been but I don't suppose they cared.'

The Crusades.

De Clari the Crusader, who became *StClair* from Picardy.

Sinclair. Winston Sinclair, the unknown relative who'd sent Ogilvie's journal to Picardy House, the Tebbit family home.

A bit of jigsaw clicking into place with beautiful precision.

Debbie was talking again. 'And that's about it. You see what a superior lot we are to you riffraff. Harry, are you there? Is this stuff any use to you?'

I'd rustled up a bachelor dinner and Zola had appeared from upstairs in a stunning red dress which almost matched the colour of the wine I was pouring. Candlelight – from power-cut candles, not romantic dinner ones – was reflecting off her earrings and a mock-diamond necklace. The puttanesca sauce had come out of a jar but it was surprisingly good, and I was looking forward to my zabaglione improvised from a sweet sherry rather than *marsala al'uovo*.

She sipped at the wine, looked at me curiously over the top of her glass. 'I think Debbie has a teenage crush on you.'

'Nonsense. I'm just a big cuddly teddy bear. I think she sees me as a surrogate uncle.' I sat down and started to twirl spaghetti. 'Look, Zola, I ought to move out of here once we've eaten. I can stay in a hotel in the village. We can't have Mrs Murgatroyd ruining your reputation.'

Her eyes widened incredulously, and then she giggled. 'And all these years I thought the dinosaurs were extinct. I happen to be a Capricorn, Harry. I'm impulsive, loving and passionate. What about you?'

'I'm a Leo, I think.'

She pulled a face. 'You're loyal, but cold and analytical. No risk to my virginity, dammit.'

I thought, *the room's getting hot.* I said, 'The Sinclair connection.'

'The Sinclair connection,' Zola repeated thoughtfully. 'Coincidence?'

'Neither of us believes that. This Crusader, de Clari. I'd like to find out what he got up to.'

Zola nodded thoughtfully. She said again, 'I know someone.'

122

21

The 'someone' Zola knew turned out to own the Oxford Museum of Antiquities, amongst a few other toys of that ilk, including, I'd read, islands in the Aegean and the Caribbean. At my suggestion we'd arranged to meet in a pub, one of a large number I knew in the area from my Oxford days. It was just off Parks Road and was run by the Paczynskis, a retired Polish couple. Zola gurgled her Scimitar into the car park at ten o'clock precisely. He was already waiting.

The pub had once been used briefly in the Inspector Morse TV series, and black-and-white photographs of the grey-haired landlords in the company of the principal actors, happily reflecting their glory, were scattered here and there on the dull panelled walls. Mrs Paczynski was looking much the same, except that her hair was now white.

Zola's 'someone' was fiftyish, with thin, balding hair and thick spectacles. He was dressed in an open-necked yellow shirt and a blue windcheater; I found it hard to reconcile his Oxfam cast-offs with the fact that he regularly hovered around the fringes of the *Sunday Times* rich list. His face lit up at the sight of Zola, the embrace was rather intimate, and I wondered just how well they knew each other.

We sat around a circular table. It was too early for alcohol but I ordered a lager anyway. Zola's friend had a companion: the man opposite me was in his early thirties, black Jamaican, with short, neat hair and a round, smooth face. He was dressed in a grey suit and the only hint of something lurking underneath the conservative exterior was a silver tiepin in the shape of a guitar. He spoke in a shy, hesitant manner which fooled me completely at this meeting.

Each of us had a photocopy of Ogilvie's journal and we all kept referring to it as I talked. I talked so much that my mouth almost dried up, and when I'd finished I quickly sank half of my pint.

There was a thoughtful silence. It was a lot for them to take in.

The Oxfam man turned to his companion. 'What do think, Dalton?' He was looking for a confidence trick.

The Jamaican gave me a shy glance before addressing his companion. 'I suppose the first thing, Sir Joseph, is to be sure that the document is authentic. Think of Hitler's diaries.'

Sir Joseph looked at me impassively. 'How do you respond to that?'

He knew Zola, and he'd have checked up on me: he would know that if there was a confidence trick we'd be victims, not perpetrators. 'I'm convinced of its authenticity. The micro-cracks around the ink would be impossible to forge. Likewise the paper. And it's been looked at by Fred Sweet not a couple of miles from here.'

Zola was on my left with a red Martini. She said, 'There are several inconsistencies with the accepted record of the Roanoke voyage.'

Sir Joseph raised his eyebrows. 'What are you saying?'

'That no forger would make such mistakes, Joe. They're too easily checked. The historians have been getting it wrong. Another thing. The Roanoke expedition was in 1585, but Ogilvie's writing his account in a form of shorthand which wasn't published until 1588. Now he might just have written his journal years after the events, but it has an immediacy about it which suggests he was usually writing things up a few days after they happened. Again, a forger wouldn't have made such a mistake.'

'What then?' Sir Joseph asked.

'Almost certainly, Ogilvie had access to the shorthand system before it was published. Some of the best brains in England were on that ship, and they probably knew about the system from Thomas Bright before he wrote it up. There was no copyright in those days.'

Sir Joseph nodded. 'And, as you say, we have an independent authority in the form of Mr Sweet.'

'And I'm holding the original manuscript,' I said. 'Forensic tests on the ink and paper can be carried out any time, subject to the owner's approval.'

Sir Joseph seemed to come to a decision. 'Very well then. I'm inclined to believe that the journal is genuine and the diarist, this young man from darkest Scotland, is giving a straightforward account.' He played with his glass of orange juice. 'And you think the intense interest in getting hold of the journal has something to do with the relic described in it?'

'There's nothing else. And "intense interest" is an understatement.'

'Yes, that's quite a bruise. Dalton, what's your assessment of the artefact?'

Dalton's voice was soft, almost gentle. It had a slight Jamaican twang. There were the rounded vowels of the standard Oxbridge accent, but I thought I detected a slight tinge of something else: French perhaps, even Parisian? 'If this journal is genuine, it's telling us about something I can hardly take in.' He fingered his tie and then began speaking in a low, enthusiastic voice. 'The artefact which James Ogilvie describes is a perfect match to a relic which has been missing for almost a thousand years. Part of the Cross on which Jesus Christ was crucified. The True Cross.'

I felt an electric tingle in my spine. We waited. Dalton sipped at a glass of Coca-Cola, cleared his throat and continued. 'The True Cross has caused more death and destruction than any other relic in history. Regaining the cross from the Moslems was one of the prime motivations for the Fifth Crusade. If it really exists, if a piece of the genuine Cross of Christ were to turn up' – Dalton glanced at his companion – 'I imagine museums, rich individuals or even religious groups would pay a fortune to have it in their possession.'

'A fortune?' Zola interrupted.

Sir Joseph said, 'As a ballpark figure, my museum would pay ten million dollars.'

I said, 'Nice try, Sir Joseph, but what would the Getty Museum pay? Or a rich American preacher? Or even the Vatican? I was thinking more of fifty million.' He gave me an oblique look.

Zola said, 'Think of a genuine piece of the Cross of Jesus in the possession of some right-wing American evangelist. It would confer tremendous authenticity on him. These guys sell religion like soap and the bigger their flock the more cash they rake in. He'd corner the whole evangelical market in the States. There's big money in this.'

'If it's seen to be genuine,' I said. 'But I understand that most relics are fakes.'

Dalton nodded. 'That's absolutely right, Mr Blake. In medieval times there were fifteen foreskins from Jesus, three heads of John the Baptist and enough bones from saints and apostles to fill a warehouse, not to mention phials of blood from Christ, and so on. A European king with a piece of material touched by Jesus or Mary had something which conferred his divine right to rule. Also, relics were used to cure diseases and suchlike. It was a tremendous commercial thing. They were the focus for a lot of robbery and murder. Which was one motivation for the Iconoclasts.'

'Iconoclasts?'

'Literally, icon shatterers. People who fought against religious images. But even they made an exception for the Cross.'

'But if the relics are nearly all fakes,' I asked, 'what makes the True Cross any different? Presumably there's enough wood around from the supposed fragments to make dozens of crosses?'

Dalton smiled faintly. 'Actually, no. The definitive work on the relics of the True Cross was written by Rohault de Fleury in 1870. He chased up and catalogued all the claimed fragments of the Cross and added up their volume. It came to about four litres, which is probably just two or three kilograms since wood is lighter than water. The real Cross would weigh, say, seventy-five kilograms.'

'But we're still dealing with medieval fakes, surely.' I was beginning to sound like a broken record.

'Almost certainly, in my opinion. Except for this one. I think this particular one is authentic.'

'Come on.' Blake the sceptic.

'I'm very serious, Mr Blake.' Spoken quietly and confidently.

'You have my undivided attention, Dalton.'

'The discovery of the Cross goes back to about 327 AD. After the Emperor Constantine guaranteed there would be no further persecution of Christians, the Bishop of Jerusalem – a man called Makarius – carried out excavations to find the location of various holy sites, like the tomb of Christ and the location of Calvary.'

'Did he need to excavate after just three centuries?'

'The Emperor Hadrian had covered over the holy places. But this actually served to preserve them until Makarius uncovered them. Keep in mind that the precise locations would be very well known to the local Christians. The positions would have been handed down through the generations. It was during these excavations that the wood of the Cross was recovered.'

'Is this real history or just legend?'

'It's for real, Harry. The excavations are mentioned in various inscriptions dating from just after that time. St Cyril of Jerusalem writes about the discovery of the sacred wood in 347 AD, just twenty years after these excavations. An inscription dated 359 AD mentions that a fragment of the True Cross was found. The *Peregrinatio Etheriae*, of Silvia, whose authenticity nobody doubts, mentions that the wood of the Cross was venerated in Easter ceremonies in Jerusalem about 380 AD.'

'That's quite a recital, Dalton.' I thought, *this guy knows his stuff*.

'But there's more. These same excavations also turned up the supposed Tomb of Christ. The level of credibility of the tomb is about the same as that of the Cross. Okay?'

'Okay.'

'Okay. Now if you visit the Church of the Holy Sepulchre in Jerusalem, you'll see queues of people at the traditional site of the tomb. But now the evidence gets harder. Non-invasive archaeology by Biddle at Oxford confirms that there is in fact an ancient tomb at the traditional site. Its age is about right for being Christ's tomb.' Dalton leaned back, swirling his Coca-Cola. 'The documentation, the history and the archaeology are all saying the same thing. There's every reason to believe that the wood which was excavated came from the Cross.'

'So the True Cross isn't in the same league as the fifteen foreskins of Christ and the three heads of John the Baptist?'

'Absolutely not. There's an excellent chance that the Cross which was recovered after these excavations was the genuine article.'

'What happened to it then?'

'Constantine built the Church of the Holy Sepulchre over the holy places, and the Cross was kept there until 614 AD. Then there was a war, and the Cross was captured and taken to Persia. Then there was another war and the Roman Emperor Heraclius recaptured it and the Cross eventually ended up back in Jerusalem. The Christians swiped it during the First Crusade in 1099. Then Saladin got hold of it when he captured Jerusalem in 1187. The story is that he would ride through the streets dragging the captured True Cross behind him, tied to his horse's tail. But now we're getting into legend.'

'What happened to it then?'

Dalton paused to clear his throat, sipped at the last of his Coca-Cola. 'At this point we begin to lose the thread. The beam itself was lost during the Fifth Crusade. But fragments which came off were supposed to have been collected and brought back to Europe after the Crusades. These fragments disappeared too.'

'In any case they were fakes.' The needle was still in the groove.

Dalton nodded his head. 'That would be my guess. It was faking time by then. But, as I say, not the Ogilvie relic.'

'Why not?'

'The fake relic business was in the West, in Rome or Barcelona or Venice, and it was a medieval practice. Ogilvie's description is a perfect match to a fragment of the Cross predating the Crusades by nine hundred years. Go back to St Cyril, who described the recovery of the Cross in 347 AD. He also tells us that fragments of it were distributed over the known world. These fragments are long gone and nothing is known about them. Except for one.'

I grunted.

'The one being a description literally unearthed a few years back from a scroll hidden in a recess above a pillar in St Sofia. Not the one in Constantinople, but a little one in Mitra, in southern Greece, where the late Byzantium scholars fled in the fifteenth century. The scroll's an inventory of treasures held by a small church in Byzantium before the Crusaders despoiled it. It includes a description of a holy triptych which contains wood from the Cross. It matches Ogilvie's icon to perfection. It also describes the wood as being retrieved from a monastery in the Atlas Mountains.'

'So?'

'So in a place called Tixter in the Atlas Mountains, not far from the town of Constantine in Algeria, an inscription has been found listing local relics, one of which is a fragment of the True Cross. The inscription is dated 359 AD.'

I thought, *The jigsaw's complete.* 'So wood from the Cross was recovered around 327 AD. It's reliably known that some of it was chopped up and spread around shortly thereafter. We know that some went to a monastery in the Atlas Mountains and was returned, one way or another, to Constantinople. It was made the centrepiece of a holy triptych whose description we have from some late Byzantium outpost. The description matches exactly that given by Ogilvie.'

Zola said, 'Bingo.'

'And a Crusader in the direct lineage of my client, de Clari, took this triptych as plunder from the Byzantium church, and it's been hidden by some members of the Picardy family for centuries.'

Dalton said, 'In my opinion it's a piece of wood from the True Cross. The only piece we can feel secure about.'

Sir Joseph said, 'The king of holy relics.'

Zola said, 'Carbon dating would settle the question.'

Dalton said, 'First catch your icon.'

Sir Joseph smiled thinly. 'Precisely, Mr Blake. After all, it's still lost. Which brings me to a proposition.'

I was used to spending £1,000 in the search for £500 maps and had all but taken vows of poverty. I tried to appear nonchalant while awaiting a proposition from one of the wealthiest men in England.

He said, 'If this really is a bit of the True Cross, or even likely to be venerated as such by a large proportion of the population, then the commercial possibilities are immense. Imagine what a museum could do with it.'

Not a word about its religious significance, I noticed.

'I would like to commission both of you to find this icon if at all possible. I will give you full financial backing, as much as you need. If you find it, and carbon-14 dating dates the icon to the time of Christ, then we have it independently valued. I buy it at one half of its monetary value, to be divided as you wish between yourself and your colleagues.'

'And if the dating shows it to be a medieval fake, contrary to our expectations?'

The man smiled. 'Then I have lost some money and you have wasted some time.'

'Out of the question. If we find the icon it becomes my client's property. In any case, the Getty Museum would be in a position to offer well over valuation, and probably would, if necessary, to acquire it.'

'But can you find another backer at short notice?'

'Actually, yes. My client.' I was probably lying. It was more likely that the capital in Debbie's estate would be tied up for months, while the lawyers crawled through the fine print and Uncle Robert stuck his oar in wherever possible.

Sir Joseph sighed. 'Very well, let me make another proposition. Allow me to finance your inquiry, and in exchange give me first refusal on the Cross. If Getty or the Vatican offer more, the loss is mine.'

Zola was nodding her head.

I said, 'No again.'

'I could send Dalton out in competition with you. It's not at all clear to me that your client is the true owner of the relic. It could be a case of finders keepers. It would be much better if we co-operate and agree a division of spoils beforehand.'

Zola said, 'I'd like to have a word with Harry in private.'

Outside, the sky was grey and the air was chilly. We sat on the car park wall. 'What the hell are you playing at, Harry? Look at the stakes! We need to get out there right away.'

'I was looking for expert advice on the triptych, not a financial backer. Debbie will finance us. We don't need this guy muscling in.'

'The backing of a major museum could be very important, Harry. We might need this Dalton's expertise. I'm not sure I'd even recognise this holy triptych after four hundred years.'

'But can we trust this Dalton? He's acting for Sir Joseph. If we find the icon he might just disappear with it, leaving us high and dry.'

'Come on, Harry, I've known Joe for years. It's high time you started to trust someone.'

'But I can't agree to a damn thing without Debbie's permission. She's entitled to everything if she's the legal owner.'

'*If*. So telephone her.'

'With Uncle Robert on the prowl? If he gets a whiff of this he'll cut us out. More to the point, he'll cut Debbie out.' I added, 'Which maybe explains why he's so keen to get the journal and keep me away. Let's go back inside. And leave me to do the horse-trading.'

In the pub, I told Sir Joseph, 'Your proposition would not be in my client's interests.'

'But your client, I understand, cannot be reached and you need the money now. Others may be on the same trail. It seems that realism calls for a little flexibility. In any case, the ownership of the icon is one which, I'm sure, could be disputed for years at great expense.' He was hinting at something.

'I have an obligation to a client.'

'Which you cannot fulfil for lack of capital. Will your client be happy if you lose the item altogether to another party?'

I spoke to Dalton. 'If this triptych still exists, somewhere in Jamaica, where would you start looking?'

'I guess the Jamaican lawyer would be a good starting point.'

'Exactly. But with Tebbit as his client he wouldn't speak to you. You're screwed up before you start.' I turned to Sir Joseph. 'I have a counter-proposal.'

A cautious 'Yes?'

'I look for the item in question, with my client's interests at heart, and you finance the whole operation. In exchange for this I advise my client to give you first refusal on the item, based on an independent valuation. That way you don't get into a bidding situation with the Getty Museum or the like.'

'You assume your client will own the icon if it is found. But it's not clear that she will have any right at all to the property. There may be other claimants and complications to do with treasure

131

trove, landowners' rights and God knows what else.'

'The icon has been in her family for a thousand years.'

'We could make lawyers very rich arguing about this. And what if your client is unwilling to take your advice? Perhaps even unwilling to sell, assuming she even owns it?'

'You take that chance. You have to, otherwise I pull the plug on the whole investigation.'

There was silence while Sir Joseph calculated the odds. Then he was saying, 'Your deal could leave me with nothing but a bill for Jamaica.'

'Correct. We're all taking chances here. And I have one further condition. Put twenty thousand pounds sterling into my client's account in advance, to cover the expenses. I'll ask her to transfer the money through to Jamaica once we're there.'

'I too have a further condition. Dalton here will accompany you. He will represent my interests. And I will put the question of ownership to an independent silk should you retrieve the icon.'

'What do we get out of it, Harry?' Zola asked.

'We'll negotiate separately with Debbie. We'll agree a percentage of the sale, once Sir Joseph has bought the icon.'

'You're a tough negotiator,' Sir Joseph said.

'What we all lack is time. There are others on the trail of this thing.'

Dalton said, 'I guess we're a team, then. I'll try to get flights to Jamaica.'

I said, 'I'd better get back to Lincoln. Passport, toothbrush, stuff like that. What about you, Zola?'

'Passport's in my handbag, and I'll pick up travel stuff on the way.'

Zola and I passed the pub a few minutes later, having done a U-turn to avoid a traffic jam. Dalton and Sir Joseph were still there. They were in intense conversation with a third man.

22

Around nine o'clock on a grey, wet morning, Dalton was waiting for us inside Manchester Airport. The conservative grey suit and black shoes were gone. In their place were calf-length trousers and an over-long turquoise sweater and sandals.

'Where are your dreadlocks?' I asked.

He grinned. 'I keep them in a box.'

The first surprise of the day came in the international departure lounge. Dalton and Zola disappeared into the duty-free shop and I wandered aimlessly along the concourse. Somehow, out of the hundreds of people milling around, my eye·was drawn to a young woman, with brown sweater and over-tight elastic slacks, staring out of a window at the rainswept tarmac. She was chatting into a mobile phone. Her outline and hairstyle looked vaguely familiar, a fact which at first I put down to my increasing paranoia. But as I approached, she turned and there she was, Ms Debbie Bloody Tebbit. She gave me a wave and a big smile and was off the phone by the time I reached her.

'What the hell!' I didn't need this sort of complication.

'Hello, Harry. You might say you're pleased to see me or something.'

'Debbie, you're not coming with us. I want you to go home. Leave this to me.'

'Why?'

'Because you're paying me to do it. Because you must have family affairs to see to.'

She gave the same teenage-angst pout I'd seen her use in her father's study. 'Father was buried yesterday, if that's what you mean.'

'I'm sorry. Look, if your Uncle Robert finds out, he'll have me up for child abduction.'

'Harry, you said we're in competition for this icon.'

'We are, Debbie, and with some extremely nasty people. Which is another sound reason for keeping you out of it.'

'That's just awesome, Harry. Awesome paternalism. You should have been a Victorian mill owner or something.' She slipped the mobile into her handbag and sat down, gazing at me with big, brown, speculative eyes. 'You think they killed my father, don't you?'

'No, of course not.'

'I thought so. Maybe I'll get to meet them.' She spoke the words casually.

This was getting out of hand: the last thing I needed was a homicidal teenager on the team. I tried to keep the worry out of my voice. 'Don't be absurd, Debbie. Please go home.'

She rolled her eyes but otherwise didn't bother to reply.

Surprise number two hit me somewhere just short of the mid-Atlantic ridge, to judge by the map on the video screen showing the aircraft's position. Debbie's unexpected appearance had been an unwelcome complication, but number two was deadly.

Introductions over, Dalton and Zola had shared what Air Jamaica called lovebird seats on the Airbus. Debbie was dozing, stretched out on a row of seats by herself, and I was making my way to the toilet at the rear of the aircraft.

This time, the unexpected female was Cassandra. She was at a window seat on her own. She glanced up from a magazine as I passed, gave a slight, cold smile and carried on reading.

In the toilet, I locked the door, put my head against it and shut my eyes, feeling drained.

I had no way of knowing whether she had followed Debbie, somehow tapped into her phone, or whatever. Had she seen me in the concourse, speaking to Debbie? Did she know about Zola and Dalton? More to the point, was she alone? Would we be met by nasty people at Montego Bay? I thought not: I hadn't known myself we were Jamaica-bound until yesterday. Maybe Cassandra's job was to keep track of us until help arrived. In that case we would have to move swiftly. I toyed with fantasy images of armed Jamaican Yardies waiting for us at the airport, maybe even Jamaican police arresting me because of some story concocted by Uncle Robert.

I tried to look nonchalant as I passed her again, but it was a wasted performance: she hardly bothered to look up from her magazine. Her apparent indifference scared me as much as her presence. Back in my seat I scribbled a note: *Don't look round. Unwelcome company to rear of aircraft. Numbers uncertain. Pretend you don't know me. Suggest we clear off quickly at Montego Bay.* I gave it an hour and wandered off to the front toilet, dropping the folded note into Dalton's lap without looking at him. When I passed on my way back he and Zola were sitting upright, alert and staring intently out of the window into the blackness. Debbie was a tougher proposition to reach as we were both in full view of Cassandra, but shortly afterwards Dalton walked to the back of the aircraft and gave me the tiniest nudge on the shoulder as he returned.

Nine hours after taking off, the big aircraft was crawling bumpily over the Jamaican coast, outlined by scattered lights seen here and there through dark clouds. Montego Bay was a big cluster of lights with a black bite taken out of it by a giant shark.

There were half a dozen queues at the immigration booths. I found myself wedged inside a cluster of immensely fat black women who were chatting boisterously. Over to my left, Cassandra was queueing behind a wedding party. Debbie, Dalton and Zola were separated but in the same queue to my right. A thick yellow line, like a starting line, separated the queues from the immigration booths. An exhausted child was bawling somewhere behind me.

Debbie was through. She had the sense to disappear downstairs towards the baggage area rather than wait for us. In front of me, two of the fat women were beginning to argue with the immigration official. Cassandra and I eyed each other up like a couple of gunfighters, our respective queues inching forwards. She gave me another cold smile. Now just the wedding party lay between her and the exit. Voices were being raised at the booth in front of me:

there was something wrong with a document. My queue had stalled and Cassandra smiled some more.

But then my fat women were suddenly through and the wedding party was snarling up at Cassandra's queue. There was no time to gloat. I trotted swiftly down the stairs, my heart thumping in my chest. Dalton and Zola already had my suitcase on a trolley. Debbie had vanished.

'Where the hell . . . ?' I asked. We made our way quickly to the exit. Outside, the air was like a furnace. There was a little square and a chaotic scattering of small buses and taxis. There were limited places for concealment. But then Debbie was waving and we made our way to a taxi, its doors open. The driver, a man in his thirties, bundled our suitcases into the boot with agonising slowness. Debbie took the front seat while Zola squeezed in between Dalton and me.

'Ocho Rios, okay?' Debbie said, turning to face me.

'Ocho Rios,' I agreed. Clever girl: we had booked into Sandals in Montego Bay.

The driver said his name was Stormin' Norman and proceeded to demonstrate why. The coastal road was narrow, potholed and littered with stray cattle and goats, all of which he saw as a challenge. To the left, powerful yellow flashes were lighting up clouds. Not English wimp lightning, I thought: real tropical stuff. I couldn't hear any thunder, but then Stormin' Norman's radio was playing lively pop music at maximum volume. The roadside was littered with shacks, lit up from within by naked lightbulbs or the flickering blue of television sets. In Falmouth, the taxi slowed to a crawl and picked its way through a square choc-a-block with young people, some of them dancing, others banging pot lids together. A youth, with dreadlocks hanging down from a red and yellow cap, slapped at my window, grinning happily and showing yellow teeth. His eyes were wide with excitement. Stormin' Norman explained that some folks was getting steamed up on account of the election, but it was nothing like 1980 when there was eight hundred killed in shootouts. We cleared town and headed swiftly into the dark. The gearbox was making whining noises. I looked out at the palm trees and the tiny wooden shacks, and wondered what we would do if the car broke down.

After two hours of this, with my nerves getting increasingly ragged, Debbie said, 'Up there,' pointing at an illuminated roof poking over some trees. Stormin' Norman took us through a security gate and up a long winding hill to a sprawling resort hotel surrounded by high illuminated fencing, like a prisoner of war camp. After Norman's air conditioning, the heat hit me all over again. The shrill screech of insects came from the forest surrounding us.

There was a self-catering apartment to spare. We were too exhausted to talk. Dalton and Zola took rooms with single beds, Debbie made for one with the king-size double, and I was left standing uncertainly in the kitchen.

Debbie reappeared. 'Harry, you have no place to sleep.'

'That's all right, I'll just stand here.'

We found some blankets and I spread them on the settee. I stripped to my underwear and slipped under a sheet. The insect noises were like a hundred squeaky fan blades. In the dark, a solitary firefly flashed on the ceiling.

Another image forced itself into my mind as I sweated on the couch and listened to the night sounds. Cassandra at the airport exit, asking about the distinctive party of four – they've left a wallet, where did they go? – finding the name of the local taxi driver who had driven them off, making a telephone call; Stormin' Norman, who liked to talk, talking too much; the Yale lock being quietly forced in the early hours of the morning.

The half-dream stopped there as exhaustion overwhelmed me. The last thing I remembered was the firefly, bright and silent, heading for me like a little cruise missile.

23

The sky was just growing light when Debbie, dressed in a diaphanous white negligee, glided into the kitchen like a ghost. 'Wake up, Harry!' A light went on and she began to clatter cupboard doors noisily. 'No coffee!' *Clatter.* 'No nothing!' *Clatter.* I pulled my trousers on under the sheet, suppressing my embarrassment.

Dalton appeared, wearing his Cool Jamaica gear. 'We'd better get away from here. They could trace us through Stormin' Norman.'

Debbie said, 'Surely that's just a fantasy.'

'Maybe. Would you like to bet your life on it?'

I said, 'I thought of it last night just as I was flaking out. They could be waiting for him to turn up at the airport this morning.'

'Or they could have got his phone number from the tourist desk in the terminal last night. Maybe even his home address.'

Debbie put her hands to her head. 'Holy Christ.'

'Get dressed, Debbie,' I said. 'We're going into town. And bring your purse.'

Debbie and I walked briskly past the swimming pool, out of the compound and down the hill we'd been driven up the night before. The air had been oven-like overnight, but now, with the tropical sun rapidly soaring into the sky, the temperature quickly rose into the nineties. Even the two-mile walk into Ocho Rios was exhausting and I began to feel lightheaded. At the edge of town a white cruise ship towered over the buildings like a giant in Lilliput.

We followed directions along the main street, already crowded and noisy, past craft markets, hagglers, tourist-junk shops. A mile along, beyond walking range of the cruise ship tourists, the town underwent a distinct change of character: it became a noisy, crowded, exuberant piece of Africa. We turned down a side street, stepping around a young man lying on the pavement, stretched out on a cardboard bed, and there was Sunshine Rentals, just where the receptionist had said it would be. An elderly, toothless Indian led us round to a back yard, kicked a squawking hen out of his path and waved his arm at a scraped and battered white Toyota, half covered with leaves from an overhanging papaya tree. Debbie rented it for the week and paid up front in US dollars. The man said it never give him no trouble but phone Mr Claybone if we get stuck.

Back at the resort, Dalton and Zola were waiting at the reception desk, baggage packed. Dalton's face was expressionless behind his cool shades; Zola was plainly anxious. We loaded the boot quickly while Debbie checked out. Then she took the wheel and drove us down the hill. Coming up the hill was a taxi. It had almost passed us before I recognised Stormin' Norman at the wheel. I couldn't make out the people in the back.

'Did you see that?' Zola asked.

'Yes,' I said. 'You think he saw us?'

'I don't think so. But I'm not sure.'

We waited at the security gate while the guard chattered to a friend. Debbie hummed under her breath, her fingers strumming the wheel impatiently. Then the barrier was up and we curved swiftly onto the road. I said, 'Hit the boards, kid,' and Debbie sang a verse of what sounded like a Norwegian Girl Guide song.

Debbie drove swiftly, and Dalton navigated from the back seat. He took us through Fern Gully, dull even in the Jamaican sunshine because of overhanging trees. Then it was a straightforward road, if winding and potholed, through the middle of Jamaica from north to south. We passed bauxite mines, the earth orange, drove along gorges, through a dozen little towns and past a thousand ramshackle homes and roadside stalls. The heat outside was tangible and I was grateful for the air conditioning in the old car. In a couple of hours we were through Spanish Town and on to a broad road taking us into Kingston, on the south coast, with the Blue Mountains soaring beyond and the Caribbean Sea sparkling to our right.

Kingston was not tourist Jamaica. Kingston had no sundrenched beaches or palm trees. There were no resort hotels, with holiday-makers carefully screened from the locals by high metal fences. Kingston was a Caribbean port bigger than Liverpool and twice as busy, and its traffic was not so much exuberant as lawless. Debbie was surprisingly calm in the midst of the chaos, and even managed a delighted squeal when we passed the Bob Marley Museum. It was a useful landmark: we passed it twice more over the next half-hour. Finally I saw something I recognised from the *Rough Guide to Jamaica*: the blue and white façade of the Ward Theatre. The lawyer's office, I knew, was close to it. Debbie took the car round the side of the building and parked. Zola stepped out to stretch her legs while Debbie, Dalton and I went on a lawyer hunt. After the air conditioning of the car, the heat was like a sauna.

'You know where you are?' Dalton asked. He had put on sunglasses and merged totally with the environment.

'Kingston, Jamaica,' I said.

He pointed. 'You're on the edge of Jones Town. With Trench Town just beyond it. Six hundred murders a year. It's one of the most violent locations in the Western hemisphere.'

'Thanks, Dalton. I feel a lot better for knowing that.'

The notice was white-painted on a strip of wood:

Chuck Martin
Attorney-at-law

Underneath was another strip of wood:

Caribbean Sparkle
Agricultural Services Ltd
registered office

Some nail-holes in the plasterwork suggested there had once been more registered companies. Next to the notices there was a narrow flight of stairs, cool after the sweltering heat of the exposed street. A short veranda on the first floor was protected from the outside world by a heavy metal grille. There was an open door and a stout woman behind a desk. Debbie said, 'My name is Debbie Tebbit. I would like to see Mr Martin, please.'

'You have an appointment?' the woman asked, looking doubt-fully over her spectacles.

For all that she was a mere nineteen, Debbie could put on an imperious air when it suited her. 'No, but I've come from England to see him.'

The woman said, 'Oh my goodness. Wait here a minute,' and disappeared through a back door.

In a moment a small, wrinkled, thin man with grey hair appeared at the door and waved us in. His office was like something out of a Dickens novel, all dark 19th-century furniture and bundles of papers, yellow with age. He peered at us curiously over half-moon spectacles.

Introductions over, Debbie opened the conversation. 'You sent my father some papers from a late client of yours.'

The lawyer nodded. 'That is correct, Miss Tebbit. A Mr Winston Sinclair. It would've been nice if you'd telephoned ahead.'

'There wasn't time.' The Tebbit touch was again creeping into her voice.

Martin asked, 'Has your father given you authority to discuss this matter?'

'My father died last week,' said Debbie in a matter-of-fact tone. 'I've inherited all his property.'

'Your father died? I'm sorry to hear that.' The lawyer made a good show of looking sorry over the death of a man he'd never met. 'But I'm forgetting my manners. Would you like a coffee, or maybe a nice cold Coke?'

'No thank you. I'd be grateful if you could tell us a little more about this Winston Sinclair. You see, we never knew this relative existed.'

Chuck Martin leaned back, took a metal tin from a drawer and a pipe from a rack. 'The truth is, neither did I until two weeks ago. The man was a poorist. He had no family that we're aware of. He lived alone on West Road in a one-room apartment. West Road is in Trench Town. Not even Jamaicans go there. The landlady found him dead in bed with an empty bottle of rum. She cleared his room and found the papers in a box with your father's name and address on it, and she brought it round here. That's all there is to tell.'

'He must have come from somewhere,' I said.

The lawyer smiled bleakly. 'Sure. The landlady said his skin wasn't Ghana-black. He had some white in his blood from way back. Sure, Winston Sinclair came from somewhere.' He opened the lid of the tin and started to pull dark tobacco into the pipe with his forefinger. I thought I was detecting a chip on the man's shoulder.

Dalton asked, 'And there's no way to say where he got the papers from?'

'Lacking evidence to the contrary, I'd say he inherited them himself.' Now he was compressing the tobacco, pushing it into the bowl. 'So how he got your father's name and address, Miss Tebbit, and why he should think he was related to the Tebbits, is a mystery to me.'

I said, 'The journal was a diary, Mr Martin. It was an account of a voyage to America in Elizabethan times. The writer was stranded in Carolina. How it got from America to here is an even bigger mystery.'

'Well he sure didn't walk. I guess the journal must have been picked up by some passing Spanish warship or slaver.' The lawyer touched the leg of his spectacles and looked at Debbie as if he was trying to focus them. 'What's your purpose exactly, Miss Tebbit?'

'Genealogy.' It wasn't exactly a lie. 'Our family tree goes back a thousand years on the European side. We just didn't know there was an American branch.'

'You've come quite a way to search for your family tree, Miss.' I wondered if the man believed her. He searched amongst the clutter on his desk and found a matchbox. For some reason he struck the match on the underside of his desk. He started to puff at his pipe. Blue smoke drifted around the little office and he leaned back with an air of satisfaction. 'Jamaica was under the control of the Spanish in Elizabethan times. If you want to chase this up, you could try our National Archives. I'd say it's a mighty long shot. The only people in Spain then were Spaniards and slaves and the Arawak Indians. I don't imagine your family is descended from any of them.' He smiled to show that he was joking.

'Where are these archives?' Debbie asked.

'Spanish Town, of course. No point in going there today, they'll be closed soon. But my feeling is it will be a wild goose chase. You may have come a long way for nothing, Miss Tebbit.' He was tapping down burning tobacco.

We thanked him and went back down the narrow stairs and out into the intense heat. Half a dozen young men were rocking the car from side to side and Zola, inside it, was gripping the seat in front. One of the youths, with yellow string vest and baseball cap worn back to front, leered at Debbie and said, 'How 'bout you climb aboard the big bamboo, white gal?' She gave him the Tebbit look.

Dalton had adopted a sort of Trench Town swagger; he approached the man close up, right in his face. I thought, *we don't need this, they might have knives*. But then Dalton was speaking in a soft, conciliatory tone. 'Bredda, nuh badda wid di war vibes, wha you say?'

The effect was magical. The young men stepped back respectfully, and then we were in the car and accelerating away, Debbie at the wheel. I turned to Dalton and gave him an astonished look. He grinned.

'I want out of here,' said Zola, tense and tight-lipped. I wasn't sure whether she was referring to the car, the city or the island.

'They were just fooling around,' Dalton said.

Debbie seemed to be driving purposefully. 'Where are we heading?' I asked.

'The Blue Mountains. I've booked us into a hotel. It's called Moonlight Chalets and it's just past a place called World's End.'

'Why there?'

'I read in *Hello* magazine that Mick Jagger uses it as a hideaway.'

'That's a recommendation?'

'Find World's End on the map if you can, Harry. If Mick Jagger can use it as a hideaway, so can we. It's nowhere.'

'So, you're from Jamaica, Dalton?' I asked.

'Actually Birmingham.'

The transition from bustling city to isolated mountain was surprisingly abrupt. There was a busy square, queues of people at bus stops, and then suddenly just a single-track potholed road rising steeply towards the Blue Mountains. Within ten minutes we were into Maroon territory; we could have been a million miles from anywhere. The descendants of escaped slaves looked at us morosely as we drove past their shacks.

The road steepened even more. At first there were low parapets, but even these eventually vanished. Debbie took us round hairpin bends with no telling what was coming in the opposite direction. Here and there, boulders were strewn over the road, the end results of heavy rain and landslides. I sat beside her with sweaty palms and a jaw painful with tension, while she took the wheels to within inches of thousand-foot drops. There was dead silence in the back of the car. Near the summit we ran into thick cloud and Debbie used headlights. At least now I couldn't see what lay beyond the edge of the road. Finally, out of the mist, as if from a Dracula movie, there emerged tall gateposts with a notice saying: Moonlight Chalets. It seemed about as remote, and hopefully as safe, as any place on the island.

'How could they possibly have known about Jamaica?' I asked.

We were spread around a circular jacuzzi, its water warm and bubbling. We had tall glasses with pink rum punches on a ledge. At this altitude the air was cool. Kingston was mapped out by a million twinkling lights far below us, and the dark Caribbean lay beyond. The moon broke through cloud and I could just make out the silhouette of mountains around us, with fingers of cloud glowing gently between them. Underwater lights lit up the jacuzzi, the inverted illumination making faces look mysterious, even unnatural. An elderly couple, Americans, were enjoying the pool some yards away.

'I wasn't followed, if that's what you mean.' Debbie was wearing the skimpiest of blue bikinis. 'Picardy House can't be seen from the road and nobody would know who was coming or going.'

'Harry and me likewise,' Zola told her. 'We took precautions.'

I nodded my agreement. Dalton said, 'And they don't even know I exist. At least, I hope they don't.'

'Did you tell anyone you were heading for Jamaica, Debbie?'

She looked at me sharply. 'Of course not. Do you think I'm an idiot?' Then she added, 'Only Uncle Robert. We had a flaming row about it. He thinks you're a trickster after my money in some way.'

So that was it. Uncle Robert.

Debbie looked suddenly aghast.

Zola asked, 'What can you tell us about your Uncle Robert?'

Debbie waved a dismissive hand. 'I know what you're thinking and it's just silly. Why would Uncle Robert give anything away? How could he even know these people?'

Zola exerted a gentle pressure. 'Tell us anyway. About your uncle. How did he get on with your father, for instance?'

Debbie made a face. She was beginning to sound a bit distressed. 'They had rows every time Uncle Robert came to the house. I wasn't supposed to hear them, but I did and I know what they were about.'

'Top up your drinks, people?' The pool attendant had appeared out of the dark. He was carrying something like a long fishing net. We shook our heads and the man disappeared into the blackness like a ship in the night.

Debbie continued, 'It was about money. Uncle Robert owned horses. He kept racing them, and he kept betting on horses, and he kept losing money and he kept getting into trouble. I think Daddy bailed him out for years. With my money,' she said, 'or at least money that would have come to me.'

Zola said, 'That makes your uncle an idiot, nothing more.'

I didn't know how to raise the next bit. The question of inheritance.

'You have inherited Picardy House, I suppose?' Dalton asked the question casually.

'I expect so. So what?'

I was beginning to feel like a lobster. 'Debbie, if you fell under a bus, who would inherit?'

'This is so stupid.'

I waited. Then Debbie was saying, 'Uncle Robert, of course. Daddy had no other brothers or sisters.' She started to cry.

Dalton said, 'We're all exhausted, jet-lagged and everything else. I'm for sleep. What about you, Debbie?'

Debbie nodded tearfully. When they had gone, Zola said angrily,

'Did it occur to you that Uncle Robert may be the only family Debbie has? And you're suggesting he's trying to grab the icon. Maybe even wants her bumped off?'

'Why else is he so hostile? Am I the only person with sense hereabouts?'

'Sense? She's a child who's just lost her father, and you, Harry Blake, are the most insensitive idiot I've ever come across.'

24

George the Third by the Grace of God of the United Kingdom of Great Britain and Ireland, King and Lord Defender of the Faith. To my trusty and well-beloved Patrick Smith and William Farrell, esquires, know ye that we have constituted, authorised and appointed and by these presents do constitute, authorise and appoint each or either of ye to administer an oath unto Thomas Higgins and William Middleton, gentlemen, that they shall well and truly, according to the best of their judgments and consciences, inventory and appraise all and sundry of the goods, chattels, rights and credits of Edward StClair, late of the parish of Trelawney, landowner, general practitioner and physical surgeon, deceased . . .

(signed) on behalf of his Grace William Duke of Gloucester, captain general and governor of our said island, and lieutenant of Iago de la Vega. This 11th day of November anno domini 1715 and the 56th year of our reign.

George Clayton, secretary.

'Hey!' Debbie hissed excitedly in my ear. 'StClair!'

We were in the air conditioned coolness of the National Archives, sitting at a heavy circular teak table. Next to us was a trolley filled with bound volumes, each about three inches thick and eighteen inches tall. The volume opened in front of us had a distinct spicy smell. The paper was brown with age and the ink was faded; here and there it was almost illegible.

I said, without really believing it, 'Could be a coincidence, Debbie. Let's look at the inventory.' We read on:

Inventory and appraisal totalling £13,110, the bulk being the sum of various slaves as follows:
  59 female slaves named and valued as follows:
  Nancy £100, Phoebe £150, Nefertiti £75, Agnes £75, . . .
  97 male slaves named and valued as follows:
  Tom £100, Old Howe £30, Billy £100 . . .
  Total value of slaves £11,600.

  One bull at £30
  12 cows at £15 each = £180
  5 cows at £12 each = £60
  Five bull calves and three cow calves at £5 each = £40
  Total value of cattle £250.

  44 hogsheads of sugar, as shipped by William Baker on the Kingston consignment to Robert Message and sold by him as appears by the account of January for the sum of £2303 11s 2d.

Several pages were devoted to 'sundry items':

Portion of rum £20.
Medical instruments £30.
A gold watch with gold chain £10.
Sundry books £10 each = £160.
Ship's compass £30.
Navigation device £2.
Two journals £1 each = £2.
Two mahogany tables = £13 4s.
24 chairs, 4 mirrors, 4 wardrobes, 4 beds, assorted bedding and clothing, two portraits, three Bibles, assorted kitchen utensils and pots = £50.

And so on.
For some reason there were a few more slaves in the list of 'sundries', but that wasn't what was suddenly holding my attention.

'Do you see it?' Zola asked. There was a feverish gleam in her eye. She pointed to an entry. 'Two journals.'

'And a navigation device, Zola. What possible use could a GP cum plantation owner have for a navigation device?'

Debbie was bubbling over. She was having difficulty keeping her voice quiet. 'These are my ancestors! We're on the trail, we're on the trail! How far back can we go?'

I flicked the pages back. 'We need a lot more than this for your genealogy, Debbie. And let's keep our eye on the ball here. What we want to know about is the other journal. The one that could lead us to' – I lowered my voice – 'you know what.'

'I'm hiring you, remember?'

'There are nasty people on our trail, remember? We can't hang about here longer than necessary.'

'How could they possibly find us here?'

'The lawyer?'

'But how could they know about the lawyer?'

'Your Uncle Robert?'

'You know, Harry, I hate you so much.'

'I know.'

Zola broke into the tense silence. 'There are slave registration returns.'

'The Sinclairs weren't slaves,' Debbie said. 'They were slave owners.'

'But the returns will show the owners,' Zola pointed out. 'Let's ask the archivist.'

The archivist was about thirty, with a round face, heavy spectacles and shiny black hair to match her skin. 'Are you with the other people?' she asked.

'The other people?' I suddenly had a sinking feeling in my stomach.

'The people who were here yesterday. They been asking the same question.'

'That's a rival academic group,' I said. 'Yes, we are in competition. I'm sorry if we're making you duplicate your work.'

'That's okay,' she said. 'What can I get you?'

Over the next hour we gave the archivist a hard time. The table began to pile up with slave registration returns, electoral office

records, tax rules, jury lists, baptismal registers and more plantation inventories. We skipped lunch. We forgot that Dalton was
outside the register office, keeping an eye out for Cassandra and
friends. We forgot about the clock until, in the late afternoon, the
archivist politely cleared her throat. 'We close at four thirty,' she
said.

Damn.

At four fifteen, we made our second crucial discovery. It was on
a platt record, a map showing the boundaries of a plantation. The
ink was almost gone and we could make very little sense of it. But
one name stood out amongst the others.

Plantation map drawn to a scale of 5 chains in an inch . . .
Charles Atkinson Esq & Company.
  . . . Martin Tebbit.
1250 acres no. 247, St Ann's, Jamaica.

There was a map showing some irregularly shaped property
bounded to the south by a river and to the north by coastline. The
compass points were marked. We could hardly make out the text
below:

  . . . to which an Order unto me directed by the Hon. Charles
Thomas Lynch, Kent,
    . . . his lieutenant governor and commander in chief of the
island of Jamaica . . .
    . . . and laid out unto Martin Tebbit senior . . .
    . . . a mountain and land situated in the precincts above and
in the form and manner described by the platt and council
and . . .
    . . . on the site thereof as performed April 10 1674.
  Cyned John Horn.

Tebbit.

The archivist was clearing her throat again. Zola leaned forwards.
I got a whiff of perfume. 'We need more time,' she said in an urgent
whisper.

'What can we do? It'll have to be tomorrow.'

'Harry,' she hissed. 'Are you forgetting the bad guys? They're a full day ahead of us.'

Debbie pulled her chair back and walked over to the archivist. There was a lot of animated muttering and shaking of heads, and then they approached an older, grey-haired woman. Zola and I watched, mystified, while the archivist left the room and the grey-haired woman lifted a telephone. Debbie gave me a mischievous wink. Then there was more chat, and now heads were nodding, and Debbie was telephoning, then writing something. She joined us again. 'We'll grab a snack and come back at six o'clock. They're opening up for us until midnight. The security desk are prepared to work overtime and the archivist will stay on to keep an eye on us.'

I gaped at her. She gave a triumphant smile: 'I just donated twelve thousand US dollars to their Repair and Binding Section. It's Sir Joseph's money, of course. Fancy a McDonald's?'

Outside, in the quiet street, Dalton was sitting in the car next to a couple of cannon flanking a bower made of white Italian marble and shading a statue of some admiral underneath it. Dalton's face was wet with sweat. We headed downtown, past a cathedral and a grim, walled prison. Men waved at us through a big grill. 'About fifteen men waiting to die in there,' Dalton volunteered, and I wondered how he knew.

We found a McDonald's in a busy shopping mall. Dalton excused himself and made for the toilets. I gave it a couple of minutes and left the queue, heading in the same direction. As I turned a corner he was about thirty yards ahead of me, speaking into a mobile phone in businesslike fashion. He turned, saw me, and dropped the phone into his back pocket with a smile. There was something odd about the action, but I couldn't have said what.

After a quick snack, Dalton joined us in the National Archives: since we were working past its official closing time, Cassandra and friends would not expect us to be there. We were now buying time at two thousand dollars an hour. Gradually, as the archivist wheeled hefty volumes back and forth, a Sinclair family tree emerged. There was no Ogilvie, no clue as to how he had reached Jamaica, nothing

151

to lead us to the True Cross, if it even existed any more. But running like a thread through the plantation records had been a single constant theme: two journals, handed down from generation to generation. Winston Sinclair had given us one of them. I needed the other one like a man in the desert needs water.

'I've been reading up on this,' Debbie said. 'It was the British who introduced the plantation system and they didn't conquer the island until 1655. They won't have anything earlier than that.'

'It's not quite like that, miss.' The archivist was holding about twenty kilos of records in her arms. 'It's true the British invaded in 1655 and they destroyed Iago de la Vega, which we now call Spanish Town. But the Spaniards had time to clear out and they took their valuables with them, and probably a lot of records too. They held out on the north of the island for another five years, round about Ocho Rios.'

'You mean . . .?'

'Chances are some documents survived and were carted to the north side of the island, and from there to Cuba. It seems a lot of the Spaniards thought it was only a matter of time before Spain reconquered Jamaica. So they buried their valuables and money. There are rumours of tunnels right under your feet. Anyway, an official list of the hiding places was drawn up. In the nineteenth century a historian by the name of Edward Long was told that the official list still existed and was somewhere in Cuba. Nobody knows where.'

'But the Spaniards never came back . . .'

The archivist smiled. 'Meaning that there's treasure buried all over Jamaica.'

Debbie said, 'Wow!'

'You people aren't looking for buried treasure, by any chance?' The archivist tried to make it sound like a joke.

'Of course not.' Debbie carried off the lie with total conviction.

Zola said, 'You mean you have no records going back earlier than the British conquest?'

'That's about it. But so far you people have just been looking at the public and ecclesiastical records. You could try the private ones. We have letters and accounts written in Spanish, Portuguese,

Dutch and even Latin. It happens we have some stuff donated from Cuba recently, from Santiago de Cuba, just across the water.'

We hit it an hour before midnight.

While Debbie and Dalton had moved back in time through the centuries, Zola and I had moved forwards, tracing the journals as they were handed on through the generations. My throat was parched in the dry air and the centuries-old dust of the records. Debbie was pencilling in gaps in her family tree. The archivist, bleary-eyed, had wheeled in a tea chest of documents recently donated by the Eldridge rum factory.

The StClairs had built a rum factory on the grounds of their plantation. Winston Sinclair, the last of Debbie's Jamaican line, had drunk the products and gone bankrupt, dying in Trench Town poverty. The new owners of the rum factory had handed over the paperwork to the National Archives. It was the end of the line for the journal, if it still existed.

I bent over the tea chest. Why I don't know, but my eye was caught by a thin heap of quarto-sized papers tied together by a pink ribbon. I thought I recognised the writing. I lifted the bundle out and undid the ribbon. My hands were beginning to shake. I flicked through a few of the faded, browned sheets. I felt as if an electric current was trickling through me.

I said, 'Hello, old friend.' I'd said it quietly, but my voice seemed to penetrate every corner of the building. The others froze.

Pure Caribbean gold.

Ogilvie's second journal.

25

'We'll never copy this before midnight.'

'I have a camera in the car,' Dalton said.

'No photographs,' said the archivist. 'We're quite strict about that.'

I flicked carefully through the fragile sheets. 'With four of us on it, we could get through this in two or three hours.'

'The deal is we close at midnight, sir. That's in fifty minutes.'

Debbie said, 'Pity. I'd have loved to donate another two thousand dollars to your Repair and Binding Section.'

The archivist said, 'Since you put it that way, I'll speak to the security girl.'

'So will I,' said Debbie. 'What's her name?'

'Ruth.'

I split the pile into four. Dalton, Zola and I got busy copying as quickly as possible. Debbie came back a minute later. 'Ruth's mother is looking after the baby, but she was staying the night anyway. Ruth's not allowed to accept a personal gift but the double time suits her nicely. And there was nothing in the rules to stop me donating something to Grandma.'

Around two in the morning, we thanked the weary archivist and Ruth at the security desk, and emerged from the building into a blustery wind. Debbie took the wheel as before: she seemed to enjoy driving. The early hours Kingston traffic was light but anarchic; Debbie drove swiftly through it. I was beginning to get the hang of this exuberant city and I used a map to navigate us up the Old Hope Road to Matilda's Corner before turning right and taking the road skirting the University of the West Indies. By the time we were starting on the mountain pass the wind was gusting strongly and I began to worry about falling trees, not to mention the prospect of being blown over the edge. We reached our 'hideaway' safely at about three o'clock in the morning. Subdued lighting lit up the steep, bush-lined driveway; the pool and the jacuzzi were still illuminated. The insect noises had gone; instead we had the rushing of a powerful wind through the trees.

Our 'chalet' – actually a substantial villa – was one of half a dozen scattered over a few acres of ground cleared from the rain forest, with a deep gorge to its rear and the swimming pool out the front. Debbie spread her notes on the big dining-room table. Dalton disappeared into the kitchen and Zola emerged from her bedroom in the same pyjamas and dressing gown she had worn in her Greenwich flat.

We'd reached that state of exhaustion where we couldn't stop. We sipped at tea while Debbie, lost in concentration, started to sketch out her family tree, the occasional *Wow!* or *Yes!* disturbing the peace. After an hour of that, she came through the door and said, 'Come and see.'

We leaned over her little tree. James Ogilvie had married a Fiona McKay and they'd had three children, all girls. The youngest, Agnes Ogilvie, had been born in 1630, late in Ogilvie's life. Marmaduke StClair, meanwhile, had married Inez Teriaca, presumably a local Spaniard. Their child, Eduardo StClair, had married Agnes Ogilvie. The families must have been close. The products of this marriage were Inez StClair (b. 1649) and Eduardo StClair Jr (b. 1651). Inez StClair had married a Robert Tebbit, and the Tebbit line had continued through James and Martha Tebbit, eventually dying out in Jamaica. The line through Eduardo StClair Jr had continued all the way to the recently deceased Winston Sinclair.

Zola said, 'Well done, Debbie. So the Ogilvie and StClair families were united by marriage, one of the descendants married a Tebbit giving a Jamaican Tebbit line, the other giving a straight line to Winston Sinclair.'

'One mystery solved,' I said. 'The Tebbits were the nearest relatives to Winston.'

Dalton was leaning over Debbie's chart, Rommel studying a map. 'It proves we're on the right lines. Nice one, kid.'

Zola said, 'That is amazing. But how could James Ogilvie and Marmaduke StClair possibly have reached Jamaica in the first place?'

'Exactly. How did they get here?' Debbie asked. 'And anyway, wasn't Jamaica under Spanish control at the time? Why were they allowed to settle? Why didn't the Spaniards burn them at the stake or something horrible?'

'Maybe Ogilvie's notes will tell us.' I was itching to get at them.

'Maybe.' Zola was sounding even more impatient than me.

'And James Ogilvie married Fiona,' I pointed out.

'His childhood sweetheart?' Debbie smiled, enchanted by the romance.

'Must be.' I wondered about that, tried to visualise him trudging up the long road to Tweedsmuir, only to turn back again with his child bride. More likely he had sent a letter, on the basis of which the young Fiona had left home and family to cross an ocean by herself. 'Whatever, it was quite a journey for a young girl in those days.'

Zola said, 'And Marmaduke married locally. The families must have been close – their sprogs eventually married.'

'I wonder why they didn't go back to England?' Debbie murmured.

I yawned. Every muscle in my body was exhausted. 'I'm played out. I'm going to bed with Ogilvie's journal.'

'Can I join you?' Zola asked, and we all laughed.

In bed, I looked at my watch. It was four o'clock and I was bone weary. I put my light out, closed my eyes and listened to the high wind in the trees and the creaking and groaning of the villa. I drifted into an exhausted sleep.

What wakened me an hour later I don't know. I lay in the dark, listening to the wind, which was now even stronger. I dragged myself up and half-staggered to the window. I don't know what I expected to see. There was a car at the entrance to the driveway, about thirty yards to the right. It had no lights but its outline was just visible in the subdued light from the pool. Someone was leaning into it, talking to the driver. As my eyes adapted to the dark I saw there were two people in the car. Then it was reversing, and disappearing quietly back down the steep road, silhouetted against the lights of Kingston as it went.

And walking back from the car, a bundle of papers gripped firmly to his chest, was Dalton.

26

You cannot know how I have longed to tell this story. I hope that one day it will be read by someone of my own country. The adventures which befell me in the Americas are so strange that I can hardly credit them myself. Let me begin by describing the fears which were aroused in me as we approached that distant continent, and how these fears were first dispelled, and then returned with double the fury.

'What is *auto da fe*?'

'In God's name, does Scotch know nothing?'

The Turk said, 'It is the Spanish for "act of faith", James.'

'Why is it so feared?' The sails were cracking gently but the sea was good and I was swaying gently in my hammock. The hatch above was open, but the cool air we had been used to was gone, and now a heavy, sticky heat was settling down on us from above. The Northern Crown was outlined in the great oblong of the overhead gratings, the stars coming and going through the little squares as the ship swayed. I thought I could count five or six faint stars within it.

'He knows nothing,' came from a corner of the berth. 'Nothing.' This was followed by a hacking cough.

The Turk said, 'Have you not heard of the Hawkins expedition?'

'No,' I said into the dark.

Somebody laughed. Someone else said, 'Ha!'

'It was a disaster.' I recognised the Hog's voice. 'English mariners were captured by the Spaniards in Mexico. The seamen were Lutherans. They were first imprisoned in a pigsty and made to eat pigs' food. For liquid they were given vinegar wine. Then they were made to dress in yellow cloaks, and carry green candles, and led to a marketplace with ropes around their necks where their sentences were read out to a howling crowd. Some of the mariners were burned to ashes. Others were flogged for hour after hour until the flesh was gone from their backs. Others had their limbs broken. This is the *auto-da-fe*, Scotch. It is the Christian charity of the Inquisition, and it is what you must expect if you are captured by the Spanish.'

'At last you can see why the dregs of prisons sleep around you, Scotch,' the Turk said. 'It is the only way Raleigh could man this voyage.'

'Thank you, Turk, for inviting me to join it.'

The Turk laughed quietly in the dark.

Over the next few hours I watched the Crown drift out of my oblong of sky and the mighty Hercules take its place. There was much to mystify me. I wondered about the beauty I saw in the celestial vault overhead, and the unfathomable depths of the abyss on which I floated. I wondered about the cruelty which men inflict on each other in the name of a God of love. I lay in my own sweat and smelled the filth and listened to the creaking of the ship and the coughing and snoring of the tavern dross around me. And I wondered, not for the first time, whether I would have been better to spend my days in ignorance, tending sheep in the cool, silent valley of Tweedsmuir.

By the eighteenth day after the storm, the weather had become unbelievably hot. According to Mr Harriot, we were now approaching hostile Spanish territory. The lookouts were more alert, and Sir Richard and Fernandez spent more time on deck, peering at the empty horizon.

On the morning of the nineteenth day, there was an excited cry from aloft. A sailor was pointing to the sky. There was a solitary bird, far larger than any I had ever seen. It approached the ship and circled lazily around the masts. There was an outburst of shouting and cheering. Shortly afterwards the musicians came on deck and struck up some tune to which several of the sailors began to dance, leaping grotesquely around the deck.

'We'll soon sight land!' Mr Bowler was grinning happily.

For a moment I allowed myself the sin of pride. 'Of course, just as Mr Harriot and I expected from our observations of the stars.' I felt my face going red at my own arrogance, but Mr Bowler just laughed and slapped me on the back.

Presently more large birds joined the first, and then we saw a tree trunk bobbing on the waves, near-submerged. There was a buzz of excitement on the ship: sails were trimmed with more enthusiasm; more energy went into the scrubbing of the decks; conversation in the galley was livelier. Even Mr Salter, I thought, was in danger of smiling.

On the twenty-first day, a long, low irregular shape appeared on the horizon: 'Land withall!'

The next day, Sir Richard turned us north-west. The turquoise water was broken by white thundering surf, and there was an island thick with green trees, with a long stretch of beach. We dropped anchor. I was tingling with anticipation, but then to my disappointment Mr Salter instructed me to stay on board. While the mariners were allowed ashore to enjoy the feel of land under their feet, I was required to carry out an inventory of the food. I spent the day scrabbling and sweating in the stinking, dark hold, while all around me was the squeaking and scurrying of rats. The stench was almost unbearable. The cheese had long since turned rancid and the biscuits had a thick layer of fur on their surfaces. Little white worms were swimming in the barrels of water and indeed I swear there was more worm than water. The rats had picked holes in the sacks and were clearly gorging themselves on the seeds and multiplying at a great rate. I counted the barrels and sacks as quickly as I could, trying not to retch in the vile air. That night I slept on deck, catching the whiff of wood-smoke from bonfires on the beach, and listening to the musicians.

The following day we made sail, heading for a bay where Sir Richard expected to find his other ships at anchor. But there was nothing. We dropped anchor again, and Ralph Lane spent a week constructing a fort in case of a surprise appearance by the Spanish. In all that time I did not leave the ship, having this or that task to perform: it was clear that Mr Salter bore a grudge against me. But the *mal de mer* incident was long in the past. I began to wonder if Mr Bowler had been right, that the man resented my ability to read and my learning, little though it was.

Shortly after the fort was built, the lookouts saw a mast appearing over the horizon. Soldiers hastily returned to ship, we weighed anchor and set off in pursuit. It turned out to be the Elizabeth. We fired cannon and discharged muskets in celebration.

Shortly, we chanced upon another Spanish ship whose captain was so terrified of us that the crew immediately fled in longboats. The ship was full of cloths but had little in the way of food or water. By now, the shortage of provisions was becoming desperate. Without fresh fruit and livestock it did not seem that we could reach our destination. Finally, on the first of June, we arrived at an island known to the mariners as Hispaniola. It was said to have a strong garrison of Spanish soldiers, and only desperation could have driven Sir Richard to anchor at this place.

We dropped single anchor about a half-mile offshore, tense with anticipation. We could smell the land. The older men muttered about fever coming in on the wind, and Mr Bowler tried to frighten me with stories of boils, yellow jaundice and deadly contagions blowing in from the shore, but I was too excited to care, and all that assailed my nose was the rich, fetid vegetation of the Tropic. Crowds of people lined the shore, some of them waving. We must have been a fearsome site to the Spanish, with our ten cannon and two demi-culverts, and the sun glistening off the armour of a hundred soldiers.

Presently a boat appeared, rowed by ten sailors. As it approached, I saw that the man standing to the rear of the craft had dark, leathery skin, no doubt a combination of sun and natural colour. He had a dark grey beard and held himself erect in spite of the swaying of the ship. It was my first sight of a Spaniard. He seemed as proud and haughty as I had heard the mariners describe his people.

Fernandez and Grenville appeared at the side of the ship. There was an exchange of conversation in loud Spanish. Then our own longboat was manhandled over the side of the Tiger and several of the officers climbed on board. To my surprise, Grenville snapped his fingers at me. I climbed down a rope ladder and joined the gentlemen in the rocking boat. I guessed that my knowledge of livestock was to be put to use.

It was strange indeed to feel solid ground once again under my feet. Stranger still were the faces which met us. Many were black. Some were, I think, Chinese.

'What are you thinking of, boy?' Marmaduke asked me, grinning, as we walked along the quayside.

'Sir, I'm thinking of solid land, and cabbages and cauliflowers, and melons and oranges, and clean fresh water without worms. I'm also thinking that we're at the mercy of these people, and from what I have heard of the Spaniards—'

'We are under a flag of truce, laddie,' interrupted Mr White.

'Aye,' said Sir Richard. 'And I have a few cannon to back it up.'

I did not for a second think that the ship's cannon would save us if the Spaniards decided to burn some heretics, but it would have been folly to say so.

We were escorted – I think that is the word – by about a dozen heavily armed Spanish soldiers. Goats were running loose in the crowded street. A priest made the sign of the Cross as we passed, a gesture which gave me no comfort at all. Many of the gaping spectators were strikingly dressed, with bright red and yellow coats and colourful handkerchiefs around their necks or tied round their heads. We were taken to the steps of a church. There was an awning, and underneath it a small, burly Spaniard with an air of authority was waiting for us, surrounded by soldiers and civilians. An exchange of civilities took place, and there followed a long conversation in Spanish, with Fernandez translating for Sir Richard. I was not privileged to be in the shade of the awning, and stood thirsty and sweating in the glaring sun, embarrassed by the grinning and giggling of two young girls, who seemed fascinated by my jacket and breeches.

At last Mr White beckoned me forwards. 'Go with this boy,' he said. 'Pick out two bulls and ten of the best cows you can find, and bring them to the quayside.'

I walked with a boy younger than me through dusty streets lined with brightly painted wooden houses. Some of them were quite grand, with balconies from which men and women looked down and shouted comments which I did not understand, but which I am sure were not complimentary. At the edge of town there was a wooden stockade, and in it about a hundred white cattle of a type which I had never seen. In truth I could not tell which cattle were the best and which the worst, and so I chose the largest, since these would have more meat. The boy and I punched our way through the cattle, avoiding sharp horns, until I had chosen ten which we then led back along the street towards the quayside. It was a task not without difficulty, since the cattle were as stupid as those of Tweedsmuir but a good deal wilder. A Spanish pinnace was waiting, and we steered them up a broad gangplank onto it. We returned to another pen for the bulls. This second transport proved a much more hazardous business.

It was a long, hard day, but at the end of it I had the satisfaction of having twelve white cattle, twenty pigs, as many sheep, and about a hundred chickens, complete with feed for a month, on board the Tiger. I worked overnight by the light of lanterns, coralling and organising my animals, while from the shore came the sounds of laughter and music as the gentlemen were entertained on long tables set up on the beach. Other seamen were heaving fresh water and beer and beautiful green vegetables and wonderful fresh fruit onto the ship, and risking punishment by sampling the wares. I too tasted sin, in the form of a melon so delicious that it must have come straight from God. By dawn I had completed my task, and went to my hammock exhausted but with a feeling of great satisfaction.

We stayed in Hispaniola for three days. I found it difficult to reconcile the horrific stories of *auto-da-fe* which the mariners had told me with the hospitality which I met during several trips ashore. The two girls who had laughed at my clothes were Isabelle and Regina de Angulo, the daughters of the military governor of the island. They knew no English, but in the governor's great house, filled with fine furniture and paintings which I cannot even describe, such was their beauty, they taught me games with painted cards, and also a strange game in which a ball was hit with a bat over netting. It was exhausting in the heat, but it was a happy time for

163

me. I must admit that when I left Hispaniola it was with some regret, and I thought that a life spent tending sheep in Tweedsmuir would have been rather limiting after all.

On the seventh of June, the Tiger and the Elizabeth set sail from Hispaniola. Two weeks later we sighted the great continent and sailed up its coastline with care. Amadas and Barlowe had been before us, and the coastline was known. It was dangerous in the extreme, with a line of sandbanks lying between the ocean and the land like a barricade. This was also part of the Atlantic where storms could arise quickly. Being close to land, Master Fernandez became the navigator of the ship. His aim was to sail over the sand bars and reach the calmer waters between the sand and the mainland.

Unfortunately the navigator made a great error, misjudging the depth of the sea. The Tiger became grounded on the sand and would not be moved off. The captain of the Elizabeth and another two prize ships were also stuck fast. And now a storm suddenly sprang up. The waves were huge and the Tiger, being broadside to them, was pounded without mercy for two hours. It looked as if the great ship would break up. We all thanked God that when the tide came a huge wave lifted her clear.

When the fierce storm had subsided, the damage became clear for all to see. My livestock had plunged into the water and had swum ashore. But the ship's keel had been so battered that seawater had flooded the hold. Our biscuits, rice, corn, seeds for growing, all were ruined. Far from growing crops and feeding ourselves, the colony of over a hundred souls would now depend for its existence on the charity of the savages.

After much repair work, we were able to refloat the Tiger. Our fleets being restored, we boarded the ships again and sailed ten leagues to the north, to a deep gap in the Outer Banks. This time the ships stayed a safe distance at sea while we emptied them, rowing our supplies first to a depot on the Outer Banks before landing on the island of Roanoke where we would construct our settlement. This island was fertile, protected from prying Spanish eyes by the sandbars and separated from the mainland by a league of calm water, giving us some protection from attacks by savages. We were within sight of their villages, across this stretch of water.

At this point Ralph Lane became governor of the new colony. He constructed a house on the Outer Banks and supervised the continuing transfer of our supplies from the ships to Roanoke island. A fort was built on the north of the island, which was about two leagues long and half a league wide. The fort was a poor thing of sand and timbers, nothing like the castles I knew of in my native Scotland. When this was done, we began working on our houses. The gentlemen built themselves fine structures, but the mariners, colonists and soldiers created houses for themselves even more primitive than those of Tweedsmuir.

I will not describe the troubles which we had. The gentlemen would not work, being busy with exploring, sketching and measuring. The other colonists refused to work for them. Many of the soldiers behaved like wild animals. It was not long before Ralph Lane introduced severe discipline, and more than one soldier was left to rot, hanging from a tree. Overhanging all of this was hunger, a dwindling food supply and a relationship with the savages which, although it started well, soon became uneasy.

All this time, I was alert to discover the true purpose of the colony. That it had something to do with the gentlemen present seemed obvious. Never were men less suited to the practical work of planting, digging and building. On clear nights, Mr Harriot would measure stars with his cross staff. And on one such night, I had an idea. We were on the beach, I with slate and lantern, and Mr Harriot with cross staff and compass. He was measuring the position of a rising star, Aldebaran, in the constellation of the Bull.

'Sir,' I said. 'You have told me that to determine longitude, you need a clock which will give you the time in England which you may compare with the local time.'

'That is true, Ogilvie.' My master was squinting along the needle of the compass. 'And I also said that fame and fortune awaits the man who builds such a clock.'

'But there is no need to build it,' I said in excitement. 'It already exists!'

Mr Harriot took his eyes away from the compass. In the dimmed light of the lantern, I could see him studying my face curiously.

'There, in the sky!' And I pointed to a thin crescent moon. 'Do you not see, sir? The moon can be used as a clock. Its movement against the background of stars is like that of the hands of a clock around a dial. If you know that the moon will pass a star at midnight in England, and we see it passing the star at six o'clock in the evening here, then we have our longitude. A quarter of a day, or ninety degrees.' I could hardly stop myself from jumping up and down with excitement.

Mr Harriot laughed. 'Calm down, Ogilvie. What do you think Kendall and I have been doing with all these star sightings? But I fear the method is not working. We cannot predict the movement of the moon against the stars with enough precision, and we do not even have star charts with enough precision.'

I felt myself shrinking with disappointment. But my defeat only filled me with resolve. Some day, I would find the solution to this great problem.

I could never penetrate the secret purpose, and began to think it would not be fulfilled until the colony had been well established. I also began to suspect that the purpose of the conspirators was to destroy the colony from within. For murder was still being committed, and the fear which permeated our group did not arise simply from the growing hostility of the Indians.

Great relief, even joy, spread through our little community when the murderer within was finally identified and arrested. But of all the adventures which befell me in America, none troubled me more, or had a more lasting effect on me, than the trial of the apothecary, Abraham Rosen.

27

There was a threat of thunder in the black clouds piled on top of each other, and indeed, when I left Mr Barlowe's house with an armful of his notes, a fork of lightning far out at sea dazzled my eyes, reaching from the high clouds to the ocean in an instant. The sea was dark green and rough, and white-capped waves pounded rhythmically on the sandbanks. I could see the masts of the Tiger and Roebuck swaying to and fro.

My morning routine, of copying the sketches of the gentlemen and transcribing the rough notes of Masters Harriot and Barlowe, was interrupted by the arrival of Anthony Rowse. He was carrying some thick book under his arm and his face was grim. 'Young Scotch, leave that. You have another duty this morning. Take writing materials to the chapel this instant. A goodly supply.' The parliamentarian disappeared abruptly while I hastily gathered up parchment, pen and ink.

A long, coarsely cut table had been set up on the dais of the chapel, facing the congregation. There was a smell of freshly cut timber. The front pews were occupied by a dozen or so of the gentlemen. Behind them, labourers, mariners, tradesmen and soldiers took up the remaining space. There was hardly room for a mouse. The crush at the back of the chapel, where there was room only to stand, meant that the doors could hardly open.

Ralph Lane, the governor of the colony, took his place at the centre of the table. On his left was Mr Kendall; Mr Rowse sat on his right. I thought of the Holy Trinity with Governor Lane as God, but quickly dismissed the blasphemous thought. I sat at the edge of the long table, on the far left of Ralph Lane. The duty of which Anthony Rowse had spoken was now clear. Having learned the art of swift and short writing, I had been assigned the task of notary at a trial. I was both proud and nervous. As to the nature and purpose of the trial, my mystification would be removed soon enough. In front of me I had laid out my goodly supply of parchment, pen and ink. The table was otherwise bare, except for the book which had been under Anthony Rowse's arm and which now sat in front of Ralph Lane. With a thrill of apprehension I saw that it was the *Malleus Maleficorum* – the Hammer of Witches.

My mentor, Thomas Harriot, sat at the front between Amadas and Sir Edward Cole, the lawyer. Governor Lane snapped his fingers at a soldier, John Vaughan, near the back. Captain Vaughan disappeared out the door, leaving us suspensed in a state of curiosity and excitement.

In a minute there was a buzz of conversation and all eyes turned. Abraham Rosen, the apothecary, was being dragged in between two soldiers, who were using elbows and shoulders to clear a path. The apothecary's hands and feet were in chains. There was a rope around his neck, held by one of the soldiers, and he was being led like a dog on a leash. The man was limping and bruised, and seemed to be in pain. I had heard cries of pain overnight and the source was now clear to me: the soldiers had been doing their work. He was clearly terrified, and as he was dragged towards the dais his eyes were looking wildly from left to right, as if for some means of escape.

Ralph looked up and down the length of the table and then fixed a cold gaze on the apothecary. 'Do you understand the charges against you?' he asked.

'Yes, and I am innocent of them.' The apothecary's voice was both faint and frightened, but it carried a note of determination.

'Read them out.' Ralph Lane slid a piece of paper towards me.

I read, and I think my voice was shaking a little, 'You are accused, first, of belonging to the Society of Witches. Secondly, you have used your secret knowledge of sorcery and poisons to destroy the body of Simon Holby of York. Third, you murdered John Barnes the carpenter by occult means. Fourth, you poisoned Simon Fludd of Exeter. Fifth, you poisoned David Falconer. Sixth, although a Jew, you have been Jesuited and corrupted and have

168

been induced by Spain to destroy this expedition from within and are thereby accused of treason.'

There was more excited muttering. Lane growled, 'Silence.' He nodded to Sir Edward Cole, a tall man, dressed in black satin and a white ruff. He had a short grey beard, little hair on top and a withered left arm. He stood before Governor Lane but placed himself so that he spoke both to Lane and to the congregation behind him, sometimes more to the one than the other.

'The matter before this court, Governor, is one of a monstrous nature. To murder any man is abomination enough. But to commit such an act through secret knowledge and sorcery is to connive with the Devil himself in carrying out the deed, and is in effect to act against God. To attempt to destroy this expedition, which has the approval and license of Her Majesty, is to act for the enemies of Her Majesty, that is Philip of Spain.' At this point Sir Edward fixed a stare on Lane, whose hatred of Spain was legendary.

Sir Edward now pointed at the trembling apothecary with his good hand. 'This wretch must face the accepted penalty for traitors. He must be hanged, cut down while still alive, have his privy parts cut off and burned before his eyes and his bowels removed while he still lives. His body must then be burned to ashes, as is the custom for a witch.'

There was a rattling of chains as the apothecary's arms and legs began to tremble uncontrollably. But Sir Edward's voice was pitiless. 'He is *sine religione, sine sede, sine fide, sine re, et sine spe* – he is without religion, habitation, credit, means and hope. He has been abused, corrupted and Jesuited: I never yet knew a treason without a Roman priest in the background.'

Sir Edward now faced Ralph Lane.

'You have before you the *Malleus Maleficorum*, the undisputed authority on the Society of Witches. The *Malleus*, Hammer of Witches, is accepted by both Catholic and Protestant jurisprudence and all the greatest authorities, writers and jurors throughout Europe. It is a book of deep scholarship and great wisdom.'

'What European authorities do you speak of?' Rowse asked.

'I refer, for example, to Jean-Bodin, member of the French

Parliament and one of the outstanding philosophers of our day. He has written this.'

At this point Sir Edward started to read from a paper, which I thought odd. Either he had anticipated the question, or there had been collusion between the advocate and one of the judges. He read: 'There exists a great conspiracy and society of witches. This society has tremendous wealth. It is cunningly guided, with cells in every town and hamlet. It uses espionage in every land and has informants ranging from high-placed courtiers to humble estate workers. It maintains a relentless, secret war against the established orders of religion and government. No act of treachery is too cowardly or too base to be used. They possess an ancient and secret knowledge, including knowledge of poisons, handed down from the time of the Egyptians and even before.'

The lawyer looked up from the paper. 'Thomas Harriot will tell you that he does not believe in witches. Yet there are those who would see Thomas Harriot, with his interest in necromancy and membership of the School of Night, as part of this conspiracy.'

There were gasps from around the courtroom. Mr Harriot, his face grim, made to stand up, but the lawyer waved him down. 'I do not say this myself. Perhaps the difference between us is only a matter of words. I believe that witches communicate by supernatural means, perhaps he does not. Perhaps Thomas could be prevailed on to accept the existence of witches at least as a secular and evil organisation.'

I felt that, in some clever way which I could not quite understand, Sir Edward had issued a threat. He was saying to Mr Harriot: Accept witches at least to this extent, or you may be thought to be one yourself. But I had no time to think further about this. Sir Edward was speaking again, and it was all I could do to keep up with him even with my swift and short writing.

'Keep in mind, then, that the best minds of our day, throughout Europe, are convinced of the reality of the Society of Witches. We cannot be so foolish as to ignore this stable consensus of opinion which has held throughout the years. The *Malleus* itself goes back to 1486 and has been repeatedly issued by the leading continental presses. Even the pontiffs have accepted the existence of witches, who are especially active in northern Germany.'

I wondered why Sir Edward had mentioned northern Germany, but my curiosity would be satisfied soon enough.

The governor raised a hand to stop the lawyer's flow of words. 'Thomas, do you have anything to say?'

Mr Harriot, on the front bench, shook his head. 'Very little. It is true that many authorities have argued for the existence of witches. I can only say that I find no room for them in my system of the world, and increasing numbers of men of science believe the same.'

'Men of science,' Sir Edward repeated. 'Men who dabble in the occult, perhaps? Men who believe in the existence of atoms which are immortal, indestructible, and which in combination constitute everything in the world? Characteristics which, according to men of faith, belong to God alone?'

Again that subtle threat, hidden beneath a veil, which I did not quite understand. But the governor was saying, 'Thomas Harriot's opinions are not on trial, Edward.'

The lawyer nodded curtly. 'I now request the court's permission to question the physician.'

'Proceed.'

The advocate pointed a finger towards the back of the hall. There was a disturbance, and Mr Oxendale was being pushed through the crowd by some of the mariners. He wore a close-fitting velvet hat which covered his ears, and a long coat whose purple matched that of the hat. I heard Anthony Rowse muttering to Ralph Lane: 'Why is the fool in court dress?' The physician sat in a chair positioned edge-on to face both the lawyer and the bench. He was nervous and his accent was hard for me to follow, I think he came from Devon or Wales, but I took his words down as accurately as I could, guessing some of them.

The advocate stood over the doctor of medicine. 'Who are you?'

'I am Peter Oxendale.'

'Your trade?'

'I am the physician, as you know.'

'And your qualifications?'

'I belong to the Guild of Barber Surgeons, or the Fellowship of

Surgeons as it was known before we united with the Barber's Company. We have the royal charter.'

'That is qualification enough, Mr Oxendale. Now describe, if you will, the events leading to the death of David Falconer.'

'Mr Falconer came to me after dinner on Thursday night, five days before we reached Puerto Rico. He said he had a feeling of restlessness and felt he was being suffocated. His pulse was very high. I felt at first he was a victim of bad food.'

'But you changed your diagnosis?'

'Yes, when his face muscles began to contract. He looked as if he was grinning. I took him to his bunk but his body began to contort violently. There was a period of respite, during which he lay exhausted and fearful, but then increasingly violent contractions overcame him and he was clearly in great agony. His back was so arched it looked as if it would break and his jaw was locked open. By this time his pulse was higher than I have ever seen in a patient. Eventually he died during a convulsion, simply, I think, from an inability to breathe.'

'Did you examine the body after death?'

'I did, sir.'

'And what did you find?'

'His extremities were grey, his blood was dark and thick, his stomach had a red congestion and he was bleeding under his skin. Liver, bowel and heart smelled of bitter almonds.'

'These are symptoms of what poison?'

Mr Oxendale threw a sidelong glance at the apothecary. 'I know of a berry whose juice creates these symptoms in the tiniest doses. It is colourless and so powerful that even the volume of a pinhead is fatal. Sometimes, I am told, death occurs within twenty minutes.'

'And how long did Mr Falconer take to die?'

'Three hours. For most of that time he was conscious and in great pain, but unable to speak because of the locked jaw.'

Sir Edward stood back to show that he was finished.

Ralph Lane looked directly at Thomas Harriot. 'Do you wish to question the physician?' Mr Harriot simply shook his head.

Sir Edward said, 'In that case I will proceed to question the prisoner.'

Mr Rosen's eyes were wandering in his head, as if he was suffering from some fever. His brow was damp with sweat.

Sir Edward's tone, it seemed to me, was domineering. 'Your name?'

'Abraham Rosen.'

'You are a Jew, then?'

'I am, sir.'

'And what is a Jew doing on a Queen's expedition?'

'Sir, I was pressed into service with Frobisher two years ago. I believe I served well, and gained experience with maladies which may afflict mariners in the tropic latitudes, as well as with the treatment of many wounds. Because of my experience I was approached by a messenger and agreed to serve again.'

'And where do you practise your trade?'

'I own a pharmacopoeia in London.'

'North or south of the bridge?'

'South.'

'In Southwark?' Sir Edward raised his voice as if in surprise, although I do not doubt he knew the answer before he asked. 'You live with thieves and whores?'

'My trade is needed there as elsewhere. And a Jew is not always welcome in the fashionable parts of the city.'

'As an apothecary, you have knowledge of herbs?'

'I have. And of balms and plasters.'

'Do you practise the medicine of the Galens, or do you belong to the reformers?'

'In truth I do not know. No herb has ever cured the great pox or plague and I believe that the reformers should be allowed to develop their methods. But I take whatever *materia medica* I believe to be appropriate to the disease, whether the herbs of the Galenists or the chemicals of the Paracelsians.'

'You have a knowledge of herbs, then?'

'Indeed.'

'Do you claim to know more than Mr Oxendale on these matters?'

'In truth?' The apothecary glanced nervously at Ralph. 'In truth, I think Mr Oxendale knows little of these matters.' I sensed a trap and was surprised that the apothecary did not see it. No doubt his mind was clouded with fear. He added, with a touch of pride, 'I have studied under both Peter Severinus and Thomas Erastus.'

Sir Edward now sprang his trap. 'And does this deep knowledge of herbs include poisons?'

'Poisons?' The apothecary's voice quavered.

'Poisons.'

'I have some slight knowledge of them.'

'I see. A deep knowledge of herbs but only a slight knowledge of poisons.' Sir Edward now nodded to a wrinkled man in a black leather tunic, sitting behind the gentlemen. The man scurried to the advocate, handed over a small black box and retreated to his seat.

'You recognise this box?' Sir Edward asked. There was a hint of triumph in his voice.

It seemed impossible, but the man's face, already ruined with distress, grew even more distraught. 'It is part of my medical store.'

'Indeed.' The word was delivered in a mocking fashion. 'It was taken from your quarters yesterday.'

The lawyer placed the box on the table in front of Ralph Lane, who opened the lid and peered in. The governor pulled out a small glass phial containing dried, blackened leaves.

I gasped with the shock of recognition. For I had seen such leaves before, in the secret bulkhead over Marmaduke's berth. I knew in an instant that Mr Rosen was an innocent man and that the murderers were Marmaduke, Rowse and Kendall, two of whom were the apothecary's judges! And I also knew that, to reveal my knowledge and save Mr Rosen, I would myself meet the hangman. I glanced around surreptitiously but nobody had seen my sudden alarm: all eyes were on the glass jar. What was I to do?

The governor's gruff tone brought me back from my horrible dilemma. 'What is this?' he asked the prisoner.

'Those are the leaves of the monk's hood,' said the apothecary, who seemed ready to faint. The weight of the chains round his wrists seemed to be pulling his arms out.

The lawyer anticipated Ralph Lane's question. 'Tell us about the monk's hood.'

'It is medicinal.'

'And if you were asked to eat a leaf?'

'Taken in excess, it is *veneficia*.'

'*Veneficia*? Which is, in the vulgar?'

'Poison.'

'Speak up.'

'Poison.'

The prisoner nodded abjectly.

Poison.

The room could have been filled with corpses. Sir Edward stayed silent for some moments, a sneer on his face. The word poison spread through the air like a miasma. Then he said, 'This plant, is it not poisonous in the extreme?'

'Yes, but only in excess.'

'How much excess? If we were to place some on your tongue now, how much would you allow to sit on it?'

The apothecary was trapped. He whispered, 'It will kill in very small quantities.'

'Again! Speak up!' Lane commanded sharply.

'With a tiny dose?' Sir Edward asked.

'Yes.'

'Indeed. And so when you say "in excess", in fact you mean a tiny spot?'

Mr Rosen nodded miserably.

'Describe the symptoms of poisoning by monk's hood.'

'Death.'

A ripple of laughter briefly broke the tension in the room, quickly stilled by Lane's glare.

'And before death, would you not say, first, a numbing and tingling in the mouth?'

'Yes, starting within minutes of taking the poison.'

'A mere tingling in the mouth? An easy death, then? Or does the tingling spread?'

'It spreads to the throat and then the whole body. The victim loses sight and hearing, although his mental faculties remain.'

'He is blind, deaf and paralysed, and yet remains aware of what is happening to him?'

The apothecary nodded helplessly. 'His pupils become dilated. He will eventually die through an inability to breathe.'

'Eventually? And how long will this take?'

'Minutes to hours, depending on the dose.'

The lawyer nodded. Ralph Lane was looking at the contents of the box with something like horror. He picked out another phial. It was filled with bright green, hard-shelled and dessicated insects. I had seen these too, in Marmaduke's secret panel.

The apothecary, his brow wet with sweat, said, 'Spanish fly.'

'Spanish fly? A poison again?' The governor's brow was furrowed.

'Yes sir, but . . .'

'And this?'

'It is a plant from South America. I obtained it on my voyage with Captain Frobisher.'

'A poison, no doubt?' The governor's eyes were filled with accusation.

'Yes, sir.' The apothecary's voice was now barely audible, and I had to strain to hear him.

'This?'

'Berries.'

'I can see that they are berries.'

'They are of the type which the surgeon-barber thinks killed Simon Fludd.'

Another phial. 'I think I have seen this.'

'Yes, sir. Those are the leaves of the belladonna plant.'

The governor pulled out the cork. 'Sir,' the apothecary interrupted quickly, 'the poison can enter the body through the skin.'

Lane hastily replaced the cork and dropped the phial back in the box. 'And the symptoms of belladonna poisoning?' he asked, his voice grim.

'There is a difficulty in swallowing, the skin flushes, there is increasing headache leading to hallucinations. Later there is paralysis leading to death.'

'And the eyes?' the lawyer asked. 'You fail to mention the most conspicuous feature of death by belladonna.'

The apothecary briefly covered his face with his hands, as if this would make his terrible predicament disappear. 'The pupils are dilated, so much so that the eyes appear black. It is indeed the most distinctive feature of the disease. In small doses it is used to enhance the beauty of women's eyes. Hence the name, bella donna.'

Sir Edward seized the opportunity for ridicule. 'And you possess this because you propose to beautify the eyes of the mariners? Or perhaps the soldiers? Or the female savages?' A ripple of laughter went through the crowded chapel. Mr Rosen remained silent, his face a mass of misery.

'And when the surgeon-barber and you attended to the unfortunate Mr Falconer . . .'

'His eyes were black with the distension of the pupils.'

'And do you agree with Mr Oxendale's diagnosis, that Mr Falconer was poisoned?'

'I do, but not by a single substance. In my opinion the symptoms are better described by a combination of poisons.'

'Indeed? You correct the opinion of the physician? It seems your knowledge of poisons is more extensive than you would have us believe.'

There was a murmur of assent around the chapel, quickly stilled by a look from the governor. Thomas Harriot stood up. 'I wish to question the apothecary.'

Sir Edward bowed ironically and stepped back.

Thomas approached the bench and picked up the phial of dried green insects. 'What are the medicinal properties of the Spanish fly?' he asked, turning to the apothecary.

'In small quantities the crushed shell is an aphrodisiac.'

Ribald laughter filled the chapel. Even Ralph Lane smiled briefly. Sir Edward interrupted, his voice full of exaggerated sarcasm: 'What need is there of an aphrodisiac on this voyage?'

'None, sir. But it also eases blisters on the skin. Several in this chapel will testify to its benefits.' There was a murmur of agreement amongst the crowd.

Thomas continued, 'And the belladonna?'

'It can be used in tiny amounts to treat sickness arising from the motion of a ship, and I have used it to the benefit of several mariners, and even some of the gentlemen. Marmaduke StClair will verify this.'

'And the berry? The thing which may have killed David Falconer, on its own or as part of a combination?'

'I have been using it as rat bait. From my experiments I have found it to be very successful. I believe that larger quantities of the berry carried on future expeditions will be extremely useful.' There was a murmuring from the crowd. Rats were the bane of our existence and destroyers of our food. The governor leaned forwards, his eyes narrowed with concentration. I was filled with admiration for my master. Two minutes ago, it had seemed certain that the apothecary was doomed. But with a few deft questions the whole issue of his guilt had been turned around. Surely the court could not now find him guilty?

Mr Harriot continued, 'And what about the plant from South America?'

There was a tiny hesitation from Mr Rosen. 'It is used by some tribes because it causes excitement, or visions of flying or floating. I have it simply because I wish to deepen my knowledge of herbs.' Mr Harriot looked at Ralph Lane for some seconds, without speaking a word, and then returned to his seat.

Sir Edward now stood up and turned to face Mr Lane. There was anger on every line of the lawyer's face. I sensed that he was not truly so but was acting the part to influence the judges by emotion. His voice was raised in this pretence of anger. 'The apothecary condemns himself with his own mouth. You see how he twists reason? A box full of deadly poisons becomes medicine for blisters or sea sickness, or rat bait, or a subject for curiosity. We see here, demonstrated before our eyes, the cunning of the witch. See how he conceals his true intentions with clever words. But the very cleverness of the words are themselves evidence against him. He stands condemned by his own mouth.'

'I am not a witch!' Rosen cried in despair.

'But would a witch not say the same? Are we to expect truth from the mouth of one?' Sir Edward approached to within two feet of the terrified apothecary. 'How do you come to live in England?'

'I fled persecution in Bremen.' The apothecary's voice was anguished. 'I found my way to England after many adventures.'

Sir Edward nodded. He stepped forward to Ralph Lane's desk and placed his hand on the *Malleus*. 'This book, Governor, was written by Kramer and Sprenger on the instruction of the pontiff Pope Innocent the Eighth, because of the extent of witchcraft which existed throughout Germany, particularly in Cologne, Mainz and *Bremen*.' He stepped back. There was a tone of finality in his voice. 'I do not believe I need to say more. The deadly poisons found amongst the *materia medica* of this wretch, his arrival from the nest of witches which is Bremen, his casuistry under questioning, which would do a Jesuit proud, these things are evidence enough for me. And they should be enough for this court. That he is a murderer is surely now proven. But it is his attempt to destroy our expedition which is his crime amongst crimes. No Englishman, this. He is an agent of Spain and must suffer the consequences.'

Mr Harriot stood up again and walked towards Ralph. The apothecary followed my master with eyes full of hope and desperation. Thomas spoke in a quiet, almost gentle voice, in stark contrast to the strident tones of Sir Edward. 'It surprises me to hear Sir Edward speak of Heinrich Kramer and James Sprenger as if they were the touchstones of wisdom. They were Dominicans! Has he converted to the Catholic faith? As to the prevalence of witches in Germany, since witches do not exist in the first place, this can reflect nothing more than the gullibility and proneness to suggestion amongst the people of those provinces. And as to the poisons, what nonsense Sir Edward speaks!'

The lawyer glared at Thomas but my spiritual mentor ignored him. 'An apothecary must of necessity carry many herbs and substances which are poisonous when taken in excess. Mr Rosen has given adequate explanations for his possession of them. And in any case, who is to say that he alone had access to them? No witness saw Mr Rosen, or for that matter anyone else, administer them. The man is innocent. Mr Lane, let the apothecary go free.'

The governor absently stroked his beard, looking between the prisoner, the lawyer and my master. 'We will take time to consider the matter.' He stood up. There was a bustle of noise as the audience rose to its feet. The judges filed out towards a room at the back of the chapel. I wondered whether I was expected to follow them, but nobody looked in my direction, and I simply gathered up my notes and waited.

Gradually noise and laughter spread through the courtroom. Everyone seemed to speak to everyone else, as if it were market day. Everyone, that is, but Mr Rosen, who stood with his head bowed, just occasionally looking up and staring from left to right, wild-eyed, like a man who has lost his mind.

After the best part of an hour the judges filed in again. The prisoner seemed close to fainting. 'Abraham Rosen,' the governor said in a grim voice. A mouse could have been heard in the chapel. In my excited state, my hand shook as I wrote his words. The jangling of the chains around the apothecary resumed. 'Of all forms of killing, that of the poisoner is the most vile. It is insidious and unclean. It uses dark and unnatural forces. The perpetrator lives in the shadows and slinks back into them when he has done his work. We find you guilty of the murders of which you have been accused. But you are not only a murderer. You are also a traitor to the country which harboured you, and to the Queen under whose protection you have lived in England.'

At this point Mr Rosen gave a great cry. 'No! I did not do this! God is my witness! I am an innocent man!'

I knew this from the contents of Marmaduke's secret panel. And now the apothecary's distress was so great, and his protestations of innocence so obviously sincere, that surely the court would believe him too.

Ralph Lane let the uproar and the man's cries subside. And while the apothecary sobbed, he pronounced sentence without a hint of mercy in his voice. 'Sentence appropriate to high treason will be carried out this day. You will be hanged and taken down while still living. Your private parts will then be cut off. Your bowels will be removed while you still live, and you will be beheaded as you die. Captain Vaughan, see to it with despatch.'

28

'Chuck Martin? Harry Blake here. I got your e-mail message. It was lucky I checked them. But how did you know where to reach me?'

The lawyer ignored my question. 'I'm glad you phoned, Mr Blake. Very glad.' He lowered his voice. 'Are you free to talk? I mean, are you out of hearing?'

I glanced out at the balcony. The wind and rain had eased during the course of the day, and now the only evidence that it had ever been was vapour rising from the occasional puddle. Dalton was taking a break from the decode and splashing around in the pool. He had the trim body and flat stomach that goes with hour-a-day workouts and that I could only envy. Zola was on a garden bench in the shade of a papyrus tree, wearing a yellow towel, dark glasses and a broad-brimmed straw hat. She was scribbling on a pad. Sheets of paper next to her were held down by a glass of pink fluid.

'What's the problem?'

'Can you get away from your companions this evening? Say for a couple of hours?'

'Ho hum. What's going on, Mr Martin?'

'I want you to meet some people.'

'I don't like the sound of this. What's going on?'

'Believe me, Mr Blake, it's in your best interests. Look, there's an open-air jam near Matilda's Corner tonight. Lots of people partying. Can you be there?'

'Maybe,' I said.

'It gets underway after dark. That's in an hour or so.'

'Just who are you representing, Mr Martin?'

'I see my client as Miss Tebbit. But she's little more than a child,

Mr Blake, and I'm not sure she could handle the information I want to give you. It's in her interests as much as yours that we should meet.'

Dalton was out of the pool and drying himself. The sun, with its usual tropical speed, was already low on the horizon behind Kingston, surrounded by technicolour clouds.

I didn't like the situation, but on the other hand didn't see what else I could do. I grabbed wallet and car keys and headed for the Toyota. Zola looked up in surprise.

'Going into town,' I explained.

'What? But what about the cipher?'

I didn't bother to reply. I sensed Zola's eyes on me all the way to the car. The Toyota was under the shade of a papaya tree, big pink fruits threatening to squelch down on it, but the steering wheel was still painfully hot to touch. I took it gingerly down the mountain pass while the sun touched the sea in a blaze of red and yellow clouds, the fleeing remnants of the storm, and finally sank under it.

I made my way along the Old Hope Road to Matilda's Corner and parked the car in a side street. A deep, thumping rhythm was echoing off buildings. A stream of lively teenagers was heading for the source of the noise and I followed them. There was a park, lit up like a fairground. I joined a queue and paid three thousand Jamaican dollars to a fat man with an enormous knitted cap with red, gold, black and green stripes. He was smoking a large, hand-rolled joint. Then I was under an archway with DIS AND DAT in blue letters, and into the park along with at least a thousand others, nearly all of them younger than me and nearly all of them black-skinned. At least I stood out in the crowd.

I jostled my way to a jerk chicken stall and filled a paper plate with odds and ends. Coloured lightbulbs were strung between trees, swaying in the wind, and the air was light with ganja and spice, and Caribbean chatter and dancehall music of a sort coming from awesomely large speakers. Young men with guitars were leaping around on a brightly lit stage. I felt a hundred years old.

There was no sign of Chuck Martin. But would I ever see him in this mêlée?

A fantasy thought struck me: that Cassandra and her friends might be pulling the lawyer's strings. Short of a knife in the ribs, I didn't see what they could do in this crowd. It was a safe place to be. That, of course, would be just what they wanted: me to feel safe. Suddenly nervous, I decided to give it ten minutes and clear off. In any case, much longer than that and I would have permanent hearing damage. I finished my food and grabbed a rum punch from a bar counter: the entrance fee, it seemed, paid for the drinks. I started to ease my way back towards the exit.

'You wanna dance?' She was about twenty, dark-skinned, with a short yellow top which exposed her midriff and most of her bosom, and a short yellow skirt which exposed a lot of thigh. *Nice thighs,* I thought. She had a wide smile which exposed perfect white teeth. She wore a gold necklace and earrings, and white mules.

'Not really,' I said, loud enough to be heard over the music.

'I don't bite,' she smiled.

'And I don't dance.'

'You just have to move your feet.'

She took my hand. It was small and warm and I thought, what the hell. I put the rum punch down on a table as I passed and then we were mingling with the hot, densely packed dancers. There was a smell of rum and jerk, and sweat and ganja, and the night air was hot. Her dance was an uninhibited affair of undulating hips and pelvic contact. I tried to imitate her movements but couldn't get the rhythm. She said, 'Well it ain't Cool 'N' Deadly. I told you, you have to move your feet.'

'What's your name?'

'Helen. I think you don't like parties.'

Here it comes. The invitation to go someplace quiet. 'Got it in one, Helen.'

'We could go someplace quiet.' That smile.

'Tell you what. You find someone more sociable and I'll go home to bed.'

This time she laughed. 'You don't get rid of me so easy. Come on.'

She took me by the hand again and we made our way through the crowd. She was still dancing to the music, wriggling her bottom and swinging her shoulders rhythmically. The group came to some sort of climax and a DJ started to mouth some rubbish in half-English, half-patois, with a horrible mid-Atlantic accent.

She'd be aiming to get me into some quiet, dark spot. The trick would be to see what was lying behind this pick-up without going the way of Tebbit. I was sweating. Either she was just a girl after my wallet or she was leading me to someone. Or maybe she was just being friendly and the earth was flat after all. She led the way past the stalls and bars to the edge of the park. It was darker here. There was a high fence and an exit, and beyond it a road with a stream of cars, and beyond that a concrete wall and a row of dirty, shuttered, one-storey buildings. Alarm bells were ringing in my head.

She felt my hesitation, put her arm in mine. 'Don't be nervous. Come with me.' She wasn't smiling any more.

'What do you do for a living, Helen?'

'Not what you're thinking, Mister.'

We walked on to the street and she took me across the road, judging a gap in the heavy traffic, and along the street, still with her arm in mine. There was no conversation; the pretence of a casual pick-up was long gone. About fifty yards on, she glanced behind us and took me around a corner. Here the street was narrow and dark.

A man emerged from the shadows. Helen, if that was her name, would try to hold onto my arm when he attacked, to stop me running. My plan, for what it was worth, was to punch her unexpectedly on the nose and take off. I was a split second from doing so when I recognised Chuck Martin. He had company: two men, in their late thirties. The shorter of the two had a dark, Mediterranean complexion and pockmarked cheeks. The other was tall, stooped, slightly awkward, with spectacles. I couldn't see him as a physical threat.

Martin said, 'I'll leave you gentlemen to it.'

'Nice meeting you, Harry,' said the girl. Then she was into a big four-wheel-drive jeep. The lawyer climbed into the passenger seat and she waved as they drove off.

The tall man opened a wallet and showed a stamped Polaroid photograph of himself next to some writing which I couldn't read.

He said, 'Inspector Wotherspoon, United Kingdom, Special Branch. And this is Inspector Menem of the Turkish National Police.'

Special Branch? Turkish Police?

Wotherspoon said, 'Sorry about the clandestine stuff, Mr Blake. We had to be sure you weren't being followed. A casual pick-up at a dance party and a trip to a quiet lane was the best we could think of at short notice.'

'This is bizarre.' In the circumstances, it seemed a lame comment.

'We've been following your progress with great interest, Mr Blake.'

'Are you telling me I've been under surveillance?'

Wotherspoon sidestepped the question. 'We're here to ask for your help.'

'How long have you people been watching me?'

'It's a long story.'

'This is something to do with Dalton, right?'

There was a quick exchange of glances. Menem asked, 'Was that a guess?'

I didn't reply. 'Can we find someplace air conditioned?'

Wotherspoon said, speaking to nobody in particular, 'So he's calling himself Dalton.'

'Naturally. It's his name.'

'Exactly what is your connection with this so-called Dalton?' Menem asked.

'If we've been under surveillance, surely you know?'

Menem waited until a man and a miniskirted woman had sauntered past. The man was counting a thick wad of Jamaican dollars. 'We'd appreciate it if you just answered the question.'

'And I'd appreciate it if you'd tell me what this is about.'

'You seriously claim you don't know?' Menem's tone was becoming openly hostile.

'Goodbye.' I actually turned away, but Wotherspoon grabbed me by the arm. He attempted a soothing tone. 'I think maybe we're all getting a bit hot out here. Let's find that air-conditioned café and start again.'

We had to walk several blocks before we got away from the party noise. We ended up in a pool hall with a few busy tables. A bunch of youths were clustered noisily around an arcade game in a corner. A TV over the bar was showing a martial arts movie. We sat on stools and I asked for a milkshake; the policemen settled for coffees.

I took the initiative: 'Where do the Turkish Police come into the equation?'

Menem said, 'The position is that we ask the questions and you answer them.'

I was trying to control my temper. 'No, the position is that I'm a free citizen in a free country and you can go to hell.'

Wotherspoon sipped at his coffee. He made a face. 'You're right, Mr Blake. But we've come a long way, we're jet-lagged, and we'd greatly appreciate the answers to some questions. You have no idea how urgent this matter is.'

I wondered if this was the good-cop, bad-cop routine I'd seen in TV dramas but had always assumed was a creation of fiction writers.

Menem asked, 'How do you come to be associated with these people?'

I was still angry at being jerked around. But I told them, 'I've been commissioned by an old Lincolnshire family to investigate a manuscript. It has things in it that need specialised knowledge. Zola's a marine historian, and Dalton is an expert on religious relics. What we've learned so far has taken us out here.'

'You claim to have no prior connection with this Dalton?' Menem's voice was carrying the tone of authority that went with the job; he was definitely getting on my nerves. Maybe it was my fault: I have that anarchic streak that would have made me a disaster in any organisation requiring teamwork.

'Absolutely none.' *Special Branch. Turkish National police.* I voiced a thought which had been slowly crawling out of my subconscious for days. 'Are you people by any chance thinking terrorism?'

'Interesting you should say that,' Wotherspoon said. I waited for an answer. Instead he asked, 'Are you people looking for something?'

Menem shot him a look, as if he'd said too much.

'How did you know that?' I asked.

'A lucky guess,' Wotherspoon said, stirring his coffee. He didn't expect me to believe him and didn't care.

Inspector Menem said, 'It happens that my country is at a crossroads between East and West, Europe and Asia. To the west, our neighbours and ancient enemies are the Greeks. To the east are Armenia and Iran, countries which hold Turkey responsible for past genocides. We have, unfortunately, a bloodsoaked history.'

'Thanks, but in my job I pick up a little history as I go. Can we get to the point?'

The policeman put three spoonfuls of sugar into his coffee. 'As I said, there are some things which we cannot explain to you.'

'You flew out to Jamaica to tell me that?'

Menem said, 'We'd like to know what you're looking for, and what progress you have made in finding it. You and your friends.'

'Why should I tell you anything?' I was still unsettled, and alarmed, by the revelation that I'd been under surveillance.

Menem sighed. 'Mr Blake, I belong to a specialist unit of the Turkish National Police. The geography and history which I have told you about make our country something of a meeting ground for all sorts of extremists. We have to deal with Kurdish separatists who explode bombs in the Misir Bazaar, Muslim fundamentalists who try to penetrate American Air Force Bases, Greek militants who—'

'What does this have to do with me?'

'For some time now we have been involved in the investigation of a group of people. To say that these people are dangerous would be to understate.'

I felt my scalp contracting. Menem continued, 'They and you are looking for the same thing and it is vital to them that they find it before you.'

'I don't know what you're talking about.' I knew perfectly well what he was talking about. I was shivering slightly, but it might have been the air conditioning.

'This is a violent little island. The death of three tourists would be seen as just another unfortunate incident in a country which saw eight hundred murders last year.'

The point had occurred to me as soon as I'd stepped onto Jamaican soil. No, it had occurred to me in an Oxford pub, just as soon as I'd realised I had to get out here. 'You said three tourists.'

'Zola, Debbie and yourself. Not Dalton.'

I thought about that. 'Not Dalton?'

Menem shook his head. 'Not Dalton.'

I slurped the last of my milkshake, and noticed that my hand was trembling slightly. Inspector Menem's eyes were like hard little marbles. I said, 'If we hit it lucky we could have answers in a day or two.'

Wotherspoon nodded his satisfaction. 'All we ask, Mr Blake, is that you keep us informed of your progress. Anything you find should be reported to me through Mr Martin's office. Not through the consulate, which is as leaky as a sieve.'

'And what about Dalton?'

The policemen glanced at each other. Menem nodded briefly and Wotherspoon said, 'Your friend Dalton is for hire.'

'What does that mean in plain English? Is he a hired assassin or what?'

Wotherspoon said, 'Much more than an assassin. He has at least half a dozen names and the same number of passports. You'll find him in Iraq, Iran, Palestine, Turkey – wherever there is a need for a knife in a dark alley or an atrocity in a marketplace. He lives in a crypt and comes out after dark.'

Menem pulled a small brown envelope out of his back pocket. He passed over a black-and-white photograph. Dalton stared at me from the picture. It looked like a London street, and the cameraman had been in a car across the road. There was an official stamp with a number and the name underneath was Leroy Abo.

'Is this the man you know as Dalton?'

'Yes. He's Leroy Abo?' I was beginning to feel nauseous.

'Amongst many other names,' Menem said. 'And these are some of his works of art.' He handed over a couple of newspaper clippings, both in English. There was a picture of a wrecked bus, and debris and people scattered over a busy street, and ambulances. The blasted market, the cars and the people placed the scene somewhere in the Mediterranean or the Near East.

'He escaped from prison in Ismir three years ago. At the moment he has connections with extremists in the north of my country. We believe that whatever you are looking for, it is in some way symbolic to these people. We think he has been commissioned to retrieve it. We also think that its retrieval will be used to trigger some major terrorist incident.'

I felt my face going pale. 'This can't be right. He works for Sir Joseph himself, the Director of the Oxford Museum of Antiquities.'

Wotherspoon said, 'He does not. You can check this for yourself. Look up the museum's staff list on the Internet.'

Menem managed a half-smile. 'Ah yes, Sir Joseph. The virtuous, the impeccable, the wealthy Sir Joseph. Now we really enter realms where I simply cannot divulge certain facts.' He gave me a few seconds to let my imagination run riot, and then asked, 'Have you noticed anything odd about Dalton's behaviour?'

I thought about that. Little things came back to me. 'Yes. Yes, I have. Phone calls, with the receiver going down when I entered a room. Unexplained absences.' I turned to Wotherspoon. 'They killed Tebbit and made it look like a robbery, right?'

The Inspector gave me a blank stare.

'But knowing this, you've still been quite happy to use me as bait.'

'Don't feel too badly about it, Mr Blake.'

'There's something else,' I said, my throat dry. 'Zola swears she saw Dalton speaking to a man in a café. Not a casual conversation; something with purpose.'

The smile vanished. The policemen exchanged glances. 'He's not acting alone, then.'

'Maybe Zola, Debbie and I should just clear off.'

Wotherspoon said, 'I won't hide the fact that the situation is extremely dangerous for you. I'd hesitate to put even one of my field officers in your position. But I ask you not to walk away. There may be many human lives at stake.'

'You people have been using me as bait since the Tebbit murder, right?' I repeated.

Wotherspoon was stirring his coffee to death.

189

'What should I do about Dalton?' I was having trouble relating the cheerful, shy young man I knew, to the fanatical creature they were describing.

'Tell him nothing about this meeting. Give no indication that you know who he really is. Above all, don't let him get his hands on whatever it is you find.'

I shook my head in bewilderment. 'I'm not sure how I can prevent that.'

Menem said, 'But the moment he has it in his grasp, you and Zola and Debbie are of no further use to him. You become a liability. He'll crush you like insects.'

'What do you want me to do?'

Wotherspoon said, 'Let us know when you're about to retrieve this thing. We'll try to arrange protection.'

I stood up. My legs were a little unsteady.

'By the way, where are you staying?' Spoken casually.

'We have a hideaway.'

'Not good enough. We need to know exactly where it is.'

'A villa in the Red Hills.' I hoped the lie was convincing. 'It's a hundred yards past the Shell station, on the right. You can't miss it, it's a big white building with balconies. I thought it was a safe house.'

'It probably would have been, without this viper in your midst.'

On the street outside I waved at a taxi, reggae pounding from it in competition with the heavy bass from Matilda's rhythm track. Menem said, 'Once we know the nature of your find, we will better understand why the Kurdish terrorists are so keen to have it.'

They stood on the busy street while I haggled with the elderly Rastaman over the price of a taxi ride to the Red Hills. Wotherspoon waved as I took off. After a couple of hundred yards I looked back, but they were gone, lost in the crowds.

When we reached Constant Spring, I steered the driver back the way we had come and then along to Beverley Hills. We trickled slowly around quiet streets lined with million-dollar houses guarded by tall fences and maneating dogs. After a few tours I was persuaded that nothing was following us, and I took us back through the city to Matilda's Corner and stopped him a block from the Toyota. The wind was getting up again and the party was hot.

'Gwine a di disco?' the Rastafarian asked. I said, 'Yeh man, keip di change.' He said, 'God bless,' and took off, Bob Marley's inheritance echoing off the houses.

I was back in the villa in half an hour. In the big kitchen, Zola was doing her thing with a pineapple, snappers and a sharp knife, and Debbie was being the kitchen skivvie. Dalton, in his Cool Jamaica gear, was poring over the Ogilvie manuscript. He greeted me with a friendly wave and a shy smile, which I just couldn't connect with the broken bodies sprawled over the streets of the Misir Bazaar.

29

My watch said nine o'clock: I'd had about three hours' sleep.

The melodious sound of a West Indian voice came up the stairs, above the moaning of the high wind in the trees. There was a frying smell.

I dressed in sweater and shorts and clattered down the broad wooden stairs to the kitchen. Debbie and Dalton were at a big table, drinking coffee. Dalton waved and Debbie gave me a sweet, innocent smile. The villa, it seemed, came with a young black maid. 'How you do sah, mi name is Pearl. Ounu reddy fi brekfus?'

'Try something traditional,' Dalton suggested.

Pearl's eyes lit up. 'You cain hab cornmeal a banana porridge, saltfish an' ackee, bammy, cheese amlet. . . .'

'Thanks, Pearl, but I'll settle for toast.'

She pouted. 'Got no toast. You cain have fried plantains.'

'Fine.'

'Arite.' Pearl smiled and in a moment I heard a frying pan rattling on to a cooker in the kitchen.

Debbie was dressed in black sweater and slacks. She poured condensed milk into her coffee. 'I've got it all worked out,' she said. 'My family tree on the Jamaican side.' She slid several sheets of A4 paper towards me. 'Daddy never told me about them. I think he must have been ashamed of them. There were unions between planters and their slaves.'

'He didn't know about your Jamaican relatives,' I said, and believed it.

I picked up Debbie's list but hardly had time to look at it before Zola came skipping into the room. She too was waving sheets of paper. 'Look at this, Harry. It's in cipher.'

192

I looked at Zola's sheets and recognised it immediately: the Babington cipher. I said, 'This is Ogilvie's writing. I recognise it.'

Debbie's eyes were filled with romantic notions of buried treasure. 'This is what it's about, isn't it? Harry, you must decode this right away.'

'Eat dem while deh hot,' Pearl ordered. She headed up the stairs, I suppose to make beds.

'I'm not a code breaker, Debbie.' The plantain in my mouth tasted as if it had been fried in Scotch bonnets. The world's strongest pepper, someone had told me, and I was ready to believe it.

There was something disturbing about Dalton's steady smile. Without taking his eyes from me, he said, 'But it is an Elizabethan code, isn't it?'

'I think it's the Babington cipher,' said Zola.

Damn it, Zola. Don't tell Dalton!

'But you must have known that, Harry.' Zola's eyes were suddenly wary. 'You wanted to decode it all by yourself, didn't you? Maybe you even wanted to find the True Cross all by yourself.'

Still that steady, disconcerting stare from Dalton. I began to wonder if he suspected I'd seen his confab in the early hours of the morning.

'Don't be daft,' I said, attempting a light-hearted tone. 'Yes, it does look like the Babington cipher. Strictly it's a nomenclator, a mixture of substitution symbols and words. We should be able to download it from the Internet,' I said, still trying to deflect the suspicion which was now thick in the air. 'Why don't you look around? See if there's an Internet café in town, or even in the hotel. While you're looking I'll complete what I can of the Ogilvie journal.'

Dalton said, 'Zola and I will get busy on that.'

I didn't like the thought of Zola alone in Dalton's company. I said, 'Actually, I'll come along.'

'Why?' Zola's voice was still heavy with mistrust.

'To make sure the pair of you don't run away with the buried treasure.' There was no point in trying to make it sound like a joke. The air was electric.

Zola poured herself a coffee. She spoke with ice in her voice. 'You must have known that was the Babington cipher, Harry. You pretended you didn't know. There has to be a reason for that. Maybe something to do with collecting a thirty-million-dollar icon for yourself.'

I couldn't explain with Dalton there. I said, 'The reason was that I had about three hours' sleep. If you read meanings into every idiotic thing that I say or do . . .'

Debbie was scrutinising her family tree enthusiastically. 'Did you know that my middle name is Inez, as in Inez Teriaca?' She tried to draw herself up like a haughty Spaniard, and added more condensed milk to her coffee.

'I can see that Harry's worried,' said Dalton. 'There must be an Internet connection here. Let's be nice to the manager and stay on-site.'

I looked out at the bending trees and the driving rain. The wind was making little waves on the pool. 'It's not jacuzzi weather. I'll head upstairs and see what the young James Ogilvie has to tell me.'

After the trial of the unfortunate Mr Rosen, we had hoped that the mysterious poisonings would stop. The apothecary had cheated the executioner in the most spectacular way possible. On the pro-nouncement of the word 'guilty', he had snatched his neck rope from the soldier's grasp, leapt to the table, seized the jar of black petals and poured them into his hands, rubbing them together and smearing the black dust over his face and chest. None dared approach him as he held his hands up, wild-eyed, and we stood transfixed, wondering what would happen next. Within moments his breathing became difficult, his back arched and he fell to the ground, cracking his head, seized with a terrible spasm. His face turned purple and contorted and his limbs became stretched, as if he was being racked. Within two minutes his breathing had stopped, although his eyes were still staring horribly and he was twitching and there was so much space between his back and the floor that a dog could have walked under him. Then there was a dreadful choking noise and his body sagged to the ground, lifeless.

And with Mr Rosen's terrible death, I had a surge of relief. My conscience was relieved of the responsibility of saving an innocent man at the cost of my own life. And yet, had I spoken sooner, before the verdict had been delivered . . . Suffice to say that over the years I have had more than one bad dream, more than once wakened in the night with Mr Rosen's eyes staring wildly into mine, pleading and accusing.

And yet, within a week, there was another murder. A young man on sentry duty was shot in the dark. We never found the gun which fired the ball, or the finger which pulled the trigger. And within days of that, the poisonings began again.

Suspicion then fell on Joachim Ganz, the mineral man from Prague who, like Mr Rosen a Jew rather than a Christian, was treated with suspicion in any case. Mr Kendall let it be known that, when he entered Mr Ganz's room, the Jew had hastily hidden a jar containing green leaves. This I confidently believed to be a lie, but mutterings soon began amongst the colonists: Mr Ganz had been seen entering the cabin of a man who had later died. I knew now that the killings were the work of one or more of three men: Marmaduke StClair, Anthony Rowse and Abraham Kendall. And I also knew that to reveal my knowledge would be to hang myself. The game they played was not my game, nor was its outcome my concern. So I told myself, in an attempt to assuage my own guilt.

But my agonies of conscience overcame even my sense of self-preservation. One wet morning I approached Mr Harriot in his cabin and told him that I believed passionately in the innocence of Joachim Ganz, dreading that my master would interrogate me about the basis for this belief. What Mr Harriot knew or suspected I cannot say, but I am forever grateful for his discretion. He simply listened quietly, and then told me that no harm was likely to come to Joachim. Mr Ganz had shown the English how to smelt copper, desperately needed in the production of bronze for the cannon which gave their ships an edge over the iron guns of the Spaniards. Mr Ganz was a good friend of England. Mr Ganz, so Thomas Harriot told me, had made a great deal of money for persons in the Privy Council, and even on this very colony. And so it proved. The mutterings against the Jew died away.

Meantime the work of the colony went ahead. Mr Harriot has described this in his journal, which I have seen, and there is little I need add to it. I note that he expunged all mention of the attempts to destroy the colony from within. I suspect he did not want people to inquire too closely about the purpose of our expedition. We had all hoped that Joachim Ganz would discover precious stones or gold. He did find copper ore, too poor to be exploited; otherwise all he found were pebbles. And Ralph Lane, who had grandiose plans for building a fine fortress surrounded by stone bulwarks and curtains, had to settle for constructing a fort which was no more than a bank of sand and a deep ditch.

Late in August Sir Richard Grenville sailed for England, promising to return in the Easter with supplies and leaving a hundred of us behind. A feeling of depression settled on our little colony as the Tiger and the Elizabeth disappeared over the horizon, leaving us alone on the continent.

Over the next few months, Ralph Lane and Thomas Harriot mounted several expeditions into the interior. Always I had in mind the mysterious *longitudem dei*, the secret purpose, the *iacta est alia* of the English Queen. I myself accompanied Mr Harriot and Mr White on one of these expeditions. We took a rowing boat out into the big waves of the Atlantic before turning towards Chesapeake Bay. We found the land here to be fertile and the savages friendly. And although it was winter, the climate was mild and we were even able to sleep outdoors on the ground. We stayed for over a month, but when we finally returned in spring we found the colony in a bad way. The assassinations had continued. There had been much violence. The savages had become hostile and grown weary of our constant demands for food. If the purpose of the conspirators was to foment trouble and destroy the expedition, they were succeeding.

By the summer our food was gone. Even Ralph Lane's mastiffs had gone into the cooking pot. And now the savages were seeing their chance and threatening to exterminate us. Governor Lane led an expedition against them. It was a vicious and bloody business, at the end of which he brought back the head of the Indian chief, Wingina. But I suppose it gave us breathing space from their increasingly bold attacks. And within a week Captain Stafford brought us wonderful news: from the Outer Banks he had sighted a huge English fleet. Sir Francis Drake had come to our rescue with twenty-three ships: the colonists were to be taken home. It was salvation for them, but it was to prove a disaster for me.

No sooner had Sir Francis Drake anchored than a storm began to blow up. The waves beyond the Outer Banks began to grow frighteningly high. A number of longboats set sail from the fleet. We began to drag Mr White's drawings, and the chests of minerals and plants collected by us, as well as the personal belongings and chests of the gentlemen, towards the shore.

And now, sadly, discipline began to break down. The colonists, including many of the soldiers, had been barely under control these past months, Governor Lane keeping discipline only by virtue of the occasional hanging. But now, as the storm started to blow, they were overcome by fear that Drake would weigh anchor and disappear over the horizon, leaving them to starvation and the mercy of the savages who now had good reason to hate them. Drake's own sailors were so fearful of the storm that they threatened to leave the colonists behind.

Governor Lane was the first to climb aboard the waiting pinnace, followed by the other gentlemen. Their chests and trunks were on the shore, left in the charge of the sailors. I had been frantically packing belongings into the chests of Harriot, Rowse, White and the others, leaving my own secret journal to the last. But now, as the fleet masts were swaying dangerously in the growing storm, I left Mr White's cabin and ran through driving rain towards my own small hut. I had no time for my collection of pebbles and strange seashells; I pulled my straw bedding aside and picked up my journal, protecting it from the rain by putting it next to my chest. I ran out.

'Ogilvie! Over here!' Marmaduke was beckoning urgently with big sweeps of his arm. I ran to him and followed him into his hut. 'For God's sake help me with this. And be quick!' He was trying to squeeze an absurd volume of belongings into his chest. A child could have seen that it was impossible to close the lid.

I said, 'Sir! This will not do!'

'A curse on your impertinence, Ogilvie. Sit on the damned lid.' But nothing we did would close it. As the minutes passed he finally swore, threw the lid open and began to go through his clothes, picking and choosing what to leave behind. Unfortunately he seemed to wish to take everything with him. I was becoming frantic with anxiety. I cried again, 'Sir, we must move.'

'Then help me pull the damned thing.' We began to drag the chest across the floor. It would scarcely move, it was so heavy. We forced the hut door against the wind. As I looked out I saw to my horror that the last rowing boat was being pushed offshore. Men were punching each other to get aboard. Already the waves were white-capped, and I was beginning to lose sight of Sir Francis's fleet through the rain.

At the sight of this, Marmaduke gave a cry of despair. He dropped the chest, pushed roughly past me and sprinted towards the boat. I followed, racing behind him with the blood thumping in my ears and my heart hammering in my chest. But it was too late. As we reached the shore the longboat was already three hundred feet out. It was being tossed by the waves and threatening to founder with the weight of men on board. One man alone remained, crying and waving, the waves sometimes going up to his neck. But the sailors were ignoring him: they had enough to do just to stay afloat. Eventually he stopped waving and stared forlornly as his salvation receded. Eventually he turned to wade ashore. It was Simon Salter.

As the last longboat headed out, I recognised one of the sailors: the Turk. He saw me too, and took his hand off an oar long enough to give me a forlorn wave. As it passed the sandbanks I could see the chests simply being heaved out. The specimens and seeds laboriously collected over the last year, the diaries, the maps and paintings, all were being tossed into the sea.

Something was happening on the Outer Banks, but at first I did not see what it was. But then, during a lull in the squall, I saw a horrifying sight. Slaves, black men and women, were being thrown over the side of one of the ships. There was fierce struggling on the deck. A cluster of rowing boats, threatened with crushing by the ship, was disgorging sailors, who were climbing up netting on its side. It seemed that the ship was being emptied of its slaves to make way for the sailors. I could see that many of the slaves were unable to swim. They formed a dense, black, frothing, drowning mass on the waves. Some hundreds had managed to struggle ashore, packed closely together on the narrow sandbank.

'How can Christians do this?' I cried to Marmaduke.

'Don't be a fool, Ogilvie. They are only slaves.'

'But they have no food and no weapons. The savages will cut them to pieces.' I knew the stories. The women were the worst, skinning prisoners while alive with sharp seashells or spreading their bowels over the ground for dogs to chew.

'Be more concerned for your own fate. This should not happen to us, not to civilised people.'

Salter had now waded ashore, water pouring from his breeches and torn shirt. He looked like a man who had been sentenced to death. He joined us and we watched in silence while the masts of Drake's great fleet swayed dangerously, fading into the rain storm and finally, one by one, disappearing from sight.

We looked at each other, wordless and aghast. Three white men – the only white men on this land – abandoned without resources on a continent filled with savages.

30

At first I think it's a noise in a dream. It's a big fluffy dog scraping on a kitchen door.

Then I'm being shaken awake. Zola, her head inches from my ear. 'Harry!' She is whispering urgently. 'There's someone trying to get in.'

I'm out of bed and pulling on my trousers in a second. Precious seconds pass while I scramble for my sweatshirt in the dark, but then I find it and I'm pulling it over my head. I follow Zola barefoot to the bedroom door and listen. At first all I hear is the wind in the trees, but there it is again, the quiet, systematic scraping, like a dog trying to get in.

Dalton pads quietly along the upstairs corridor. 'I've wakened Debbie.'

'Have you called the hotel?' I ask him.

'The phone's right next to the door. And mobiles don't work here.'

I wonder briefly how Dalton knows that. I think maybe if we go to the window and yell we might scare them off. Debbie appears, fully dressed and shivering in spite of the hot night. 'Why don't we put the lights on?' she suggests in a whisper. 'Scare them off.'

I run quickly to my bedroom window. There is a big four-wheel-drive jeep at the entrance, glowing in the subdued lights from the pool and the hotel. It seems to be empty. The drop from the windowsill to the veranda below is only about ten feet. I turn back and almost collide with Debbie.

'I think they're in.' Her voice is distorted with fear.

I grab her by the arm and guide her quickly towards the window. She looks down, hesitating, and I say, 'I'll hold you.' Then she's over the windowsill and I'm holding her by the wrists and she drops. Zola follows. I turn to Dalton but he pushes me to the window and then I'm out, landing with a clumsy thud on the veranda.

A yellow flash in the dark, lighting up bushes and trees, and the roar from some gun. At first I don't even know I've been shot. I'm aware only of a sudden push on my left arm which sends me sprawling face down. I get up and risk a glance behind me, dodging as I run. Two faces at the window.

Debbie and Zola are ahead, zig-zagging along the driveway.

Now I see an alarming dark patch on my shirt sleeve. An aching numbness is beginning to spread through my arm.

I haul the jeep door open. I had thought to free-wheel the car down the steep hill but the fools have left the ignition key in the vehicle. Debbie and Zola have vanished somewhere in the trees to the left. I have no idea where Dalton is. I switch on the engine and crash into second gear, putting my bare foot hard down on the pedal. For some panicky seconds I'm driving in the dark while I struggle for the headlight switch. I'm acutely aware of the lethal drops at the edge of the road. But then there is a tunnel of light ahead of me and I'm taking the car down as fast as I dare.

A minute later the thing I'm dreading appears on the mountain behind me: headlights. They must have taken the Toyota keys. I push the jeep some more, but the hairpin bends are terrifying. Now and then, at the corners, the beams light up the tops of trees; more often they are staring out into blackness.

I have about ten minutes of this. I'm beginning to feel lightheaded and the blood, running down my arm, is making the steering wheel slippery. The Toyota is more nimble than the jeep and I reckon it will be on me in about five minutes.

The pain is starting now, from the inside out of my arm. I'm getting dizzy and I know I have to stem the flow of blood, but how can I, racing the jeep down the most dangerous road in the Caribbean?

There is a sudden, almost 180-degree bend. I slow to about fifteen miles an hour, terrified. The Jeep tilts outwards. There is a scree of boulders on the road, a mini-landslide from the recent rain;

I swerve to avoid it, taking me right to the verge, but my front left tyre hits the boulder at the very moment that my right one thumps into a pothole. I feel a sense of unreality as I realise that the right wheel has gone over the edge. The jeep slowly begins to tilt, as if I am in a turning aircraft. Blackness looms up underneath me. I believe I'm about to die. I jump for the passenger door, which is now above me. The jeep is still in contact with the road but it is juddering and slewing as it tilts. It hits something and the engine stalls.

There's a metallic crunching noise as the jeep begins to go over the edge. It's a slow movement at first. I jump again for the passenger door and this time I get out, but the jeep vanishes from under my feet and I'm following it down in the dark, weightless in freefall, stomach floating inside me, arms and legs waving, down to whatever grave is waiting below.

A bird, a beautiful thing, soaring in the mountain air.

And another, and another. I suddenly become aware that they're circling me. I panic, but I can't move.

One of the vultures has landed. It's about twenty yards away. Others follow, flapping down noisily.

Now I manage to move a finger. It's enough for the moment. The food is still alive.

Something very close behind me. I force myself to move an arm. And that's it. I have no energy left. But the vultures keep their distance, for now.

I hear a male voice. It's Jamaican, and it's saying something like, 'Lawd sah!'

Through badly swollen eyes I can make out a black face peering anxiously into mine. Then there are hands under my armpits and I'm being heaved up to a sitting position. Now the man is attempting a fireman's lift, and for the first time I see the ground around me. I have fallen about fifty feet, except that it is more of a steep tumble down to a broad, flattish piece of land. The jeep, however, has rolled beyond this flat ledge and disappeared over its edge. I catch a glimpse of banana trees and coffee bushes. Then the man is staggering under my weight towards a shack, with corrugated iron roof and veranda. A small, grey-haired woman is leaving the shack, hurrying towards us, but then all I see is rich, bush-covered ground.

Now I am being bundled into a small truck, filled with what seem to be leaves. The woman holds me upright, while the man crashes into gear. We are driving over a shallow stream and up a steep, stony slope, and then we rejoin the road. I more or less faint and recover, faint and recover.

At first there is only brilliantly lit green hillside interspersed with black shadows, but then I begin to see the roadside stalls and even a little cluster of shops with names like Tek it Eazy, Katie Rouge Kitchins and Yaso Jerk Center. More brightly painted wooden shacks: a butcher's shop, a food emporium, a post office with notices about Melodious Explorers and the dangers of diabetes. I wonder about my own life expectancy. Then suddenly we are in town and turning left past a busy bus station, and there is the St Thomas Aquinas Church and a long row of stalls, and the truck swerves right towards low, pink buildings with a notice saying: UNIVERSITY OF THE WEST INDIES HOSPITAL.

A blurred, black face, peering closely into mine.

'Yuh name?'

'Thomas Aquinas.'

'Yuh gi mi yuh name or deh wi charge mi fi murda.'

As I focus, I see I'm in a big room with a dozen or so people milling around. Some are dressed in white, others are lying on trolleys. Somebody is having a bloodstained shirt cut open: a young man, his eyes rolling in his head, and moaning loudly. Clusters of people surround him; he is connected to a baffling array of plastic pipes, wires and tubes.

'I need to know your name,' she says, trying English.

'Harrius Blakeus.'

'Where you from, Mr Blakeus?'

'On holiday, staying at the Terranova. I won first prize, a weekend with Miss Jamaica.'

'You behave yourself now. What happened to you?'

'I was in the Blue Mountains, hiking.'

'On your own?'

'No, with Miss Jamaica. I was robbed.'

The nurse sticks a thermometer in my mouth. 'Suppose God treat we like how we treat one anedda? Foolish, foolish, on your own up there. You're lucky to be alive, Mr Blakeus.'

A doctor approaches; at least I suppose he is a doctor from the white coat and the stethoscope and the air of authority. He is about fifty, with a black, wrinkled face and white hair. He dispenses with the stethoscope and feels my pulse. 'You lost three pints of blood. Lucky it was just a flesh wound. Lots of bruising around your ankles but nothing broken. Rest for two or three days and you'll be dancing the hornpipe.'

My sheet is damp, I can feel sweat on my brow, but still I'm shivering. The doctor volunteers, 'And you got a touch of a fever.'

'Where am I?'

'Kingston ER. We have more experience with bullet wounds than UWI.'

The boy with the chest wound is starting to shout something in a thick Jamaican patois. The doctor floats out of my vision and I drift back to sleep.

Two men, dressed as ambulance orderlies, also floating. The ceiling, all damp patches with big lights, rotating like the night sky.

'Can he be moved?'

'Yes, but keep the drip on him.'

My voice booms around the big room and along the hospital corridors: 'They're not ambulance people! They're abducting me! They're taking me away to kill me!' I think my lips move.

The nurse leans over me as they lift me gently onto a trolley. 'What's that you say, Mr Blakeus?'

'They're going to kill me,' I managed to whisper. 'I know where to find the Cross of Jesus.'

'That's okay. You stay cool now.'

I grab her sleeve. 'Don't let them take me.'

The nurse disengages my arm and pats it reassuringly. She speaks quietly to the doctor. He glances in my direction. In a moment he approaches with a syringe six feet long. 'This will calm you down a bit.'

I try to pull the drip out of my wrist, crawl off the stretcher and flee for my life down the corridor. I almost reach the drip but the nurse has a grip like a gorilla. 'You lost a lot of blood, Mr Blakeus. And too much hot sun isn't good for Europeans.'

There is an outburst of shouting from the corridor: another young man, moaning and holding his head, surrounded by friends. I think I see exposed brain.

'This ain't no place for Whitey, Mr Blakeus,' the nurse says gently. 'Yuh gawn to a nice private nursing home.'

'I like it here,' I manage to whisper.

'We need the space here.'

Then the ceiling starts to drift past and the young man with the chest wound, now covered with a massive bandage, is complaining loudly about his torn shirt, and the trolley is squeaking along a corridor and curious faces are looking at me and I'm shivering with cold, and floating, light as a helium balloon, and then there is hot sunshine on my face and I'm being wheeled over rough ground into a space shuttle and flying high over the Blue Mountains and Jamaica is shrinking to a small green dot on the turquoise Caribbean and there is a smell of perfume from Miss Jamaica, only Miss Jamaica is a Trench Town Yardie and he looks like one of the killers in the woods.

A quiet room. Light sheets; warm, dry air. A breeze blowing through an open, shuttered window. Curious rhythmic tapping from outside, like tennis balls being hit. A million insects clicking and buzzing. One of them, an iridescent dragonfly, hovers uncertainly at the window, looking for food. It darts away. Female laughter, and a man's voice.

Room light, airy, pleasantly furnished with wicker chairs. I drift back to sleep.

Darkness when I wake again. A gentle swishing from outside, which I recognise as waves. I try to move but my arms weigh a ton each. Do I mean a metric ton or am I talking British Imperial units? Soon will have to relieve myself. I close my eyes and sleep for a month.

*　　*　　*

On the second day I was well enough to sit up and start thinking about escape. Which was optimistic, as they'd had to support me to the toilet and back the day before. The two ambulancemen, that is. With revolvers in the waistbands of their shorts.

31

My head was a cannonball. Someone had replaced my blood with mercury and my arteries with lead piping.

It must have taken half a minute to pull the sheet off and ease my legs over the edge of the bed. My head whirled as I sat up. Swollen fingers protruded from a thick bandage wrapped around my arm.

I gave the dizziness time to settle before I tried to stand upright. I felt a sense of achievement as I wobbled over to the open window and supported myself on the sill. The smell of coffee drifted in, mingled with damp tropical earth.

There was a path, winding down to a small rock-enclosed cove, turquoise and calm. There was a short jetty, a rowing boat and a powerful motor cruiser about a hundred yards offshore, bristling with aerials. I could just make out its name: *New Millennium*. Beyond the cove, the white-capped Caribbean stretched to the horizon.

Down to my right was a blue, kidney-shaped swimming pool. A man was lying face down in it, on an airbed. He had a broad, hairy back which glistened with sweat. His arms were dangling in the water and he was completely motionless. He might have been dead.

At the edge of the pool was a white table shaded by a pink summer umbrella with a Martini logo. A woman, apparently naked, sat at the table, drinking orange-coloured juice through a straw. Her breasts were deeply brown, with the nipples a dark shade of pink. She glanced up, smiled and waved. 'Breakfast?' she called up. She nodded to someone out of my line of vision, underneath the red sunshade below my window.

In a moment there was the squeaking of shoes on stairs. A completely bald man with an open-necked shirt – one of the ambulancemen – took me by my good arm and led me down wooden stairs. Still that black revolver in his waistband. He looked like a young Kojak. Every window and door in the house was open, and a warm, gentle breeze was blowing through the rooms. By the time I'd been propped up at the table the pool man was out of the water and towelling himself, and Cassandra's breasts were covered by a red string bikini top.

'You should eat,' the man said in a deep voice. His face was wrinkled and his English heavily accented. Kojak disappeared through French windows into the shady interior of the villa.

'Coffee?' Cassandra asked, pouring me some. I had to use both hands to lift the cup. I drank the brown, sweet liquid greedily.

The man lifted a packet of Marlboro from the table. I shook my head. He and the girl lit cigarettes. Kojak came back with an English breakfast, everything deep-fried. He leaned over me, serving up the plates. I was within two feet of the revolver tucked into his shorts but the fact wasn't worrying him; I had problems enough lifting the fork. They watched me in silence as I ate. I felt better after the food. Kojak took the plates and cups away and disappeared back into the villa. It was a big, white, boxy house, like something made of Lego, all verandas and gingerbread frills.

I sat back. 'What now?'

The man leaned back in his chair, blew smoke, looked at me thoughtfully. 'My name is Apostolis Hondros. I'm a priest of the Greek Orthodox Church. I tell you this because if you survive this encounter you will identify me from some Interpol photograph. If you do not, well . . . either way, nothing is lost by giving you the information. You see, I am open with you. I need your help, Mr Blake.'

'And I suppose you have ways of making me give it.'

'Correct. I intend to find that icon, Mr Blake.'

'It may not even exist.'

'We are confident that it does.'

'What about the others?'

'Your colleagues? Debbie and Zola are both here, resting.'

My stomach flipped. 'Dalton's one of your people, right? Leroy Abo.'

The Greek laughed harshly. 'I see that we fooled you completely. He was in fact a member of the British MI6. They were using you to get at us.'

'And where is he?'

The man waved his cigarette casually. 'He is dead. As the ladies will be shortly.'

'Oh God.' I sank my head on the table.

Cassandra pulled me up by my hair. 'You too,' she added conversationally, looking at me through cigarette smoke. Her eyes were glittering with pure sadism. 'If only you'd given me the journal in Lincoln.'

'If you help us,' Hondros said, 'we might reconsider your future.'

I pushed her hand away with an effort. I leaned back in the garden chair and looked at them. Their eyes showed as much pity as those of the vultures. Even talking was an effort. 'Once you get your greedy hands on the relic, Debbie, Zola and I are finished.'

The Greek nodded. 'Could be. But my magnanimity is your only hope. What else is there?'

I nodded at the heavy silver cross on his hairy chest, held around his neck by a thick chain. 'Is that a cross or a swastika?'

Hondros smiled. 'You're being naughty, Mr Blake. You hope to provoke me.'

'No chance, with someone as self-satisfied as you. I'm just curious to know what brand of lunacy drives you. I think I'm entitled to that.'

'Lunacy?' Hondros adopted a puzzled expression. 'Is obedience to God the act of a lunatic? Or perhaps you don't believe in God. Perhaps you think the world sprang into existence by itself.'

I sighed. 'This is bad news. You're a religious nut.'

'Some of us prefer to spend our limited time on this earth planning for eternity.'

I looked out at the motor launch. I said, 'You may be just passing through, but you sure like the waiting room to be comfortable.'

Hondros gave a contemptuous half-smile. He stubbed out his cigarette in a little marble ashtray and took another one from the packet in front of him. 'You are a traveller, are you not?'

'It's my job. I look for antique maps in the back streets of the world.'

'Do you know Venice?'

'Not very well.'

'St Mark's Square?'

'Uhuh.'

He flicked at a little green lighter, held the flame to the cigarette and puffed. Grey smoke spiralled upwards and he inhaled with satisfaction. 'Do you know St Mark's Cathedral?'

A memory came back. 'Vaguely.'

'And the four gilded horses from the Hippodrome which grace the façade of that building?'

'I remember them. So what?'

Another puff. I noticed for the first time that his fingers were brown with nicotine. 'Now there we have art, in the Byzantine style. True beauty. Go to Venice, Rome or Barcelona, Mr Blake. Look closely at the wonderful statues which decorate these cities. Look at the paintings of the saints, the egg-shaped heads and the pinched faces, a style adhered to by the Byzantine artists for a thousand years. Oh yes, the Byzantine style, because these things were stolen from that great civilisation in 1204.'

'1204?'

'Yes, by the Latins of the Fourth Crusade. On their way to fighting the Moslems of the Holy Land, they raped Constantinople, the centre of Byzantine civilisation. The Byzantines were fellow Christians, but they were guilty of an unforgivable crime.'

He paused. I obliged: 'Which was?'

'Their crime, Mr Blake, was that they were a civilised people, a bright flame burning in a world of barbarity. They loved art and literature and things of beauty. They bathed rather than smelled. And after the Latins had stuffed their ships with gold and silver and precious fabrics from Constantinople, and melted down its bronze statues to make cannon, and stolen the Crown of Thorns, they burned that wonderful city to the ground.'

I had the feeling this was a well-rehearsed spiel. He was searching my face to see how I reacted. I said, 'That was nine hundred years ago, for Christ's sake.'

He shrugged. 'Walk amongst the ruined columns of the Constantine of Lips monastery, my friend, and the ghosts of the murdered monks will walk with you. You will feel their living presence. You will know that the conquest happened yesterday. In any case, the desecration continues to this day.'

'I'm too tired for this.'

'It continues, Mr Blake, because after the Crusaders came the Turks, who entered our city on May twenty-ninth 1453, and who occupy it to this day. Go to modern Constantinople and what will you find? Mosques built on the ruins of churches. The Church of the Holy Apostles, the most famous church in Constantinople after the Hagia Sophia, was plundered by the Latins and then, after the Turkish conquest, smashed by the dervishes of Mehmet the Second. Smashed for fourteen hours, Mr Blake. A holy place, smashed for fourteen hours with iron bars. Go to the site of that church today and you will find a mosque, built on the sacred ground of the Holy Apostles. The Jesus Christ Pantocrator monastery, having been looted by the Venetians, is also now a mosque, the Imperial coffin in it used as a footbath by the Turks who enter. The list of desecration is endless and the Greek government does nothing.'

'Are you real?'

'I have saved the greatest injustice to the last. I refer to the Vatican's fraudulent claim to have a line of succession from St Peter. Do you know your religious history, Mr Blake?'

I said, 'Here we go. Some distorted rubbish.'

Hondros continued, 'You probably do not know that the Vatican's supposed apostolic succession from Christ is based on nothing more valid than torture and murder. The elimination by violence of the true Roman Orthodox bishops – Celts, Saxons and West Romans – was a process begun in the seventh century and which has continued ever since. This happened throughout Spain, Portugal, Italy, Germany and England as well as Gaul. Only in the east, in Greece, did the true succession from Christ survive. Today's papacy is the Antichrist, imposed by murder. Not distorted rubbish, Blake, historical fact. Cassandra, more coffee for our guest.'

Cassandra obliged, and I sipped at the liquid. It was lukewarm. I said, 'Who cares? It's all in the past.'

'An antiquarian cartographer with no sense of history? How very Western! But we must give the Antichrist credit. He acts consistently. The Franco-Latins have pursued their policy over the centuries down to the present day. In 1923, when Italy seized the Dodecanese islands from Turkey, it replaced the Orthodox bishops with Vatican ones, forcing the faithful to either accept clergy ordained by these impostors or do without sacraments.'

'Okay Hondros, I'm persuaded. You've established your credentials as a lunatic. So where does the icon come into it?'

The Greek's eyes were gleaming. He stubbed out the cigarette and leaned forward. 'You know the history of the True Cross. You know that it was found by the Emperor Constantinople, stolen by the Persians, handed back three hundred years later, stolen again by the Mohammedans, then by the Latins, and finally reaching this island after eighteen centuries of travel. But you will retrieve that cross for us – at least the one surviving part of it. Either that, or the three of you will die.'

'And having found it for you?'

'It will be returned immediately to Constantinople. Certain events will then take place.'

It took a second, but then a horrible anticipation began to sink in. Hondros grinned. Cassandra lit her second cigarette with tense, nervous movements of her hands.

I said, 'Since I'm a dead man anyway, why not tell me?'

'Are you a dead man?' He leaned back, peered into my eyes thoughtfully. 'Yes, perhaps I should not insult your intelligence by holding out false hopes. But you will help me find the icon in order to prolong your life, hoping that "something will turn up". Am I right?'

'Absolutely.'

'Very well. The return of the True Cross is a symbol. In three days a brave young woman will drive a truck loaded with explosives into the Blue Mosque in Istanbul. The Suleymaniye, perhaps the finest mosque in the city, will suffer the same fate. A ferry, crossing the Bosphorus to Uskadur, and packed with tourists come to admire the fishing villages and the old Rumeli Hisari fortress, will at the same time explode and sink. And a trail of evidence, carefully laid by us over many months, will lead back to the Opus Dei.'

'The who?'

'Your ignorance continues to surprise me, Mr Blake. Opus Dei are a branch of the Catholic Church distinguished by their outrageous wealth and a long-standing suspicion of their true motives. They have often been suspected of fascist connections. A lie, of course, and they deny it, but what does a protestation of innocence matter against a willingness to believe the worst? Think of the outrage throughout the Muslim world.

'A few days later a light aircraft with Bosnian registration will take off from an airfield in Bosnia. It will be loaded with explosives. It will cross the Aegean, flying under radar until the last moment, when it will crash into the dome of St Peter's. Other churches in Venice, Barcelona and Rome will be destroyed. An act of revenge, the media will cry, Muslim retaliating against Catholic. Hatreds which have simmered just below the surface for a thousand years will erupt. In the present climate, with tinder awaiting a match throughout the region, who knows where it will end? But we of the Orthodox faith will see our ancient enemies tearing each other to pieces. We will enjoy it all on CNN as we drink coffee in bars and cafés from Athens to Olympia. You have a saying, Mr Blake, revenge is sweet. It will be sweet. And the True Cross, placed in our hands by God, will symbolise the justice of our cause.'

'Sort of a divine seal of approval.'

He gave me a cold stare. 'If you like.'

'Very good, Hondros, a first-class performance. For a moment I almost believed you.' I turned to Cassandra, who was looking at me with a puzzled frown. 'Actually, he's just after the Cross for its cash value. He'll sell it to the Getty Museum or the Vatican for a fortune. But by the time the fact dawns on you, he'll be blowing your brains out.'

Hondros smiled and shook his head. He started on another Marlboro. 'What a pathetic effort.' And Cassandra threw back her head and laughed.

Part Three

Star Sign

32

'I need to see them. Prove to me that they're alive.'

Hondros shouted something in Greek. I peered into the dim interior of the villa. In a few moments Debbie appeared, a short, stocky man behind her carrying a revolver. She was pale-faced and had a fist-sized, yellowish bruise on her arm. Her white sweater was stained green, as if she had slipped on wet grass, but it was neatly tucked into her jeans. Her face lit up with pleasure when she saw me. 'Harry!' The gunman held her arm to stop her running forwards.

'Satisfied?'

'What about Zola?' I directed the question at Debbie.

'She's all right. We're sharing a room. What are they going to do to us, Harry?'

Hondros made a gesture of dismissal and the gunman pulled her away. 'Harry!' But then she was gone, pushed out of sight along some gloomy corridor.

'Don't think I'm without sympathy,' Hondros said, showing no sign of any.

He opened a folder in front of him and slid a few sheets of paper over. I flicked through them with my good hand: they were photocopies of Ogilvie's second journal. 'Photocopies,' he said. 'No doubt we could decipher them in due course, but time is short and you have been doing such an excellent job so far. Work on this. Tell us what it has to say about the icon. You have until, let us say' – he pulled Cassandra's wrist towards him and looked at her watch – 'nine o'clock tomorrow morning to reveal the secret.'

'Don't be stupid. It could take weeks to crack the cipher and I'm not even an expert.'

'Nine o'clock. If you have not told us where to find the icon by then, we will shoot Debbie. You will then have another three hours before we kill Zola, and three more before we write you off as a bad job.'

'You can't seriously—'

'And if you utter a single word of complaint about this, I will shorten the time available to you by one hour.'

'Give me Debbie and Zola. Three heads are better than one. They've already been crucial, Debbie with her family knowledge and Zola as a marine historian.'

'There may be something in what you say, Mr Blake. I see no disadvantage to your proposition.'

'We won't be able to work with your gorillas breathing down our necks.'

Cassandra said, 'Why the velvet glove, Tolis? Persuade him with a hammer on his bad arm. More coffee, Harry?'

'No thanks. Have I mentioned that your breath smells?'

'Let's be civilised, please,' said Hondros. 'I'm not a fool, Blake. I understand that pain clouds the mind, that where an intellectual problem is concerned there is a need for an environment conducive to thought. You can have the whole of the downstairs part of the villa, and the ground surrounding it as far as the fencing. Touch the fencing or the gates and you will be shot. Put a toe into the sea and you will be shot. Step onto the jetty and you will be shot. Venture upstairs unaccompanied and you will be shot. Does that seem reasonable?'

'Downright generous. I thank you. And if we lead you to the icon?'

'I will feel well disposed towards you.'

'You'll smile when you pull the trigger?'

'You're wasting time, Mr Blake. I suggest you get busy.' He shouted something into the interior of the house. There was a long exchange in Greek; I assumed that the characters within were being briefed.

I managed to stand up and walk unsteadily into the house. There was a big living room, air-conditioned cool after the blistering heat outside. Debbie came running in and almost knocked me over with a hug that sent shooting pains up my injured arm. And Zola, in a light summer dress, gave me a squeeze. 'What happened, Harry? Are you badly injured?'

'I got a bullet in the forearm. Lost a lot of blood, mainly, and ruined my shirt. The crazies abducted me from the hospital. What happened to you?'

'We ran into the trees but there were four of them.'

'And Dalton?'

'I have no idea. They say he's dead. There was a lot of shooting.'

Debbie's face was showing strain. 'They've told us what they want, Harry. And what will happen to us if we don't deliver.'

'We'd better get on with it.' At that moment all I wanted to do was crawl back into bed.

There was some splashing from the direction of the pool. Cassandra and Hondros had dived in. Hondros was swimming like a paddle steamer and Cassandra was floating face down. The wooden quay lay at the end of a descending path which passed the pool, and the motor boat was at the end of the quay. Cassandra's revolver was still on the poolside table.

It looked so easy.

'Forget it,' I said. 'There'll be some gorilla at the upstairs window.'

I walked to the poolside table, Debbie putting her arm in mine and keeping me steady. Zola picked up the sheets, frowned at the array of symbols. I was within arm's length of the gun. Debbie said, 'You're wrong, Harry. It's two gorillas.'

'How can we possibly hope to decipher this?' Zola wondered.

There was enough splashing that they wouldn't hear me, but still I spoke quietly. 'Your suspicions were right, Zola, I think it's the Babington cipher.'

'The what?' Debbie's eyes were full of misplaced faith in her Uncle Harry.

'It goes back to the failed plot against Elizabeth. Remember your history, Debbie? Mary Queen of Scots was up to her neck in it. The English Catholics believed that Mary was the true Queen of England and they had a point.'

'How come?'

'Elizabeth was the daughter of Anne Boleyn, but the English Catholics didn't recognise Henry VIII's marriage to her because they didn't recognise his divorce from Catherine of Aragon, because it hadn't been agreed by the Pope. That made Elizabeth illegitimate and not entitled to the throne. It's all quite logical.'

'I really don't care about stuff like that, Harry. All I want to do is stay alive.'

'Stuff like that could be vital to our survival. The plot was headed by a young man called Babington. The conspirators were all young, charming, naive Catholic gentlemen, and they all died horribly after the plot failed.'

'Just like Marmaduke StClair,' Zola said to me.

'Who's this Marmaduke?' asked Debbie.

'Never mind, there isn't time. The conspirators intended to bump off Queen Elizabeth, incite a rebellion and put Mary on the English throne. Babington needed Mary's approval and there was an exchange of smuggled letters between them. Coded letters, Debbie, in case her jailer discovered them. All this happened in 1586.'

'The Roanoke expedition was in 1585.'

'You're beginning to get it, Debbie. Babington pulled together his conspirators in March 1586, but he must have been thinking about it long before then. Marmaduke and the others went on ahead, so to speak, on the Roanoke expedition, so that when Elizabeth was assassinated they would announce that Mary's relic had been buried at seventy-seven degrees. The whole Catholic world could then claim North and South America and the new calendar. It would be a moral rout for the Continental Protestants.'

'And the code, the one that Babington used . . .'

'. . . would have been known to Marmaduke. That has to be where Ogilvie got it from.'

I waved at Hondros, and shouted, 'I need to make a phone call.'

We were set up in a few minutes. Cassandra, glistening wet, was standing over Debbie and pointing a gun at the back of her head. I had a cordless telephone on the table, and Hondros was smoking again. Zola was next to me, staring levelly at Cassandra and exuding pure hatred. I hoped she wasn't going to do anything impetuous.

First I got through to Directory Enquiries. It was three o'clock in the afternoon in Oxford, but I knew Fred had an easy schedule, and he was on the telephone within minutes.

'Fred? Harry here. I'm calling from Jamaica. Need to pick your brains again.'

'Jamaica? What villainy takes you to Jamaica, Harry?'

'You were right about Thomas Bright, Fred. And the journal has led me out to a second journal, also by Ogilvie, but written in a different cipher. I suspect it's the Babington one.'

'Babington? In Jamaica? What in— what's the story behind this?'

Cassandra pulled back the hammer of the revolver. It clicked loudly. Debbie began to shake.

'I'll tell you when I get back. Meantime, Fred, I need to know what the cipher alphabet was, or even if it was Babington at all.'

'Give me some of the symbols.'

'There are numerals like 2, 3, 4, 7, 8 and so on, the sign for infinity, the Greek capital delta, the Jewish Nabla, and lots of symbols that don't seem to belong to any alphabet, for example a double S like a Waffen-SS symbol.'

'Definitely Babington.'

'Fred, I need a favour. Can you scan in the Babington cipher and fire it through to my e-mail address in Lincoln? I'll pick it up from there. I need it urgently.'

'I don't know,' Fred said teasingly. 'It sounds like a two-pint favour.'

'I'll bring you back a case of Red Stripe.'

'It's a deal. You should have it within the hour.'

'Thanks, Fred.'

With eight of us in it, the upstairs bedroom was crowded. I sat at a corner desk with computer and printer, fired through to my own computer and pulled down a GIF file. The cipher was as I remembered it: a simple letter substitution for the most parts, with symbols replacing a few common words. With a few pages of encoded text it could probably have been cracked in an hour, even less if you were expert. I ran off several copies on the printer.

Hondros picked one up. His cigarette had burned down to his fingers and he dropped it on the wooden floor, grinding it with his foot. 'Well, ladies and gentlemen, now that we have the cipher, it seems we no longer need you.'

Cassandra said, 'I like the next bit.'

I felt myself freezing up with fear. Debbie's face had gone chalk-white and Zola was tight-lipped and alert as a cat. I seriously wondered if she was going to dive at Cassandra. But there were three other young men in the bedroom, all of them armed and all of them beyond reach.

Hondros said, 'But just in case of any complication . . . translate the remaining text.'

I said, 'I'll get busy on it.' It would buy us time. Beyond that, I didn't know. The thought of being dead in a few hours was just too hard to take in.

I went down to the pool table again, supported by Debbie. One of the young men tossed a notebook and pencil in front of me and swaggered off. Debbie and Zola sat on either side. In the living room, Cassandra and Hondros had started on the message. Cassandra was reading it out a symbol at a time and Hondros was looking each one up in the Babington cipher. They were excruciatingly slow.

'We have to do *something*,' Debbie whispered.

I looked around. Gunmen were strategically scattered around the grounds: one was standing at the jetty next to the boat, cigarette in mouth, eyeing us impassively through dark glasses; one was leaning on an upstairs railing, looking out over the sea; and one was stretched out on a deckchair at an upstairs balcony, a newspaper on his head to keep the harsh sun at bay. He was sipping a long drink and grinning down at us. I said, 'Let's beat these idiots with the translation.'

33

Having been abandoned in the New World by Sir Francis Drake, we found ourselves in a position of terrible danger. There were three of us, Marmaduke StClair, Simon Salter and myself. No sooner had the flags of St George disappeared into the storm than I urged we flee the island on the instant, before the savages were fully aware of what was happening. Otherwise we would be captured within hours. After the massacre of the week before, and with no fear of vengeance from the departed colonists, the fate they would deal us did not bear thinking about. I must admit that we all felt terror bordering on panic.

Marmaduke insisted on running back to his chest for what he called the relic. Simon and I too ran as fast as we could from hut to hut, gathering what scraps of food we could find. On the west of the island, after our bloody raid of the week before, Wingina's village was deserted. Unfortunately we were in full view of Wingina's mainland village, a league distant across the water. Rather than paddle away, since we would surely be seen and pursued, we each dragged a canoe back across the island. The hunting canoes were simply too big and heavy for this, and we each hauled a small dugout with a single-bladed paddle. Great fear gave us great strength. We prayed that news of the disembarkation had not yet reached the Indians and that they would not understand what we were doing.

In agonised fear of discovery, we hauled the canoes eight furlongs to Shallowbag Bay on the west of the island, and hastily filled them with the few provisions we had found. Some of the black slaves had miraculously reached the island a few chains to the north. How, I do not know. As we approached the western shore they saw what we were about and ran towards us, at great speed. Several of them splashed into the water behind us, and one, a strong swimmer, was able to reach Marmaduke's canoe and grab hold of it. He was a young man, of about my age. I hated Marmaduke when he raised his heavy wooden paddle and brought it down with force on the slave's skull, splitting it open, while at the same time not knowing what else he could have done. We left the man floating face down in the water, blood spreading from his head, and paddled away with all our strength.

We paddled for over a league down Roanoke island, with the Outer Banks protecting us from the big Atlantic waves. All this time we were in terror of Indian canoeists rounding the south of the island and intercepting us. But we reached the dangerous shallows of Port Ferdinando, where we crossed the Outer Banks into the ocean, this being the furthest gap from hostile Indians. We were swamped almost immediately. I used my outer jacket first as a scoop and then as a sponge. It would not be long before we capsized, and we were forced to turn back in towards the Banks, keeping as close to the shore as we dared, and in constant danger of capsizing in the stormy waves. But we had no thought in our minds other than to get away from that hellish place and its murderous inhabitants, and we paddled as if all the devils of hell were pursuing us.

After an hour we approached Croatoan island. Suddenly we were met by a hail of arrows from the trees and were forced out into the dangerous waves.

And then the thing that we feared happened. As we passed the island, a dozen canoes appeared, threatening to cut us off from our southward flight. To turn back would be fatal, for we would surely be trapped between two groups of savages. To go out into the sea would be to drown as the big waves swamped us. We paddled furiously on as the Indians tried to intercept us. The distance between us closed rapidly. They were making strange, high-pitched cries.

We passed them, Marmaduke and Simon in front, while I trailed about twenty yards behind. I did not dare to turn, even for a second, but I heard the splashing and the whoops at my back. I paddled with all my might but my companions were slowly drawing ahead of me, and I could hear the savages gaining. They were maybe fifty yards to my rear. I was almost sobbing with exertion but it was making no difference. Slowly, they were catching up.

And then Simon Salter did an extraordinary thing. He glanced behind, bawled encouragement at me, and then seeing I could do no more, turned his canoe completely around and drove it towards the savages. His face was contorted with rage and fear. As he passed I shouted, 'Sir, no!' but he cut me off with a roar: 'Get out of it, Scotch!'

The whooping redoubled. Marmaduke glanced back and then carried on paddling as if possessed by a demon. I dared a glance and saw Simon surrounded by screaming savages in their canoes, paddles rising and falling like cudgels, his own landing hard on a neck. But then I turned to the business of fleeing and saw no more.

A mile further south Marmaduke and I began to risk backward looks. There were no signs of pursuit. The coastline was now unfamiliar. We were utterly exhausted and at the same time too terrified to stop. After another hour of paddling we pulled over onto the Banks and lay on the sand, not caring about the rain or cold, just worn out by fatigue and fearful that the savages, having dealt with Mr Salter, might turn their attention to us. My knees were raw and bleeding from kneeling in the canoe, but I was alive.

We hauled the canoes across the Banks into the calmer water between Banks and mainland, and continued to paddle south. Here the mainland was swamp and we saw no signs of habitation. Presently thirst and hunger began to nibble at us, but we were still too fearful of the Indians to wish to land. Finally, with the wind easing but the rain still falling heavily, and with darkness approaching, we crossed to one of the few sheltered coves we had seen. I was almost senseless with tiredness, and yet we slept little. I wept awhile.

The following morning, we found that the canoes had acquired an inch of rainwater. We were also highly alarmed to discover the footprints of savages in the sand. We gorged ourselves on the water and then risked a short trip inland. We soon found a small freshwater lake and gorged ourselves some more. The lake was rich with fish but we caught none. We then found driftwood which we used to build makeshift seats for the canoes, saving our raw knees. We took more flattish pieces of driftwood aboard to use as scoops and then carried on south, tantalising our hungry bellies with a few pieces of sodden bread which Simon had tossed into my canoe at Roanoke. By the end of that day the storm had passed, our food was finished and we were again thirsty and freezing. The sea salt drying on our skins was forming white cakes around our eyes, ears and hands, making paddling quite painful. Again, we slept on the Banks, shivering with cold. But our fear of pursuit had almost gone.

Marmaduke and I awakened the following morning. Both the relic and my journal were still with us, each of us having slept with our treasure next to our chests. We ventured inland again, found another freshwater lake, and this time were able to catch some fish with ingenuity and stones to make a small dam. We ate them raw, head, bones and all. They tasted excellent.

I will not detail our canoe voyage south. It lasted forty days, which I counted by marking little notches on the rim of my canoe with the help of my ballockknife. There was time for me to ponder on why Mr Salter, whom I saw as a cruel and ignorant man, having no love for me or anyone else, should have sacrificed his life for mine. It is a question I have pondered many times in the years since, but to which I have found no satisfactory answer. I can only say that, if there is a heaven, I am confident Mr Salter is there. Indeed, the populations of heaven and hell surely contain many surprises.

As we moved south, the weather became warmer and the sea grew calmer. Our skins first peeled, and then became dark brown, in the heat and glare of the sun. We made good progress in the gentle sea and found we could survive by raiding the coastal lands. From time to time we would see savages. Whenever this happened we would hasten back to our canoes and paddle away quickly. We always lived with our wits about us and our eyes wide open.

It was on the forty-first day that we were captured by the Spanish. I was awakened by a boot kicking heavily at my ribs. We were surrounded by about half a dozen soldiers. There was a longboat and a great ship, I believe a galleon, half a mile offshore. An officer started to question me roughly in Spanish, of which I understood not a word, a fact which caused him to slap me after each question. I thought it wise to keep my ballockknife in its place.

Marmaduke then astonished me by speaking to the officer in fluent Spanish. He drew the officer aside and spoke to him quietly for ten minutes or so. The officer's arrogance gave way to astonishment. He marched over to the relic, took it away from the other soldiers and opened the silk cloth carefully, making sure no one could see what was inside. When he approached me again, his attitude was entirely different. We were ushered onto the longboat and taken out to the deep-rolling waves and the ship. Marmaduke held the relic in his lap, and my journal was hidden next to my chest. At the time I did not know how much had survived the soakings and drenchings of the past six weeks.

The deck of the ship was crowded with soldiers, much as was the Tiger. We were ushered down a hatch and into a small cabin, into the presence of the captain. Again, Marmaduke spoke with great fluency in Spanish, and again the initially hostile attitude of the Spaniard gave way to astonishment and then respect.

That evening, we dined with the captain and his officers. There was a great deal of wine and hilarity and jovial conversation, much of it centred around Marmaduke. For me, not understanding a word, the joy was in the silk shirts and breeches I had been given, and the soft cushioned seat, and the hogsmeat, and the boiled rice, and the silver cutlery and goblets, and the beer, which I drank to glorious excess, and the fact of being served rather than a servant.

And that night, lying on a glorious bunk, feeling again the rhythmic sway of a ship, listening to its hundred creaks and groans, Marmaduke, drunk with wine and excitement, talked too much.

That the Roanoke expedition had a secret purpose I had long known. But now that purpose was made clear to me. By establishing a Protestant colony in the New World, at precisely seventy-seven degrees longitude west, Queen Elizabeth would have been able to announce a new calendar, devised by her astronomer John Dee, the prime meridian of which passed through the colony.

This new calendar was greatly superior to the Gregorian one then being introduced by Rome. It would cycle through 33 years, pacing the life of Jesus so that a man would know he had been born in, say, the fourth year of our Lord. Easter, that most sacred of days, would follow closely the biblical prescription, and it would match the passing seasons with great precision. The prestige of Elizabeth would be enhanced amongst her Protestant neighbours, and as the advantage of the new calendar became apparent it would be adopted by more and more nations, to the humiliation of the Pope and the embarrassment of Spain, stuck with an inferior calendar.

The colony, therefore, had to be made to fail. Marmaduke, Rowse and Kendrick were the spies in its midst, assigned this task. Kendrick was the poisoner, and Rowse fired the shots which killed the soldiers. Marmaduke brought with him the True Cross, which had been in his family since the Crusades. There was therefore a Catholic plot within the Protestant one, but there was even more to it than that. A relic from Christ, kissed by a monarch, confirmed that monarch's divine right to rule. The relic had been so kissed. But it had been kissed, not by Queen Elizabeth, but by Mary Queen of Scots. Buried at seventy-seven degrees west, it would confer her divine right to rule the New World in anticipation of overthrowing Elizabeth.

That Marmaduke was a Catholic we all knew. But that he was part of a plot to overthrow Queen Elizabeth and put her cousin Mary, Queen of Scots, on the throne, took my breath away. I wonder that he told me this even in his drunken state. But the reason was soon clear. To save my life, he had had to introduce me as his assistant in the enterprise. Otherwise, as a Protestant, I could expect nothing more than the *auto-da-fe*. My security lay in my acquiescence, and I had to know the plot should I be questioned about it. As indeed I was, later, by Dominican monks.

The ship is headed for Jamaica, Marmaduke told me. There we will stay until the Protestant Queen has been overthrown and the true faith has been restored to England. The Spaniards do not know the full story, he added. I have told them only that we were destroying the Protestant expedition from within. Mendoza, the architect of the plot, knows my story and will confirm my part in it by letter from Spain.

And the True Cross? What will happen to it?

They have been told that the thing I carry is a family heirloom. They do not know that it is part of the True Cross. Better that they never know. It will stay with me on the island.

And so, patient reader, this old man has come to the end of his testament. As the world knows, the plot against Elizabeth failed. The Queen of Scots was executed. Walsingham's torturers extracted the names of the plotters. Marmaduke's was never mentioned in public, but that might have been a ruse to entice him back to England. He was never able to leave the island of Jamaica.

In due course, after many adventures, I sailed to Spain. I travelled by wagon overland through France to Calais, and crossed to Dover in a fishing boat. Having by then some money, I purchased a horse and made my way back to my native Tweedsmuir.

The valley in which I had grown up, and which had filled my young world, now seemed to me small and insignificant. Much had happened in it. My mother had died of a fever and my wretched stepfather, I am glad to say, had drunk himself to death. My beloved brother Angus was now a prosperous farmer, married to Jean, the smiddy's youngest daughter. I found that I was now an uncle. Dominie Dinwoodie, now quite white-haired, welcomed me as a long-lost son, and he and I spent many an evening exchanging stories.

Fiona had grown into a beautiful young woman, as yet un-married. I asked her to become my wife and to come out to Jamaica with me, where, I explained, I too was becoming a prosperous farmer, on fertile land abandoned by the Spaniards. To my joy she agreed, and we took the long trip back through France and then Spain and across the wide Atlantic Ocean. In the course of our lives we have crossed that ocean more than once to Scotland, but only to stay a short while. Our true roots are now here in Jamaica. And here we shall stay, with our three children, until we die.

Stewardship of the True Cross was given to me by Marmaduke StClair as he lay dying, in trust for his family. And here, at last, for Marmaduke's family only to understand, is where it is hidden.

34

I, James Ogilvie, son of William Ogilvie, shepherd and farmer of Tweedsmuir, leave this document as my final testament.

In accordance with the instructions of my friend Marmaduke StClair I record herein the location of the True Cross of our Saviour Jesus Christ. It will serve as a reminder to his children and their children, who will be tutored in the meaning of what follows and who may pass on its hidden meaning to later generations of their family. And to ensure that the Cross remains in the hands of the StClair family and none other, I write only this:

THE BOOKKEEPER
THE STAR OF THE WHEELS OF TIME
THE POLYGON

May God grant you peace. These are my last words.
James Ogilvie

'Oh thank God.' Relief flowed out of Zola.

Debbie, still pale-faced, was looking bewildered. I explained, 'It buys us more time, Debbie. They'll have to keep us alive until we solve Ogilvie's conundrum.'

'But can you solve it? What does it mean?'

I stared at Ogilvie's clues. *Polygon.* A young man, fond of geometry. *Stars.* Taught the art of celestial navigation by one of the leading men of the age. But *Wheels of time? Bookkeeper?*

I shook my head. 'I've no idea. But no way will the crazies be able to crack this. We have a definite bargaining counter.'

Zola said, 'I doubt that, Harry. As soon as we tell them what it means, they'll get rid of us. Sorry, Debbie.'

'I have to agree they'll bump us off. But they won't do that until they have the icon safely in their hands. Between then and now we have to find some way to escape.'

'And get to the icon before them,' said Debbie. I looked at her in astonishment: with practically no chance of survival, she was still determined to retrieve the family heirloom.

'Come on, Harry. Our lives depend on this.' Zola was running her fingers over Ogilvie's message, her eyes intense.

I shook my head again.

Debbie astonished me some more. 'Why don't you work on the code, Harry, while Zola and I think of some way out of here?'

Zola said, 'Did you see the keyring on the dressing-room table? It said something about the Royal Yacht Club.'

'Be realistic, Zola. You'll be shot if you go upstairs. There's a gorilla on the jetty, two looking at us from upstairs, and one more out of sight. Presumably he's round the back somewhere. Not to mention Cassandra and Hondros.'

'You have a better idea?'

'I can hardly walk, let alone run. I can't get away from here. I'll make it a condition of handing over the decode that the pair of you walk out the door.'

'Be realistic, Harry. As soon as you admit to decoding the message they'll use pain to lever it out of you. If not on you, then on us. And then they'll kill all three of us anyway.'

Zola had a point. I didn't want to think what they could do to Debbie.

'I don't want to die,' Debbie whispered, fear in her dark eyes.

And now Hondros was approaching. His face was grim.

'Bookkeeper? The star of the wheels of time? The polygon? What does it mean, Blake?' His voice was trembling.

I shrugged. The casual gesture infuriated him.

He spread his fingers on the table, over Ogilvie's message, and his eyes bulged with anger. 'And will I be stopped at this stage? Seventeen centuries after the thieves took it from us? By some shepherd boy's fondness for puzzles? Find the meaning, Blake, and find it quickly. I will give you until midnight tonight.'

'That's absurd—'

'And then the velvet gloves will be put away, and we will start on your friend Debbie, and you will hear her screams while you work on the problem, and we will continue on her either until she is dead or you have given us the solution. Understood?'

I looked at him bleakly and nodded. I understood.

35

The bookkeeper; the star of the wheels of time; the polygon.

At first, when I'd wandered around the Lego house, I'd sensed eyes viewing me with suspicion from all directions. But by now I had done it so often, head bowed in thought, that the gunmen were becoming blasé. I wondered if I could exploit the fact in some way, but couldn't see how. I could hardly walk and the circuit soon exhausted me. There were four of them, one standing at the jetty, one at the rear gate, and two who seemed to wander at will, sometimes disappearing into the house, or leaning out over one of the upstairs balconies, or sometimes sprawling on poolside chairs. They were never without their ugly black revolvers. I couldn't see any way out.

There was about an acre of ground around the villa, enclosed in a fence about nine feet tall. There were two cars at the side of the house, one of them the battle-scarred Toyota we had hired, the other a black Chrysler jeep: it seemed they'd had no trouble replacing the one I'd sent tumbling down the Blue Mountains. A single rough track led through a heavy wrought iron gate up a hillside and over the summit a few hundred yards away. In the early afternoon I'd seen a white cruise ship far out at sea, heading no doubt to St Lucia, Grenada and points beyond, Jamaica having been 'done' that morning. At no point was I out of sight of one or more of the guards.

I went back into the living room and flopped on a couch, letting the cool breeze from the air conditioner flow over me. Cassandra, in dark glasses and red bikini, was reading a paperback at the poolside. Now and then she would put the book down and spread suntan lotion on her arms and legs. Hondros spent half his time on a mobile phone: it seemed he had left the task of decipherment to us. Zola and Debbie were nowhere to be seen, but then it was a big house.

Something in the back of my mind, trying to get out. Something about Ogilvie, and stars, and calendars. I stood up, closed my eyes, tried hard to think. I needed that bargaining point.

Who needed a bookkeeper in 17th-century Jamaica?

Debbie came sailing through. 'There's a cold drink in the kitchen, Harry.'

Spoken casually. I got the message. Zola was sitting on a work surface, tapping her heels on a cupboard door. There was no one around but still she spoke in a hushed voice. 'There's a fuse box outside. I think it needs an Allen key to get into it, but we might manage to open it with a nail file. If we could maybe fuse the house after dark.'

'It won't fly. We'd need to get away either by car or boat, and for that we need keys. They're upstairs on the dressing-room table, along with Debbie's mobile phone. Can you imagine running upstairs with the key, running back down and outside, fiddling with the key for the gate, starting the car and driving out, with these armed thugs running around looking for us? Anyway, there's always at least one of them upstairs.'

'Do you have a better idea?' Zola asked coldly.

'Yes. I crack Ogilvie's code and use it as a bargaining counter.'

'We've been through that, Harry. They'll torture it out of you, or put a gun to Debbie's head, or mine.'

'It's ten past four. They're going to shoot me at midnight if we haven't cracked the code,' Debbie reminded me. She was trying for a matter-of-fact tone but desperation was edging into her voice. 'How are you getting on with that, Harry?'

'Yes, Harry, how are you getting on with that?' Hondros was standing at the open door, a mobile phone in one hand and the inevitable gun in the other. His hairy stomach was overlapping the belt of his red swimming shorts.

I wanted to say something defiant, throw some insult at him. Instead I said, 'I have some embryonic thoughts. Ogilvie's information is pretty minimal.'

'Naturally. It was designed to be impenetrable to anyone outside his little family circle.' He looked down at his revolver and gave the barrel a spin. 'Share those embryonic thoughts, Blake.'

I said, 'Where in Jamaica, in Ogilvie's day, was there a need for a bookkeeper? Jamaica in Ogilvie's day was just a trading post. Passing ships would pick up food and water. That had to be recorded, and that's where a bookkeeper would come into the equation. By the time Ogilvie reached Jamaica the Spaniards had abandoned New Seville to the north and moved their administrative capital to Spanish Town. They were using the harbour at Port Royal. Wherever the icon is buried, it has to be somewhere in that area, on the south coast. That's as far as I've got so far.'

Hondros gave a thoughtful nod. 'Very good, Blake.' Then he pointed the gun at Debbie's head, holding it at arm's-length and squinting along the barrel.

There was an awful stillness.

Hondros had an expression like a hanging judge. 'But what I want is the True Cross, not embryonic thoughts. You have seven hours and fifty minutes remaining to deliver it.' Then he padded out of the kitchen in his bare feet as quietly as he had entered, leaving a trail of water. Zola wrapped her arms around Debbie. Debbie wasn't making a sound, but her shoulders were shuddering.

'He actually bought that rubbish, Harry.' Zola was patting Debbie's back as if she was a child.

'It's not Port Royal?' Debbie's voice was muffled. She was hiding her face in Zola's chest and her arms were around Zola's neck.

'No chance,' I said. 'The StClair family's property was on St Ann's, on the north coast of the island. Remember what Ogilvie said? That he developed land which the Spanish had abandoned?'

Zola was still patting. 'And the earliest plantation on the island was Sevilla la Nueva, on the north coast. They'd abandoned it by the time of Roanoke.'

Debbie disengaged herself from Zola's embrace. 'On the north of the island?'

I nodded. 'Just west of Ocho Rios. And a plantation would need a bookkeeper. The starting point for the search isn't the south of the island, Debbie, it's the north. You go along with that, Zola?'

'Absolutely what I've been thinking. Sevilla la Nueva, not Port Royal.'

Debbie patted moisture from her eyes with her sweater. 'You're going to give the crazies a false trail?'

'We're going to screw them up totally. We'll head off north while they head south.'

'That means we're going to escape? Do you have a plan, Harry?'

'That's your job.' I hated saying that, hated seeing the hope go out of her eyes. 'The star of the wheels of time,' I said to nobody.

'Something to do with the Nothing Days?' Zola wondered. 'The *Nemontemi*?'

I said, 'It's not my field, but I don't think a star was connected with them. My guess is he's talking about the big wheel, the fifty-two-year cycle.'

'Would you people stop talking gibberish? What are these wheels of time?' Debbie demanded.

I said, 'The Mayan and Aztec civilisations were obsessed with calendars and the passage of time. It dominated their lives for centuries—'

Debbie interrupted impatiently. 'So what? I'm sorry but I keep thinking about torture starting at midnight and my brains getting blown out, and what are you doing about it? All you do is talk about Aztecs and wheels of time. Even I know the Aztecs came from Mexico, not Jamaica. And they didn't have wheels.'

Zola said, 'But the Arawak natives must have come from Central America.'

'Zola isn't getting it quite right, Debbie. The native Jamaicans were Taino, not Arawak, but who cares? Whoever jumped into canoes and paddled to Jamaica brought their culture with them, a culture which was obsessed with measuring time. It would have been irresistible for Ogilvie to use their calendars in his coded message. Calendars were what the expedition was about.'

Zola had to have the last word. 'Stop splitting hairs, Harry. The Taino family included the Aztecs. But there's a problem with what we're both thinking – the Spaniards had worked them to death by the time Ogilvie arrived.'

'There must have been a few of them around,' I said. I needed the last word, too.

'Will you two stop squabbling? Where is this getting us?' The despair in Debbie's voice was deepening.

'This could save your life, Debbie,' I said. 'The Aztecs used two calendar systems. The first was a three-hundred-and-sixty-five-day cycle, divided up into eighteen months of twenty days each, with five days left over. These were the Nothing Days, the *Nemontemi*. During those five days there was no fire, no food and no sex. But they had a second calendar, a sacred one of two hundred and sixty days, made up of thirteen months with twenty days in each. So after three hundred and sixty-five days you're back to the beginning of the first calendar, and after two hundred and sixty days you're back to the beginning of the second one. And after fifty-two years you're back to the beginning of both of them together. Two big wheels with time marked on them.' I was trying to illustrate by rotating my hands like gear wheels, but without much success. 'But listen. Because the three hundred and sixty-five days isn't exactly the length of the year – it's about six hours out – it turns out that at the end of the fifty-two-year cycle the two calendars have slipped twelve days against the seasons.'

'Okay, Harry, but so what? How is this going to keep me alive?'

'Because to keep the calendar in time at the end of the fifty-two years they stopped counting for twelve days, during which they had a great ceremony, a long procession to the Hill of the Star, and the midnight sacrifice of a prisoner. He was stretched out, his heart cut out and a fire kindled in its place. And this is where it all comes together, Debbie. The ritual took place when a sacred star reached the overhead point at midnight. That's the solution to Ogilvie's second puzzle. He's referring to the sacred star, the star of the wheels of time.'

'Otherwise known as the Star of the Fire-Making,' Zola said. 'I expect this is on the Aztec Calendar Stone, described by Humboldt in 1810.'

'No, that gives the world ages through time. More likely it's in de Landa's 1566 book.'

'I thought that was lost, Harry.'

238

'It was for three hundred years, but then it was rediscovered in Madrid. Surely you knew that.'

'Stop it!' Debbie's fists were clenched with frustration. 'This is life or death. What was this star?'

'Aldebaran. The Eye of the Bull. A bright red star in Taurus.'

Zola paced up and down for some moments. Then she blew out her cheeks. 'We could be on to something. Find something to do with a bookkeeper on the old Spanish plantation, and draw a line towards the rising point of Aldebaran.'

My wounded arm was pulsing. 'As far as the nearest polygon, whatever that turns out to be. And there, at the polygon or maybe buried under it, you'll find the icon.' I turned to Debbie. 'I think we've done it.'

Debbie said, 'Well that's just terrific, that's really wow. Okay, now you two giant brains have solved that one, finding a way out of here should be easy.'

36

I did a few more orbits of the villa, my head bowed as if I was deep in thought, while looking around casually from time to time. The sun was a big pink oval touching the horizon, going down in a glory of crimsons and yellows and streaks of black. I was finding it hard to take in that this could be my last sunset.

The pattern was clear: a man at the jetty, a man at the back gate – Kojak, as it happened – and two upstairs. All young, Greek-looking men, all with instructions to leave us alone. Not an inch of boundary fence out of their sight. And yet they had to eat and they had to relieve themselves and they had to drink: in this heat, they had to drink a lot.

It wasn't long before the sun began to disappear and the insects in the hills around us began their imitation of squeaky fans. As the sky darkened, Cassandra and Hondros appeared, elegantly dressed as if for an evening out. Cassandra had a long, slim pink dress, a cocktail handbag and a clutter of gold jewellery. Hondros was dressed in black trousers and a black silk shirt, with the swastika cross around his neck and his thinning hair sleeked back. Hondros ignored me, Cassandra gave me a sultry sideways glance. They climbed into the four-wheel Chrysler, stopped at the gate. Kojak opened it and I watched the red lights disappear up the hill. One or two stars were beginning to come out, and I reckoned it was about five hours to midnight.

There was a faint clunk from an outhouse, and the grounds, the swimming pool, the jacuzzi, the fence and the villa were suddenly flooded with light, like a car park in a shopping mall.

I still couldn't see a way out of this, and my perambulation was exhausting me.

On my next orbit the kitchen light was switched on and I saw Debbie busy at the sink. After a while the smell of cooking began to drift out. Zola appeared. 'Harry, do you want to eat?'

I didn't, but there was something in her voice. I made my way round the side of the house to the French windows.

'What about you?' she asked curtly, looking at Kojak.

The man took his gun out of the waistband of his jeans and waved Zola and me towards the house with a sweep of his arm. He shouted something to his colleague on the balcony.

On a long kitchen table, places had been set for seven, presumably the three of us and our four guardian gorillas. Candles had been lit, which I thought was overdoing the hospitality to people who would shortly be firing bullets into our bodies. The two hoodlums had come down from upstairs; the man at the jetty had not yet appeared.

The kitchen was sweatily hot. Debbie was peeling potatoes in a basin of water at the kitchen sink. Zola slid a heavy frying pan on to an electric cooker. She glanced at me over her shoulder and said, 'Just like my Greenwich flat, Harry.' It was a second before I connected her comment with the frying pan.

'Debbie and you are cooking something special,' I said. My heart was starting to hammer in my chest.

'Right on.' *Something special.*

'I think we're close to solving the problem,' Debbie said to the young man standing behind her.

'Ya,' he said, showing no interest whatever. He was standing back from her, running his eyes openly up and down her body.

That was the problem. None of them were within arm's length, and all of them had guns in their hands. I couldn't see how the ladies were going to solve that one.

Zola agreed. 'Yes, I think we've got it worked out. Harry, do you want to cut some bread? We need to make Melba toast.'

There was a bread box on a kitchen unit and I went over to it, exaggerating my weary state. Kojak stepped back; he was eyeing me carefully. I looked around for a breadknife, found one in a drawer. 'Are you sure you're up to this, Harry?' Zola asked, and at last I began to see what she meant.

'Definitely.' Army conditioning was kicking in.

'There's too much going on here,' Debbie said. She was coating fillets of fish with batter and piling them up on a plate. Zola bustled over and took the plate over to the cooker, brushing aside one of the gorillas.

And at last I see the whole pattern. Zola with frying pan; me with breadknife; Debbie, I'm convinced, about to ask for help. Sure enough, she turns to the man behind her, manages a honeyed smile. 'Peel the potatoes. I'm saving my nails.' He puts his gun into his waistband. Debbie moves towards me, takes a couple of slices of bread. Our eyes meet, the barest glance.

I'm cutting more and more bread. My knuckles are white with the strength of my grip on the knife, and my wounded arm is aching with the tension. It has to happen in the next few seconds or I'll have no more bread and no more excuse to hold the knife.

Debbie puts the bread into the toaster, a big, hideous yellow thing near the kitchen sink. The man is next to her, up to his wrists in water.

Zola suddenly gripping the heavy frying pan with two hands.

Debbie picking up the toaster.

Zola's frying pan swinging through the air, a vicious two-handed swipe, oil and slices of fish spiralling out, and my breadknife thrusting towards Kojak's bladder with as much force as I can give it, Dominie Dinwoodie's voice inside my head: 'There is no defence against a thrust upwards, like so.'

All this in slow motion.

Debbie swipes the toaster into the sink. There is a buzz like an angry bee; the lights flicker and dim. My man is buckling towards the floor, his mouth opening wide with the sudden pain and fear. Zola's frying pan is making hard, fast contact with her man's face. Debbie's man is arching backwards, his eyes threatening to shoot out of their sockets and his short, black hair standing on end. And then the lights fail completely and I see the reason for the candles on the dinner table.

Debbie leaps over the quivering body of her man. I start to run after her but Zola is shouting, 'No, not that way. Round the back!' Pointing to a door behind me. I run through a short, dark pantry, its shelves stacked with tins and sacks. Zola is behind me and then we are out, into the hot night air and the noisy insects and the star-filled sky.

The man on the jetty is shouting. He is out of sight. He shouts again, closer this time. Debbie appears between Zola and me, breathing hard. I hear the slight jangling of keys in her hand, hope the sound hasn't travelled.

The Toyota is at the end of the house in full view of the jetty man. Zola peers round the corner and raises a hand in the near-dark to stop us. We wait in agony. The sound of Kojak moaning comes from the back door. It must be Kojak: the other two are unconscious or dead.

Then Zola is frantically flapping her arm, waving us forwards. Bent double – I don't know why – we sprint towards the car. Debbie takes the wheel, turns the ignition and slams it into gear while Zola and I are still jumping in. 'Where's the bloody headlight switch?' she shouts.

'Keep them off! The gates are open,' I shout back. We can just make out the tall gate pillars in the dim light and Debbie aims the car between them, engine and tyres screaming. The track is a ribbon of light dust.

'He's out!' Zola shouts from the back seat.

I look back: yellow flashes are coming from the side of the white villa, but we are already far up on the hill, the car hammering into potholes every few seconds. Beyond the Lego house there is a cruise liner far out at sea, lit up as if it was Christmas. And then we are over the top of the hill, the track broadens, Debbie has found the headlight switch and she is swerving the car like a stunt driver, trying to avoid the black potholes. Then in a few hundred yards the track is passing through trees and there is a tarmac road, and Debbie turns right and puts her foot down, and Zola is laughing like a thing demented, and my gunshot wound is giving me hell, and I think about electrocution and stabbing and braining, and a line from a Jane Austen book jumps into my head, something about ladies being delicate plants indeed.

37

'Stop!'

Debbie pulled over at a row of stalls on the edge of Orocabessa and Zola ran into Harvey's Hardware Bazaar. The owner ambled round from the side of the hut. Zola emerged some minutes later with three torches, an armful of spades, a pickaxe and, bizarrely, a calculator. The road didn't need much navigating as it skirted the sea nearly all the way. Once I suggested we turn off to avoid a long peninsula and we ended up lost, following a lorry without lights for twenty minutes while Debbie fumed and Zola fired off a lot of sarcasm about a map dealer who couldn't read maps.

But at last we were back on the coast road and Debbie took the car up to an alarming speed, weaving around potholes and using the horn on stray cattle and goats.

Zola said, 'I need someone to hold the torch.' I clambered into the back seat and lit up her page. She was drawing little spheres with triangles on them, and writing out an equation. I recognised sines and cosines from my schooldays. 'Spherical triangles,' she said. 'Essential to celestial navigators. You recognise the cosine formula, don't you, Harry? I thought not. Let's hope my calculations are better than your navigation.' She drew another celestial sphere and wrote down some numbers. The bumpy ride made them look as if they had been written by a drunk. 'The sun's in Taurus at the end of May.' Then she started jabbing at the calculator. 'Good. Which puts Aldebaran between fifteen and twenty degrees north. Say, declination eighteen degrees. I don't suppose you know the latitude of Jamaica?'

'Eighteen degrees north,' I told her. 'Surely you knew that, the great navigator?'

More numbers. Then, 'Got it. At this latitude Aldebaran rises about seventy degrees east of north.' She looked out at the dark countryside. 'Where are we?'

Debbie said, 'Coming up to Ochi.' Her voice was strained. 'Pothole— too late.' There was a jarring thump.

'Okay,' I said. 'If Zola's sums are right, we find this Spanish plantation, look for something to do with a bookkeeper and see what lies along a line of sight at seventy degrees azimuth. If there's a polygon, we'll find your icon.'

A single red light emerged from the dark. Debbie braked and fell in impatiently behind a cement truck, water trickling from it. 'This is like something out of a pirate story. X marks the spot. We really are looking for buried treasure in Jamaica.'

'On the nail. But so is the competition.'

She said, 'Bugger this,' pulled out, put her foot down, pressed the horn and flashed the headlights, scraping past with a few inches to spare. Within the hour we were hurtling through Ocho Rios, past the Jerk Chicken Center, past another illuminated cruise ship, past the resorts and restaurants and along the same coast road which Stormin' Norman had sped us along three days ago in the opposite direction.

I said, 'Seven or eight minutes at this speed.'

Five minutes on I leaned over Debbie's shoulder. 'Slow down.' Then in the headlights there was a notice: Nueva Sevilla. Debbie slowed to a crawl and turned left.

I said, 'Switch off your lights.' A half moon gave us enough light to see a narrow, gently climbing road. It wound up towards a long, low white building, softly lit up by spotlights.

'The Great House,' Zola suggested. 'Every plantation had one.'

A track led off to the left from the road. Debbie trundled the car a few yards along it and stopped. We sat quietly, looking around. Zola said, 'Nobody.'

'I wouldn't expect anybody. They were depending on us to solve Ogilvie.' I said it cautiously.

'Anyway, you steered them to the Port Royal, didn't you?' Debbie's nervousness was reflected in her voice.

'So how come we're all strung up like violin strings?' Zola asked.

I said, 'Debbie, why don't you clear off awhile? Zola and I can meet you somewhere on the main road.'

'Are you kidding, Harry?'

Low, ruined buildings were scattered over the plantation as far as the skyline about half a mile away. We stepped out, closing the car doors quietly. I thought, *there's no logic to all this quiet stealth.*

Debbie was looking over the parapet of the bridge. I could hear water gurgling. 'What are we looking for, Harry?'

'Anything to do with a bookkeeper.'

'A bookkeeper? Where the hell do we find a bookkeeper here?'

'Whatever, let's be quick about it.'

We split up, our torchlights spreading over the open ground as we dispersed. I was getting close to the Great House and beginning to worry about security guards when there was a restrained shout from down the hill. Debbie, in an excited state. 'Over here! I found it!'

And there it was, with a notice to say so:

THE BOOKKEEPER'S HOUSE

Constructed using the Spanish walling technique. The bookkeeper was the work supervisor. On large estates such as Seville, there were usually two overseers; one to supervise field operations and the other to oversee the factory work.

Zola ran up and hissed, 'Yes! Yes!'

I saw that the sea horizon was visible from our elevated position. The sky was sprinkled with stars and the Milky Way arched overhead. It was easy to see that Aldebaran, a brilliant red star, would have been a natural marker for Ogilvie.

'Is that the pole star?' Debbie was pointing at Arcturus.

'No. There's the Great Bear and there are the pointers. That's Polaris.' It was low in the sky, over the sea. I stretched my arm out. 'And this is seventy degrees azimuth.'

But Debbie trotted smartly over the grass and jumped over a low wall. My heart was thumping in my chest. We really were looking for buried treasure. It seemed unreal.

The directions took us back to the path onto which Debbie had turned the car. The track crossed a bridge and there it was:

THE NUEVA SEVILLA SPANISH CHURCH
1524–1534

In 1524 construction began at Nueva Sevilla, of a stone church on the orders of the Spanish Abbott Peter Martyr . . . Hans Sloane saw the church in 1688 and described it: 'the church had three naves with rows of pillars and a very fine west gate'. The Gothic style church also had buttresses. The chapel was polygon in shape. Several fragments of carved work in stone, such as mouldings, festoons, cherubs have been found . . .

'This is it, isn't it, Harry?' Debbie was whispering. Not thirty yards away was a small row of houses, lights showing through curtains.

'A polygon.'

Zola whispered, 'And I'll bet the icon's buried plumb in its centre.'

'Maybe the relic's long gone. Maybe some workmen dug it up centuries ago.'

Debbie, next to me, said, 'Oh, Harry. Not after all this.'

We crept quietly round the side of the ruin. The night screeching of the insects had started. Zola shone her torch into a door gap and said, 'Hey!'

An archaeological dig. All the paraphernalia was there: the tarpaulin, the terraced earth, the buckets, the trowels, the string marking off neat rectangular grids. We stared, baffled, our torch beams searching every corner. My head was whirling.

'Weh yuh ah luk fah, sah?'

Debbie gave a little scream and I nearly jumped out of my skin. A boy of about fourteen was standing behind us, holding a jamjar of water with big transparent shrimps swimming inside it.

'You gave me a fright,' Debbie said. It was an understatement.

Zola said, 'Have the archaeologists been here long?'

'Mi granpa wi no bout dat. Cum yah so.'

We followed the boy along the track. There was an isolated house in a field, with a porch and a corrugated iron roof. He opened the door and waved us in. 'Weh Grampa?'

There was a fit of coughing from the back of the house and an elderly man with walking stick appeared. He said something

247

incomprehensible, but waved us in welcomingly. The boy went ahead and disappeared in the direction of a cooking smell from the back of the house.

The living room was small and lit by a single naked bulb hanging from the low ceiling. A television took up one corner and there were a few boxes with cushions and a single armchair. There was a sideboard with family photographs and a couple of candles. On the wall above the sideboard was a mirror. To the left of the mirror, sellotaped on the wall, was a picture of Haile Selassie cut from a magazine, and to the right, hanging on nails, was the True Cross.

There was a raised female voice from the kitchen: 'Yu too damn likky likky cum out a di kitchen. Go ketch sum wauta.'

The silver frame of the medieval description was gone. There were holes where, presumably, precious stones had once been. The three parts of the triptych were still together, however. On the two outer parts, faded but still recognisable, were two paintings. On the left was a mother and child. She had the enlarged eyes, elongated face and thin pointed chin of the Byzantium artists. The right-hand panel depicted Christ on the Cross. The centre part was plain. Recessed into its wood was another piece of wood, a rectangle about six inches by twelve. It was old and gnarled, like a piece of driftwood. Or like a piece of wood two thousand years old.

Apart from the missing silver and jewels, it was just as Ogilvie had described it.

The old man reacted to our stunned faces as if he had been struck. 'Dat neva cum from di dig,' he said in an outraged, defensive tone. 'Hi inna di family fi ah long time.'

Debbie said, 'I'd like to buy it from you.'

'Ow much?'

'A hundred US dollars.'

'As far back as mi gran puppa,' he said. And probably a lot further, I thought.

'I can go to two hundred US, but don't ask me for more.'

'Mi gi yuh it fah three hunner dallar.'

'It's a deal.' Debbie spoke coolly. She turned her back, fumbled in her sweater, and when she turned round again she had a stack of

American dollars in her hand. Zola and I exchanged the briefest of glances. Zola's face was white; I felt my own wet with sweat.

Grandpa suddenly grinned. 'Neva did like it.'

The triptych was held in place by nails through the holes where gemstones had once been. The old man leaned his walking stick against the sideboard, eased the relic from the wall and handed it over to Debbie. It folded easily. She tucked it under her arm and counted out the cash, putting a note at a time into Grandpa's extended hand. It took a hundred years. When she finished I became aware that I hadn't been breathing. I gulped air.

He waved at us from the doorway. 'She ah wan tuff bargaina,' he called into the dark. He was using irony in the Socratic style, Ogilvie would have said.

'This doesn't seem right.' Zola's voice came from the dark. 'It's as if we're cheating the man.'

'I am Deborah Inez Tebbit and this has been in my family for a thousand years. This is my property. It's mine.'

I'm breaking into a sweat. I can't take it in. I can't believe we have it. All we need to do is reach the car and clear off. We are literally seconds away from pulling it off. The others are thinking the same. We walk briskly; and then we trot; and then we break into a run.

Past the Spanish church; over the little bridge, water trickling underneath; the car just visible in the dark, about thirty yards ahead. Almost there. We keep our torches off. Debbie is ahead of me, fumbling with keys. I look around, peering into the trees. We're going to pull this off! We really are going to pull this off! Debbie is still fumbling. I see moonlight reflecting from the windscreen of a car a hundred yards or so further up the hill; it's almost hidden behind a ruin. I just have time to open my mouth before a voice, speaking good Mediterranean English, comes from behind us, from the little church we have just passed. 'Thank you all, most sincerely. I would never have found it without you.' And we are lit up in the beams of four torches, neatly coming from the cardinal points of the compass: north, south, east and west.

38

'It's not like forensic entomology, for example.'

The Professor – at least that's what I'm mentally calling him – is looking at the triptych laid out on the table in front of him. He is scanning the wood with a large magnifying glass, and droning on about wood and DNA. I place him in some third-rate North England university, stretching his minimal talents into a zero career and getting his professorship, if he has one, through his adeptness at screwing funds out of public trusts and councils.

They had expected us to escape, wanted us to. They had followed us without lights, a convoy of cars along the dark coastal road, all the way to the *Sevilla la Nueva* plantation. Hondros had taken the icon out of Debbie's hands: a thousand years in her family and she had held it for less than a minute. The cars had appeared from odd corners and we had been bundled into them, a car each. The convoy had taken us through the dark night, back through Ocho Rios, back along the deserted coastal road, back towards the Lego house. I sat between two men I'd never seen. Both were smoking heavily, but the nausea I was feeling wasn't altogether due to the smoke. The Lego house was easily seen, even in the dark; its whitewashed walls were glowing faintly in the starlight. The big motor boat was still in the lagoon, and again I had some brief fantasy idea about jumping into it and escaping into the wide ocean.

And now the electricity is restored and the stabbed, brained and electrocuted men are gone – dumped in the sea, probably – and we are sitting on the living room couch, which, being low, we have to struggle to get out of; any idea of a sudden leap is out of the question. And there are fresh people, again, I think, all Greek, or at least Mediterranean in origin. 'Inspector Menem' is with us; he has a gun in each hand, which seems excessive for three unarmed captives. And in the opposite corner a young black man with dreadlocks is rolling a large joint. I presume he's a local contact who supplied the guns, as easily obtainable in Jamaica as a packet of cigarettes. Cassandra catches my eye and gives me that cold smile.

Hondros and the Professor are about ten feet away, on the far side of the table. Cassandra in one corner, and the young black Jamaican in the other, are each about fifteen feet away from us. Debbie, on my left, is breathing in big gulps. I feel a sense of helpless rage, mixed with guilt, that she should find herself in this position. She is trying hard to keep herself under control.

The Professor's drone reaches its conclusion, delivered with all the smug certainty of a mediocre mind. Hondros asks for confirmation: 'It could be the Holy Relic?'

The Professor nods. 'Of course proper verification would require carbon-14 dating.' He smiles triumphantly. 'But I can safely rule out some sort of elaborate modern forgery.'

It's our death sentence.

'Thank you, Doctor.' Hondros folds the triptych shut. 'I think you can leave us now. Cassandra, would you see to the Doctor's fee?'

The Professor gives a slight bow of his head. 'I would like to be well clear of this island before' – he glances briefly in our direction – 'before there is any unpleasantness.'

Hondros smiles smoothly. 'Have no fear, Doctor. You will be long gone before anything happens here.' Cassandra walks slowly across the room.

He gives us another glance, this one slightly anxious. 'They have seen my face, you know.'

'Doctor, you have absolutely no worries in that direction.' She raises her gun.

At first the Professor doesn't take it in. When it finally becomes obvious, when Casssandra's finger is tightening on the trigger, he gives a high-pitched, complaining cry and raises his hands as if to ward off the bullet. There is a harsh *Bang!* and he suddenly becomes an inert weight and drops to the ground, his head cracking against the marble floor. A splodge of red, centred on his chest, begins to run down his tie and shirt. Cassandra says, 'Doctor Kaplan has been paid.' She says it calmly. Next to me, Debbie is sobbing quietly. The red blood makes a little puddle, begins to spread over the floor.

Hondros scratches his head. 'He did like to talk.'

'You people are inhuman.' I know it's wrong to say it. I know you don't provoke, don't draw attention to yourself. I just can't help it.

Hondros pays no attention. 'And that, ladies and gentlemen, would seem to be that.'

There is some Greek chatter. Someone is cracking a joke and there are glances in Debbie's direction. The young black man takes up his weapon and looks at us through the smoke with narrowed eyes. If I dive under the table I will have momentary protection. I'll pull Hondros off his feet, go for his gun and point it at his head. While the armed gang are thinking about that, Debbie and Zola will clear out. I know it's stupid. I know it's a zero-hope tactic. But what else is there on offer?

I wonder about old-fashioned pleading for mercy but dismiss the thought: the tactic would have had more chance with the vultures.

'What now?' My words come out almost as a croak.

Hondros glances at his watch. 'Time is short, for all of us. I want to be off this wretched island and safely back in Europe by tomorrow. Now, who should we dispose of first? You, Blake? Or would you rather see your friends go, prolonging your own pathetic life by a few seconds?'

I can't speak. He snaps, 'Answer now.'

'It's probably best if I go last. Save distressing the others.'

'How noble. Cassandra, dispatch Mr Harry Blake first.'

Debbie's mobile phone rings. There is a stunned silence. Everyone in the room is on their feet, except for Debbie, Zola and me. Debbie says, 'I'm expecting a call.' Her recovery of composure, her presence of mind, amaze me.

Cassandra says, 'Ignore it.' She swivels her revolver from me to Debbie.

The mobile keeps ringing.

And suddenly I know what's coming. I know it with certainty, with crystal clear certainty. My heart is hammering in my chest. She says, 'I have to answer the phone. They're expecting it.'

'Who?' Hondros is bristling with suspicion and alarm.

'Special Branch,' I say, desperately trying for an air of conviction. 'They're expecting us to call around now.' Say anything, any rubbish to keep them focused on the mobile, anything to keep their attention away from the French windows. The urge to look at the windows – even a glance – is almost overwhelming, and I have to force myself to keep my eyes on Hondros. I'm screaming inside, waiting for it to happen. Cassandra approaches Debbie, gun in hand, waiting for the word. Not just Cassandra: there are seven guns pointing at us, the click of hammers being cocked everywhere.

And then it happens.

The French windows shatter. At the same instant that three men burst through them, another two rush through the kitchen and bedroom doors. They have flak jackets up to their necks, black helmets and ugly black carbines. Cassandra opens her mouth to scream but the carbines roar and her body collapses lifeless to the floor. The carbines keep roaring. The young black man, joint dropping from his mouth, is emptying his gun into the armed Greeks.

Zola's fingers are digging deep into my forearm.

Hondros alone is left standing, his gun on the table, a fine spray of Cassandra's blood over its surface. People are bawling at him: '*Armed police! Freeze!*'

He seems not to hear. He looks at the True Cross, says, '*I ecclisia trefete me to ema ton martyron.*'

'*On the floor!*'

He turns to me. There's some sort of expression in his eyes, some sort of fire, but I don't understand it. He says, '*Makari o Theos na sou sterisi Galini kai Iremia.*'

'*Face down! Spreadeagle!*'

And without haste, he reaches for the gun on the table.

Five carbines roar simultaneously. Hondros's face and chest disintegrate and hunks of brain and flesh and splinters of white bone splatter against the wall and the Jamaican artwork behind him. A vase shatters into powder, a picture falls from the wall, riddled with holes. The momentum of the bullets drives him backwards and his smashed body hits the floor and slides across it, leaving a bright red smear. I lose my hearing, and it's some seconds before I become aware that Debbie is screaming.

39

Another convoy took us through the same dark night. This time it turned left at Ochi, taking us into the interior of the island. The headlights occasionally lit up houses and shops, protected behind wrought iron. In between, there were long stretches of nothing. I had no idea what to expect at the end of the journey. I was squeezed between two policemen, still with flak jackets and helmets and carbines between their knees. They were effectively mute. The driver chain-smoked all the way. I shook for the whole journey and told myself it was just a reaction.

The journey ended at a modestly-sized blue and white building. There was a lot of door slamming as Dalton, Debbie, Zola and I stepped out of our separate cars and stretched our legs, and I took in lungfuls of fresh night air with relief. A white-on-blue notice said: *Jamaica Constabulary Bog Walk*. It was two o'clock in the morning but the place was as busy as a Saturday market.

Debbie, full of tears, threw her arms round Dalton and buried her head in his shoulder.

'Nice one, Dalton.'

'They told us you were dead,' Zola said.

Dalton grinned and gently disengaged Debbie. 'They exaggerated, Zola. But you already knew that, didn't you, Harry?'

'I guessed it. But how did you find us?' I asked. 'And how did you infiltrate them?'

Dalton put a finger to his lips. He ushered us round to the car park at the side of the building. People were tossing flak jackets and helmets into cars, and carbines were being loaded into a Ford Transit van. There was a lot of animated chatter and some laughing.

'They needed guns. They couldn't import them so they acquired them locally. It was a couple of days before we located the supplier and at that point all we had to do was quietly arrest him. They were looking for someone to clean up the house after they'd gone, get rid of the guns and so on. Enter Dalton, the supplier's friend, looking for a few hundred US.'

'That sounds highly dangerous,' I said lamely. 'They could have recognised you.'

'They'd never seen me close up.'

'I nearly didn't recognise you,' Debbie said. 'Those dreadlocks.'

Dalton grinned. 'I told you. I keep them in a box.' We drifted towards the porch; sweaty policemen were milling around us.

I asked, 'How did they find us at Moonlight Chalets?'

'They must have followed you, Harry. What else?' Dalton lowered his voice. 'We'd tapped the lawyer's phone and we knew about your meeting. He'd been duped into arranging it.' He added, 'But we lost you after the raid. That was worrying. It took GCHQ to locate you.'

'I'm tired, Dalton. I don't get it.'

'We had a team scouring the island, but it was pretty desperate.' He hesitated and then said, 'Well, Harry, the technique's in the public domain, and I guess you'd work it out sooner or later. Hondros used a mobile phone. We picked up his calls by satellite. London have some pretty smart voice recognition software. It took a few calls to pin him down. Then it was down to a regular police operation.'

'Seven dead is a regular police operation?' Zola asked.

'It seems so. The people who rescued you are the Crime Management Unit. They're used to coping with heavily armed gangs.' He lowered his voice. 'Their human rights record makes Ghengis Khan look like Snow White. But at least they got to us.'

'In the nick of time,' Zola said. 'What would you have done if they hadn't, Dalton?'

'There was no Plan B. I was just praying along with you.'

'So, when did you first start tracking us?' I asked.

'Just after *Sevilla la Nueva*. Hondros used his mobile in the car to tell his pals they had you. By the way, that gave us another lovely bonus. They had several teams out here, scouring the island for you. Thirty people in all, in four villas from Negril to San Antonio. The Jamaica Constabulary are bringing them in now.'

Debbie was still shaky, but there was determination in her voice. 'The police have taken the True Cross. They're calling it material evidence or something.'

Zola said, 'They can't have it. Not after all we've been through.'

Dalton frowned. 'Unfortunately, it *is* material evidence.'

'But they could hold onto it for months.'

'Years, Debbie. The judicial system moves slowly in Jamaica. We might never see it at all.' He thought for some moments. Then: 'I'd like to try something.'

We followed Dalton into a crowded backroom. Half a dozen telephones had been installed. The room was filled with the smell of sweat, cigarette smoke and coffee; the phones were ringing constantly. Through the open door we saw a car draw up. A door was opened and a high-ranking, bleary-eyed policeman stepped out. I knew he was high-ranking from the air of deference around him, and from the swagger of the man. He fixed a sideways stare on me as he strode into the room. He had bulging eyes and heavy lids and there was only one possible name for him: Mr Lizard. It was a natural. He began a quiet conversation with the local police sergeant.

Dalton pulled out a little diary and dialled a number. He jabbed a finger at two telephones. Debbie lifted one, Zola and I shared the other. An elderly female voice answered: 'Yes.'

'I'd like to speak to Sir Joseph, please.'

'I'm sorry, but he's asleep.'

'Would you waken him up, please?'

'I beg your pardon?'

'Tell him that Dalton is calling.'

There was a long hesitation, and a touch of ice in the voice when she replied. 'One moment, please.'

There was the sound of footsteps coming and going, and then Sir Joseph came on the line: 'Dalton? Do you have it?'

'Yes and no, Sir Joseph. I'm calling from a police station in the Jamaican hinterlands. It's being held by the local police as material evidence. We won't see it for years, if at all.'

'And our Balkan friends?'

'Up to their necks in it. Seven dead, and they're bringing people in from all over the island.'

'I'll try to contact the Foreign Secretary. Where exactly are you?'

'It's called Bog Walk.'

'Sit tight. Be as unhelpful as you can to the local police. Tell them nothing about the icon. If I can't contact the Secretary I'm afraid you're in for a long night.'

Mr Lizard was watching me from the corner of his eyes. He muttered something to the sergeant, who was licking his lips nervously. The sergeant came over. 'Why are you using an official telephone, sir?'

I put the receiver down and shrugged. The sergeant said, 'Would you follow me, sir?'

'What you doing in Jamaica?' The policeman had dispensed with statements about rights.

'I was on business.' The interview room wasn't much bigger than a broom cupboard and most of its space was taken up by a small, square table and four chairs. I sipped at the coffee; it was half-cold and flavourless.

'And the nature of your business?'

'I was looking for something on behalf of a client.'

'God Dem you, Mr Blake,' said the sergeant impatiently. 'Just answer the questions properly. What exactly yuh looking for?'

'An old family heirloom, which my client thought might be in Jamaica.'

'What sort of heirloom?' The sergeant was shouting now. Maybe he thought this would impress the superintendent.

'Just a family antique.'

For a moment I thought the man was going to hit me. But Mr Lizard interrupted the flow. He lit a small cigar. 'Mr Blake, the position is this. We get a phone call from your Special Branch in England to say y'all are being held by an armed gang. They even tell us exactly where. We get you out of there, risking the lives of my officers in the process, and I have seven carcasses on my hands. Now, you don't expect us to just walk away from that situation, surely? Do you?'

258

'Of course not.'

'I'm glad you see it that way. We already have Amnesty International breathing down our necks on account of some people think we have a bad record when it comes to defending ourselves under fire. What am I to tell the Police Commissioner? That all this was over that piece of wood we found on the table? Now we are going to need to know who these people were and what they wanted and where you come into it. Give me some help here, Mr Blake.'

The man's question was reasonable and his tone was urbane, even civilised. He was scaring the hell out of me.

'And I don't want you taken to East Central Kingston for a more formal interrogation. Want to avoid that if we can. Much better if we can clear everything up here. So.' His tone became businesslike. 'What is it about this piece of wood?'

40

The British Ambassador turned up in person. He was a young man, surprisingly unstuffy, and he was accompanied by two men even younger than him. His arrival was announced by an extremely nervous policeman who tapped at the door of the interview room and put little more than a nose round it.

'Of course I have no authority here,' the Ambassador agreed with Mr Lizard. 'But I'm expecting your Police Commissioner to call at any time.'

As if on cue, there was another knock at the door and the same nervous policeman announced to Mr Lizard that, 'There a call for yuh, suh.' We left the stuffy little interview room. There was no sign of Debbie or Zola and I had to assume they were being interviewed in stuffy little cupboards elsewhere. Mr Lizard took the receiver, and I watched with satisfaction as his vinegary expression melted, thawed and dissolved into a sullen acquiescence.

'Where is it?' The Ambassador wanted to know.

'Sir?' The Lizard was pretending not to understand.

'The Ambassador is referring to the piece of wood. You know, the one you've been questioning me about for the past hour.'

The policeman looked blank.

'Perhaps we should telephone the Commissioner,' the Ambassador suggested smoothly. 'I'm sure he won't mind being called out of bed again.'

'Sergeant Mortimer, see to it. And arrange an escort for our witnesses.'

An escort. But where to? I didn't want escorting anywhere, not with the Lizard in charge. I wanted out of it and far, far away from here. A surge of anxiety washed over me. I put it down to tiredness setting my imagination into overdrive.

Her Majesty's Ambassador was either reading my mind or ahead of me. 'Thank you, but I'll be taking my people back in the Rolls.'

We waited for the Ambassador next to the Rolls-Royce. It was bottle-green and had a little Union Jack, and it felt reassuringly British, even if the firm was owned by BMW. In a minute he appeared with the triptych. It was three o'clock and things were beginning to ease. Inspector McIntyre, who'd led the raid, told me they'd netted thirty people that night. They were being held at more than a dozen stations dispersed round the island.

The Ambassador emerged from the porch with his minions. Dalton arrived at the car seconds later. 'You go ahead. I have things to clear up here.'

'Unbelievable,' said the Ambassador. He had an overnight stubble and a slightly bewildered look about him. The car was moving with monastic silence and gliding over the potholed road like a hover-craft. His assistants were in the front. 'The Foreign Secretary explained it to me just an hour ago. I can hardly take it in. What did you tell the local constabulary?'

Zola said, 'Some tale about being chased by thieves into the Blue Mountains. It was totally incredible and nobody believed it for a second.'

Debbie said, 'It was all we could think of at two o'clock in the morning.'

'Especially as we'd been swimming in blood half an hour earlier,' I reminded him.

The Ambassador grunted. 'Never mind. It worked.' He patted the triptych on his knee. 'This could go out by diplomatic bag later today. Where would MI6 like to send it, Mr Blake?'

It took a few seconds to dawn. Zola caught my eye for the briefest of moments. I hesitated. The Ambassador said, 'Of course. I'm stupid at this hour.' He pressed a button and a slab of thick glass slid quietly up between the driver and passenger compartments.

'Picardy House?' I asked Debbie.

'Better not. Uncle Robert. I think we'll just hold on to it.' Something in her voice told me there would be no point in arguing.

The Ambassador nodded. Debbie took the triptych from him and rested it on her thighs. She glanced at me and smiled. I thought, *After nine hundred years.*

Zola said, 'What do you know about this operation, Ambassador?'

'Only what your people have told me.'

'But I'm not sure what that is,' she said. 'We've been out of touch for the past day or two.'

The Ambassador glanced uncertainly at Debbie. Zola said, 'It's okay, Debbie has access to the same material as us. You can speak freely.'

'Okay, let me give you a resumé of my briefing. I knew nothing about any of this until it arrived a couple of hours ago. What I'm told is that a couple of years ago the Israeli police questioned a priest of the Greek Orthodox Church in Jerusalem about gun running. They released him for lack of evidence, but the incident was enough to tickle the interest of British and American intelligence. It turned out that he wasn't a priest at all, but a clerk in their Arabic department. Can't remember the name.'

'Apostolis Hondros,' Zola said.

'That's it, I remember. That's his adopted name, right? He was actually born Enver Bayal. Turkish by birth but converted to Greek Orthodox around the turn-of-the-century. The story is that he tried to enter the priesthood but was rejected. According to the Bishop Aristarchus of the Greek Patriarchate, his opinions were becoming ever more extreme, he was developing a fanatical hatred of the Vatican and was violently opposed to the 1993 agreement between the Orthodox and Vatican churches. He was equally opposed to the country of his birth for political reasons which I just skimmed over for lack of time. Something to do with support for the Bosnian Muslims. How am I doing?'

Zola said, 'Very good so far, Ambassador. They seem to have given you a thorough briefing.'

'The Turkish police associated him with several assassinations of

Muslim clerics in Istanbul in the late nineties, but nothing was ever proven. He disappeared for some years, but at the turn of the millennium founded a group calling itself the Byzantium Circle. It has the usual cell structure which makes it hard to penetrate, and it attracts the usual mish-mash: religious extremists, nationalist extremists, young idealists, naïve academics, the rootless, the resentful and the disturbed.'

'They're all disturbed.' I said that because I wanted to keep the Ambassador talking.

'It's their goal.' The Ambassador shook his head. 'I can hardly take it in.'

'What goal is that?'

Don't push your luck, Zola!

The Ambassador looked momentarily puzzled. 'They don't have more than one, do they?'

'How much did they tell you about it?' Zola asked.

'Not much. I don't suppose you can tell me anything?'

'Sorry, Ambassador. Official Secrets Act.'

It occurred to me that Zola hadn't lied once throughout the conversation.

We'd had about three hours' sleep – three hours seemed to be my ration these days – when Dalton turned up, hammering noisily on doors and telling us that we just had time for the Caribbean sunrise. It was all pink and gold and high mare's tails and we watched it and yawned as we had coffee and breakfast baps on the veranda. The Ambassador, it seemed, had the baps flown in from England every morning.

'We were bait, right?'

'I'm sorry, Harry, but it's not customary for MI6 to say anything at all about its operations. In fact if the Ambassador hadn't slipped up you wouldn't know—'

'Or maybe I was the bait and Zola and Debbie were unexpected complications. Either way, HMG has no right to put its citizens in jeopardy like that.'

Dalton said, 'The rules are changing, Harry. We're living in dangerous times.'

'And my father?' Debbie asked. 'He wasn't killed by burglars, was he?'

Dalton shook his head. 'I'm so sorry, Debbie, I wish I could tell you. But I'm just not at liberty to say. There still has to be an inquest.'

'Bend the rules this once, Dalton,' Zola snapped. I think it was loss of sleep. 'It means a great deal to her.'

'Dalton means yes,' I said to Debbie. 'I can read his body language like a book. Cassandra was in on it.'

Debbie said, 'You think so, Harry? In that case I'm satisfied.' She looked dreamily out over the sea, and her eyes moistened. 'Very satisfied.'

Dalton said, 'I'm that bad an actor, am I? No matter. You're all going to have to sign the Official Secrets Act.'

Zola said, 'Guess some more, Harry, so we can all watch Dalton's body language.'

'Piece of cake.' I gave Dalton a look. 'You knew there was a major terrorist operation brewing. You knew they were after Ogilvie's manuscript but didn't know why. Maybe you knew they'd killed Debbie's father but warned off the local police. They had my description of Cassandra. So you let us run with the manuscript to see where it would lead. Okay so far?'

Dalton was spreading butter on his bap and pretending not to hear. He was making little swirling patterns with his knife.

Zola said, 'That sounds plausible, Harry, except for one thing. Where does Sir Joseph come into it? I just asked him for expertise on the Crusades issue and Dalton appears, as if by magic. Dalton, who happens to know all about religious icons and also merges into the Jamaican background. How could Joe have that on hand?'

'He didn't, Zola. But if I was under surveillance by MI6, so were you. I don't doubt that your call to Sir Joseph was monitored and that Sir Joseph, in the national interest, was persuaded to recruit Dalton, who was no doubt given a crash course in relics, crusades, medieval bigotry and religious fanatics.'

Dalton was spooning marmalade on to the bap. 'If I were guessing the way you're guessing, I'd say that MI6 can already call on people with expertise in these areas. Ancient hatreds are a big thing with us these days.'

'Where did Cassandra come into it?' I asked.

'She's just another crazy like Hondros, of course,' Zola said, spreading butter on a croissant. An early morning hummingbird was moving in fast, iridescent little jerks around a Mexican creeper on the wall.

'Or was she in it for the money? Of course, it can be hard to say. But let's not compromise our MI6 colleague here. He's a high-flyer, keen to stay on the fast-track promotion route.'

'They were all driven by conviction, not money,' Dalton confirmed. 'I shouldn't be saying this, but you'll be reading it in the newspapers by the time we get back to England. The Byzantium Circle, as it was called, had been preparing the operation for at least two years, before anything was known about the True Cross.'

I said, 'So, when they learned there was a paper trail which might lead to the True Cross . . .'

Zola wiped a spot of jam from the corner of her mouth. 'Learned from . . . ?'

Debbie completed the sentence. 'Uncle Robert?'

'No. Your Uncle Robert was questioned while you were getting suntans here. He guessed that the journal might have something to say about the lost family icon and he had ideas about going for it on his own.'

'Stealing from me.'

'But he had nothing to do with the Byzantium group. Harry and Zola's suspicions were wrong in that respect. We think Hondros was informed by someone in the office of the Jamaican lawyer, Chuck Martin. Someone who looked into your family's history, found out the story about de Clari and then alerted Hondros or Cassandra – how, we don't know. Presumably the party involved was looking for a percentage. The Jamaican Constabulary are investigating.'

I said, 'Something you don't know. The longitude of the Bog Walk police station. It's seventy-seven degrees west.'

'What?' Debbie gasped. 'That's amazing.'

'And *Sevilla la Nueva*, where they buried the icon, is about the same.'

Zola was saying, 'Do you think Ogilvie—?'

I interrupted. 'Let's think about that later. Meantime we should get off the island quickly. We're holding an icon worth a fortune and stories will be getting around.'

Dalton said, 'I thought you'd never catch on, Harry. And there may soon be other claimants turning the screw on the Police Commissioner. The Jamaican government itself may have ideas. You don't seriously think I got you up early for the sunrise.'

Debbie said, 'We can't lose it, not now.'

'While you people were sleeping I booked us on a mid-afternoon BA flight to London which we won't be taking. We'll be on a chartered yacht to Cuba by eight o'clock this morning.' He glanced at his watch. 'That's in one hour and nine minutes.'

Debbie said, 'Go, go, go.'

I gulped down the last of my coffee. 'I've never sailed a yacht in my life. We'll capsize and get eaten by sharks.'

'Don't be such a wimp, Harry,' said Zola. 'Sailing a yacht is easy, I expect.'

Dalton stood up. 'Move it, folks. Pack up and hand in the key.'

'Don't forget the Cross,' I said. 'Not after all this.'

41

It was like one of those Agatha Christie mysteries with the suspects assembled in the drawing room.

We were crowded together in Zola's little Greenwich kitchen. Sir Joseph was perched on a high stool with a tumbler of milk; Debbie, in dark skirt and sweater, was sitting on a work surface next to the kitchen sink. Her face was flushed with excitement. Dalton, Zola and I were on chairs at the little circular table. My gunshot wound had more or less healed and I was wearing a short-sleeved shirt to show it off, like a duelling scar. It made me feel heroic. There was an unopened champagne bottle in an ice bucket, and a cluster of glasses.

The True Cross had been taken briefly out of its Bank of England vault, and Zola, Dalton and I had taken three tiny splinters from it before tucking it away again.

'I've taken advice on the ownership issue,' Sir Joseph declared. 'Want to hear it?'

There was a chorus of assent.

'It's not simple. It depends on how long it was lost, whether it was searched for by successive generations, and how it was searched for.'

'How can you search for something if you don't know where to start looking?' Debbie asked.

'There's no absolute answer to this. It depends on the actions of your ancestors down through the generations. If, say, a couple of generations, or even one generation, of your ancestors gave up looking, even for a period of ten years or so, it could be argued that they had given up the claim. In that case, if someone else finds it, that someone else is entitled to it.'

'The story that we had the True Cross hidden away somewhere has been handed down through our family from generation to generation. The icon has always been seen as part of our heritage. De Clari of Picardy hid it away somewhere – it was hidden, not lost. Someone knew where it was. The proof is that Marmaduke StClair went out to Jamaica with it. And Marmaduke StClair is an ancestor of mine.'

Sir Joseph nodded. 'Good point. Another point in your favour is that instructions for retrieving it were given to your father, albeit indirectly, by a direct descendant of Marmaduke.'

'It belongs to the Tebbits, then. It's mine.'

'But if you're handing something down from one generation to the next, it's not enough to say, "I bequeath everything to you." You have to mention a specific item. Marmaduke merely buried the Cross and left a coded message for his descendants to find. It's pretty obvious that successive generations failed to understand the code, and so it might be argued that the Cross was thereby lost to your family.'

Debbie said, 'How can you know it was lost? Maybe they just kept it hidden. And even if it was lost, you can be sure that successive generations tried to crack the code. That's looking for the Cross, isn't it?'

'But the Cross was never mentioned in your family wills. We can be sure of that. And there are rival claimants.'

'The Jamaican poorist?'

'For one. Where did he get it from? Did he really dig it up from the ground? Has it really been in his family for generations, in which case he may have a claim. And if it was buried on Jamaican soil, especially on property owned by the state, which the *Sevilla la Nueva* plantation now is, then the Jamaican government may claim it as treasure trove. Public law may also then be involved and the complications become, forgive me, Byzantine.'

I interrupted: 'But Debbie bought it from him.'

'Thereby, possibly, admitting that she didn't own it in the first place.'

'But destroying the Jamaican poorist's claim. He sold it.'

'It might be argued that you cheated him. Offering him three hundred dollars for a thirty-million-dollar item.'

'That was three hundred dollars more than he was entitled to,' Debbie said determinedly.

'Maybe so. But if the poorist dug it up from the ground this may strengthen the Jamaican government's claim on the icon. And there's another problem.'

Debbie said, 'Another problem? How can there be more problems than this?'

'Who's to say that de Clari was entitled to the Cross in the first place? After all, he stole it during the Crusades. Possession by theft doesn't confer ownership. The Church may argue that the Cross belongs to it and that the Tebbits were never entitled to it.'

'Which Church?' Zola asked.

Sir Joseph frowned. 'Now we get into dangerous territory. Constantine, or one of his minions, discovered the Cross in Jerusalem in 327 AD and took it to Byzantium. That would seem to make it the property of the Greek Orthodox Church, who would claim the True Cross from this act.'

'Joe, are you saying Hondros and Cassandra were entitled to the icon all along?' Zola was open-mouthed with surprise.

'I'm only anticipating what expensive lawyers might say. On the other hand, the Catholic Church makes the claim of apostolic succession, and their expensive lawyers would say this establishes their client as the true inheritor of the Cross of Christ. I wouldn't like to be the judge who has to make a decision between these two powerful rivals.'

'I'm not so sure either Church could make a claim,' I suggested. 'After all, the Cross was stolen and held by the Mohammedans for centuries, during which time the Churches stopped looking. From what you say, they therefore gave up on the claim.'

'But the Catholic Church tried to retrieve the Cross. That's what the Fifth Crusade was about.'

'It was an excuse for plunder, not a genuine attempt to retrieve it.'

Sir Joseph sipped at his milk. 'Possibly. Who can know for sure what went on in the mind of some pope eight hundred years ago?'

'So where do we go from here?' Zola asked.

'We stick to the deal. My legal team is looking into the question of ownership. But others may well make claims to the icon and the issue could drag through the courts for months at enormous expense. Keep in mind too that after the emancipation of the slaves, people had to fend for themselves. Many went into the interior of the island and then just scraped a living on whatever land they could; there was no question of lawyers defining land boundaries or creating deeds.'

I said, 'The deal was that I persuade Debbie to give you first refusal on the Cross, based on an independent valuation.'

'Correct. I've had it valued at twenty million dollars.'

'My people put it at forty plus. I can't advise her to accept less.'

Sir Joseph waved a dismissive hand. 'Debbie, I'm prepared to offer you ten million dollars for the icon, should it turn out to date from the time of Christ. That's to say, you drop all claims to ownership in exchange for ten million dollars. I take the heat of the legal actions. If it turns out you own the icon, you keep the money and give me the icon. If it turns out you don't own it, you keep the money anyway.'

'And if it turns out to be a medieval fake?' I asked.

'Debbie gets nothing.'

Debbie turned to me. 'Harry?'

I said, 'A quiet confab, Debbie.'

We sat at opposite ends of a big couch in Zola's living room. Debbie had dismay written all over her. 'This doesn't seem right. It's been in the family for centuries.'

'Okay, Debbie, but if you go through the courts and it turns out not to be legally yours, you could lose two or three million sterling in costs. Do you have that sort of money?'

'Picardy House might be worth that. But there's all the hassle, and Uncle Robert sticking his nose in. It's not worth the gamble.'

'And if the icon turns out to be a fake, you don't have anything anyway. I think you're being offered a reasonable deal. My advice would be to take it, subject to a lawyer getting the details nailed down. But it's your decision, not mine, not Uncle Robert's, and not a lawyer's.'

'Harry, look at me. Do I look the type for a pearl necklace and a cashmere sweater? Someone who'll marry a Hooray Henry with nothing up top but the social column in *Country Life* and the price of silage? Do you think I want to spend the rest of my days rattling around inside a family pile?' She shook her head firmly. 'Daddy's gone and it's time to move on. I want out of Picardy House. And I want rid of the icon.'

I gaped. 'What? Something that's been in your family for centuries?'

'And what good has it done, to us or anyone else? I've given this thought, Harry. The best thing I can do for my six children when I have them, and all the Tebbit generations to come, is stick it in a museum where it belongs.'

'The Curse of the Icon,' I said stupidly.

'Sell the damn thing. I'm going to sell Picardy House and buy pads in London, Paris and Monte Carlo, and I'm going to enjoy life. I'll see the Jamaican poorist all right, and you get ten per cent for acting as my agent. So do Zola and Dalton.'

'Dalton's a public servant, he can't take anything from you.'

Debbie sniffed. 'Ten million dollars is a lot of money. Eight after you and Zola have your cut. Let's go for it.'

'Final answer?'

She hesitated, pondered the options, little lines of tension puckering her mouth. Then she gave a little smile. 'Final answer.'

Sir Joseph had finished his milk and was trying to look nonchalant. I said, 'I've advised Debbie to reject your offer.'

'That is foolish.'

'The icon is probably hers and its value is in excess of forty million dollars. I can't in all conscience advise her to accept a quarter of its value.'

'But can Debbie afford the fees when the legal actions start? They'll be astronomical.'

'We'll find a no-win, no-fee law firm. They'll be queueing up for this. Sorry, Sir Joseph.'

'I can go to fifteen.'

'Twenty.'

'Fifteen and that's my final offer. Accept it now or all offers are withdrawn.'

271

'Twenty million dollars and it's yours.'

'You're calling my bluff?'

'Uhuh. You're not the only museum owner in the universe.'

Sir Joseph looked at me thoughtfully. For some seconds the loudest noise was the ticking of the clock on the kitchen wall. Then a grin and, 'A wonderful piece of brinkmanship, Harry, congratulations. I agree your terms. If you ever need a job . . .' We shook hands on it, then Debbie shook hands with Sir Joseph and everybody was shaking hands with everybody else.

Twenty million dollars. Fifteen million sterling, enough to buy Debbie a herd of horses. Less my commission of 1.5 million and the same to Zola. A good morning's work.

Sir Joseph was saying something, and I dragged myself back from some stupid fantasy about swimming pools and Aston Martins. 'I'll have my people draw up the papers. All this is conditional on the icon being the correct date. Two thousand rather than one thousand years old.'

The correct date. Carbon-14 was the key. We had each taken a tiny splinter from the Cross and sent it to separate laboratories. Mine had gone to one in East Kilbride. Dalton and Zola didn't tell where theirs had gone, and I didn't ask. Three separate samples, three independent groups, and the True Cross still there in case of any dispute.

They'd explained the business to me in East Kilbride. It was all very technical. It seems that radioactive carbon, or carbon-14 as it's called, is created in the atmosphere when cosmic rays hit ordinary carbon atoms in the carbon dioxide of the air. These radioactive atoms decay with a half-life of 5,500 years. There's a balance between the rate at which the radioactive carbon is created by cosmic rays and the rate at which it decays spontaneously. The carbon dioxide is ingested through the leaves of plants and so enters the food chain. When the plant dies, or the herbivore which eats plants dies, or the carnivore which eats herbivores dies, it stops taking in carbon-14. The remaining carbon-14 in the bones of the animal, or in the dead wood of the tree, then goes into decline, with no food coming in to replenish it. If you measure the proportion of carbon-14 in the remains, you get the age of the plant or animal from the moment of death. A lot of carbon-14 in the bones means a recent death and a noisy Geiger counter; a little means an ancient death and a quiet counter.

There's a complication. There always is. Sometimes more cosmic rays come in from space, sometimes fewer. Most of the cosmic rays come from the sun, and the sun, for some reason, has a 200-year cycle of activity. This puts little 200-year wiggles in the graph, which, if you don't allow for them, can put you out by a century or two. But the smart men allow for these little wiggles; they assured me they could date a splinter of wood 2,000 years old to within a century, maybe even fifty years. Some enthusiasts thought they could do better.

The difference between a medieval fake and the True Cross is a thousand years. The smart men said I was asking them to hit a barn door from six inches away.

I smiled tensely at Dalton over the top of the unopened champagne bottle. 'What has this meant for you, most of all?' I asked him.

'Nailing the villains'. That was simple enough. Hondros had been communicating with his Byzantium Circle through movies on the Internet. Each frame of the movie could have a million pixels, and if you knew the algorithm you could pick the right pixel, putting dark=0, light=1 or whatever, and so could send a message in binary with an unbreakable code if the other party knew which pixels to look at. It was a long, long way from Babington and his letter substitutions. But they'd found a CD in Hondros's Lego house, the NSA had cracked it in a couple of weeks, and from that point on Hondros's home movies had become an Aladdin's cave. A massive operation was now underway, nasty little terrorist cells being broken up in Greece, Turkey and Italy. You could follow its progress every night on CNN. The Pope's regular vacation in Castelgandolfo Palace had been cancelled without explanation, and rumours of an aborted assassination plot had spread 'like the plague', as Ogilvie would have said. It had to be the highlight of Dalton's young career.

'And you, Zola?'

'Reaching out and touching history. Ogilvie's journal bringing it to life. And I loved that yacht sail to Cuba. I'll buy a yacht, fifty feet long with all the trimmings. I'll call it *Aldebaran*. *Debbie* for short.'

I looked over at Debbie, who was tapping her heels against a cupboard door. 'This is what Daddy would have wanted me to do.' I understood. She might be rejecting Picardy House and the family icon, but she was still defining her life in the context of the family; she was still Deborah Inez Tebbit. And she'd had an experience she'd remember for the rest of her life.

I looked at Sir Joseph. He said, 'Do you need to ask? To have recovered a piece of the True Cross of Christ for my museum. And what about you, Harry?'

'If the Cross turns out to be genuine?' I let my fantasies out. 'First I'll get rid of the overdraft and the loans. Then I'll go mad. I'll buy a house with a few acres of garden and a swimming pool, with a Porsche or an Aston Martin out front. And once I've got that out of my system, I'll settle down and devote the rest of my life to my passion.'

'Your passion.'

'Seeking out ancient maps and manuscripts in the back streets and bazaars of the world.'

'Sounds good,' said Zola. 'Maybe I could join you now and then. We could sail to the Bosphorus in *Aldebaran*, and scour the Book Market in Istanbul.'

Said lightheartedly. But was there an undercurrent of something? Ancient hormones stirred. She was reading my mind, smiling slightly.

I said, 'Just don't ask me to make any more paella.'

Sir Joseph gave me a puzzled look.

Debbie said, 'They all depend on the dating, don't they? All these dreams.' She had come down the previous evening, and the ladies and I had spread ourselves around the little flat in sleeping bags. Sir Joseph had turned up at the crack of dawn, Dalton an hour ago. The three laboratories had all promised an answer by mid-morning. It was mid-morning now.

'Would anyone like a cup of tea?' Zola asked. Nobody replied.

The telephone rang. It was starting on its second ring by the time Zola had cleared her chair and was picking up the receiver. We were all on our feet. Sir Joseph had knocked over the stool. I realised that my fists were clenched tight, but for the life of me I couldn't loosen them. There was muffled talking, and then Zola was handing the receiver to me. Her voice was agonisingly stressed. 'It's the East Kilbride people.'

I took the phone, said, 'Harry Blake here. Good morning, Jim. I'm handing this over to a third party. Tell her everything.' I turned to Debbie. 'It's your icon. You take it.'

Debbie listened. The muffled voice went on for about a minute. Then she was saying, 'You're absolutely sure? . . . Give or take fifty years . . . Thank you very much then . . . Goodbye.'

She put the receiver down, closed her eyes and leaned her head briefly against the wall telephone. Then she turned and looked around, wide-eyed. She seemed surprised to see us there.

I was screaming inside. 'Well?'

She looked at me and smiled. The smile broadened. Then she put her hand over her mouth and giggled, and then she was leaning against the wall and laughing. Then her laughter drifted into something like hysterics, and it was infectious, and she was sliding down the wall, and in spite of ourselves we were laughing at her out-of-control laughter.

'For Christ's sake, woman!' I managed to say.

She paused, looked at me, spluttered, threw her head back and shrieked some more. And at last, when she had regained control, she said, 'You owe this to Doctor Dee, Harry, the Elizabethan 007.'

'You mean . . . ?'

She gave me a warm, happy smile and said, 'I'd go for the Aston Martin.'

275

Acknowledgements and Notes

That Raleigh's 1585 voyage to North America had a hidden purpose is a serious if controversial proposition, due originally to Simon Cassidy. The secret calendar of Dr John Dee is central to this proposition and I am indebted to Simon Cassidy and Duncan Steel for discussions about these and similar matters. The machinations involved, along with the amazing significance of calendars throughout human history, are superbly described in *Marking Time*, by Duncan Steel (John Wiley and Sons, 2000).

I am grateful to Daniela Rohr for an introduction to the legal complexities which would lie behind claims of ownership of the holy triptych of the novel. Mike Bartle gave me valuable information on Elizabethan sailing and shared some of his knowledge of ocean canoeing with me. The staff of the Jamaica Archives in Spanish Town, and of the public library in Armagh, Northern Ireland, were extremely helpful, as was Sue Wales, administrative officer of the Bodleian library. Alecia Hyatt of Tropical Tours at Ocho Rios helped me with Jamaican patois, as did Apostolis Christou with Greek. And I am indebted to Jay Tate, formerly of the British Army, for a description of what it is like to be shot in the arm: much as I enjoy carrying out first-hand research for my novels, this was one area where I preferred to rely on the experience of others.